"A masterclass in concise storytelling… The book whips along at a rapid pace and characters are cleverly rendered. A fantastically easy read."

SciFiNow on *Firewalkers*

"Filled with relatable ideas and foreshadowing, the narrative wills a sense of foreboding that compels you to keep turning the page."

Grimdark Magazine on *Ogres*

"Dramatises the conflicts between rich and poor, right and left, public and private in a brutally satirical fashion. At the same time, it's an enormously entertaining story."

SF Crow's Nest on *Ironclads*

"If you're a fan of plausible futures and cutting edge storytelling, you owe it to yourself to check this one out."

At Boundary's Edge on *Firewalkers*

"Can easily stand proud with dystopian novels such as Orwell's *1984* or Margaret Atwood's *Maddaddam Trilogy*."

Fantasy Hive on *Ogres*

"The wars of Tchaikovsky's future are brutal, inhuman, and strangely awe-inspiring in their horror."

Locus Magazine on *Ironclads*

TERRIBLE WORLDS REVOLUTIONS

TERRIBLE WORLDS REVOLUTIONS

Ironclads
Firewalkers
Ogres

ADRIAN TCHAIKOVSKY

SOLARIS

First published 2023 by Solaris
an imprint of Rebellion Publishing Ltd,
Riverside House, Osney Mead,
Oxford, OX2 0ES, UK

www.solarisbooks.com

ISBN: 978-1-78618-888-5

10 9 8 7 6 5 4 3 2 1

A CIP catalogue record for this book is available from
the British Library.

Designed & typeset by Rebellion Publishing

Printed in Denmark

IRONCLADS

With thanks to my special military advisers
Harry Cattes, Shane McLean and Rick Wynne

CHAPTER ONE

STURGEON SAYS THAT, way back when, the sons of the rich used to go to war as a first choice of career. He says that, back then, the regular grunts were basically just poor bastards with a knife and a leather jacket—only he's got that annoying-as-crap patronising look that says he's dumbing stuff down for me—and no training, and no clue, save what lies they got told.

But the rich guys: Sturgeon says they had all the time in the world to learn stuff, and all the money in the world, and they bought the best armor that no poor bastard was going to stick a knife through, and they would just wade in and make a game of how many poor bastards they could cut up on the way. And even if things went really bad for them, they didn't die, Sturgeon says. He says they just let themselves get captured and ransomed, and had a fine old time telling jokes to the rich guys who grabbed them about all the poor bastards they killed.

What Sturgeon says is that things swung round—the science of killing a man sort of galloped ahead of the science of stopping him being killed. Guns, mostly. And suddenly the sons of the rich didn't like the idea of being soldiers, not once it was them getting shot up with the rest of the poor bastards. The clever ones went to war with a crapton of gold braid on their sleeves and a crapton of space between them and the front lines. The rest went into stock-brokering and lawyering and running companies, where the money was better and the chance of getting shot was less, and you still basically got to say how the war went, if you were in the right industry.

But they missed it, when it was gone, Sturgeon says. There's something you get from shooting a guy, from ripping his head off, from just wading in and showing the poor bastards how much better you are than them in the most simple, physical way. He reckons it's a kick you just don't get with raiding the company pension pot or evicting tenants or throwing a prostitute out of a window and getting away with it cos your uncle's a police chief and your grandfather's a judge.

Sturgeon says things have gone full circle. Sturgeon says a lot of stuff, though. Usually he doesn't get this far into his spiel before Franken slugs him. Sturgeon, as far as I'm concerned, is full of shit.

WE TOUCHED DOWN in England February 9th with about two thousand other tough guys out of the 203rd to rapturous applause. 'Rapturous applause' is Sturgeon again, but he was right: the limeys loved us. Mostly, they loved the fact we had money, which wasn't something the old country had much of. Everyone knew that a GI on shore leave anywhere in the English Territories had struck lucky. Women and booze were dirt cheap there, and if you got into a scrap and broke a window or an arm then the cops knew to look the other way. But that didn't happen often, or not on my watch. Weird thing how fond most of the guys were about England. Now it was part of the Union everyone was all 'the old country' and feeling mighty protective of the place, like all our ancestors had come over on the *Mayflower*.

My ancestors had come over from the greenish island next door, far as I know, and I reckoned I was let off feeling sentimental about the English on that count. Still, it was going to be a solid two weeks R&R before the 203rd got shipped off again to take the war to the Nords.

We got dumped off at the big base near Reading, leave shifts downloaded to our hub and the first mob of us already fixing to hit London and stuff some good solid dollars down some kinky dancers' panties. For the rest, it looked like half of England had come to us. There was a regular shanty town outside the base—they had a whole load of girls come here because it meant they could earn some cash to send home, and a bunch of older folks who had sad little stalls and carts and tents, selling everything from beer to little tin statues of Big Ben, from the wisdom of the druids to the family silver. They looked… they looked thin and dirty and tired. That was what England looked like to me. Thin and dirty and tired, and with those bad teeth you hear about—that Sturgeon says was never a thing back then, but sure as hell is now. And smoking. Everyone smoked there, the cheapest, nastiest cigarettes you ever ended up stinking of. Which they called fags, which was good for a laugh at least.

Sturgeon has a bundle to say about that, as well. Of course he does, the mouthy bastard. Sturgeon says that it wasn't much more than twenty years after they voted in their Independence crowd and cut themselves right off from Europe, before those same politicos sold the whole shebang to us. Turned out England couldn't stand on its little Union Jack-gartered legs the way it once had, but that was fine: its new leaders had already got themselves a place on the board at a dozen US corporations, so they were all right. Anyway, England became a territory of the Union, and the media said everyone was happy about that.

Later, it became our stepping stone for taking the good fight into Europe, when it turned out that we had what Sturgeon calls irreconcilable ideological differences with some of the governments there.

The base was busy—they already had the 12th Mountaineers and some armor there, and a whole load of the 170th were just being flown out. We were all getting billeted—and more than ready to get down to other things too, the moment we had the chance—when I remember Franken punching me in the shoulder, which is how he gets your attention.

"Sarge, lookit," says Franken.

I lookited, and I saw what he was talking about, and it's a hell of a sight: no fewer than three Scions striding through the press of the base like it was nothing, and everyone else getting the hell out of their way.

The English call them 'the Brass,' but to us they're just Scions. This is who Sturgeon was bitching about, with his dumb history lesson. I squinted at them as they strode past, looking for the logos; looked like a pair from the pharma giant Sayline and one—the biggest one— from the agricorp Buenosol, who are pushing so much of the action over in Nordland. They were eight feet tall, give or take, and you couldn't have gotten the edge of a razor anywhere into the joints of their armored shells. One of the Sayline boys was like an egg on spider legs but the other two were built like men, two arms, two legs on a big armored box where the actual lucky guy would be sitting with all home comforts. They had more guns each than a whole squad, and there was nothing the 203rd was equipped with that would have got through that plating of theirs, either. It felt like a privilege to be this close to them and everyone had gone quiet when they came through. Some, like Franken, pushed close to get a touch, a hand on that expensive metal, because if you were into that stuff the Church of Christ Libertarian went on about, these guys were the Deserving. These guys were rich because it was God's plan, just like if any of us got rich, that would be God's plan too. Just like any one of us might get rich, somehow. We could be the president too. Everyone said so. We just had to work hard and wait our turn.

Anyway, the three Scions just shoved their way through us all, not giving us a glance, and Franken was practically drooling, no doubt imagining how it would be to fight a war from inside a metal shell like that, with a comfy seat and porn on demand and a machine to wipe your ass for you. And I heard Sturgeon do one of those 'tsk' noises he does, because, like I've probably made clear, Sturgeon's an asshole with Ideas and Opinions, and neither of those things is much use for an infantryman these days.

Ninety minutes after touching down at Reading, me, Sturgeon and Franken got our orders to get on a heli for London, and none of us had the faintest idea why. My best guess was that Sturgeon's mouth had got him into trouble, and that Franken and I had been luckless enough to be within earshot. Nobody told us what was going on, we just got passed hand to hand, airport to car, car to city center, along the Embankment road with those bigass barriers to stop the river coming in all their posh lobbies, and then we ended up at the top of a glass-steel tower in whatever they called Wall Street over in London, waiting in a boardroom where the chairs probably cost more than any of us would earn in ten years.

Franken was looking knives at Sturgeon. To be honest, so was I. Sturgeon was a tall, narrow-shouldered New Yorker with a nose like an elbow, and when he wasn't about you'd have said he had glasses on—even though nobody in the army wore glasses—just because he was like so many speccy nerd guys in old TV shows. He wasn't a computer geek or a business wiz or any of those useful sorts of nerds, though, or he wouldn't have been slogging about with a gun like the rest of us. Sturgeon was just a guy who'd had way too much education and then found he had way too little money, like all of us had way too little money. These days the army was often the best, sometimes the only, way of digging yourself out of that hole.

Franken was blonde and from Kentucky and the size of three Sturgeons mashed together, which was a fact he'd had cause to impress on Sturgeon more than once in the time I'd known them. I'd been with them both in Uruguay and then in Canada, and I'd always reckoned that we'd end up going our separate ways after one tour or another. And yet, whenever I got back off leave, it was their ugly faces I was showing the family photos to. The three of us had been on 203rd HQ's Recon platoon through more clusterfucks than I cared to remember.

Sturgeon opened his mouth and I could see he was going to say something clever, meaning something that would get us into trouble. "They're listening," I told his open mouth, and he shut it quickly. No sense getting us into worse than we already were.

"What, then?" Franken demanded.

"We might not even be in the shit," I remember saying, without much enthusiasm. "Maybe they just need security or something. Maybe this is it: easy street for the rest of the war."

"Us?" Franken pointed out. "The three of us get a soft security detail? Because, stop me if I'm wrong, don't they have their own people for that? You know, the real corporate guys, rather than army?"

"Yeah, well," I started, and then the Man came in.

I called them to attention, but I didn't have to, we were already on the way there: me, Franken, Sturgeon, one after the other. You always stand to attention when a Scion's there. A Scion always outranks a regular soldier.

He was seven foot tall and must have weighed six hundred pounds in his suit; not all the lightweight alloys in the world could bring that down. These days, every boardroom in the west had reinforced floors and extra-wide doors. His suit shone like it had just been polished. There was a head on top—it wouldn't have had the guy's head in it, it was just for show—that was square-jawed and good-looking as a film star, and the whole chassis was moulded like the muscles of a weightlifter. I'd run into a few Scions by then, and his was by far the nicest piece of kit I'd seen: fancy enough that I reckoned it was his peacetime civvies, and that he probably had a spikier suit for wartime. A lot of the Scions didn't get out of their shells unless they were inside their compounds, behind a dozen walls and a hundred guards. After all, there was still the occasional bomber out there, home-grown or foreign national. Sons and nephews of the corporate board members were too valuable to take risks with, even here in London City Central.

On his shoulder, like I had my stripes, there was a little logo, but I didn't know it. Scions from companies you hadn't heard of were Big Business. If a company was too small for you to have heard of it, it couldn't afford Scion shells for its gallant warrior sons. If a Scion came from somewhere that wasn't a household name, that meant it was one of the big, hidden companies; the companies that owned the companies that you knew.

When he spoke, a face came up over the cold steel of the mask. Probably it was his face; what would have been the point else? It was a good looking, well-groomed regular guy sort of face, just like they all had when they were rich enough. It wasn't the sort of face anyone was born with, but one that had been measured and tweaked and shaved until it said: *I Am Right; and You Can Trust Me.* You liked that face, just looking at it; you trusted it; you wanted it to like you.

"At ease, Gentlemen. Thanks for coming," said the projected face. His voice was just as well crafted, elocuted and touched up. You'd have done a lot, if that voice asked you. "You would be Theodore Regan, I take it?"

"Yes sir, Sergeant Ted Regan, sir."

He smiled at me, one of those magic smiles where all the condescension is invisible. "I'm a Ted too. Ted Speling, looking after the family interests over here while the war's on." He didn't offer to shake hands. With Scions, it was a habit that had fallen out of use. "Sergeant Regan, you're in a position to do my family a favor."

He said that, and I already wanted to help him any way I could. Plus, of course, that sounded like there was money in it. And then he said: "My cousin Jerome has gone missing, Sergeant. Something happened to him three days ago, out on the front. Nobody knows where he is. You men come highly recommended. I need you to find him, or find what happened to him. Will you do that for me?"

Of course I would. I was already agreeing to it. I didn't choke over that 'highly recommended' bit (because, *really? Us?*). I didn't even see the Big Thing in what he'd said until Sturgeon finally burned through his ability to keep his mouth shut and said, "Your cousin was on the front, sir?"

"That's correct, soldier," said Rich Ted.

Even as I—Poor Ted—was shooting a glare at him, Sturgeon's mouth went right on motoring. "Was he out of his shell, sir?"

And I stopped, because he was right: any cousin Jerome that Ted Speling might lay claim to wouldn't have been within a hundred miles of the front without a shell.

"Well," Rich Ted said philosophically. "It so happens you've hit on the very heart of the problem."

Even then I thought that Cousin Jerome must have decided to get out of his shell, take the breeze or something; maybe there was some pretty little Nord girl tricked him into it. It's pretty much the only need that those suits only fulfil halfway, after all. But no; Cousin Jerome hadn't been pressing his *dwat de sey-nyer*, as Sturgeon called it. The enemy had done something, and his shell had just cut out and shut down and stopped telling anyone where it was.

You see, that never happened. There was a lot of tech in the world, and while we poor grunts got just enough to do our jobs, the Scions got everything money could buy. They had all the money, after all. Sturgeon says— here I go again with what Sturgeon says, but—he says that back when soldiers were soldiers, there was a whole lot of money put into making sure we had all we needed to let us return in one piece—it was lost votes and bad PR if all your brave boys didn't make it back to the Land of the Free. Of course we've had the means-tested voting reforms since then—what the newspapers when I was a kid called the 'Elephant in the Room', on account of how so many people had just become something nobody talked about. Now, on account of regular soldiering being a good job for people with no other options, Sturgeon says, when we get cut up, it doesn't impact on the election so much. This is when he starts saying how the government doesn't look after us any more, and this is usually where Franken starts hitting him.

But sure, it's no secret that your regular grunt does not get the dollars spent on him that the corporate squads do, in terms of gear and support, and it's true we get the crap jobs that they don't, because if things do get hot for us, it's the government footing the bill, not the corporations. And I might have some thoughts and feelings about that, but because I'm not so damn smart as Sturgeon, I keep my mouth shut.

And Scions—Scions have no limits, or certainly the models made in the US of A don't. Those shells are the battledress of the sons of corporations. No man of means is going to send his heir or his spare out with anything less than the best—just like they wouldn't be seen dead in anything less than the biggest car, or perfect teeth, or what golf club you belonged to. When I was in Canada, I saw... well, when our shining boys came through, you should have seen the Canuck infantry run like rabbits. And when their maple-leaf ironclads came stomping the other way, we couldn't hold, even though everyone said they weren't as good. We couldn't dent them.

Sturgeon says that we could have done, only they didn't give us the tools for it. He says that all the corporate types go to the same clubs, and that it's not in their interests to kill each other off when there might be a merger the week after. Like I say, Sturgeon says a lot of things.

Nonetheless, this is beyond dispute: better than the regulars, better than the best-equipped corporate guard, better than mechs and drones and biotech is the armor and the weaponry of the battlefield Scions.

Which brings us back to Cousin Jerome, because all that top flight tech had just fucked off and deserted him, and now he was either dead or caught. Rich Ted was pretty sure he was caught; Jerome would be a big old bargaining chip for the Nords, after all, except that apparently nobody was even asking for a ransom.

That made it our job to go get him. Or to find his body or records of his demise. At no point did he say anything about finding out how the hell they screwed over his shell to winkle him out of it, but that was kind of hanging in the air in a 'bonus payment' sort of way. I reckon they wouldn't honestly have trusted us with that one as a mission objective, but if it fell into our laps we surely would be bringing it to Rich Ted's rich attention.

"Why us, sir?" I asked, and he explained that we would be going in as a small, covert team. He talked about the fact that we three had come through some of the nastier global knife-fights of the last few years without a scratch, and with commendations—he didn't mention all those times Sturgeon got put on a charge for opening his big,

big mouth, or when Franken almost got court martialed for punching a captain. He said a lot of things, but I was used to Sturgeon, and so I could cut through the crap. "You want this done, why not send a few unstoppable Scions?" I could have asked, and the answer he would never have given me was: "Because we're scared they'll do it to us."

Two hours later we were on a plane heading seaward toward the fighting, detached from 203rd's Recon company and leaving the rest of the lads behind. You'd think one of the officers might have made a fuss, but everyone knew that when the Corporates said "jump," you basically didn't come down without orders in triplicate. We were there to fight the war their way, and if their way was sending the three of us off on a rescue mission then that was what was going to happen.

There was gear for us in the plane—and it was brand new, not the hand-me-down crap we normally had to work with. Franken complained, of course. Franken liked his own stuff, worn by long use until it was a comfortable fit in his big hands and smelling mostly of Franken. For me, I appreciated the downpayment. This was Rich Ted investing in Poor Ted, at least a little.

We slept on the plane; live this life long enough and you sleep when you can. The plane's descent woke us and when we looked out, we saw Nord country.

CHAPTER TWO

STURGEON SAID, ONE time, about how the barriers broke in New York when he was a kid and suddenly the whole city was fighting a desperate rearguard action against the sea; when the Hudson burst its banks and swallowed Bloomfield and half of Newark, and made an island out of Newark Liberty Airport. It was the same on both coasts, the defining images of the decade as all that denial came home to roost. But not for Nordland, apparently. Sturgeon said that it was geology, basically; that all this mountainous, fjord-cut land was still riding high even as the sea clawed at it, keeping just ahead of the tide while Thailand and New Orleans and the Netherlands went the way of Atlantis.

The beachhead was a place called Gotham-berg—or that's what everyone called it. The place was thoroughly home-away-from-home. We came in to a chorus of accents from Texas and New England and everywhere in between, and the first thing that met our eyes when we got off the plane was a Mickey-D's. The fighting was way north and east of there. Gotham was thoroughly pacified and brought round to our way of thinking. Of the rest of the country...

Sturgeon got really obsessive about it, when we talked about fighting the Nords. Then he got hit, mostly, but basically there are a lot of Nords, and we're not fighting all of them. The bit just over the sea west of Gotham hasn't weighed in yet, and there's another lot up in a long strip on the west coast who are apparently still mulling it over, with a buttload of Marines waiting just offshore in case they come to the wrong decision any time soon. All the middle of Nordland is the bit we've got problems with, basically: Sweden and Finland, say the maps. Sweden is where the fighting is, and the other place... Finland is weird. Finland is different. Nobody I met in Nordland was looking forward to when Sweden had given it over, and we were left looking at the Finnish border and all the ungodly shit that was waiting on the other side.

We got orders pretty much as soon as we hit tarmac: we had to meet the rest of our team. What rest of our team, you might ask? Apparently Rich Ted didn't want to rely on us quite that much, so we cooled our heels in the vast expanse of Gotham that had been given over as a staging post, waiting for the pair of them to pitch up. We got to watch our boys and the armor and the gleaming god-statues of the Scions march off to stick it to the Nords, and we got to watch a fair number of our boys come back bloodied, though we reckoned we were giving far more than we got.

What it was—this is Sturgeon again—after all the levees broke, after the big economic crunch that hit when half

our coastal cities turned into swimming pools, everyone
needed to pull together. Pulling together, here, meant
buying American, supporting the big corporations that
were our only hope of rebuilding. The problem was that,
over the pond, there were a whole load of governments
who'd taken the same knocks and gone the other way,
taken their god-given democracy and abused it to vote
in the socialists. A whole bunch chucked out all those
promises they made under the Transatlantic Free Trade
Agreement. Corporate assets were seized. There were
bombs, too—full-on terrorist attacks on the property
of multinationals. They were fixing to take all that good
stuff our corps had built up and grab it for themselves,
just hand it over free to every Bjorn and Benny. It was,
everyone says, an assault on our freedoms, on our very
way of life. Everyone except Sturgeon, anyway, and I
guess probably the Nords.

We kicked our heels for two days, which was fine—if
there was anyone who knew how to have a good time on
a US military base it was us poor bastards. Then Lawes
and Cormoran turned up, and we were a team and ready
to go.

Lawes and Cormoran had obviously been given the
chance to get to know each other before they reached
us, and there was a distance between them that told me
neither of them had much enjoyed it. Lawes was a little
guy, smaller than Sturgeon even, and there was nothing
neat about him. I never saw him clean-shaved and his
uniform was darned and filthy, dotted with old stains he
hadn't been able to get out, and his shoes scuffed. He
had brown teeth, huge in his thin face, like he'd been
designed to gnaw through cables we'd find we needed
later. He was a corporal in the English expeditionary

force that got sent over when our boys first landed; he'd been here since the start, which made him our best shot at local knowledge. When I saw his gear, there was some serious snake-eater covert ops stuff there—gear that would make him room temperature to thermals and screw with motion sensors. He was someone who knew all the holes and the gaps in the fences; there was more than a touch of the rodent about Corporal Lawes.

Cormoran was a different beast altogether: some kind of predator, a panther maybe. She came with a metal suitcase that looked like it weighed a ton, and she had a lean, lanky body that could lug it around like it didn't weigh anything. Her fatigues were grey and expensive, and there was a shimmer about them that said they could do all sorts of things, just like her headset and the gadgets in that case. Cormoran was a woman, and black, but the truth was that Cormoran was corporate, and that set her apart from the rest of us far more. She got paid more, and she got better gear, and most of all she would surely have some personal mission to fulfil, or why would she even be here? I reckoned that going on a mission with Cormoran would be like travelling with a time bomb. We'd always be waiting for her to suddenly decide her objectives were more important than ours.

Not that we had a choice about taking her. We'd need her anyway: she was a drone specialist. Whilst mostly that should have meant she got to fight the war from a hundred miles behind the lines, these days the Nords had some good electronic countermeasures, which meant that a lot of fancy drone work was best done from inside the range of a gun. Lucky Cormoran; lucky all of us.

They shipped us out to the front. The 96th Armored and its friends were pushing east just then, taking ground from a Nord army which was mostly just backpedalling and letting them have it. Convoys would get us as far as the troops got, and after that we'd be on our own as we broke the line and headed into enemy territory. All we'd need to do would be to keep our heads down and stay clear of anything that had a Swedish flag while we closed in on Cousin Jerome's last known position.

"Except," Lawes told us on the way out, "it ain't as simple as that, is it? I mean sure, Swedish national army, easy enough. There ain't exactly that many of them, and the way I hear, your lot've got 'em on the back foot anyhow—if it was just them. But this bloody country— who'd've thought they'd got so much fight in 'em, eh?" He spat, smoked, twisting together horrible roll-ups with stringy tobacco from a yellow tin. "Stockholm's lost control, is the problem. There's Nord corporations fighting on both bloody sides—I got shelled by the 1st fighting corps of fucking Ikea last year!—and there's all sorts of wankers coming in from mainland Europe to fight for the Swedes—men and mechs and White Walkers. And the *locals*. Wherever you end up there are partisans, just civvies who've grabbed up whatever gear they can. And when the Nord army gets its orders to pull back, you think the partisans go with them? Don't you believe it. Every fjord and stream and hill and rock'll have some Sven or Olga with a gun. And then there are the Finns, always the bastard Finns."

"I heard about them," I told him.

Lawes fixed me with his rodent stare. "You ain't heard nothing. They ain't human any more, what they send over the border."

After that he tried to interest people in a card game, and Franken took him up on it and lost a few dollars—

meant less to him than the win did to Lawes, but that's the English economy for you.

I tried to get Cormoran talking, picking a question just too flat-out rude to be ignored. "So how come someone like you lands a job like that?"

She gave me a look that said it wasn't the first time she'd heard that. "Summa cum laude out of MIT," and then, because she saw something in my face, "Yeah, before they changed admissions policy. Last class of Alpha Kappa Alpha, me." I didn't know what she meant, but I looked it up later.

I tried to push a little more, but she was having none of it, her dark, bony face closed off. There was something I saw there—the look of a woman who doesn't think it's worth getting to know you, in the short time you've got.

After that it got interesting. I was woken up when something exploded outside the plane and for a moment I didn't know where I was or which war I was fighting, just crunched and taut and bracing myself against everything, because it was all dipping and diving around me. Franken was swearing, but that didn't narrow it down because we'd been serving together a while and that was kind of his baseline.

Cormoran was the center of attention. She had her briefcase open on her lap, and there were two screens lit up on the inside, along with a handful of control tabs. She was running her drones, I realised—more with headware than fingers, from the way her eyes went in and out of focus.

Sturgeon brought me up to date. "Half a dozen attack drones latched onto us five minutes ago," he said, eyes fixed on Cormoran's screens. "One of the engines took a hit but it's still going."

"I can tell that," I said without much patience. There was another cracking report from the blind space outside the hull. From Cormoran's twitchy smile it was one of theirs, not one of ours. "This a hunter pack?"

"Just flak," Sturgeon said, meaning raiders set on autopilot and released in the general direction of our side, rather than tracking us down in particular. Just bad luck then, but Cormoran was more than equal to the challenge. Human-led is better than automatic still, in most fields. Her drones would have their own hair-trigger decision-making software, but she was feeding them a strategy moment to moment, keeping them unpredictable and managing the hacking war that must be going on between the little flying machines. It took her ten more minutes to strike out all of the enemy, using just two of her own. I guess that meant we could rely on her right up until the moment she sold us out.

A COUPLE HOURS after, we were being offloaded right where the 96th had its mobile command post. Orders had outstripped us, so that while there were all sorts of prickly officer types just dying to know who the hell we were, our corporate credentials meant they didn't get to ask, and there was an unmarked M1000 Trojan with my name on it, a nice compact ride with reinforced tyres and armor plate, and a minigun up top that Franken was instantly all over.

"Lovely, reliable rides, the Trojans," Franken said, letting it hang there.

"Their only drawback is that, when you're inside one, you feel like a dick," Sturgeon came back, right ahead of Lawes's. "It's what soldiers get into just before they get fucked." It's a testament to how some people just don't think it through before they name stuff.

The Onboard was loaded with our maps already, showing us where the Scion's signal had given out.

"This won't take us far," Lawes warned us. "Once we're out on our own any vehicle just draws attention. You can never mask the heat signature of something like this, and the partisans will have rockets and drones all over us the moment they guess who we are. And the terrain is a bloody bastard. You're a sitting duck on the road, and off the road, most of it's still forest, can you believe that? Like it's the bloody Middle Ages out here."

"Worse," Cormoran put in. She had her briefcase open again, and for a long moment I couldn't even work out what was on her screens. Then it started animating, frame by stilted frame, and I worked out that some parts of what I was seeing were a satellite view. The vast majority of what should have been contested Swedish soil was smeared with roiling dark clouds that obscured any sight we might have had of what the enemy was doing.

"Seriously," Sturgeon hissed, "what *is* that?"

"Is that the flies?" Lawes asked gloomily.

"Yeah." Cormoran gave us a bright look. "Gentlemen, this is a gift from the Finns. They breed these little bugs, midges, they chip 'em and ship 'em, and every so often the Nords release a batch. There are millions of the little critters each time, and they basically just block the view of our satellites—and we can't see a thing—no one can. So every time our forces advance, we're going in blind. Makes for all kinds of fun."

"They bite?" Franken asked uneasily. We were all

thinking it: mosquitos, disease, some kind of Finnish lab-grown plague that zeroed in on the stars and stripes.

"Not yet," Lawes told us. "Jolly thought though, ain't it?"

The 96th were moving out that day, so we synced our helmet HUDs, got in our Trojan and tagged along. Scuttlebutt said light resistance—drone intel put the national Nord forces pulling back, but everyone reckoned they'd have left mines or mechanicals or something for us to have fun with. I had Franken drive and we found a place toward the back of the convoy. Sturgeon patched into the 96th's comms and we listened to what seemed like every individual soldier pinging us to try and work out who the hell we were and why they were letting us come to the party. Our corporate credentials were obviously suitably imposing. Nobody pinged us twice.

The 96th had their own drone wing out scouring the land ahead, and Cormoran was keeping her toys in their box. A squad of jets went screaming over once, but the fly-screen up above, which blocked the satellites and dulled the sun, had a trick of fouling jet intakes and abrading rotors; air support would be patchy at best.

There was an attack. Of course there was an attack.

I remember in Canada it was civilized warfare. There were skirmishes and shoot-outs; we took towns and villages, and we froze our asses off. We went head to head with the Canuck troops and the French troops and some severely tough Russians that nobody told us were there, and our Scions and theirs stomped about and played their own games with each other, and we tried to stay out of the way. That's war, and when we'd pacified a region, they knew it, and stayed pacified. It's not exactly the worst fate in the world, to have a few corporations putting drilling rigs and mines and sawmills on your land. It brings in money and jobs and solid libertarian values, and if you work hard, like they say, then you'll get paid. But the Nords didn't see it that way.

So, the attack. First off, everything stopped, because the lead scout vehicles had got bogged down. This was nothing natural—the retreating Nords had gone in for some serious improvised irrigation and suddenly we were looking at a crapton of swampland that hadn't been there a couple of days ago, and hadn't looked like anything to write home about when the drones overflew it. This wasn't the first time for this trick, and so the advance scouts were already converting their vehicles for amphibious work. What it did mean, though, was that everyone stopped. No prizes for guessing what came next.

Cormoran's briefcase lit up like the Fourth of July, all these alarms and lights, and then there were rockets coming at us. The Nords—probably Lawes's partisan irregulars—were in the trees and upslope to the south. They were a mile off at least, but they had a whole mess of handheld anti-armor kit, the cheap disposable stuff you could get for a song these days. You couldn't aim them for crap, and I reckon at least half must have gone wide of the entire convoy, but someone had gone on a serious shopping spree to kit out this bunch because everywhere was exploding at random. We had a front seat view of it from inside the Trojan—every camera was just showing us flash-bang and the air full of sprays of dirt, clods of earth being chucked around. Cormoran was trying to get her drones clear for a better picture of what was going on, but from her face I guess she didn't fancy her chances—there was just too much crap being thrown about for clear flying.

"Is this it?" I asked. "This can't be it," because it was all sound and fury out there, but the rockets weren't making much headway against the armor of the transports; we got bounced around, but hell if they were actually getting through to us.

Then we saw a vehicle ahead of us—it was a big Powell Defender transport, a score of men inside and it just leapt sideways with a flash so bright the cameras cut out for a second. Sturgeon was listening intently to the comms chatter. "Limpets," he reported, eyes wide.

"How the fuck are *they* getting drones through this shit?" Franken demanded.

"Because they're slow and they only need to drop them on us," from Cormoran.

"Disembark," Sturgeon relayed.

"Fuck that," was Franken's thought. I was in two minds. The rocket barrage, horribly inaccurate as it was, was slackening as the Nords burned through their toys. If a Limpet found the Trojan and latched on, it would burn us up quicker than the Powell had gone. And Limpet drones wouldn't be targeting men.

I went up into the little shell turret of the Trojan and got behind the gun, cameras giving me a 360 view of the field around us. The bigger armor was already retaliating, sending salvos off toward the partisans' positions. The transports were mostly yakking out their troops, men sprinting for cover or scanning the skies. I saw a Limpet coming in, like a bumblebee the size of my head, and picked it from the air with a quick burst of fire. A couple of our cars were gone—the air now getting thick with smoke as well as the last of the pattering dirt thrown up by the rockets, but we were taking back the initiative. Overhead, someone was risking a gunship, hovering and tilting above with its guns spitting sporadically. I hoped they were watching out for the fly-swarm if it suddenly dropped on our heads.

I heard Sturgeon shout out something from below. I didn't know it, but we'd had another gunship out there, and it had just set fire to a mile-long strip of forest to the south to try and dislodge the rocket-men. Then *something* had got it—it caused the same sort of devastation crashing down as it had when it was up and spraying phosphorus— and that *something* was coming for us.

"Oi, Sergeant!" from Lawes. "I reckon this is where we make our move."

"We're in the middle of a fight," I yelled back to him.

"Not our fight, remember? Higher calling, eh?" I swear sometimes Lawes just sounded like Dick Van Dyke to spite me.

Then company arrived, filling a big part of the sky. Because the fly-swarm didn't stop the *Nords* putting stuff in the air.

"*That*'s something you don't see every day," Cormoran said, sounding more impressed than I'd like.

"Move us out," I told Franken, sending a best-fit course to the driver's panel.

Cruising in at treetop height was probably the biggest gunship anyone had ever managed to get in the air. In Canada they'd had three of them across the whole front, and they were called something like Jodorowskys. Of course just being big didn't actually count for a whole deal, but they were built with that modern Slavic approach to engineering, all redundancy and hard-wearing components and no regard whatsoever for looking pretty. They took a lot of pounding before gravity took offence and yanked them down to earth.

This one was coming in all guns blazing—a blistering wall of counter-munitions fire to lock down the crap we were launching at it, and then its own ordnance bursting free of that firestorm to lance in at the transports. The incoming fire was focusing on the infantry transports, not the armor; they knew that armor took towns but men held them. That was today's war all over, though. These days, men were the cheapest part of any national army, the bit that was most easily replaced, least easily repurposed by the enemy, most easily forgiven when everyone shook hands over the treaty table.

Everyone was scattering now—the transports were nothing more than targets for the firepower the gunship was turning out. Those who were out and free to run around were getting cut up too, but it was incidental—they simply didn't rank highly enough as targets.

Franken was guiding us out from between a couple of tanks, both of which were incandescent as they threw all they had at the Jodorowsky. If we'd had a corporate detachment with us we'd probably already have won, but these days the main line army just doesn't get the best toys.

"You never said there were so many Russians here, Lawes!" I yelled.

"You ever know a fight in the last ten years that wasn't bloody crawling with White Russians?" he hollered back, and that was true enough.

Our own remaining gunship had pulled out, or at least I couldn't see it and I hadn't seen it go down. I was torn. Orders were that this wasn't our business. But these were our people. It didn't feel right just to skip out on them, for all we couldn't do much to help.

That was when the cavalry arrived. I hadn't realized

we even had Scions with the 96th until three of them came vaulting through the smoke. Something I'd seen a hundred times before, sure, but you never get used to it. You always catch your breath, if you've got even a sliver of soul left in you. They were like gods: human figures head and shoulders over the soldiers around them, made of gleaming silver and gold and darkly menacing black steel. And they *were* gods, in a way. This was what human ingenuity could achieve, when price was no object. The corporations wouldn't shell out to give us common grunts that sort of protection, but it was only the best when their sons wanted to play soldier.

They were unleashing a barrage of firepower at the Jodorowsky, and suddenly the tables had—not just turned, but been completely flipped over. The weapons built into those beautiful shiny shells cut through all the counter-ordnance the gunship could muster, striking strings of explosions off the enemy hull. When the Jodorowsky replied in kind, the Scions were briefly enveloped in fire and shrapnel, but when the flare cleared, two of them still stood, and the third was getting back to his feet. I almost expected him to brush his metal chassis down like he was dusting off a tuxedo.

The soldiers around them hadn't been so lucky, of course. Bitter thought.

We were pulling out by then, heading off and ignoring the pings and queries of the column officers who wanted to know what the hell our business was. Behind us, I saw the Jodorowsky falter in the sky for a moment—as if physics had suddenly served it with a cease-and-desist, but then it was backing away, ponderously thundering upward, driven away by three boys who had shinier suits and richer folks than its pilots did.

And then we were clear of it all. Sturgeon had filleted the scout intel about the impromptu swampland the Nords had thrown up, and luckily it looked as though we could bee-line it for Cousin Jerome's last known whereabouts without getting ourselves bogged down.

"Got one question, though," because of course Sturgeon always had questions. "What the hell was our guy doing so far in front of the fighting?"

Somehow none of us had thought to ask that before. I came down from the turret and saw looks passing between them that spoke eloquently of just how none of them really trusted each other. Oh, Franken and me and Sturgeon were a team, but the other two were loners. I'd pegged Lawes as someone who very greatly valued his own skinny little hide, and Cormoran... Why did I think that if only one of us got out of this alive, it would be Cormoran?

"Spying, maybe?" Franken suggested, making me realize that the long pause on his part had actually been because he was thinking. It was a good call—Scions did a lot of espionage work, mostly industrial. Cousin Jerome could have been off stealing Nord secrets when they zapped him with this new anti-Scion thing of theirs. Maybe that was the actual secret he'd been after.

"Just get us there," I told Franken. "Cormoran, you're our eyes. Lawes... what do we need you for exactly?"

The Englishman gave me his rat's grin. "I don't know about your Scion, Sarge, but I've been kicking about in this bloody country since before the war. Think of me as your multi-tool, to get you out of whatever you get into."

"A tool for every occasion, right," I agreed, which was wasted on him.

We had a jolting and uncomfortable time of it for

the next hour or so, which was fine by me. I'll take 'not being shot at' over 'dead in comfort' any time. "So do the Nords know we're here?" I asked Lawes, partway in.

"Someone will know we're here," he confirmed, in a sour mood. He had tried to light up inside the Trojan three times, by then, and after the stench of his uniquely horrible tobacco had brought the rest of us close to vomiting, I'd ended up taking his tin off him. "Thing is," he went on, "it's not like they're all talking to each other, over there. Between the initial bombing runs and the ECM slap-fight last year, most of the comms infrastructure's buggered, so they're basically down to carrier pigeons over half the country. So maybe some partisan cell or a corporate scouting detachment's seen this one US scout car lost in the woods, but who're they going to tell? We'll only know about it if they come and give us a kick. Which they will, soon enough."

"Gentlemen," Cormoran told us abruptly. "I see them."

She was flying her drones high, hanging them just below the fly swarm's lower reaches, spying out the trees ahead. Pure visual showed nothing, and they had set camp with a mess of heat-baffling tarps above them, but there was still just enough signature leaking out to show us someone was there. Mind you, Cormoran was corporate; she had superior gear.

"They've seen us?"

"Probably." Cormoran shrugged. "They're not moving on us with anything mechanical, but they might send men out." Sending men out was like trying to map out a minefield with a long stick: nobody cared what happened to the stick and you could always get another one.

"Go round?" Sturgeon suggested. If they were going to show an interest in us, that was unlikely to help. Franken had throttled down our own heat, running as cold as possible, but the Trojan was still going to stand out.

Lawes was peering at the images. "They got drones out?"

Cormoran skimmed back through images on one screen and pulled up a shot of a silvery disc-looking flier glimpsed between trees. At Lawes' behest she zoomed in and then more until it filled the screen—fuzzy and blurred but still visible for all that.

Lawes gave a thoughtful grunt and settled back. "Shanks's pony," he suggested, which apparently meant go on foot if you were English.

But we weren't ready for that yet, or I wasn't. I had Franken take a detour, and Cormoran keep a long-distance eye on what the enemy were doing, whoever the enemy were. We crept on at a snail's pace, cool and quiet as possible, and nobody stirred from the camp under our drones' watchful gaze.

I took a nap for a while and—as happens far too often in this line of work—the fighting woke me. Not an attack from outside, but the entirety of my team trying to kill each other right there in front of me.

CHAPTER THREE

I AM ASHAMED to admit that I thought *Mind-control gas!* first off, even though the Trojan's filters would have kept anything like that out, and nobody had used gas weapons against military targets since the Luobu debacle. Weapons that can be screwed over by a change in the weather are never worth the bother.

It wasn't mind-control gas—if there even was such a thing—it was just my dumbass squad being fuckwits.

Sturgeon was already on his ass with his hand pressed to his temple. He hadn't actually been in the fight, I discovered later. Franken had been going for Lawes, and had elbowed Sturgeon in the head by accident as he lunged as if his body was so conditioned to slapping his comrade around that it had suffered a targeting error. Lawes had a knife out, and was backed right into the back corner of the Trojan, half-hiding behind our gear. Cormoran was nursing a cut hand, which suggested she and Franken had become unlikely allies.

I asked them all to tell me what was going on, which sounds a damn sight more polite than it came out at the time.

"That little fucker's sold us out!" Franken yelled, tensed to spring for Lawes.

"Oi, listen—" the Englishman started, but I shouted him down.

"Cormoran, report."

The corporate gave me a somewhat mutinous look but complied. "Your man there caught an outgoing signal. Lawes was talking with the enemy."

"Just hear me out—" Lawes tried again, but I snapped, "How long for?"

"No idea," Sturgeon got out, grimacing. "He was encrypted on some weirdass short range frequency." There was a beauty of a bruise coming up about his eye. "I was just messing with comms. I was bored."

I had my pistol out and at Lawes without really thinking about it. A shot inside the Trojan could do a lot of damage if it starting bouncing around, but I reckon it wouldn't do half as much if Lawes ate it first.

"Jesus Christ, will you just listen?" the Englishman demanded, and then flinched back when Franken half went for him.

"Don't blaspheme," I warned. "He doesn't like it."

Lawes' eyes bugged out a bit. "Seriously?"

"First Church of Christ Libertarian is *very* serious about taking His name in vain," I confirmed. It was odd to see that rattle Lawes more than the gun, but they were weird about religion where he came from. "Now how about you start talking?"

"That lot out there, I know them," Lawes got out

quickly. "They're Nord corporates, not the nationals. That means they're not fighting us."

"Plenty of Nord corps are fighting us," Sturgeon snapped.

"Not them—look, seriously, when you lot first weighed in here it was only 'cos you were asked in by a bunch of Euro-based multinationals who were getting their stuff nicked, right? Now, I agree that once the real fighting started, a lot of the Eurocorps had to at least pretend they were fighting for the national interest, but most of them are just clockwatching. After all, when the war's done, they'll all be best friends again, right? This lot are Skaalmed special forces, and what they're mostly about is watching over their corporate holdings until it's safe to go back to business as usual."

"So?"

"So they won't fight us, for starters," Lawes pressed. "So they can take us right where we want to go, escort us there—the partisans and whatever other fuckery they have, they won't go for us if we're with 'their' people," and he did that thing with his fingers for the 'their'.

"And why would they do this?" I asked him.

He gave me a sickly smile. "I know them; they know me. We've done business together before. There are plenty Skaalmed boys owe me a favor."

For a moment the situation balanced on Lawes' knife edge. "Cormoran," I said. "Get yourself patched up."

"Already on it." And of course she had some crap in her that let her heal fast. Somebody had *invested* in Cormoran.

"Okay," and I lowered the gun. "Last question, Lawes. Why not just *tell* us?"

I caught his face naked then; there was no subterfuge in it, none of that ratty cunning, just complete surprise.

He'd never thought to; it just wasn't in his nature. I guessed he'd been playing his own games out here for so long that he'd run out of people to confide in years ago.

"If you want to go off-script some time, you clear it with me," I told him, "or I will serve you to Franken. You got that?"

He nodded, servile as you like, but I wondered. I wondered what sort of business he did with Nord corps, and just how much that was going to bite us in the ass. If we were going to go eat breakfast with the Nords at Lawes's invitation, I was sure as hell going to keep close enough to snap his scrawny neck if things went bad.

I had him put me in touch with the Nord commander, and she and I—it threw me a little that she was a she and maybe it shouldn't have—had a little chat. It was the first test of our translation software, too, so I let the woman's Swedish wash over me, with all its improbable vowels and weirdass inflections, while a pleasantly urbane male voice spoke over it, giving me the Nord's deal with a Californian accent. This was Överste Rurisksdottir of Skaalmed AB's Asset Protection Division. Skaalmed were big business, and so Rurusksdottir probably had serious hardware at her disposal, and sufficient Swede cred to warn off the locals. If Lawes could be trusted, then his deal sounded good.

I wanted to ask for orders right then, but trying to hail the 96th's column might give us away to other enemies, and might not go down well with Skaalmed either. Besides, unless Rich Ted Speling was anywhere within earshot, there wasn't exactly anyone who *could* give me orders.

So I trusted Lawes, in the end. I promised myself not to make a habit of it. We went to break bread with the Nords.

* * *

Överste RURISKSDOTTIR WAS one of those women who drew your eye whenever she walked into the room. It might have been the enormous chrome exoskeleton. She was a Skaalmed Scion, but whatever else she might have been, she was sure as hell trying to connect with her inner Viking. There were spiky runes edging the plates of her shell, and she had an actual hammer—something it would have taken four men to lift—magnet-locked to her back. There were horns on her headpiece, and I leant over to Sturgeon and told him that if he was going to pass some comment about Vikings and history and horned helmets—he'd done it three times since we set foot in Nord country—then no power on earth would save him from the consequences. And for once he kept his mouth shut.

Most Scions are built well enough to put over body language when they want to, and Ruriskdottir's suggested strongly that she wasn't impressed with us. The Skaalmed detachment numbered about a hundred, but they were toting some serious gear: not just the disc-shaped drones we'd seen, but some miniature armor that could switch from tracks to legs for the rough terrain, and packed considerably more punch than our Trojan. They had mechs, too—that stilty Netherlands type that look like Martian war machines and were such a pain in the ass in Mexico. One of them was active and patrolling, and every time it passed it stopped and stared at us with the cluster of camera eyes clumped in the center of its round body. A Skaalmed logo flanked them on the left, and the red arrows of Ruud, the manufacturer, on the right. And a nasty pair of gun barrels below, which kind of dominated my attention.

As for the troops themselves, they were neat and disciplined and ready, and edgier than I was expecting. Corporate elites, with all their fancy gear, you don't imagine them being jumpy, but this lot kept their eyes on the forest and cast a broad net with their drones. About one in three were women, which was an odd thing to see these days. I'd served with plenty of women in my time, but back home the creed of Christ Libertarian had very strong views about a woman's place, and it wasn't on the battlefield. Congress hadn't made it illegal for women to sign up, but current regs didn't make it easy for them.

The Överste and I had a carefully phrased conversation through our respective translation software.

"You won't tell me what you're coming out here for," she told me. Like all Scions, her mech body could stand still forever while she reclined inside. That meant I had to stand too, if I wanted her to take me seriously. We were at one edge of the camp, and I took in the darkening treescape, listening to the faint hums of the drones, the whine of insects and the staccato chatter of birds.

"We've got somewhere we need to be," I explained. "If you're sharing, any intel would be appreciated. If we're allies."

She made a grating sound that I recognized a moment later as a sigh. "I've not known what we are from day to day for about a year, Sergeant Regan. Back when we kicked all this off, they told me it would be over within three months of your lot being invited in. The socialists would fold under popular pressure, they said. Nobody thought the *people* would back them to the hilt—until way after they would have preferred to surrender, in fact. The Swedish army is still in the field because it's become a point of national pride, of national *identity* even, that we fight. And nobody thought the Finns would back us. And nobody thought it would be such a god-damned *cause celebre* in the Euro-union either." And I have no idea whether she actually said that bit in French or whether my translator was getting above itself.

"That must make it awkward for you," I said diplomatically.

She whacked one immense fist into the armored palm of the other hand, making me jump back, and drawing the startled attention of my fellows. It was just that, though, just the one motion, and the danger ebbed after a moment.

"If it were me, just me, Ada Rurisksdottir of Sandviken, then I would take up a gun and fight for my country," she told me in the male Californian tones of my software. "But my family fought long and hard to get on the board and I have a duty to our shareholders. Our shareholders are not even majority Swedish. So we sit out here and wait to see how the arguments go, over in Stockholm. If the socialists continue to be stubborn, then we are halfway your allies. If things go another way, perhaps tomorrow we are your enemies."

"But for now?" I pressed.

"For now? I have spoken to your pet English. We help you get where you need, and don't ask questions. I will give you Intel and a clear route to your coordinates, and a best guess at what's in the way."

"Who controls the country between here and there?"

"Nobody controls anything," she told me bitterly. "You're on the shores of the Vättern by then. There was some serious fighting there—your advance forces, the nationals and the partisans. This was before the lines crystallised, when you were still just dropping men and mechs wherever you liked. For a month there was even a boat war up there on the lake. There was a big factory at Tunnerstad on the island there, someone's research facility. I never did find out what they were doing there, but someone bombed it and then everything went straight to hell. Now you've got freelance Euro marauders that way, and cells of locals fighting everyone and everything, and... worse."

I knew precisely who 'worse' meant: the same faction that had gifted the satellite view with its pest problem, and half the Nord war veterans with their nightmares, to hear people talk about it. "They're active up there, are they?"

"That was where they first showed people what they'd been cooking up in their labs over the border," Rurisksdottir confirmed grimly. "Look up how the Vättern boat war ended, if you don't believe me. Nobody had any idea, before that."

We spent a night on Skaalmed's hospitality, while Sturgeon and Cormoran looked over their intel and planned our next move. Why had Cousin Jerome been out on the banks of the Vättern? Probably not for his health. Had there been industrial secrets hidden in the ruined research facility? Had he just been some privileged kid who got lost?

Did the Finns have a weapon that killed Scions?

WE GOT TO within a day's easy walk of the coordinates before we lost the Trojan. To be honest I don't think any of us had expected it to last so long.

Cormoran had her drones flying wide, which gave us a little advance warning when the enemy tried to bring one of them down with a barrage of rockets. While she was wrestling with that, Franken was taking us away, but the drone flying ahead of us reported more heat signatures— mechanicals suddenly powering up as we got close. We'd driven into a trap.

Even then we might have got out of the net: Cormoran had given us a chance, and Franken took it with both hands. We were off-road, though, and the country out that way was riddled with little lakes and streams that suddenly opened up from between the trees like mouths. The ground was unpredictably soft between them— something the drones just couldn't know beforehand. One moment we were looking good to get clean away, the next we were slewing sideways toward a dark expanse of water of unknown depth, half our wheels churning mud. Franken wrestled us clear the first time with judicious jockeying of the gas, but there just wasn't a straight path of dry ground to be had anywhere we turned. I don't know whether the locals had been damming and flooding or whether it was just the land itself we were fighting, but the enemy caught up to us just as we plowed into another mire and began to flay the armor from our right side.

Trojans are, as they say, designed for deep insertion. This meant they were designed to last long enough under fire to give the occupants a chance to get out. Lawes took the turret this time, swinging the minigun about to give an answer to all those urgent questions the enemy were asking us. I hunched by Cormoran to get a drone's eye view of who was after us. As I'd half-guessed, they were Ruuds, that same model of tripod mech that Rurisksdottir had been packing. Probably she hadn't betrayed us—you saw machines like these wherever the fighting went; they were reliable and none too expensive.

This lot were tooled up with the squat box of a rocket battery, and a minigun that wasn't much inferior to ours. I saw two of them stalking forward, broad, padded feet managing the treacherous ground better than our wheels had. They were concentrating on emptying rockets into the flank of the Trojan—the wheels there had already been shredded, but the armor was holding.

One of them was abruptly cut down, a leg scythed away and then a jagged line of holes chewed across its compact body by our gun. Then our chassis shuddered, and Lawes dropped down out of the turret, cursing. That marked the end of the Trojan's ability to defend itself.

We were ready to go by then. Sturgeon popped the side-hatch away from the Ruuds, and we crashed out into shin-deep muddy water. Lawes had the opportunity to utter a cry of despair as another of the Ruuds rose from the black lake ahead of us, close enough to poke with a flagstaff. I looked into its lenses as water ran from it and the barrel of its minigun spun up. I swear the bastard was gloating.

A bright flash lit it up, and pieces of mangled weapon pod were flying overhead to rattle from the Trojan's abused hull. Then another, so the machine staggered sideways, trying to get its launcher in line as we lurched and stumbled along our doomed transport's side. Then Franken pumped a grenade into it, right where one of its legs met the body. His aim was spot-on textbook perfect, shattering the vulnerable joint and pitching the entire machine backward to be lost in the water.

One of Cormoran's drones spun and hovered where it had been—the source of the initial hit. It was like a dragonfly as long as your arm, but it must have been packing some serious weaponry somewhere.

"There's still one out there!" Sturgeon yelled, and even as he did, something gave on the Trojan's far side and the vehicle shuddered a foot further toward the lake with the impact. We lurched out from its shadow shooting, guided by the eyes of Cormoran's drones. The last remaining Ruud was already chattering at us with its gun, and I swear Franken never came closer to being killed in his life. The Ruud was already reeling from a pair of drone strikes, though, oily smoke issuing from somewhere inside its cracked carapace. I finished it off myself, three rounds into its lenses, and then another three and another, pushing deeper and deeper until I hit something vital.

When it was down, we crouched in the mud, behind the trees, and we waited. Cormoran had her briefcase before her, spiraling her drones out further and further, looking for any more teeth of the trap that were coming late to the party. When let loose without human operators, Ruuds use a net mind—trigger one and you trigger them all. At the same time, they're not programmed for suicide. We'd just trashed three of them, so the rest of the pack might write us off as too tough to take on. Probably they'd already reported us to whoever set them out here, if they even had a live human contact any more. Autonomous mechs without a handler to shut them down were as dangerous as forgotten minefields after the fighting had finished. That was one reason we didn't tend to use them, but nobody else seemed to see it that way.

We let Cormoran do her thing for an hour before anyone was willing to call the all clear. After that, while Sturgeon and I kept an eye out, Franken set about scalping. It was a habit of his, and occasionally a useful one. With surprising deftness he took his tools to the

Ruud I'd downed, and dug until he had isolated and removed its brain.

"You have got to be kidding me." Lawes watched in fascinated horror as Doctor Franken performed his surgery. "Is he going to wear it about his neck like a trophy or something?"

I nodded to Sturgeon, who never needed an excuse to show people he knew stuff they didn't.

"Best defense against mechs like this," he explained smugly. "Their net mind is always reaching out to reincorporate missing elements, so we'll kill this one's transmitter, but leave it receiving. When its buddies turn up looking for it, we'll know. Also, Franken likes to play with them."

"Is that right?" Lawes was torn between being disturbed and impressed. It felt good to know a trick the Englishman didn't.

"They talk," Franken grunted, finishing off. "I'm gonna hook Freddo here to a translator and see what's going on in his little mind." He held up the mech's brain, ragged with severed wiring.

Sturgeon kept his eyes on Lawes' face. "The AI's pretty complex, with the Ruud models," he explained with relish. "Sometimes they beg."

Lawes' eyes flicked between the two of them. "That's cobblers," he decided.

Sturgeon and Franken grinned in unison, best friends now they had someone else to annoy.

"We should move," Cormoran said quietly at my shoulder. Being who she was, she could have tried to pull corporate rank on me, I guess, so I appreciated her discretion. Of course, whether Franken or the rest would have followed her orders is another question.

It didn't take any time at all for us to declare the Trojan out of the fight. It would take more than a puncture repair kit to get it moving again. That done, I set my three subordinates to clear out everything we could use while I took Cormoran aside. From the way she was standing about, I could see she had something to say that was just for me.

"You strike me as a smart man, Sergeant," she told me.

I regarded her doubtfully. "You've got low standards."

"Well I came in with Lawes, so what do you expect?"

I couldn't stop a smile at that one. "So what is it I'm missing, is that what you're going to tell me?"

"I've seen your records, Sergeant: long service, but it's not exactly all medals and commendations."

"So?" Of course she'd seen all our records. The army didn't say no when the big corporations came asking.

"So haven't you wondered why it's you here, and not a corp team?"

"They don't like to get their hands dirty?" I shrugged. Inside, I felt a stab of unease. It was a good question, and I didn't like to think I'd bought into that Rich Ted/Poor Ted thing so much that it had gone under the radar.

"We're trying to get back one of their own: a son of the corporate families," she pointed out, keeping her voice low. "What expense would they spare, exactly?"

"You tell me," I shot back, harder than I'd intended. "You're one of theirs, after all. You're no grunt. So whatever we're actually being sent to do, you'll be all right."

"Is that what you think?" Her face had closed up again, putting distance between us, even though she didn't move a step. I was going to deny it, just a knee-jerk, but then I didn't, and she nodded. "That is what you think, then? I'm going to sell you."

"And cheap." I shrugged. "Nothing we haven't seen before. The army gets the crap jobs. The army gets sent in whenever the corps need meat for the grinder. That's what Sturgeon says." It was pretty much just the tip of the iceberg of what Sturgeon said, but it was about as far as I would follow him.

"Yeah, well." I didn't see the tension across her shoulders until she let them sag. "Happens that way sometimes. Not this time. I'm as fucked as the rest of you, believe me."

We stared at each other for a moment, and I heard a clatter and a whine of fans from inside the Trojan, and Sturgeon chattering happily about whatever they'd just woken up.

"If it helps, I figured they were sending us because they didn't know what the hell ate the Speling boy." I guessed she wouldn't think of him as Cousin Jerome. "They aren't going to risk another Scion, or maybe anything expensive. So I did think of it that much." Not as much as I should have done.

She shrugged again. "Keep on thinking that. Maybe it'll turn out to be true."

Then our three brave salvagers turned up, and they had a pet. It was one of the BigBug load-carriers that we so seldom got to play with, a headless, squat, six-legged robot that would obligingly cart all our gear around for us. We loaded it up with rations and ammo and tents and all the rest of the salvageable gear from the Trojan. Then we set off on foot because, while I can't speak for the other two, we of the 203rd can be stubborn to a bloody-minded fault when we set our minds to it.

CHAPTER FOUR

CORMORAN HAD HER drones out as our long-range eyes, and Lawes turned out to be a surprisingly good pathfinder who kept us from getting our new boots too wet (the spares we'd all changed into after we got dumped on the lakeshore). The soundtrack for that trek was a constant muttering complaint coming from Franken's direction, though not actually from Franken. This was the brain he'd taken from the Ruud, which he'd patched through his translator into a little earphone speaker. If you leant in close, you could hear the bastard thing trying to report in that easy Californian accent, calling out for its absent siblings and then—I swear this is true—cussing out Franken like you wouldn't believe, threatening him with physical violence and Euro-law prosecution for what he'd done to it. I don't know much about battlefield AI, but I reckoned those Ruudboys had been out there a long while to get that glitchy and personality-filled.

We were due more than our share of shit, that journey, but it was the flies that started the next round. It wasn't as if our journey had been insect-free, but after four hours or so we started to realize that the air was getting busy with them, the dark beneath the trees flurrying like static with the blur of little wings. Sturgeon was casting anxious looks upward, as if that whole satellite-blocking fly-screen was just going to descend on us like weather. What tipped me off more was Cormoran: she had her briefcase on her back, and was flying her drones with a little handheld console and her headware, but from the look of it, it wasn't doing the trick.

"Give me five, Sergeant?" she asked.

I nodded, signalled Sturgeon to keep watch, and Cormoran opened up her case and tried to sort her toys out.

"What's up?" I asked her.

"I'm losing contact," she told me. "The distance at which I can actually link to them is shrinking as we travel."

"It's a power problem?"

"I charged up all the batteries from the Trojan; they should be good for days yet. It's some sort of interference…"

I swatted at the low whine of a fly, then examined my palm critically. If I'd be expecting to see tiny spilled microcircuitry for guts, I was disappointed. "Is it these bastards?"

I wanted her to laugh that off, but she just frowned.

"Is it the satellite screen come to take a look at us?" I pressed.

"I don't think so, but something from the same labs. Look."

She showed me some readings on her case screen. Suffice to say they were too technical for me to make much of them, which must have shown on my face.

"They carry a charge—the flies. Each on its own is nothing, but enough of them together and they just… cause interference, screw with our comms and my drones. I'm not going to be able to keep a proper watch—right now I can't send anything more than about a hundred yards before I lose the link, and I don't want to trust them on automatic, that's too easy to fool. If it gets worse…"

"We could get zapped by these things?"

She really wanted to dismiss that one, but then she gave another of her shrugs. "Fuck knows, Sergeant," was her frank appraisal of the situation.

Lawes got us to the edge of the Vättern after that, where all the fighting had been. Intel was patchy, so I had Sturgeon pop out all the warning tech we could get—Geiger counter, chem-hazard, everything. We were getting toward dusk then, just when we'd found some country that was no use whatsoever for hiding in. We were exposed out at the water's edge, with the dark bulk of the island hunching up the horizon across the water. There had been a lab or something there, Rurisksdottir had said. I decided that I didn't want to go find out, and looking back I'm glad that was one command decision I got to stand by.

After a brief conference with our expat Englishman, we pressed on alongside the water, more and more jumpy, picking up pace as the daylight left us, the BigBug labouring patiently in our wake.

We found some little town that had been a harbour before everything kicked off. It looked as though it would have been a nice little tourist retreat or retirement place, stuck on a little strip of low ground between the water and the trees. They'd fought over it for weeks, Lawes said. All those nice suburban homes and gardens trampled by men and mechs and Scions, torn up by shells and the treads of tanks. And for what? Nobody was there now, not our guys, not their guys. Whatever strategic objective had been served by dropping men and machines onto the shore of the Vättern had long since become obsolete. Or else everyone's guys had been driven off. Like Lawes said, like Rurisksdottir had said, there were more than two sides to this war.

We pitched camp in the broken shell of a big, ruined quad—might have been a school once, or some government office or just a really fancy house. It gave us cover and plenty of ways out if we had to bug out, which was what mattered. We got attacked in the night, too. There was a hectic twenty minutes of gunfire enlivened by one really badly aimed Molotov cocktail, followed by about two hours of occasional potshots at us. This broken place, this wrecked gravel shadow of a town, still had its residents. It's one thing you learn in this job: some people won't ever leave home. Some people will cling on no matter what; they've got nowhere else to go.

We all had night-sights, and we had Cormoran's drones. From the images she captured, I don't think the locals had anything other than a handful of scavenged assault rifles and a grab-bag of hunting weapons. I gave orders to scare them off, but there's no accounting for bad luck, and there must have been at least a couple who ducked late or took the wrong left. They weren't soldiers; they weren't even the partisans we'd been warned of. I don't exactly count it as a grand victory over the Nords.

I think they might have been after our rations as much as our blood.

Come first light, we were all eager to get going, because the alternative would be to stay and see if parts of the rubble-jagged landscape would suddenly resolve themselves into dead faces and outflung limbs.

We took to the treeline, moving parallel to the water's edge, as the interference drew Cormoran's drones closer and closer to us, until they were always a constant hovering presence or just perching on her shoulders. The robot brain kept up its muttering, which seemed to buck up Franken's spirits, if nobody else's.

There was a wrecked ship we saw, half-beached in the shallows. Like Rurisksdottir had said, there'd been a bit of a boat war on the Vättern. The wreck had been a compact gunship, and one of the turrets was still sticking one finger up at the sky. The grey armored hull had been shredded below the waterline, the damage revealed when it heeled over in final defeat. I'd never seen the like: the metal just snipped up and pulled open like someone had taken a pair of sharp pliers to a toy.

"There's probably some still alive in there," Lawes said glumly, nodding at the inky water.

"Some what?" I asked him.

"You didn't hear what the Finns brought, to clear everyone out? Crabs." Everyone was looking at him like he was mad, and he shook his head mournfully. "They just seeded the lake with them—little ones, when they did it—and the bloody things grew and grew—big as cars, someone told me. They just tore open anything that put out on the water—and any*one*." He chuckled, in that miserable English way of his. "Funny thing is, there was always supposed to be a monster in the Vättern—

like Nessie, you know?—and now it's got more monsters than anyone knows what to do with."

"You made that up," Franken growled at him, but Lawes met his gaze without a flinch.

It was within an hour that we hit our coordinates. There were no giant crab attacks that I'm admitting to.

HALF AN HOUR later and we still didn't know much more. There had been a camp there—our man hadn't just been got strolling down the lovely crab-infested lakeshore. Lawes tried to piece the tracks together, but there was little enough to find given the time that had passed. The drones picked up more. Cormoran had some kind of scene-of-crime software she set up, and I got to peer at models of how things might have been based on the marks and prints and scars that had been left behind. A tent, she thought, and thermal baffling sheets—she'd pinpointed the attachment points on the trees nearby. Soil analysis showed where a heater had been sat, and by that time Lawes had turned up a couple of empty Nord ration packets, just scrappy films of foil, but they told a story. A small team had been parked here, waiting, and then our man had come along. And then he'd vanished off the map, somehow.

Cormoran set the drones on a spiral pattern, looking for a trail we could follow, but by then Lawes had found fresher prints. They should have been none of our business—they were clearly far more recent than whatever had happened to Cousin Jerome. What got us worried was that they came out of the lake.

None of us were happy with the idea, but once Lawes had shown them to us we couldn't doubt his conclusions.

They must have been fresh that morning, and they were... How to describe them? They were almost human. Think about that: I'm not sure there's anything more frightening. Not mech tracks, not monsters. We could plainly see the imprint of toes, of fingers, but longer than they should have been. They put me in mind of werewolf movies.

"We need to move," Lawes decided. He looked at me with his big teeth bared, like a dog anxious to be let off the leash. "This is Finnish SpecOps. They could be here right now." And what was worse was, he was looking toward the water as though they might just be hanging there like drowned men, beneath the surface.

"Have we got anywhere to move to?" I demanded.

"Yes." Cormoran looked up from her open case. "I have a trail. Tracked vehicle, probably a converted PBV 5-series or similar." I had my helmet HUD call it up: a heavily armored car not a million miles from our Trojan. "It's faint," Cormoran went on. "We'll have to take it slow or we might just lose it altogether, but we've got something to follow. Heading inland, looks like."

All this time, Franken's stolen brain had kept up its mutinous grumbling—you just tuned it out after a while. Right then, though, even as Cormoran was calling her drones back, the translator's flawless Californian snapped out, "Oh you bastards are in for it now!"

Even though it couldn't reach out to them, the brain had felt the first electronic touch of its friends.

For a moment we just crouched there, weapons at the ready and listening, hearing nothing. Then Sturgeon and one of the drones caught the first heat signature through the trees at about the same time.

We got moving sharpish, skipping over terrain that was lumpy with rock and root and pocked by gaping craters that nature hadn't been able to mend. Behind us, the Ruuds would be striding forward, stilting over the terrain with their long legs. I'd seen them in action often enough to track their progress in my mind's eye. They looked awkward and teetering, but they could put in a hell of a turn of speed over rough ground.

Our heading was away from the water, because if we got caught in the open between the trees and the lake then we'd be dead meat on legs. Franken, bringing up the rear, turned to launch an incendiary in the general direction of the enemy every half minute or so, keeping them busy and screwing with their heat imaging.

"Can we sacrifice the Bug?" Cormoran asked, doggedly keeping pace with her case swinging in one hand.

I had a frantic going-on-holiday moment of trying to remember what we'd stowed where, what of the Bug's load we could reasonably carry. "Is this going to slow them or stop them?"

"Just slow."

"Free the gear and it's yours."

She was already in the Bug's systems, and it jettisoned its clasps and straps explosively, spilling duffle bags and tins and the tents over the forest floor. Everyone grabbed what they could—we'd be leaving a lot of hot meals behind us, and our next sleeping arrangements would be newly intimate. We ran on, and behind us the Bug wheeled nimbly on its six feet and then lumbered off into battle.

I didn't see what it did at the time, but Cormoran had drone footage she showed me later: the little carrier robot charging like a doomed knight toward the great stalking strides of the Ruuds. Something—one of Cormoran's somethings—meant they didn't flag it as a target until it was quite close, or perhaps they were just too fixated on us. It must have been within ten yards when the nearest of the trio of mechs stopped and started shooting at it. The valiant Bug lost two legs in that burst, but it could still hop about on the remaining four, and it closed the distance in a sudden mad rush. In my mind, it was screaming a battle cry.

It blew—the drone's cameras were just flat white for a second, and in the aftermath one of the Ruuds was down, and another was staggering and limping, one leg damaged and trailing. A half-dozen trees had been torn into as well—there was a matchwood-strewn crater where the Bug had been, with odds and pieces still pattering down.

I swear, if I knew that was a thing the Bugs could do, I'd not have gotten within twenty feet of one of them.

The last Ruud was still coming, in the drone's footage, and Cormoran was yelling that same news to me right then and there as we ran. I was weighing up the odds: probably we could turn and ambush it now, the five of us against a machine. Certainly we couldn't just keep running.

Then the forest ahead of us whomped into flames— abruptly the trees were a wall of fire, all that damp wood and earth seething and spitting and cracking in the instant inferno heat.

"That wasn't from the Ruud!" Sturgeon shouted.

We were already changing course, now running parallel to the trees' edge instead of away from it. Another incendiary shell exploded past us, lighting up a hundred yards of beach with flames that could burn underwater.

Lawes was swearing to himself. The rest of us were saving our energy for running. Except Cormoran, whose

drones were obediently feeding her images of just what
had run into us.

"White Walker!" she cried, and that's when our day
got a whole lot worse.

Like Lawes said, if there's fighting, there's Russians.
These days they're the premier mercenaries the world
over: they don't quit and they're backed by enough money
to make even a few of them a serious problem. This isn't
the government, what they're calling the Red Russians
now. This is what happened when that government
finally went all out on those rich oligarchs and their
families, took their property and drove them out to make
them everybody else's problem. Some of them were
legitimate businessmen and some were criminal families
and some were former government types who had picked
the wrong side. What they became, though, was a well-
monied class of global exiles: the White Russians.

And of course, most of them just found gainful
employment around the world, but you know what?
In my trade I never got to meet that type. I got to meet
representatives of the mercenary clans who had got out
of Russia with their fortunes intact, enough to equip
a private army well enough to go head-to-head with
corporate special forces.

And of course the favored sons of these military exiles
went to war, just like the sons of our great corporate clans.
And, just as with them, they spared no expense. Except
that while Rich Ted Speling or Överste Rurisksdottir had
shells that could get through a decent-sized doorway,
fit for a hostile takeover in the boardroom as well as a
battlefield, the White Russians thought big. What came
striding toward us through its own wall of fire was as tall
as the trees, which it shouldered aside without difficulty.

The White Walker was a brutalist, headless humanoid shape, with two arms low at the front for grabbing and crushing, and two more off its shoulders that were basically just enormous toyboxes of weapons. Its front was painted with a vastly complex coat of arms full of saints and horsemen and five different colors of eagle.

For a moment, the fire was messing with its instruments and it just stood there, receding behind us as we ran. Then it got intel from the Ruud and began following us, moving at a leisurely stomp that sent shockwaves through the ground to us and shivered the branches of the trees.

It was a Scion. We could fight men and we could fight mechs, but we had nothing that would touch it. Nobody had bought us that sort of firepower.

Sturgeon says—and I appreciate this is an odd time to be talking about what Sturgeon says, but it's crazy what goes through your head when you're running for your life—Sturgeon says that it's not even just that they're cheap. He says that they could give us common soldiers Scion-killer weapons if they wanted, but that would be putting the power in our hands. Scions fight Scions, like chess players play against chess players. We pawns are just here to get taken.

That's what Sturgeon says. Right then, with the White Walker rattling our teeth with each step, it was hard to argue with.

Another couple of incendiaries went over our heads and exploded five square yards of forest ahead and to the left; we were fleeing like rabbits with a dog after us, and I had the idea that the Ruud was running interference off to the right, closing the trap. The Walker was still some way behind us, and there was a lot of tree cover, but I was still thinking, *Why hasn't he crisped us?*

Was it the flies? Because the air was thick with them by then, and maybe they were screwing with the Walker's targeting. Or maybe the son of a bitch was just enjoying himself, the lordly Boyar out hunting peasants.

Sturgeon was in the lead, and without warning he disappeared, so completely that it was like a magic trick. More woodland real estate was going up in smoke, so any shout he gave was utterly lost. A moment later, Lawes was gone too, and then I was skidding to a halt at the edge of a big square hole, that had been covered over with branches and leaf litter before my comrades had crashed into it.

I imagined spikes. I imagined... well, to be honest my imagination was going nuts about then because I think I imagined crocodiles or something, but then Sturgeon was calling, telling us to get down there. With the Walker thundering closer, we didn't need much encouragement. Franken popped an incendiary in an adjacent tree as he brought up the rear, so that our exit would be just one more hotspot for the Walker to pass over.

CHAPTER FIVE

WHAT WE'D FOUND was a tunnel, too cramped to stand up in, which my HUD compass claimed ran north-east/south-west. We took the arm that led away from the water and put as much distance between us and the hole as we could. The crazy skimming of my gun's flashlight showed the tunnel was walled with concrete slabs, many of them defaced. My HUD translator kept picking up graffiti as we went, so that we made our escape through a cloud of overlaid Swedish obscenities.

I say, escape. That makes it sound happier than it was. What actually happened was that we came suddenly out into a big chamber lit by a couple of flickering electric lamps. The floor was some way below, and we stumbled and skidded down a rough flight of breezeblock stairs and into the muzzles of at least a dozen guns.

Sturgeon was already on hands and knees at the foot of the stairs—not shot, but the clumsy bastard had tripped over his own feet, his own gun skidding conveniently out of reach. Lawes was after him, aiming back at our new hosts, grimacing enough to show every one of his brown teeth.

There were at least fifteen of them there, men and women wearing a grab-bag of civvies and military cast-offs; armor vests and Barbour jackets and Vintersorg reunion tour T-shirts. Their guns—by far their most attention-grabbing feature given where they were pointed—were mostly surplus, assault rifles of the model before the model the current national army were toting, but there were a couple of ours there as well.

"I think we found the partisans," Cormoran said softly from behind me. "You want a flash-bang?"

She could blind them with her drones but I imagined the enclosed space with that many guns going off. If someone pulled a trigger right now, just about everyone was going to die from terminal ricochets.

"Easy now, let's not make this worse," I said, and saw that none of them understood me. They weren't Rurisksdottir's well-equipped lot; they didn't have translators, and they'd have to crowd inconveniently close to hear mine.

"Sarge?" Sturgeon asked. He had slowly tipped himself back until he was sitting on the bottom step.

"Go for it," I invited, and he tried something in Swedish that was good enough for my translator to recognize it.

There followed the expected give and take where they told us to put our guns down, and we politely declined. At the same time I was making plain that we weren't there to shoot anyone, and that we were just a peaceful little search and rescue team. It was really, really hard to phrase all of this, partly because I didn't want to tax Sturgeon's vocabulary, and partly because we were Americans, and Americans were very definitely fighting the Nord army right about then, and so it was kind of hard to put the innocent face on.

They didn't seem to be buying it, and I was keenly aware of just how twitchy people get when this sort of stand-off goes on for any length of time. Then a new voice broke in, and a lot changed as soon as it did. It was a woman's high, light voice, and the partisans shuddered when she spoke. Moreover, she was speaking some jabber that didn't sound at all like Swedish, and that my translator gave up on from the get-go.

But Sturgeon answered her tentatively, fumbling for words. He was a smart guy for languages, Sturgeon. When the 203rd had been given its marching orders, he'd been cramming like there would be a test and everyone had laughed at him. How glad was I that he was a goddamn intellectual right then? Damn glad, I can tell you.

She stepped forward, and the partisans gave her plenty of room. That would have been the time to shoot them, I reckon, but I was too startled by what I was looking at.

She was as slight as Sturgeon, and shorter, and her hair was swept back wetly like it had been gelled. She didn't have a gun trained on us, although there was a long-barreled pistol-looking weapon stuck through her belt. She had some sort of uniform on, pouches and clips and pockets but no rank or insignia. It ended at her elbows and knees, but I didn't see that at first, because the skin of her limbs was fuzzy with sleek hair. Her eyes were cat's eyes glinting in the electric light. Her feet were bare. I was being slow, right then; only the bare feet joined the dots for me. I remembered those footprints near where our man Jerome had been nabbed.

It was a fine time to discover my Californian translator didn't know Finnish.

She looked into our guns without any apparent fear, but I had a sense of a coiled spring in her, as if she could go faster than bullets.

"She wants to know why the Russian is after us," Sturgeon explained.

"You get the impression she and the Russian are best buds?" I asked him.

"Sarge, I don't know."

I looked at the woman and she looked back at me—she was real uncanny valley territory. She was beautiful—that's how they'd made her. She was beautiful and she wasn't human. She scared the bejesus out of me.

"Tell her we don't know, but he and his Ruudboys have been after us for a while."

"I thought these guys were on the same side as the Whites," Cormoran murmured, but I'd put my words into Sturgeon's mouth and he was saying them. I was playing to my gut, letting something inside me that was all instinct and no thought decode that near-kin body language of hers.

The Finn woman nodded sharply and said something to the partisans, which a couple of the more learned had to translate to the rest.

"She said we're all friends then," Sturgeon translated. "Although the rest don't seem to see it that way."

"Can't think why." I leant in close. "All right, you're always claiming you're such a smart guy, find a nice polite way of asking her why they're not shooting us dead."

The rest of us settled on the stairs, with our guns not quite pointed at the partisans, and the partisans settled at their end of the room with their guns not quite pointed at us. The Finn girl stood apart from them—and I watched them as their eyes tracked her, and at least one of them crossed himself when he thought she wasn't looking. When Sturgeon spoke to her, his hands were constantly in motion, gesturing and clutching to reach past the gaps in his Finnish. She stood absolutely still, a cat watching a mouse hole. Jesus, but she scared me.

Franken got out some ration bars, something to chew on while we had the chance. His robot brain had shut up—some time during the fight it had apparently suicided, perhaps clicking that we were using it as an early warning system.

I saw when Sturgeon got the big news—he almost jumped in the air with it, and then spent some painful minutes getting the woman to repeat whatever she'd said before hotfooting it over to us.

"What's the deal?" I was watching the partisans, who were looking more and more twitchy now that the Finn was talking to us.

"She knows we're after the Scion," Sturgeon got out.

"Fuck." Abruptly we were also tense as hell, which did nothing for the anxiety attack the locals were having. "And how? You let that slip?"

"No, Sarge. She saw him. She said she couldn't think who else we'd be out here after."

"Saw him—"

"She knows where they took him. Or her people do, anyway. I, er..." He grimaced. "From what she said, there's not much goes on around here they don't see."

I glanced at Cormoran. "Those flies of theirs, they spy stuff out?"

She looked uncertain for about the first time since we'd met. "I really want to say no, Sarge, but..." She shrugged.

"So…?" I prompted Sturgeon.

"She's ready to go. She's ready to take us."

"Why?" Franken broke in. "Why would she? Got to be a trap, Sarge."

"Yeah." I nodded, thoughtfully. The Finn woman was watching me—not us, but *me*—and I wondered if she could hear us, and if she could understand.

Sturgeon looked stubborn. "More of a trap than being stuck in a small room with a bunch of Nord irregulars, Sarge?"

"Yeah, I can think of lots worse traps than that—shit!" Because in that eyeblink between looking over at her and looking back at Sturgeon, she'd come up right close to us, close enough for me to jab her with my rifle barrel. She said something in her jabber—it was weird, that language, sounded half Nord and half music—and then she almost flowed up the stairs, aided by everyone's very strong desire not to be touched by her.

"She said to come on," Sturgeon said, and then, not that I'd asked, "Her name's Viina."

Everyone was waiting for my order, and what decided me was the thought that, with Bioweapon Viina out of the room, the forbearance of the partisans was unlikely to last very long. Swearing, I got to my feet and led the charge after her.

She took us past where we'd entered the tunnels, moving into the dark without a flashlight and letting us blunder after her. Cramped spaces and poor light make for a very tense Sergeant Ted Regan, and I swear I nearly shot her three times just from pure nerves. We broke out into the forest at last, to find that dusk had snuck up on us. I didn't reckon that Viina was one to just set up camp and wait for the morning, though, so we were all on night ops until further notice. I wondered if she needed to sleep at all, or whether half her brain napped at a time, like dolphins.

Cormoran was doing what she could with her drones; all she could tell me was that we were veering back toward the lake, but that we were probably going parallel to the vehicle tracks we'd found before the Walker and its mechs stumbled on us.

"So why's she helping, Sturgeon?" I pressed, punching him in the shoulder. "Or are we just trusting your magic girlfriend?"

He threw me a hurt look. "What I heard, the whole thing's gone to crap on their side. The Walker's been hunting the partisans down, and they reckon they've been sold out by the government—or maybe just by the corporations. They say they're the only true patriots left in Sweden, that they don't trust anyone. They want to make their own state, basically, run the place themselves."

"And so nobody can control them." I was thinking ahead, because some time in the future everyone would be in a place where we could sign a piece of paper and agree just how much of Nordland could be picked clean by the corporations—ours and theirs—and if there were a load of armed natives still determined to be at war, well, that'd be real awkward for all concerned.

"Yeah, so they've been fighting just about everybody, except the Finns."

"Why not the Finns?"

"Because whatever the crap the Finns want, it's not Swedish land," Sturgeon explained.

"How about you give me your best guess as to what they do want."

"Sarge, I have not the first idea. Unless they don't want anything, and them being here is a test."

"A test of what? Of *them?*" Because Viina was a weapon, and weapons needed testing. "So why is Little Miss Loaded Gun there leading us to Cousin Jerome?"

"I think she's curious," Sturgeon told me. "I think she wants to know what he was doing here, too."

And that was when the White Walker, which had been sitting very quietly amongst the trees, running its systems cold as the night air, suddenly rammed everything up to high gear and turned its lights on. We were caught like rabbits in the headlamps as the night was split with a thunderous screaming sound.

The Russian was coming to get us, and he was playing some serious thrash metal from his suit's speakers. Everyone's a comedian.

We legged it through the trees, with the major disadvantage that we didn't have many trees left because Viina had brought us out closer to the water than before. Behind us, the Walker rose to its full height and took its first stomping step.

We tried to keep to the forest, but there were Ruuds out there too—spindly shapes suddenly flashing hot in our sight, the Russian's hunting dogs stilting along and herding us toward the open ground. Franken lit one up with a scatter of grenades and incendiaries and left it burning, but by then we were basically out of woods, and we were a *lot* closer to the water than I'd reckoned on.

I remember turning, on that strip of ravaged farmland we found ourselves on, with the great darkness of the Vättern at our backs. One of the Ruuds plowed out of the treeline with Cormoran's remotes circling and buzzing it like hawks. It fixed on us, minigun swinging, and then one of the drones rammed it right in its camera-lens face and exploded, rocking the thing back with its chassis suddenly torn open and on fire. And all of this in silent mime because the thunder and bass of the White Walker's music was the only thing our ears had room for.

When Sturgeon's voice came, though, it came in my earphone, cutting through the row. "Sir! She's—!"

He was already halfway to the water—I caught him gesturing, but the signs made no sense, and then the Walker came out of the trees and I had other priorities. I was about to get set on fire by some oligarch's favored son.

We shot at it; of course we shot at it. We peppered it with grenades and AP rounds and incendiaries and whatever little peashooter the remaining drone had. It stood there and let us, our shot lighting it up with constellations of doomed little impacts that did no damage at all.

The music went dead. The night seemed very, very quiet after that; my ears were buzzing with the silence. The White Walker actually leant toward us a little, as though choosing who it was going to kill first. Then one of its shoulder pods spoke, and a shell spiraled madly overhead before arcing back and plowing into the forest with a flare that left jittery after-images across my HUD. Another two followed—one soaring far off over the Vättern before extinguishing itself, and another seeming to go straight up, detonating like a firework and spattering the water's edge with shreds of burning phosphorus, sending us all running. Right then I still thought he was playing with us, until I glanced up. In the Walker's lights, the air danced and glittered and seethed

It wasn't just my ears that were buzzing. Over my head, the air was thick with flies. The flares and echo-shapes on my HUD were just the edge of the vast cloud of ECM interference that were sending the Walker's targeting haywire.

"Where's the Finn?" I yelled, because she was doing this somehow; she had to be.

"Bloody hell!" Lawes' voice, far too loud in my earpiece, and then the Brit was throwing himself aside from something. I saw the shadow of it with my eyes, but my HUD told me it wasn't there, just a piece of cool night sprinting toward the Walker on all fours.

It got to within ten feet of the Walker and leapt, finding a perch up there amongst all that obsolete heraldry. I glimpsed something humanoid but not human, long-limbed and ragged with hair. Then I saw another, springing up to the Walker's shoulders. There were more; they had come out of the water behind us, silent and sleek: Viina had not been operating alone.

We stood very still, we humans, save when the Walker stomped forward and we made room for it. This had suddenly become a fight in which human beings were entirely optional. It was a battle of competing technologies.

And still I wondered how the Finns could actually achieve anything. Let them be swift and strong as bears and tigers, it wouldn't mean jack against all that armor. The flies were still coming, though, swarming through the air to settle on the Walker's hull like we were watching some piece of film run in reverse. It was like the Scion was drawing them out of the air. They were coating his weapons, his vents, every part of him that promised access to the meat below.

My HUD began to tell me a story then. The White Walker was starting to live up to its name on the thermal imaging: from red to orange, growing hotter and hotter as the thickening carpet of engineered insects blocked its heat sinks. And all the while the Finns danced across its surface, prying and wrenching.

Its shoulder pod exploded. I caught a brief afterimage of a torn near-human shape being flung away, but then all the ammunition was going up, each shell setting off the next, and the whole area became a very unhealthy place to be. We continued our escape along the water's edge, leaving the battle to forces entirely beyond us in power and sophistication.

Sturgeon says... Well, hell, by the time I stopped running and turned around, it was mostly over. I saw the Walker on the ground and on fire, and then something fundamental went off and there were pieces of armor and favored son raining down all over.

Sturgeon says that a crab the size of a Buick came out of the Vättern and scissored one of the Walker's legs off at the knee, but I'm not falling for that. Even in this world of ours, such things just don't happen.

I did a head count; we'd all made it, bar the drone that had given its artificial life to take out the Ruud. For a moment I thought—*hoped*—that we'd seen the last of Viina and her compatriots. But no, here they came, a full dozen of them ghosting without warning from the shadow and the pitch. Two legs, but they didn't walk like us; human features but animal expressions. We had our guns up, all of us, and they didn't show any fear at all. I know that the movies lie. I know that if I've got my finger on the trigger and my sights on a target, there's no way they can rush me before I punch a hole in them. That's been a point of faith for me all my professional life. Facing the dogs, then, I lost that faith. They came from the darkness like wolves from old stories, the killers that taught us to fear the night. When Viina grinned, I saw fangs. They looked at us with the arrogance of top predators. The arrogance of youth, too: how old could they have been, how quickly had they been force-grown in their labs? Or were there breeding populations of these things over the border? Had they already broken away from their creators?

Sturgeon says it was going for decades before the war: the US was tightening up on whole areas of science that the Christ Lib crowd and the other fundamentalists were crying blasphemy on. A lot of Europe was going the same way for secular or religious reasons, and there had been that outbreak in China that had suddenly made them way less keen on biosciences as the future of military superiority. The funding dried up and the laws came in, and a great many scientists just found a different area to work in, preferably for one of the agriscience multinationals, because that was where the money was.

Except there were some researchers who didn't care about breeding a new strain of wheat that would outperform its competitors and then conveniently die off so you had to buy more. There were some who had been playing with the blasphemy label since before the Christ Lib people got hold of it. Those men and women who were long on genius and short on ethics needed somewhere to go.

I have no idea what was going on in Finnish politics or academia which led to that place becoming a covert haven for mad scientists. Sure as hell it wasn't the only one, but they were maybe the most subtle. Five years before I signed up there was what the media called

Operation Frankenstein in Bolivia, when the boffins over there got a bit too open about what they were making. There was never an Operation Moreau kicking in doors in Helsinki, though, and we were face to face with the results of that oversight.

"So, what now?" I asked. I was going for defiant, but Sturgeon's shaky translation sounded pitiful.

One of the males muttered something that sounded hungry, and a couple of them laughed, cruel and malevolent as hyenas. Then Viina spoke, in that voice that sounded almost like singing. Her eyes glowed in the moonlight.

"She says, let's find your..." Sturgeon grimaced. "*Perillinen.* Which is probably Scion." He paused, listened to the next words. "She says she'll show us. She says it's not even far."

"Where are they off to?" Lawes hissed. Even as Sturgeon had been speaking, some of the Finns had just walked off into the water, as if it was the most natural thing in the world. One by one they dived and were lost in the cold lake, hidden behind the moon's reflection, and I thought, *Not wolves; otters.*

"She says..." Sturgeon was listening intently. "She says that she has... ah, *siunaaminen* something... She's..."

Viina walked forward, slipping between our guns, cutting between me and Sturgeon, close enough to brush us both with her fingers before we jumped aside. She was going for Cormoran, who backed off hurriedly as the Finn reached out a hand.

"No, it's your drone, she says she's—blessed?—your drone. She... Again please?"

Viina looked back at him with amusement and made fluttering motions with her hands.

Sturgeon nodded hurriedly. "Your drone can fly now. Your drone can follow the track. You'll see. Follow her, but send the drone ahead."

I nodded permission, and Cormoran sent her last remaining remote ahead. Viina said one word, and it was obviously, "Follow," or something close.

"What about the rest of them?" Franken demanded. "Why aren't they coming?"

What Viina had to say about that, after Sturgeon translated, well… She said there were a lot of men where we were going. Did we really want all of them dead?

CHAPTER SIX

However she did it, Viina blessed that drone good. Cormoran flew it through that fly-spattered air and never lost signal once.

The trail took us inland at the start like Cormoran had said, then it broke out of the trees and shadowed the course of a road that the fighting had left shattered like a long strip of jigsaw pieces. All this time we were following on foot, while Cormoran had one eye on the terrain in front of her and one on the drone's camera feed. We'd reached the road ourselves when she called a halt. "All right, this you've got to see."

What it was, was a castle. This was Europe, and suddenly it had become the Europe we Americans were always promised, because the bad guys were holed up inside an honest-to-God ruined castle. And in the bombed-out restaurant and parking lot across the road from it, but that doesn't sound half as impressive.

My HUD map called it *Brahehus* and it was obvious that the end had come for it a long time before anyone thought of airstrikes. It had a few intact walls, though, and the drone showed that there was a prefab cabin pitched in there, and a bigger camp outside the walls around a space that had been cleared and flattened as a landing pad. This wasn't just some temporary camp. There were plenty of men there; a handful of vehicles. They had been there a while.

"Come on," I said, and Viina was pacing back and forth like she was about to just take off without us. Cormoran was still messing with the images, though, panning and searching until at last she said, "There!"

They'd roofed off the castle with heat baffles, but the drone had snuck in under them, neat as you like, creeping into that covered space through the gaping eyesocket space where a window had once been. It took a single image before retreating, and even then the enemy security grid had started to wonder if something was wrong. Cormoran did a lot of finagling to stay undetected that long.

We got a good look at that single image of the cabin, as Cormoran zoomed and let her software's pattern recognizers do their work.

There was a shape through the window there. We couldn't exactly buzz the drone down to head level to be certain, but it sure as hell looked like an American-made Scion shell to me. We'd found our man. Or we'd found his metal clothes, but either way it was the best lead in a field of one.

IT TOOK US a day's walk to catch up with the drone, keeping under cover wherever we could and hoping that nobody else's remote eyes had been 'blessed' by the Finns. Viina kept going in and out—now loping alongside us, then just gone for an hour or more on her own business. She made it painfully clear that we were slowing her down. She looked at us as though we were… Jesus, I don't know: pets; barely tolerated cripples; last year's models.

We let the dark gather before we got too close to the castle. I mean, sure, we'd all show up on thermals—except Viina—but no sense in making things easy for them.

By that time, Cormoran had built up a picture of how security worked there and got a few clues as to who these clowns were.

"Corporate," she told us. "Not Skaalmed, and their insignia isn't flagging up as known, but their gear is good. If they were just sitting tight, I think we'd be screwed, but they're packing up."

Lawes was staring close at her screens, eyes narrowed. "'Cos the front's moving this way," he suggested. "They want to scram before our side get here."

"They're moving our man out then?" Franken put in, "Reckon we can grab him on the road?"

"They'll be traveling faster than we can, now we've lost the Trojan," I pointed out. "We're not equipped to strike a convoy."

Lawes looked up at me. "You're going to suggest we walk in there, aren't you."

"They're not friends of yours, then? I thought you knew all the Nord corporate types."

"Even the ones I know, they wouldn't exactly want me walking in on some Scion-kidnapping operation."

He wasn't quite looking me in the eyes, which I guess was normal for him, but my gut said to press him. "Who are they, Lawes?"

He bared his teeth again, that tic of his that made him look like he was trying to use bad dentistry like a threat display. "There, that badge there. That's the field operations division of LMK. The big agri boys: Lantgård Mass Kemisk."

"They're on our side, aren't they?" Franken asked slowly.

"No, no they're not," Lawes told him. "I mean, yes, there's a US subsidiary, just like there's a Nord one and an Indian one and, you know, anywhere there's money. They're one of the big players here, though."

"They asked us in," Cormoran recalled. "Or they were one of the corps requesting US help when the Nord govs turned socialist."

"And they've been pitching into the fight ever since, whenever it looked like the US corp forces were getting too much of an upper hand." Lawes glowered at the lot of us, then jabbed a finger at Sturgeon. "Ask him, he knows. If you think this is a fight between US and Nord govs then you're bloody morons. This is corps versus corps using poor bastards like us as the meat in the grinder."

"Because it's cheaper for them to have the army die in their place," Sturgeon agreed softly.

"Enough of that," I snapped. "What this *is*, is a rescue operation. Those are our orders. Let Capitol Hill and Stockholm sort out the big picture between them. We're going to go in, grab our man and get out."

Lawes stared at me. Well, they all stared at me, but I remember Lawes most.

"You're cracked," he spat out. "Sarge, sod me but you're mad. LSK are serious business from South Africa to the sodding Arctic Circle. We do *not* want to go poke them with a stick."

"No, soldier, I don't *want* to, but it looks like they're leaving me no choice," I told him.

"It's suicide."

"No, it's just us doing our jobs."

"It's suicide, just to go drag out some over-privileged nancy boy who's stupid enough to get himself caught. You think they won't just ransom him back when they're done? You think anybody's going to ransom us?"

"That's our mission," I told them.

"They've got a couple hundred men in there," Lawes snapped. "They've got better gear than us."

"And most of them aren't at that castle, they're over the road in the main camp," I pointed out patiently. "I reckon whoever's in charge just couldn't resist pitching his command in an actual castle, and so he's ended up separate to most of his force. Now, I'm not suggesting we take the place by storm. We're going to exploit their officer's dumbass ideas about living history and do this sneaky. I thought sneaky was what you did, Lawes."

"You think LSK have such toss security that I can walk straight in? We're not exactly corporate industrial espionage over here."

"Well, actually," said Cormoran, which diverted all that aggrieved disbelief from me. She shrugged. "The ECM from the fly-screen is screwing with their systems a lot. Now it's not touching mine, I can start messing with them."

"Can you cut us a gap in the fence?" I was thinking about thermal and motion sensors and just plain cameras, the sort of security even a mobile base like this would have.

She was looking at the screens of her case again. "Their systems are shielded against casual intrusion," she said, eyes narrowed. "Gonna need to go hammer some spikes in. That means someone getting there on foot and not tripping the alarm." She looked up at us brightly. "And it's not going to be me. It'll take all my concentration to open a gap, and twice that to keep it open."

"So once we've got a gap?"

She grinned, a brief flash of white teeth. "Then your handpicked elite go and see if our man's still there. Take the drone with you and get it close to their data systems. They're not open to access from outside queries, but with a bit of proximity you never know. I'll see what I can read while you're over there."

"Because you won't be one of my elite, right?"

"Sure as hell no." Unapologetic as you please.

"Fine then: spike their defenses; team go in; spring our guy; GTFO." Perhaps not one of my most sophisticated plans.

"Who gets to go spike?" Sturgeon asked. Nobody was falling over themselves to volunteer. Cormoran's spikes were little data relays someone would have to splice into the corps system. Once in, they would act as open terminals for her signals, letting her turn whole sections of their grid on and off, hopefully without being noticed.

My eyes had turned to Lawes. I'd seen the tech he was carting about with him. He squinted back at the drone image, obviously turning the odds over in his mind. "Your Mr bloody Speling better be good for the bonus," he muttered grudgingly

He upended his pack and brought out his sneak-suit, which would mask his heat signature—and fry him if he wore it for too long. It was patterned with slow-shifting shadows that broke up his silhouette and muddied his movements, all the cues that electronic or human security would be attuned to. With his skinny frame got up in that, his face hidden by goggles and a bandit-style bandana, it was hard to focus on him even standing there in front of us. There would be electronics in the cloth to screw with motion sensors, too, and even then he would have to be damn careful.

We went over the details again, the signal, the timing— he had thirty minutes to get somewhere before he'd need to pull out, or we'd assume that he'd been compromised. It was a pain in the ass that we couldn't send a drone in with him, but Cormoran would be busy redirecting their systems, and she didn't have a second drone to spare any more. Besides, if the enemy's security was any good, then they'd be keyed up to detect drone infiltration rather than human. After all, why would they expect that anyone would be stupid enough to just walk into their base?

We lost track of Lawes once he'd left us, which meant he was doing something right. Cormoran was working, and the rest of us got to just sit around. I'd already decided that I'd go in myself, if Lawes could cut us a big enough hole, and I'd take Franken with me because if Cousin Jerome really was there, and not able to just walk on his own feet, we'd need someone big to carry him. Sturgeon and Cormoran would be our cover, if we came out hot.

I'd half expected Viina to volunteer her services when it came to going in, but she was just sitting back with her knees gathered up to her chin and watching us with that cool, alien amusement. If she actually understood what we were about, there was no indication of it.

Just short of twenty minutes into our time and Cormoran said, "He's doing it. I'm getting access. First

spike is online. Yeah, that's good." Headware feeding her
the data, she nodded blindly at her own mind's eye. "I'm
in. No alarms tripped. I see the security grid... trying
to isolate the cabin from the main camp." Abruptly
she grimaced. "No, no..." Her hands twitched, old
keyboard reflexes surfacing briefly. "No, got it. Come
on Lawes, don't make me cover for you. It thinks it's
seen him... rerouting queries... The security's... well,
it's OK, I guess. Always the problem with field ops like
theirs, you never quite get the..." She went on, little
scraps of sentences, half to us, half talking to a Lawes
whose existence and actions she was having to infer from
what she saw going on in the LMK system, and who
couldn't hear her in any event. And then at last, "Yeah,
we're good, we're good. That looks stable, at least until
they do a sweep... and there's the signal. Over to you,
Sergeant." My HUD sprang up with a ground overlay
showing me the corridor she'd cut through their security.

I nodded to her and to Sturgeon, with one last glance
at Viina in case she had decided we required her services.
She hadn't moved: apparently we were doing the next bit
monster-free.

We got half the way there before Lawes popped up in
front of us, almost in arm's reach before we saw him.
A moment later he was desperately stripping away the
camouflage. Inside, he was the color of well-done lobster.

"Christ, I hate those bloody things," he hissed, and
just stared down Franken when the man growled at him.
"Fuck me, don't make me do that again."

"Stop complaining and let's move before all your hard
work gets overwritten," I told him.

The three of us followed Cormoran's invisible road,
briefly skirting the edge of the main camp before

heading up to the castle. I could already see that Bahehus hadn't exactly been Fort Knox even back in the day. The windows weren't little slits that a man could get arrow-shot through, but were great big open holes in the walls—enough that it seemed more hole than wall in parts. Most of these had been screened over, but the whole place was still little more than period decoration for whatever was inside. They were relying on their system spotting any intruder, which was their bad luck.

Lawes pulled us down, and we watched a trio of men pass along the foot of the castle wall before heading toward the main camp. They didn't seem overly alert, and they were talking amongst themselves—my translator didn't catch more than a few words, but I recognised the tone. These were soldiers at the end of their duty, eager to get back to their buddies. In the army, we said that corp forces had the best gear and the best pay, but they knew fuck all about proper discipline half the time. Apparently it was no different amongst the Nords.

Then we were creeping further in, right up to the wall, and I'll bet Franken was praying to Christ Lib that Cormoran had done her job properly or this was going to break all known records for going FUBAR. No klaxons and no red lights, though; more to the point no bullets coming our way.

There was a front way into the castle courtyard where the cabin was, but none of us felt quite that confident. Instead, Lawes took one of the screened windows, isolated a trip-switch that would have started yelling, and then cut a slit in the plastic. He sized up Franken, widened the slit a bit, then made 'after you' gestures.

"We'll need more than that," I murmured. "We might be coming out of here with a body."

For a moment Lawes stared at me blankly, but then he nodded and turned the slit into a flap, securing it with a clip to stop it flapping once we'd all clambered through.

There were lights on in the cabin, and I did wonder whether we'd end up bagging some LMK director as a hostage. If our guy wasn't there, and Cormoran couldn't trawl it from their system, then we'd need someone to point us in the right direction, after all.

It's amazing how far ahead of yourself you can get, if you're not keeping your mind on the here-and-now.

So we crept up to that cabin. The front was all lit up, but the side where we were was shadowy, and still within the footprint of Cormoran's attentions.

Lawes signaled: did I want to try the front door? I didn't, because no amount of electronic wizardry would keep us from just physically being seen.

"I'll go round the back," he said, just a whisper in my helmet receiver. "Hold here."

When he was gone, I took the chance to examine the cabling running from the cabin. Most of it was clamped to the wall with staples, and some of it would be power, but maybe some was data. I got Cormoran's drone out and moved it from one to another until it gave me a green light, like she'd said it would. Clamped there, it would try to read the LMK dataflow, and maybe it would turn up something useful if we found nothing more than an empty shell inside.

"Come round the back, Sarge, I've got it sorted," buzzed Lawes in my ear, and so we did, and we found Lawes there with a good dozen LMK soldiers, all waiting quiet as you please with their guns on us. We didn't even get the chance to return the favor like we did with the partisans.

Franken growled, deep in his chest, and I put a hand on his shoulder. Inside, I felt exactly the same, and when Lawes grinned at us I wanted to shove every one of those big teeth down his throat.

"When?" I asked him flatly.

He spread his hands. "Look, you're new in this neck of the woods, right? You think you know how it works, us, them, all that shit. Only I told you it ain't like that. Friends today are enemies tomorrow and the other way round. I've been here since the start. I've made bloody sure I kept on the good side of the big players, whichever side they were playing. You think I want to be on LMK's shit list? You think I want to get myself killed on some bloody stupid suicide mission just because some rich Yank moron's got himself caught?"

"It wasn't a suicide mission," I ground out between my teeth.

"Not until you sold us out, you little shit," Franken added, with considerable restraint. "How the fuck did you even have time?"

The Nord officer there laughed at that. "Oh, your friend here came right to us," he explained in almost accentless English. "He was telling us his whole story while my men were splicing in your spikes. He wanted us to just send men to secure your team, but that sounded too much like a trap to me. Now we have you, we'll go pick up your friends. Hopefully they won't resist."

I said nothing. There didn't seem to be much point lying about our numbers or capabilities, not when Lawes was being so obliging for them.

They took our guns, disarmed us smartly of anything more dangerous than a spoon. I'd lost comms on the instant, all channels cut. I couldn't send a warning to

Sturgeon and Cormoran, but I hoped to hell that they'd notice I was suddenly off the grid.

The LMK officer cocked his head. "Do you want to see your target, Sergeant Regan, isn't it?" He must have taken my sullen grunt for confirmation, because he had the pair of us taken round the front of the cabin and escorted into the front door. The place looked like every prefab admin hut I ever saw: desk, terminal, furniture, and a couple of bunks at the back. There was paper, too, because nobody out in the field ever relies 100% on the electronics. Every soldier knows that things always go wrong. Of course, for us they'd gone wrong all at once and without warning.

The Scion was there, too. It was seated, although the legs must have been taking a lot of the weight because the metal frame chair didn't look that sturdy. The shine of its chassis had taken more than a few knocks—it needed a polish before it was fit for the parade ground, certainly. The sculpted face, between and above its broad shoulderplates, was a good enough approximation of Cousin Jerome's to give me positive ID.

Our captor rapped sharply on its chest. In truth the armor was too thick for it to sound hollow, but I got the point. Our man was long gone to some Nord gulag or interrogation suite. Not exactly a huge surprise—my dreams of finding Jerome in the flesh and spiriting him away had always been mostly wishful thinking—but right then the Nord banging on his shell sounded like someone hammering nails into my coffin.

"So where is he?" Maybe I thought it was one of those movie moments, where the bad guys explain all their plans. If so, the Nord officer hadn't seen that kind of movie.

"I don't believe that's information you require, Sergeant."

"What happens to us?"

His smile wasn't unpleasant, in its own way. "Sent for debrief. Prisoners of war. What's the line? For you, the war is over."

I nodded, impassive, almost as if I hadn't heard him. Mostly this was because something had flashed on my HUD. It was showing me a handful of status bars: my biosigns and other data it could get from me. Everything else was blocked, though, in or out. Except something had flashed in the corner of the corner of my eye just then, a rapid sequence of characters.

Franken grunted. To anyone else it would have sounded like nothing so much as brute resentment about our position. To me, who'd known him for so long, it told me he'd had the same.

"We'd ship you out by air," the LMK officer was saying as his men ushered us out of the prefab, "but you wouldn't thank me for it. That damned muck the Finns let out into the air gets into the engines. So it'll be by road, but it won't be so bad."

And I was nodding along, but the signal came and came again. The characters blurred past very fast. 'I' was first, G last. Was it a code? Was it just a word?

We were clearing the castle walls, crossing toward the road, toward the main camp. I was concentrating so hard I tripped and almost faceplanted the path.

I-N-?????-N-G

The officer had asked me a question. I tried to reconstruct it, but I'd missed it entirely.

Franken came to my rescue. "He's just tired. We've been on the move for weeks." So the officer probably thought I was drunk, and I couldn't blame him.

"Give me a moment." Shaking my head as if to clear it.

"Get him up," the officer directed, and I was hauled to my feet. I could see he was suspicious as hell. "What's wrong with him."

It came again. I saw it—I must have been really obvious because he grabbed my helmet and yanked it, twisted it off my head and nearly cut my throat with the chinstrap doing so. It didn't matter. I'd seen the signal. I'd seen what it said.

Incoming.

Cormoran had got in. They were coming to rescue us.

This failed to fill me with cheer, because it sounded like the best possible way to get the rest of my squad captured or killed.

The officer had a pistol out and he jammed it under my chin while his men held me. "*Vad* är *du gör?*" he snarled, too angry for English and of course the translator was in my helmet. I could play dumb with real conviction.

Then he was gone. It was so sudden I thought he'd shot me. I could still feel the steel finger of the pistol at my throat even though it had been torn away. Then the killing started.

I saw the officer lying dead at my feet with his head mostly ripped from the rest of him. One of his men was twisting my arm behind my back—as if I could have had anything to do with it. The other had let go, was bringing his gun up. I heard shouting in Swedish.

I saw Viina. Just for a moment in the darkness, I saw her. She slammed into the LMK soldiers and cut two of them open, body armor and all, then turned and loosed a spray of bullets from her long-barrelled gun. Franken was free, grabbing up a rifle from the ground. I rammed my head back into the face of the man that had me, glancing painfully off his chin. It was enough to loosen his grip and I tumbled forward out of it.

My helmet was there on the ground in front of me. I could see the HUD lighting up like Christmas.

Franken was down on one knee at my side, crouched low and not lifting the gun, because right now he wasn't anyone's target and he wanted to keep it that way. "Got an escape plan," he snapped out, eyes on his own display.

"Lead," I told him, snagged my helmet, and then we were both running. We were both running *back* toward the main camp. "Wait, this can't be right!" I hollered at Franken but he didn't hear. A moment later I had my own helmet on, wrestling with the strap, seeing the path overlaid in front of me—right into the heart of the enemy.

Franken turned, let me get past him and then opened up full auto back toward the castle, not trying to kill people so much as trying to make them keep their heads down. There was all sorts of commotion in the camp, of that you can be sure.

They had Ruuds. One of them leapt up from its collapsed-stick resting pose right ahead of us, its minigun already whining. The camp lights gleamed—no, they swirled, the air dancing about them like smoke. Then I was stumbling, waiting for the gunfire. I saw soldiers ahead of me, some of them in full battledress, most of them not. They looked as terrified and confused as I felt.

The Ruud shuddered and something screamed inside its body. It did a mad jig on its three stilting legs and then just starting shooting and loosing off shells—at random? No: there was one place it wasn't shooting and that was at me and Franken.

Men were running, falling, shouting, shooting back. The Ruud rocked with a dozen impacts, but the fit was on it like it was possessed. Around its body the flies danced like stars in the searing light, blocking any attempt by the LMK techs to reassert control.

Still, there was just one of it, and plenty of them. Abruptly bullets were tearing up the ground at my feet, and me without so much as a pea shooter. Franken returned fire, which is to say he was pissing into the hurricane. I didn't even know where we were running to.

Then I did. One of the enemy vehicles was suddenly outlined in blue, the universal color of the good guys. It was starting to move out, jerky at first but then rolling forward, an armored scout car that could have left our Trojan in the dirt.

I went for it, but then threw myself aside as the suppressive fire came in. One shot struck my body armor at an angle, not enough to floor me but enough to remind me how many parts of my body didn't have the benefit. The Ruud lurched into them then, spraying shot madly, dancing like a marionette. Some of the camp was on fire from the incendiaries. Another Ruud was active, but just standing and sparking.

Viina came past us like the north wind, now on two legs, now all fours. I saw her snatch up a dropped rifle and roll, emptying it at the enemy as she came up to her knees, and then she was running—she seemed almost fast enough to overtake her own bullets. When she struck the knot of LMK men I lost sight of her. I could only track her by the bodies she left behind.

Then I bounced off the side of the armored car, and the string of text on my HUD was saying *GETINGETINGETIN*.

"Viina!" I yelled. No human could have heard me, but who knew how good her ears were?

She broke from them—again, it was only by the reactions of the enemy I could tell. She was coming, dancing through the firefight, even as Franken tried to cover her.

The possessed Ruud exploded, and then the other one, the one that had just stood there, scything shards of metal every which way. One of them spanged off the vehicle over my head, and when I'd got through ducking, Viina was down. Shot? Caught by the blast? I couldn't say, but I was running already, pelting into the killing ground because somehow, in my head, she'd become one of *my* people, and I was damned if I was leaving her behind.

I was almost at her when someone shot me high in the chest. I went down, feeling the colossal impact through my vest, like the punch of a giant. I was ten feet short of Viina, who was twisting, flapping, clawing at the ground towards me. She couldn't help me. I couldn't help me. I could barely breathe.

Then a knee came down on my chest, right where the shot had gone, and I screamed. It was Lawes, the little fucker. He had a pistol pretty much up my nose and his eyes were wide and mad. Probably he was saying something clever and English. He could have been quoting Shakespeare for all I heard him, even though he was crouching real low to deny Franken a shot.

I was willing Viina to get up and do something, but she'd been shot bad, far worse than me, though that balance was about to be redressed. If Lawes had just pulled the trigger I'd not be telling this, but I had so thoroughly screwed his plans that he had to tell me, had to explain just how much he hated me.

Then something flashed between us and basically rammed him in the face. I recognized Cormoran's drone in the moment before it drew back, the sheer fact of it dragging Lawes' gun barrel up to follow it.

I threw him off me. I had my breath back by then and he was a little guy. He staggered, tried to get me in his sights again, and then someone shot him through the groin. It might have been Franken; it might have been one of the Swedes—they weren't to know he was on their side, after all. Like Lawes always said, it was a complicated war.

I gathered up Viina, hugging her to my chest—she seemed to weigh ridiculously little, like a child or a doll. She was bleeding badly, shaking, thrashing feebly. I was hurting her more just by trying to save her. I should have left her. She wasn't even human, after all. Would I have done it for a dog? A cat?

I did it for her. I lurched and staggered and gasped my way back to the vehicle, even as the camp went mad behind me. Cormoran had coopted another Ruud and it was driving the LMK boys back, just as mad and spasmodic as the first one. I saw her drone zip like a mad wasp through the open hatch ahead of me, while Franken blew all the ammo he had to try and cover me.

Then I was dumping Viina inside and clambering in after her. In the car, Sturgeon was at the wheel and Cormoran was sitting calmly at her open briefcase like she was doing nothing more taxing than updating her relationship status.

I turned, yelling for him, and Franken came in backward through the hatch. His armor vest was all ripped up and he had lost the gun. For a moment I was telling myself it was Viina's blood on him, but it was his; it was his own.

I dragged his trailing leg in and got the hatch closed, feeling the impact of more bullets against it. Sturgeon was moving out, looking back at all the mess we'd made when he should have been looking where he was going. Cormoran scrabbled for a medical kit.

Franken was clenched, every muscle pulling against the rest. He met my eyes, teeth gritted and his face twisted so much by the pain that I wouldn't have known him. I could hear Sturgeon's panicky swearing, and I gripped Franken's hand and told him to hang in there, even as Cormoran slapped painkiller tabs on the inside of his wrists and on his neck.

And Sturgeon just drove. At first he took the road, because it was simply the best way to put distance between us and the LMK base. After that he went back into the woods, guiding the Nord vehicle between the trees until we were surely past the point where Cousin Jerome had been snatched, past where we'd fought the White Walker or met the buried partisans.

I had to hope that the fly-screen above us would screw any attempts to track us, because otherwise distance just wouldn't be enough.

CHAPTER SEVEN

AT LAST WE stopped. Franken was under, and we'd patched him as best we could, but he'd lost a lot of blood and we hadn't exactly stolen a field hospital. I'd seen him shot before, but I'd never seen him so pale, like his own ghost. The moment we came to rest, Sturgeon was bolting back out of the pilot's seat to look at him, his hands wringing at each other.

"Stupid bastard," he muttered. "What was he thinking?"

Viina, we hadn't given meds to. She was still with us, just about, gut-shot and trembling, curled about her wound and keening at a pitch that was only just inaudible, like electronics feedback. When we went close she snarled and spat, but it was weak. We could have forced some tabs onto her, but Cormoran was against it. We didn't know what they'd do to her. They'd been made for humans, after all.

"Your drone good to go?" I asked her, looking up from Franken's corpse-like form. When she nodded, I told her to get it out and scouting. If LMK were on our trail, we needed to know. If we'd got ourselves on anyone else's radar, we needed to know.

"What now, Sarge?" Sturgeon asked in a whisper. "What do we do now?"

Fuck knows. I just shook my head. We were down two and out of leads. Time to head home and admit defeat, surely. Even my stubbornness has limits.

Except heading home would rely on the world leaving us alone, and it didn't sound as though we'd be granted that indulgence. Cormoran's sudden intake of breath brought me straight over to her screens.

"What?" I couldn't see anything there, no thermal, no visual, nothing. She was frantically adjusting parameters, swinging the drone in wide circles, casting for the scent.

For a moment, no more than a second, we saw them on her screens, loping grey through the night toward us. Then they were gone like specters.

"The Finns." My throat was abruptly dry.

"They've come for her," Cormoran confirmed.

"How can they even know?" I demanded. This whole war front was a fog of misdirection and interference, except for them. They just cut through it all and they didn't even carry radios.

"I think..." Sturgeon was still crouching over Franken. "I read about some stuff—what our people think the Finns were working on, what, ten, fifteen years back? Before Operation Frankenstein went down in Bolivia and all the rest of the biolab havens stopped taking visitors. Comms through quantum entanglement, they said."

"Bullshit," I replied promptly.

"Speculation," was his mild correction. "But what they said was, nobody had got it to work, not in a man-made system, but some guy at Harvard reckoned biological systems would be better at it. Only that was about when all the funding got yanked and the Congressional Science Committee basically said it was all the work of the Devil. So we never found out. But maybe the Finns did."

"I second bullshit," Cormoran put in. "So how are we playing this? They coming to kick our asses for letting their warrior princess get killed, you reckon?"

I thought about how the White Walker had been taken down. This tinpot little Nord scout car was a cardboard box by comparison, and I had the distinct feeling we wouldn't be able to outrun them either.

"Nobody point a gun. Keep the hatch open. We come in peace, right?"

The other two nodded unhappily. Out past the hatch the night contained a thousand ghosts. Every moon-shadow, every moving branch was a Finnish werewolf.

I glanced at Cormoran. "By the way, that was good work with the Ruuds back there. I didn't realize you could even hack them that way."

She smiled slightly. "Normally? No. But I was in their system, thanks to you, and one of their techs had left the codes lying around. Strong as the weakest link, right?" She shook her head. "Even then they're no pushovers. If it hadn't been for the fly-screen blocking the LMK from getting back in, I'd never have done it. You saw that, right?"

"I did."

"I wonder if you've had a chance to think about it, because that was just something that happened, to back me up. Because it's real easy to think of these

Finn creations as if they're animals, something less than human, but they saw what I was doing instantly, long before the LMK techs cottoned on." Her eyes were haunted in the vehicle lights. "They're smart. Computer smart, human smart, who knows? Maybe smart like nothing anyone saw before."

She stopped speaking then. They'd arrived.

They slunk out of the darkness: solemn, slender, alien. Some had human eyes, and some had cats', and some the dark, featureless orbs of deer.

One of them put out a hand with claw nails, misted with wiry grey hair. The words he spoke were foreign, but I got the gist without needing a translation. *Give her to us.*

"She's all yours. She's right here, you come and take her." Slipping outside the car, giving him space to get in, it was a hard thing to do.

Two of them bore her out and laid her on the cold, root-ribbed ground, and then another was bending over her, slipping things from pockets in his fatigues. I wouldn't have been surprised to see fetishes and voodoo dolls, but they were pipettes and vials, some modern alchemy, dashed on her skin, jabbed into her veins, dropped into her forced-open mouth.

While that was going on, one of them came back to us, one of the females. She was tall, stoop-shouldered; her eyes were huge, an owl's merciless orbs, and I swear I saw the black darts of horns jutting from her fringe of tawny hair. She came and stared at Franken, and I'd seen people less dispassionate looking at road kill. But then that hunter's face wasn't made for expression. Maybe I'm doing her a disservice.

"It's not just you, you see," I told her. "It's us. We

suffer too. We've got losses too." I didn't care whether she could understand me. I didn't know if Franken was still breathing.

She said something. The words were lost, but the rhythms of her speech, a little like Swedish, a little like some language spoken by prehuman elves of a thousand years ago, they washed over me. But she sounded sad. She sounded sympathetic. The bioengineered killing machine could spare a moment to come down to our level, to taste the grief of yesterday's men.

And then she was asking me a question, and I stared into that face and could not guess what. Sturgeon got it, though. He twitched and his eyes went wide.

"She says—Sarge, she says, she says they will save him—will try to save him, Sarge!"

I looked into those predator's eyes. There was nothing written there that I could read. "Save him how?"

"I don't know, sir, but—it's yes, right? Come on, Sarge, he's almost..." Sturgeon's voice shook. I guess he was a better friend than me, in the end.

What would Franken say? "Can we... can we wake him, ask him?" But I knew the answer. He was clinging to life with such a failing grip that to tug on that rope would be to send him falling away into the abyss. So what would he say, Franken the church-goer, the devout Christ Libber? Would he want to live, even though deliverance came from the paws of demons? Questions I couldn't answer for him. I could only answer for me. Did I let one of my squad die? Did I let my friend die? Or did I make him live, and damn his principles.

I'm selfish, in the end. Most of us are.

I nodded to the Finn, and Sturgeon retreated to the driver's seat as she started her work.

* * *

THEN IT WAS time for sleep, for whatever the Finns were doing wasn't quick. It wasn't any field surgery I recognised: no incisions, no blood, no struggle. Instead they hunched over their patients, with their potions and their elixirs. They were not mending by brute mechanical force. They were growing, changing, tending the bodies of their charges like gardeners.

Sturgeon took first watch, at his insistence. When he woke me for my shift, Cormoran was up as well, watching feedback from her drone as it flew just below the fly-screen and mapped out the country around us. I told her she should sleep; she said she'd slept. Her headware kept her going on just a couple of hours, she told me.

"I'll bet that cost more than all the gear I ever got from the army."

"Probably. Nothing but the best, right?" She shrugged. "You've got a plan, Sergeant? When we're done with feeding time at the zoo, what are your orders?"

"You think we should go back?"

"You're worried what people might think?" Said with a sidelong look and an arched eyebrow. When I nodded, her expression turned pitying. "Sergeant, what they'll think is, 'Holy fuck, they're not dead!'"

"What's that supposed to mean."

"Why do you think they sent you and yours on this little jaunt, Sergeant?"

"Because we get things done."

"Oho, that's it, is it? And you get things done, what, better than a crack corporate extraction team, do you?"

I opened my mouth to say, *We're not doing so bad,*

except I was surrounded by manifest evidence to the contrary.

Cormoran snorted. "Seriously, one of their own goes missing, and what happens? They send three grunts nobody'll miss out of the 203rd and a treacherous little shit like Lawes. That sound to you that they actually even think Jerome Speling's still alive out there? That he *can* be rescued?"

"But there's you," I told her hotly. "You with your million-dollar skull candy and your million-dollar education. They sent you. So maybe the rest of us are just here to get you where you need to go and then bleed out on the ground while you do it."

"That's what you think, huh?"

"Damn straight."

"Well then let me tell you why I'm here, Sergeant Regan. I'm here because when my commanding officer thought he'd slum it and sleep with the help, I told him where he could get off. And I went on saying no right after he said he wouldn't take no for an answer." She was speaking quietly but her voice abruptly had an edge on it like broken glass. "And when he tried to put me over his desk I hacked his fucking phone and overclocked the battery so much they needed a surgeon to unmelt it from his thigh. So no, Sergeant, I am not here to perform a dance of corporate superiority over your cooling corpses. I am here to die like a dog, just as you are. So what are your orders?"

I remember how much hope just fell from me, right then. I hadn't realized that, however much I expected her to cast us off, I was still taking a lot of strength from the idea that *someone* on the team would accomplish the objective. An objective. Any objective. I'd imagined her suddenly calling down an unmarked corporate gunship to load Jerome onto, when we'd found him. And even if it flew off without me and mine—as it surely would have—at least the mission was done, then. At least I could stand up and say, "We won!" into the muzzles of the guns. Finding out she was just as damned and lost as the rest of us was a blow, I can tell you.

"I'm open to suggestions," I told her.

"Fine." She took a deep breath. "We could actually go find Jerome."

"You just said—"

"I know what I *said*. I also know that I hacked the crap out of the LMK system, and I found out where they took him."

THE NEXT MORNING, Franken was awake. Still pale, still drawn, but you wouldn't mistake him for his own corpse any more. Where he'd been shot across his chest and gut was just a load of purple bruising now, and some clenched, hard-edged scar tissue that looked months old, not hours. About his scalp, just into the hairline, I saw some livid tissue too, but right then I wrote it off, because his hair was there, and no way could they have played brain surgeon without a close shave first. I mean, that stood to reason, right?

He was sitting up, eating up our remaining rations like a starving man. When I sat by him, he managed a nod and swallowed his mouthful. His eyes headed off between the trees until they settled on some of the Finns.

"How do you feel?"

"Better," in a voice still weak, but despite that he added, "Strong." We looked at each other for a moment, and he started, "You let them...?"

I nodded, and warring expressions crossed and recrossed his face. I was waiting for him to accuse me. I wanted to say sorry, except I wasn't sorry. I expected disbelief, horror, religious mania. Instead, he took a deep breath, let it out. The factions of his face compromised on acceptance. "Fine," he said. "Right."

Viina was already about. She moved a little gingerly but, given how she'd been shot up, the recovery was little short of miraculous. I caught her looking at me occasionally. Maybe she wanted to thank me for getting her out of it; maybe she wanted to blame me for getting her into it. No way of knowing from her face or her feline eyes.

"So, what do you reckon?" I put to Franken. "You going to be OK to move out?"

"Try me. Move out to where? We got a plan?"

"The same plan." In my mind, I turned over what Cormoran had found out. "Stockholm. Trail leads to Stockholm." Meaning that if we got there, we'd have crossed the entire breadth of Sweden from where we'd landed.

But Sturgeon had been talking to the Finns. The Finns understood everything, it seemed. Maybe they could read minds.

The Finns could help us, and I wasn't turning down anybody's hand right then, even if it had claws and hair on the palm.

CHAPTER EIGHT

THE PARTISANS WEREN'T exactly crazy about the idea, I could tell. Two days out from our unscheduled stop for rest and major surgery, and the Finns had led us south-east to another band of grim-faced locals and foisted us on them. We were clear of the US advance, which was apparently focused some way south for tactical reasons opaque to me, but the locals were digging in. This bunch were better equipped than the last—plenty more body armor, plenty better guns and plenty discipline too. Still, they knew they couldn't go toe to toe with our boys, nor with any corporate forces that might decide to give them a hard time. So I listened to them talk defiance in their civilian clothes—talk resistance and urban fighting, ambush and trap, and felt like I should do something. There was no winner, I wanted to tell them. Nobody came out of that game well. Recent history told that story over and over.

I knew that if I said that—in the translator's confident

tones that even I was starting to find unbearably smug—
they'd not listen to me. I knew that plenty of them were
going to die, to drones, to mechs, to us—and they'd get
some of us, too. I knew. And a whole load of people who
weren't fighting on anybody's side would be caught in
the middle.

Don't fight, I'd tell them, and they'd stare back at me
and say, *Go home*. I wished I could.

The reason this bunch were better equipped and
led than most was standing in front of me right now,
listening to Viina through her own tinny little Nord
translator. Her name was Freya, and she was a solidly-
built woman with a round, pale face and hair gathered
up in a black beret, straight out of an old film about le
French Resistance. She was not a partisan, exactly. She
was a Nord government liaison, a political officer. She
was, therefore, the enemy. I knew it, and she knew it, but
apparently Viina didn't. Viina was trying to recruit her.

The interplay between the two women was very fast,
and Sturgeon's commentary was erratic. Freya was angry,
dismissive, incredulous, hostile. Viina was calm and
focused, the sort of stillness that precedes the pounce.
And she was patient; she let Freya rage and blow, and
steadily wore the woman down.

"I don't get it," I told Sturgeon. "Why the hell does she
think they'll do anything for us?"

"That's pretty much what this Freya wants to know,
too. But Viina... I dunno, Sarge. You've seen how the
Nords look at the Finns, right? Half-spooked and half
in awe. Monsters, but they're *their* monsters. So now the
Finns want to help us get to Stockholm without having
to shoot up locals every ten miles. And this Freya can do
that for us."

"So why are the *Finns* doing this for us?"

I saw where his eyes went, before he told me he didn't know. Franken was sitting a little apart, gun across his knees, brooding. He was at full strength now—you'd not even know he'd been wounded. His eyes were still blue and human, and he hadn't sprouted feathers or scales or fur. But Sturgeon and I watched him, and we waited for all these things. We waited for the alien to burst—*pop!*—out of his chest cavity. We waited to see what the Finns had done, when they saved his life. We couldn't, either of us, quite accept that saving his life was all they'd done. Every little thing, every word, every action of Franken went through a kind of filter, in our minds, where we thought, *Is that right? Is that how Franken would have done it, before?*

And of course the more we were off with him, the more he was off with us, and the more food we all served up to our paranoia.

And we didn't have any better idea of why the Finns were suddenly our best pals. It sure as well wasn't for our minimal role in saving Viina, and I didn't think that 'helping out invading US servicemen' was in their book of right things to do on principle.

"All right, fine!" said that cheerful Californian in my ear, as Freya threw up her hands. "I can get them on a train to Stockholm."

Viina followed that up with another patient demand, and a second round of negotiation began. Sturgeon translated this as centering on whether we arrived on our own two feet or handcuffed to a radiator.

"Fuck this." Franken stood abruptly, silencing the room. The Nords were big, a lot of them, but very few of them were quite as big as Franken. It was when I caught myself thinking, *Is he bigger than he used to be?* that I knew I'd gone completely nuts.

I went out—we were in a big warehouse or hangar or something, now repurposed as partisan barracks. Outside there was a carpool of random military and civilian vehicles, a couple of old sentry guns and, far too close for comfort, a little town of people who had yet to discover the joys of being bombed or driven from their homes because they were harbouring resistance fighters.

Cormoran joined me out there, hands smudged with dark oil stains from where she'd been adjusting the innards of her drone. "On a scale of one to screwed, where are we?" she asked.

I had no answers. Privately, I reckoned we'd gone off that scale some time back, but I had a care for morale, so kept the thought to myself.

WHEN WE WERE actually on the train—so too late for it to do any good—Sturgeon asked me why we hadn't just quit. We were already some way out of our skillset. We weren't black ops; we weren't special forces. We certainly shouldn't have been dolling ourselves up like Nord civilians and going on holiday to Stockholm. Yes, we had orders to bring back Cousin Jerome, but... at what point did those orders cease to bind us? It wasn't as if we hadn't pulled out before. Under fire? Low on ammo? Promised reinforcements suddenly got better things to do? Sometimes it's just better sense to fall back. But this... there was no line. There was no point at which I could say, "The mission's FUBAR, we're going home." The mission came so pre-FUBARed that I couldn't make the call.

Maybe if Cormoran had drawn a blank; maybe if there'd been no trail to follow, I'd have called it a day. But she scooped that intel out of LMK's systems, and so there we were on a train full of Nords who hadn't fancied either cosying up to the US army or taking up a gun and joining the partisans, but whose homes lay behind the lines, or would do any day. There we were, three US soldiers and a corporate stooge, and I wish I could say we were heading into the heart of darkness, but from what everyone saying about this war, it didn't even have a heart.

"How are you feeling?" I asked Franken. He'd bullied his way to a window seat, and the two of us sat awkwardly side by side in a car crammed with families. My hushed words came to him via an earpiece salvaged from his helmet, because it wouldn't do for anyone to hear a voice from the US of A right then. Oh yes, didn't I say? Only Sturgeon actually spoke the lingo, and he wouldn't pass as a local. Our story was that we were English socialists who'd flown out here to support the cause, because apparently that was a thing. Basically we were all going to do our best Lawes impression if it came to it.

Franken shot me a narrow look. "What?" his voice growled in my ear. "Wondering if I'm feeling *Finnish?*"

"No, no." *Yes.* "It's just... You were *shot* just a couple of days ago. So I can't ask?"

"I'm fine." He stared angrily out the window at the Nord countryside speeding past. "Don't keep asking." That sounded like Franken, anyway.

So we went on to other topics, just passing the time as socialist public transport took us further and further away from the fighting. While Cormoran dozed, clutching her case, and Sturgeon read a Nord newspaper, the two of us tried to pretend that what we were doing was normal and sane. For a couple of hours we almost managed it.

I decided I'd get some shut-eye then, and hunkered down with my shoulders about my ears. The car was rowdy with people, especially screaming kids, but I had got to sleep through worse.

Only, just as I was letting myself go, Franken said something else, soft as he could, as though he didn't really want me to hear it.

"My eyes are different."

Something clenched inside me. Outwardly, I held myself calm and still, and just cocked an eye at him.

"I never saw this well before. Never." He wasn't looking at me, seemed most of the way asleep himself. I opened my mouth a couple of times, but couldn't find anything to say.

WE GOT OFF the train outside Stockholm in a flood of tired, unhappy, unwashed people. They had camps there, outside the city, and it looked like the soldiers there—gov and corp—were very keen that this tide of displaced humanity didn't wash up on their doorstep. It reminded me of back home, how every so often there'd be some great cause, some refugees from one of the little wars in Asia or Africa, say, and everyone would be like, *Oh, why don't they do something?* And we'd wire a few dollars over and feel good about ourselves. Only, when New Orleans went under for good, somehow that was totally different. Franken and me, we were on crowd containment detail for that one. I got shot in Mexico the next year, and I still preferred that to the orders we got in Louisiana.

So the Nords had these camps. You know what? I've seen worse camps. They looked neat and orderly, kind of like you'd expect. For all I knew, Ikea was mass-producing a flat-pack lean-to called the 'Fükd' just for the occasion. It was still a camp, though. It was never going to be a happy place.

We weren't supposed to get off there. Political Officer Freya had given us papers to take us all the way to Stockholm Central, only we didn't trust her and so we went the last leg on foot, after Cormoran found the bugs we'd been tagged with and EMP'd them.

"Are we clean?" I asked her. No sense in making it easy for the Nords, after all.

"Clean as I can make us," she confirmed, although there was something eating at her, you could see.

"What is it?"

"When I was going over Franken," she said, eyes flicking over to find him. "It was like… I thought I'd found something for a moment—a signal of some sort. It was like something meshed with my headware, made a connection."

"But you zapped it."

"I couldn't find it. There was nothing there, nothing at all."

I felt I knew exactly what she was saying, but it was easier to play dumb. "You're not making sense."

If we'd got our teeth into the subject then, who knew how things would've played out, but instead Cormoran backed down, and I was too chicken to force the issue. "You're right," she said. "I must have been mistaken," and that was that.

Sturgeon found a delivery guy—just some package courier heading into the city on totally civilian business—and talked him into giving us a lift. This is the thing that, looking back, I find hardest to believe. Once we showed we'd got papers, though, the driver just didn't really care. We were going to give him a couple hundred dollars and he was obviously a pragmatist who reckoned a little US currency in his back pocket would be useful insurance. Cormoran sorted the money transfer and I had a sneaking suspicion she took the money from her old boss.

And so we were cut loose from Nordgov supervision and just coasted into Stockholm in the back of a van, and our papers held up when the checkpoint boys stopped us, and we thought we were terribly clever. The plan was that Cormoran would hack the local networks and send a bunch of netbots hunting for any mention of Cousin Jerome, and then they'd report back to her, and we'd bust in to wherever he was being held and GTFO just like the plan said. Or at the least we'd find out what we could and then call up Rich Ted and give him the good or bad news. That would also count as mission completed, as far as I was concerned.

So we were very clever. We were ingenious, even. For three grunts and a computer nerd we MacGyvered the fuck out of that part of the plan. We had every right to be proud of ourselves.

When we got out of the van, in a parking lot in the outskirts of Stockholm, Freya was there. She'd obviously been feeling lonely, because there were a dozen guys and girls with her who weren't in uniform, unless you count the fact that they all went to the same tailor for their suits. I guess individually they might not have drawn attention, but with that many of them together, it did kind of scream *Secret Government Agency*. They all had machine pistols, indicating that they'd already broken a few restraint barriers. I should remind you, we'd left most of our stuff behind to travel in civvies—no rifles, no helmets, just pistols and the underlayer of our body armor making us sweat under our shirts. Only now it wasn't the only thing making us sweat.

I thought the driver had sold us out, but Freya's people scared the crap out of him. He was on his knees with his hands behind his head the moment he saw them. A little star-and-stripe-painted part of me said, *That's what you get from a socialist government*, but then again it wasn't as though it didn't happen everywhere, gov or corp; so much for ideology.

We adopted the position too, and they disarmed us quite competently and took Cormoran's case.

"How'd you find us?" I asked. I felt it was expected of me.

"Not being complete idiots," said the translator in my ear, sounding as though he was enjoying it. Freya knelt down beside me, face to face, her gun pressed to my side.

"I don't think you're a bad man, Sergeant Regan." Now she was speaking English, crisp and unaccented. "But I don't know why you're here in my city—maybe you don't even know yourself. I don't trust anything that comes out of the US lines right now. So I can't just give you the run of Stockholm, no matter what the Finns say. Because I don't trust them, either."

"So what now?" I was wondering if I could grab her, hold her hostage. Problem was that the Nords had more hostages than I could realistically hold on to, and there was nothing to stop them putting a bullet in the back of Sturgeon's head to show me how serious they were.

"You come back to our place and we ask you some questions. Politely, the first time. But I think you know the drill."

One of them took the van man off. Another shoved us in the back of an armored car painted up in the blue and neon yellow of the local law and order. We were cuffed to the interior, with a couple guys to watch over us and another couple in the cab. The rest of the Men In Black got into other vehicles with prominent government plates. Apparently inner Stockholm is a no-car zone unless you're gov or corp or very rich, which I guess really hampers your ability to cruise about in unmarked cars being sinister and anonymous.

There wasn't much conversation in the back of the prison wagon, mostly because our guards shouted at anyone who spoke. Sturgeon looked philosophical and Cormoran was fretting about her case, I thought.

Franken looked... not good. His jaw was clenched and one of his eyes was half-closed. He looked like a man with toothache. When I caught his gaze, he winced and looked away. There was sweat on his forehead, as though he was running a fever.

I was about to make something of it—everyone's seen the movie where the prisoner's sick, so the guards suddenly abandon all pretense at security. But then we stopped—and quite suddenly—and things obviously went south outside because there was shooting.

Our captors didn't know what to do. They tried for orders, but got nothing from their radios. We saw through the grill that the two guys in the cab got out— and then one of them fell right back in, only deader than when he'd left. There was a quick meeting of minds in the back of the car, which we were not invited to attend, and then our two guys kicked the back door open and went out guns first.

They put them away sharpish, because there were a bunch of guys outside in full urban ops gear with assault rifles, waiting for them. It was the slickest work I ever saw, how they bundled the gov types away and then cut us loose and got us out. We were in the middle of the city, some old part where all the buildings looked like someone had repurposed Disneyland for offices—I saw skewed vans ahead where they'd blocked off the leading gov cars. I heard sirens, but they were going to be too late. Freya's remaining people were keeping their heads well down.

So the lot of us got bundled into more cars with gov plates—either they were stolen or faked, or there were just more govs in Nordland that I'd been led to believe. I saw Freya and some of her survivors sent off that way, and then it was our turn. Nobody was explaining what was going on, and none of the super-stealthy black ops uniforms had handy badges to tell us who these new guys were. Except better equipped and more ruthless than our original captors, which suggested to me they must be corp types of some description.

They frisked us over for bugs. They even zapped something in Cormoran's headware because they thought it would let her call out. It obviously hurt like hell when they did it—moving some sort of gadget up to her temples and letting fly. One of her eyes was bloodshot, after that, and I had the horrible thought that they'd fried some of her actual brain rather than just the tech. When she'd got over the shock of it, though, she found a moment to meet my gaze and wink that red eye. Apparently she had a trick up her cybernetic sleeve even then.

We ended up somewhere in central Stockholm, that's all I knew. We got head-bagged after a while, and we were moved between vehicles and made to bumble along on foot. We went underground for a bit, from the echoes, and we went in lifts and on moving floorways. If we'd come out of it in some secret volcano lair, I wouldn't have been much surprised.

And then the bags came off, and the cuffs came off, and we were all four of us in a board room overlooking the commercial district from somewhere high up.

CHAPTER NINE

STOCKHOLM'S ONE OF those Euro cities where most of it looks like—well, like Euro cities are supposed to, if you're from the States—all old, old stuff as though any moment a bunch of people in wigs and enormous dresses are going to pour out and start doing one of those old-timey dances.

There's a few bits in the middle, though, where the last century's caught up to it. There's one part that Sturgeon tells me is called something like 'The Wall of Glass' now—they had one big skyscraper there, and then another and another, all crammed in because other parts of the city were just too damn historical to knock down, until it was like Superman's Fortress of Solitude around there, just a great big bank of glass and steel. And all solar-collectors, of course, because this is the Nords we're talking about.

Anyway, that's where we were, and the serious-looking men who'd put us there were leaving, ceding the room to us. We had a whole-wall window onto that part of the city, all bright and lit up and advertising weird-ass Nord products on its big eyesore video billboards. Another wall was all screens, as though someone was going to ask us to make a presentation any minute.

"Everyone OK?" I asked first. Sturgeon nodded, but Cormoran was frowning. She indicated her head and then a wave of her fingers at the room around us. No connectivity, apparently.

"Franken," I pressed, because he hadn't answered.

"Fine," he grunted. He didn't look fine. His hands were fists, and I could see the muscles of his neck twitch and tic. Cued by me, the other two stared at him as well and he rounded on us angrily. "I'm fine, OK? Get off my back, for Chrissake!"

Sturgeon was going to say something at the uncharacteristic cussing, but Franken loomed at him and snapped, "*I'm* allowed, all right?"

I put a hand on his shoulder, and although he shrugged it off angrily, he stood still while I said, quiet as I could, "Tell me."

There was real fear in his eyes, deep down where only I could see. "I can hear... it's like there's voices, right at the edge of everything. It's like there's a radio inside my head, with the volume turned real low."

Then Sturgeon said, "Someone's coming," but he didn't need to. We all knew it because, despite the reinforced floors that corp towers had these days, you could still feel it through your feet when a Scion was on the way. And no wonder they'd left us alone with our thoughts, because it wasn't as though we could do much against one of them.

The seven foot chrome exoskeleton that walked in was stepping lightly, for what it was. It paused in the door, regarding the four of us. Its barrel torso was broad enough around that I guessed the rich kid was sitting down in there, and the limbs were pure mech—it could go either way, with those shells. The head atop it was bland and faceless: purely decorative, or maybe full of guns.

I came halfway to standing to attention, all three of us army types did. It was what you did with Scions, when they weren't actively trying to kill you.

"Sergeant First Class Theodore Patrick Regan," a pleasant male voice named me, well spoken and American. "Specialist Soloman Sturgeon; Specialist Daniel Belweather Franken, all of the United States 203rd Infantry Division." There was a snicker from Sturgeon because that was the first any of us had heard of Franken's middle name, which sure as hell wasn't on any of his ID. That there was no answering snarl worried me more than I could say.

"And Miss Helena Cormoran," the Scion went on, "formerly with the Special Corporate Services Division of Huesson International Technology and Logistics Incorporated." The faceless metal head made a show of scanning the room. "What happened to the other one?"

"Lead poisoning," I answered.

The Scion made an amused sound, nodding philosophically as if the head was real. It took up a position at the head of the board table, as though about to chair a meeting or call up a pie chart on the screens behind it. "I understand you've come a long way to find me."

I gave that gleaming face a long, hard stare. "Nice try."

But then it was splitting open, just peeling back, and the chest and shoulders as well, the metal hinging, folding and flexing, until the body was half-open. It wasn't something any of us had seen before; the whole point of being a Scion was that you were in your own little impregnable world. You didn't open up where us lowlifes might throw a punch. But this one did. In that office tower on the far side of Nordland, we got to see how the other half live when they go to war.

Or at least the head and shoulders of it, anyway, it didn't unzip all the way and spill him out. It was cosy in there, I can confirm, and he was cushioned by all sorts of direct interface gear—to give him instant living control of the shell, and to keep his body fit and suppress its complaining for as long as he needed to stay inside. Tell the truth, I wasn't really looking. I was looking at his face instead. Within the steel was Cousin Jerome, in the flesh, with a grin that was pure rich boy mischief.

"That's right, Sergeant."

"But your shell," I got out. "We saw it, with…"

"Yes, you did crash our friends from LMK, didn't you? Who aren't exactly happy about that, by the way. I had to leave my shell there, Sergeant. They're just too easy to track. But we made sure I had a pristine new suit of clothes waiting at this end, as part of the deal." And then it all went in reverse, and we were face to face with that shiny façade again, except now his face got projected onto it, like Rich Ted's had been. There was more than one way to show a family resemblance.

"What deal?" Franken said, sounding strained. When I glanced at him, he looked in pain, one hand pressed to his jaw. His other twitched out and touched the shell of the Scion. I'd seen it done, before a battle: the superstitious seeking some metal benediction, as if having had all that money's worth of titanium and steel under your hand would rub off, somehow. I wondered if he was praying, if he wanted the sheer concentrated wealth to drive the Finnish right out of him like an exorcism.

Jerome Speling's visage frowned and flickered. "Is your man ill?" His light-built features adopted an expression of concern.

"He got shot," I said shortly. "And what deal? We were told to rescue you. We were told the Nords got you, that they had some sort of super-weapon that switched off your suit. But you're saying that you…"

"Switched it off myself? I did, yes." The hand he lifted could have crushed iron girders. "Don't look at me like that. I'm no traitor. I came here to arrange the end of the war."

"The end…?" And suddenly it made sense. Of course he did. His corporation—that big multinational where the board and shareholders all had his nose and his chin—wouldn't want a drawn-out expensive war after all, even if the US gov was footing most of the bill. And the Nords must have seen already that their tech wasn't as good as ours. Of course we'd send someone, quiet and covert, to negotiate their surrender. It all fell into place.

Except for the pieces that just kept falling, like *us*. I was working my way to saying it when Cormoran broke in.

"When the US government wants to talk terms, they send a diplomat," she pointed out quietly. "And they don't need to go all hush hush because that's what diplomats do: they go to other countries and talk at our enemies. I'm guess you weren't sent by the White House, Mr Speling."

"There are those with considerably more at stake here than the government, after all," he agreed equably. "Come on, now, I'm sure none of you are quite that naïve."

"Wars start and stop for corporate interest," Sturgeon agreed darkly, and I shot him a warning look. This really wasn't the place for his polemic.

There was a weird thing then, because the screens behind the Scion flickered, and one of them began to play a movie, only it was a movie of Cousin Jerome talking to some other guys. Open Scion shells were behind the others, like they'd all decided to show how much they trusted each other by stepping out. What was behind Jerome was the camera, so we were mostly seeing the back of his head unless he looked left or right.

I assumed the point of this would become relevant later, so I didn't say anything about it. None of us did.

"Well, quite." It really was quite amazing how natural and human the body language of that man-shaped vehicle was, with its idle gestures, waving away Sturgeon's words. "The old nationalist way of waging war was ruinous, after all. Easier just to know from the start that it's about protecting business interests. What is our great country, after all, without its industry? And so, when it's about money from the start, then it ends when both sides know they're not going to get any richer by letting it carry on."

"Linköping," said Franken. It sounded like he was trying to clear something from his throat. The weirdest thing was that the image of Jerome on the screen kind of lip-synced with the word.

Jerome—the real Jerome—might or might not have heard him, but Cormoran grabbed at his attention as soon as he'd finished speaking.

"That still doesn't make sense," she objected. "Did your cousin not know about this deal? Because if he did, it must have slipped his mind when he was giving us our orders. We're supposed to be getting you back behind the lines…" but her voice tailed off as she said it, and she glanced at me helplessly. "Or…"

Jerome let the pause become awkward before speaking to fill it. "Unfortunately, a high-ranking Scion such as myself can't just step off the radar, Miss Cormoran."

"Ms," she corrected flatly. "So, while I can't say I had any illusions, how about you explain to the Sergeant exactly what that means, Mr Speling."

I didn't need the explanation. "We weren't supposed to succeed," I said hollowly. "The world was meant to think you'd been got. Which meant the world would expect someone to be sent after you. Which meant us, because we were supposed to have fuck all chance of actually getting this far. And, Cormoran, I'm sorry, because you've pretty much been telling me this from the start."

"Pretty much," she agreed.

"Jönåker," said Franken, more clearly this time, and it was weird, because he didn't speak a word of Nord, but he was saying it with just those sort of weird stresses and sounds the locals gave words.

And this time Jerome had heard him. The metal suit went very still and he demanded, "What did he say?"

"Hanukah, I think." Sturgeon looked only baffled.

But Cousin Jerome suddenly had a bee in his metal bonnet, and he came stomping around to tower over Franken. "You say that again!"

Franken lifted his head, and his face was agony, pale and sweat-sheened. "They say Linköping. They say Jönåker. The battles you planned." Suddenly he leapt back with his hands to his head. "Get out!" he screamed. "I don't want to know. I don't want to tell them! Linköping! Jönåker! Bergshammar!"

"What the hell?" was my contribution.

"Places, Nord places." Cormoran must have had some maps stored in her headware. "Drawing a line from our advance to Stockholm." And half the rest of the screens all lit up showing Jeromev—different meetings, different people: rich men sitting together to plan the fate of the rest of the world. Some of it was from building security cams, but most wasn't footage that anyone would have wanted recorded for posterity. But Jerome's new shell had been kept running, in case things went south and he needed to bail into it. It had recorded everything its master had done.

Then Jerome lunged forward and caught up Franken, one hand clenching on the man's arm, one at his throat, hoisting him bodily. The questions erupting out of his shell were the only things keeping Franken alive. The projected face had frozen in mid-smile, like the man inside had died.

"Tell me how you know that!" he demanded. "You can't know that. You were checked; you've got nothing that can cut into our data. You couldn't change the channels on a TV with the 'ware we left you."

"Fuck!" Cormoran leapt up from where she'd been sitting. "Oh you son of a bitch!" Whatever she was looking at was not in the room.

I remembered when she said she thought something in Franken had touched her headware. I remembered it wasn't there when she'd gone back for it. I wondered what the hell sort of shapeshifting bioware the Finns had put in Franken's skull just so he could get inside this building and let them reach out and touch the enemy's network.

There were maps springing up on the rest of the screens—troop movements, figures, documents in English and Swedish. Cormoran had put as much of the room as possible between her and Jerome, not that it would have helped.

"I'm getting their plan fed directly into my implants," she got out, shaking her head frantically. "I've no idea how. Nord forces meet US advance at Linköping, get their asses kicked. Try to hold at Jönåker, get their asses kicked. Then…" her eyes, white and red, were very wide. "Oh hell."

"Not another word!" Jerome warned her, advancing around the table with Franken still held aloft.

"Sergeant, they're going to bring down the government, the Swedish government. It's all set out, clear as day. They'll manufacture unrest after Jönåker, topple the socialists, get a corp puppet regime in place that'll do exactly what they want." She was gabbling it out, scuttling crabwise about the table to keep it between them.

Jerome put a stop to that by throwing Franken into the table, which snapped it in half and should have done the same to him.

"And what's wrong with that?" the Scion demanded. "That's what we want, isn't it? A compliant Nordgov that will do what we ask, what the Nord corps ask, whatever's best for business? Why are you saying this as though it's a bad thing?"

"Wait, so what was the other one?" I asked, into the silence that followed. "Link-thing and Hanukah and…"

"Bergshammar," Cormoran pronounced. "Bergshammar is where the Nords throw us back, in this plan. To give confidence to their new government they need a victory over our guys." It was like she was reading it from an autocue inside her head. "After that, everyone sits down at the peace table and everyone gets what they want. Except for the Nord people I guess. And except for everyone who got stage-managed to death in the fighting."

"All right, fine," Jerome said, sounding very calm again. "So let's change the topic of conversation onto *how the fuck you just did that?*" And the crazy was right back, the crazy of a man who's had things his own way since he was born, and suddenly doesn't. "There are no signals. Our techs have checked. Nothing's getting out of this room."

Sturgeon cleared his throat nervously. "You might want to get them to check again." He was standing at the window, looking out at Stockholm's swanky business district. All the billboards, all those great big electric adverts, they were showing Jerome. They were showing Jerome's maps. They were showing, piecemeal but coherent, Jerome's plan.

Jerome took two steps toward the glass wall. The attitude of the suit was shorn of all humanity, as if it had just been an act he was putting on.

"They made me do it." The voice, sepulchral, came from the wreckage of the table. Franken sat up, cut and bloody, but still in one piece. "They used me. They're in my head. They needed me to get here so they could hack your system from inside. They work best when they're close to things."

"Our system is locked down," the Scion spat out, "Nothing is getting out. The moment you got brought in we made *sure*. Just in… just in case… We killed *her* connections. We made certain. You were scanned and… scanned…" By then, his voice was almost a whimper.

"I can hear them," Franken lurched to his feet. "They're in my head, all the time. I'm in theirs. They work best when they're close to things. But them and me—even when we're far away, we're still close to each other. We're all together. We're all equal in the pack."

And then a sudden burst of the old Franken as he turned to me and cried out, "Fuck's sake, Sarge, they made me into a commie!"

I don't know whether it was that aggrieved capitalist soul of his or some instinct of the Finnish network that he was plugged into, but he just went for Jerome then. He rammed into him with his full bodyweight, and although the Scion must have weighed half a ton, Franken hit him high up and toppled him toward the windows.

And life's not the movies, and they build tower blocks pretty damn strong. Jerome hammered into the glass and cracked it a thousand ways, but it didn't give. He ended up hanging there, actually half out over the street and stuck in the crazed glass like it was a spiderweb.

I knew my cue. "Go!" I yelled.

A couple of the corp security who'd grabbed us were already in the doorway, weapons up. Franken just about used Jerome's chest as a footplate to spring at them. I saw two holes punched in him—all the way through—and then he had slammed the corp guys down to the ground. He was weeping. He threw them around like they were dolls but he was weeping. His face was knotted up like a fist with self-loathing. Blood streamed from his wounds but it was already thick and clotting. They were flesh wounds, literally: punched through muscle that was already knitting itself together.

I got one gun and Franken got the other and the four of us burst out into the next room, and then the room after, because a lot of people were getting the hell out of Dodge around then. It wasn't even Franken lighting a fire under their asses—right then the whole building seemed to be in utter chaos.

CHAPTER TEN

MOVIES AGAIN: YOU know, the ones where the hero's fighting the bad guys in a tower block. You saw that one where they're fighting all the way down the stairwell, or there's that one they remade like nine times, where the guy drops bombs down the elevator shaft and they magically know to explode just where the villain's guys are. Did you once see one of those where the hero got lost? Seriously, if we hadn't actually seen the fire escape sign we'd be wandering round there still. Nobody stopped to engage us in a complicated martial arts fight. In fact, most of the guys we saw around there didn't look as though fighting people was why they were on the payroll. They were in suits or shirtsleeves. Some of them were just running around, but a lot of them were at computers very determinedly doing something— Cormoran said they were wiping data, reformatting drives. Others were actually shredding paper documents, like they were having a flashback to two decades before. We saw a lot of LMK letterheads and logos, and I reckoned their stock was probably underperforming on the exchange right about then, because if that crap was on the billboards outside, then it would be all the way around the world by now. There'd be guys in China selling their shares in LMK even as we were trying to get out of the building.

So we found some stairs, and for a moment we stopped there, breathing heavily and listening to the sound of running feet and panicked voices. It wasn't just the stock market crash these people were worried about. While me and mine were focused on trivialities like just how many good men would die to bring about Jerome's little plan, I reckoned the Socialist Government of Sweden would be more interested in that whole corporate-assisted regime change thing.

"Franken," Sturgeon said. "Franken. *Bellweather*, you all right?"

Franken was crouched down on the steps, holding his head like he was trying to tear it off. "Don't call me that," he grated.

"Then give us a sign, man," Sturgeon insisted. "Come on, what's up with you?"

"They're telling me... they're telling me to do things," he rasped out.

"Tell them to fuck off," was my advice.

"I can hear them. They say up, we go up... up, up, up."

"Can they hear me?" I demanded, and in the absence of a cogent reply I went on, "You listen here, you Finnish bastards. You've got what you wanted. You've got your spy into this place and ripped open its guts. You can leave him alone now. We don't need you any more."

Franken's head swivelled to look at me, eyes very wide, the pupils like pinpricks. What was wrenched out of his lips wasn't English. To me it didn't sound human, but Sturgeon had his inner Finnish-human dictionary working overtime and he said, "It—he—Franken says we need to get to the roof. He says to trust... them."

Not a chance, but Cormoran was already filling in from intel they were feeding her. "Sarge, they've got army and police pulling up all around this place. What are they going to think when a bunch of Americans try to push past them."

"That we're part of the problem," I finished for her. "Fine. Okay. But what's up?"

"Helipad," Cormoran said flatly.

"We're short a helicopter."

"I reckon they'll be flying one in for the big cheeses."

I grimaced. "Fine but—Sturgeon, ask Franken—ask whoever's in there with him if we get him *back* at the end of this. Ask them if they can make him right."

"Sarge, I don't even think they'd understand the question," Sturgeon said.

Then Franken stood, and that was plainly our cue. We were up those stairs at a solid soldier's pace, glad for once we'd had to leave our packs behind.

Nobody in the world knew who we were or what part we'd played right then. But everyone knew what had been done. As we were thundering up those stairs—occasionally elbowing aside locals who were far more sensibly heading *down*—the material the Finns had hacked out of Jerome's shell and the LMK net was on a thousand websites, broadcast in a hundred countries. Sure, it was pored over by countless emergency gov and corp committees, but that wasn't the thing, because those people knew the score already. The big deal was that now everyone *else* got to see how the deals were done. Everyone else, who'd been told about national interest and liberty and freedom and ideals, was being given a chance to wake up and smell that stuff they'd always told us was roses.

And you know what? I know what Sturgeon has to say about the whole deal, but Sturgeon says a lot of things. Me? I don't get that having the gov types run the show is so great, or the corps either. But when someone has me bent over the table and tells me to smile when I get shafted; when someone has their eye on their shareholder dividend so much that they're willing to get my people killed for it; that's going to get even me into politics.

Up the stairs, and I had to catch Cormoran as she stumbled. She had a hand pressed to her face, and my stomach lurched with, *Jesus, it's catching?* as if being Finnish was contagious now. But she shook her head quickly. "Gonna have to cover for me, Sergeant," she said. "I'm... rebooting my headware. Got all kinds of shit streaming past my eyes right now. I'm trying to get a comms channel out past the burnt sectors. Not going to be much good until I'm done."

I held onto her as we slogged up and up, all the time not knowing what we'd find at the top.

And then we were up, and we were late to the party because the Board of LMK had already turned up for the evac party. There were three of them in the building at that time, or at least that was all who'd made it the roof. Probably I'd have recognized faces from the Jerome tapes currently breaking box office records all over the world, but of course their faces and the rest of them were hidden behind their metal shells. These were all Family men, scions of whatever the Swedish corporate dynasties were.

Crouched at the top of the stairwell I demanded, "So what's the plan now?" in a hoarse whisper. "Firstly, I don't see them making room on the chopper for us; secondly, how the hell is LMK even going to fly one in without the Nord flyboys taking it down? I'm willing to bet that they really, *really* want these guys to answer some questions."

"No idea about the first," said Sturgeon, "but for the second: incoming."

The air, which had been hosting sirens and the occasional gunshot from far, far below, began to thrum with a familiar thunder. It wasn't the sound of a nice corporate helicopter with all mod cons, not even the heavy lifters the Scions used. It was something bigger. 'Bigger' didn't do it justice, in fact. The only word was *Biggest*.

A vast shadow was falling over Stockholm as the largest, ugliest combat flier in the world taxied awkwardly over the city center toward LMK's doomed corporate HQ. The White Russians were bringing their Jodorowsky, still scarred from its run in with the 203rd but no less dangerous for all of that.

One of the Scions stepped forward, waving. Another took that moment to glance back, and obviously spotted us. It turned smartly and began striding toward us.

"Back down the stairs!" I ordered, and Franken promptly bolted out across the roof like a startled rabbit.

I thought he was charging the Scion, but he was cutting a path around it, close to the rooftop's railing, as if making a desperate break for the helipad. Of course we went after him, but the Scion was already between us, gaining on him despite his burst of speed.

The other two were turning, alerted by their fellow VIP. Beyond them, the Jodorowsky drew closer. I saw something strike fire off it, some Nordgov gunship or ground to air, and it replied with a contemptuous salvo, not even altering its course.

The running Scion had almost caught up with Franken when it tripped. It cracked the concrete when it came down, then lurched up to its knees. At first I couldn't see what was going on, but there were grey shadows clinging to it, three at least, and there were more coming over the edge of the roof. They climbed like spiders, four hundred feet of glass and steel. They must have been scaling the building since we were brought in. The Finns, of course. They hadn't been as far away as the voice in Franken's head had made him think.

I saw one grasped by those metal hands and ripped in two. Even the best bioscience can't toughen you up to resist the full torsion strength of a well-made Scion. The others were already at work, though. They weren't trying to get through that immaculate shell; they simply didn't have the strength. They had an ally, though—a big one: gravity.

Scions weighed most of a ton, but they were made to be as light as possible whilst remaining impregnably strong. Three Finn werewolves could hoist one in the air easily enough, and then it was over the railing with him, because even if the outer armor didn't crack open, the occupant would be so much jello when it hit the street.

Automatic fire sprayed from another Scion—I saw at least a couple of the Finns go down, injured and writhing. The rest were already on their targets then, driving them away from the helipad and toward the roof's edge.

They lost more than a few, the Finns, but they fought like… I want to say animals, but that gives the wrong impression. They fought like a pack, perfectly coordinated, each one selfless and totally committed to the cause. They had those metal men off the side of the building faster than you'd believe. All the while we just stood there, Sturgeon and I, and Cormoran crouched at our feet trying to get her head together, muttering to herself.

The Finns vanished over the edge of the roof as quickly as they'd come, job done, skittering down the building's sides like nightmares. Then it was just us and the Jodorowsky, which had come in to hover impossibly above us, like a meteorite impact about to happen. And then, even as it lurched and shifted for balance in the air, it was us, the Jodorowsky and Jerome Spelman in his metal suit.

He was pissed. I think I can say that for certain. He burst out onto the roof still spiky with glass from the window. He had geared up, too. There were a couple of weapon pods over his shoulders ready to unleash hell in our general direction.

This was the moment for noble speeches, but I had nothing. There are reasons I never made it past Sergeant.

We retreated as far as we could go, but no matter how big the tower, there was still only so much distance we could get on the roof. Jerome took three steps and braced but, because of who he was, because we had really got him riled over and above anyone in his whole life, he let us have the benefit of his opinion first.

"You've got them thinking I'm a traitor," came his amplified voice. "You piece of fucking white trailer trash! I was going to end the war! *I'm* the patriot here! You're the traitors! And now I'm going to put you in your fucking place with a fucking vengeance."

And the rooftop shuddered and flared with artillery, the whole structure of the building shaking and cracking with the fury of it. I didn't see much of the result, because I was instantly half-deaf and half-blind, crouching like a sinner at the second coming. The Jodorowsky had opened up on Jerome.

"—the hell?" Sturgeon was shouting, wide-eyed as a kid at a fireworks display. "... do that for?"

"I asked him to!" Cormoran hollered over the thunderous echoes bouncing back and forth between my ears. "I got a channel out! I called the pilot!"

"Why's he on our side now?" I demanded.

"I promised him my old boss's bank access codes!"

"Sarge—!"

Sturgeon's shout dragged my focus round to the slag and rubble that had been the other half of the roof. We could see a fair amount of the building's twisted skeleton through it, and sure as hell nobody was coming up those stairs again, nor were we leaving that way. What we could also see was Jerome.

He was crouched on all fours, and one of his weapon pods was mangled. His shiny shell was all battered to crap, but he was very much still with us. Even as I saw him, he began launching at the Jodorowsky, and although his shots looked tiny compared to the gunship's, the vast frame above us rocked and groaned when they struck. The best that money can buy, like I said. I figure that each shot Jerome took was worth a year's back pay for the whole 203rd.

Cormoran was shouting—in Russian no less—at the pilot, who was presumably trying very hard not to drop down and squish the lot of us.

Franken was already at Jerome.

I hadn't seen him go. I still don't know what drove him, whether he was a puppet of the Finns in that moment, or a loyal friend and comrade, or just so tortured by what they'd done to him that he would take any way out.

Jerome was already on shaky footing on the tangled wreckage of the roof, and the recoil from his own ordnance didn't help. Then Franken slammed into him at top speed, grappling him by the head and the ruined weapons pod.

For a moment I didn't think it had helped, but then Jerome was tilting stiffly backward, like a dictator's statue hauled down by an angry mob. I saw his arms reach for balance as he took one teetering step back and then another, but there was nothing there for that second step, and he dropped, falling away past the mangled girders and shattered concrete and the million shards of glass.

And then the Jodorowsky unrolled a metal ladder at us with a clatter, and it was time for us to make our getaway. The three of us. Just the three of us.

THERE WAS A very awkward meeting, two days after that. Present were: me, Sturgeon and Cormoran, Political Officer Freya, Viina the Finn and a Russian named Genaddy Osipov. Our lack of tech finally became a positive because they had to conduct the whole business in English, and I listened to Freya's translator speak clipped sentences into her ear with all the verve of a tax accountant, while Genaddy's murmured in a breathy female voice that seemed to be constantly on the point of orgasm.

Of the lot of us, only Genaddy was happy. A common soldier in the White Russians' mercenary companies, he had suddenly become richer to the tune of several million dollars thanks to Cormoran's hurried negotiation. He grinned at everyone and drank from a hip flask, and it wasn't entirely clear why he was there except that he was hard to shake off.

The subject of our discussion was mostly extradition. Nordgov would happily have vanished us away to an interrogation camp somewhere, I knew, but it had become fairly well known that we'd thwarted a corporate coup, however unwittingly, so we were somehow heroes of the exact nation we had come over to make war on. The one upside was that we weren't easily vanishable.

There were a lot of calls for us to go back home, some of which wanted to put us on trial, while others wanted to pin medals on us. I'd found a TV giving CNN with Swedish subtitles, and discovered that things were busy back Stateside. The revelations about how the war was being fought—about who was pulling the strings—had led to enough popular uproar that suddenly Congress and Senate were both trying to look shocked. There would be enquiries, and people were already talking about wars past: Canada, Mexico, Somalia, the intervention in Chile. Suddenly a lot of recent military history was looking fishy. The Swedish campaign was already being rolled back, our boys heading home early and in one piece. The TV was full of politicians trying to out-do each other in crusading against the very scourge of the American people that had probably put them in office. There was talk of a New New Deal, of expanded regulation, anti-trust stuff. Who knew whether it would come to anything? Meanwhile the markets were in free fall. I thought about all those expensive Scion suits and wondered how much would have to get struck from the portfolios of the wealthy before they couldn't afford them anymore.

In the end, Sturgeon accepted political asylum in Sweden. He always was a socialist at heart, and he had no faith in the reception we might receive back home. Cormoran negotiated a service tour with the Russians, because their money was good, and she likewise didn't fancy her chances in a country that had become an unwelcoming place for an educated black woman over the last few decades.

For me, I could see only one choice. The US was where I came from, and it was where I was going to. I wanted to see this through. I wanted to rejoin the 203rd. I wanted to testify to what little I knew. Most of all, I didn't want to turn my back on what Franken had believed in. I said so, to the lot of them. I said it to Sturgeon's face, after he'd done moralizing. I said it to Freya. I said it to Viina: that I would honor his memory; that Franken had always been a good American boy.

And she looked at me then, with an expression on her face—but with those Finns it was hard to read anything they let show. I tried to ask questions, through Sturgeon, but she just pretended she couldn't understand him. And yet her eyes never left me, and that look never left her. *I know something you don't.*

I chewed over that look all the way until I was waiting for the diplomatic helicopter to come repatriate me. I got to wondering just what might have happened to Jerome and to Franken when they fell. There was a lot of broken building they might have bounced off on the way. Could Franken have lived? Was that what Viina's ambiguous expression had been trying to tell me?

But by then I was already in the air, and whatever secrets Viina had, she'd taken them back to the dark, science-haunted no-fly zone that was Finland.

FIREWALKERS

CHAPTER ONE

ROACH HOTEL

THE MASSEREY-VAN BULTS were coming in all the dry way down the Ogooué Road, and, as Hotep would say, there was much rejoicing. They came in a real motorcade, big cars with windows so tinted they were like black mirrors, the back ends corrugated with heat sink fins so that M. and Mme. and all the little Masserey-Van Bults, could slide untouched through the killing heat of mid-afternoon. People turned out for them. As their fleet of cars grumbled down the Ankara's one maintained road, everyone spilled from their factories and repair shops, an impromptu half hour holiday from whatever it was put food on the table. The kids jumbled out from their shacks and shanties, from all the hand-built homes that had gathered around the Anchor like junk washed up on a high tide, never to see the sea again. They all cheered, waving scraps of cloth for flags—didn't matter the colour so long as it was bright, bright enough to see through that dark glass! They whooped and stamped, all of them, and Nguyễn Sun Mao waved and hollered just like all the rest of them because this was how you did it, at Ankara Achouka. You did it whenever the new guests arrived at the Roach Hotel, because this was the only time you'd see them. They check in, but they don't check out, which was some ad from long-back. Anyway, it wasn't Roach Hotel, not really, not to the face of the people who got to stay there, however briefly. Not to the face of the wabenzi who ran the Ankara town, controlled the jobs and who got fed. It had a fancy French name in twenty-foot gold letters that loomed over everything in the township, just like the Ankara cable loomed over them and everything, going up forever.

The motorcade was approaching the big gates of the Roach Hotel now. The first couple of cars just went in, past the guards and the guns, up the gravel drive; past the dusty space where there'd been lawns in Mao's dad's day, before the owners acknowledged that even they couldn't waste water on that kind of conspicuous consumption. Mao's dad had got to see the place pristine new, before time and dust and the heat cracked the façade. Mao's grandad had helped build it, one of that wave of labour that had converged on all three Ankara points long-back—they had locals, yes, but they got in strong backs and keen minds from all over, and it so happened there'd been plenty out of Vietnam who'd needed somewhere that wasn't underwater right about then.

The crowd's jubilation was ebbing. For a moment it looked like the Masserey-Van Bults were going to screw tradition and just pass through that gate from which no soul returned. Then, after three cars had cruised on, the fourth stopped and more men with guns got out, the private soldiers of the corporate compound noun that was the Masserey-Van Bults. And after them, some flunkies in suits, already pink and sweating in the seconds after leaving the vehicles' AC. Mao shook his head and rolled his eyes, but he kept waving his little flag because he had parents and siblings and they got hungry just like everyone else.

They had little baskets, like they were giving out lucky money for New Year: stacks of notes, a king's ransom. Sullenly, sourly, the flunkies began chucking the cash into the crowd, flashing the sweat-stains spreading like plague zones across the armpits of their shirts. The crowd whooped. Children ran up and down the line, gathering it all up. The wabenzi would redistribute it later and plenty would stick to their fingers in the process. It would all go to buy just a little less than the last, because even these good old American bucks, these sterling pounds and roubles and euros and rand, bought less and less of the less and less there was to buy.

Children, because it looked better to the guests of the Roach Hotel if it was happy kids rushing around to grab their bundles of old notes. Because nobody wanted real desperate adults slugging it out for handfuls of cash. That might suggest that they weren't *happy* with what they'd got.

Mao'd thought the flunkies were it, but there was a special treat in store for all the lucky people of Ankara Achouka. Mao saw some kind of argument going on within that great big space within the car, bigger than the room he shared with two sisters and a brother. The flunkies were protesting: *no, go back, really ma'am, not appropriate.* And then she appeared, a woman white-going-on-pink, with a broad-brimmed hat already wilting on her head. Her hair was like gold, like hair you only saw in adverts. Her sunglasses looked like poured mercury. She was waving back, basking not in the killing sun but in the adulation, listening to the crowd go barmy because some daughter of the Masserey-Van Bults had graced them with a personal appearance.

She threw something into the crowd—artless, awkward, but it reached the front ranks, almost brained some old boy, in fact. Not a wad of cash, this: something heavy. A plastic bottle, rich man's water, the pure stuff. The inside of the car was probably lined with them.

There was a fight, after that. The half-brained old boy had the bottle, his neighbours wanted it, the people next to them... Then the gendarmes had just turned up out of nowhere in their riot suits and were whaling into the crowd and cracking heads, because this sort of unruly disorder before the eyes of the guests just would not *do*. And Mao was bitterly sure that the chief of police was going to nurse a long cool drink of rich man's water this evening on his nice veranda, and that old boy was going to nurse nothing but a headache.

Then he looked at the Masserey-Van Bult girl, and she looked so stricken. She'd done a nice thing, hadn't she? She'd shown the proper noblesse oblige. Except it had all gone wrong and now her day was ruined. He thought she'd actually stamp her little foot. But then she was back inside the car with her flunkies so the cool air could get flowing again, and the rest of the motorcade was passing the gates, and everyone went back to work or back to not having work, and then Balewa turned up and punched Mao in the shoulder. Balewa and Mao had grown up together, meaning they'd hated each other from ages five to fifteen. Then Mao had gone Firewalker and Balewa's dad had pulled strings somehow to get his boy the coveted position of errand runner for Contrôleur Attah. In which role, inexplicably, Balewa had turned out to be a good friend, and to fondly remember all those times he and Mao had tried to beat the living shit out of each other. Which meant when Attah wanted a Firewalker crew, Balewa tried to get the word to Nguyễn Sun Mao.

"Attah wants you."

"Wants me, or wants someone?" Mao asked, abruptly reviewing what he might or might not have done.

"Wants you, he says." Balewa shrugged. "Between you and me, guy, Attah is on the plate with the Sonko up in the Hotel. Got bizna for you. Name your price."

Mao clapped him on the shoulder, feeling the soft there, where once there'd just been the skinny. Attah's business was feeding Balewa and his family well. Attah's business was keeping Mao's people full, too. Always happy to do business for M. le Contrôleur.

ATTAH JEAN JACQUES was one of the old wabenzi; his family been running Achouka a hundred generations, to hear him tell it—and he would. He was a short man, bald, fat: not *fat*-fat, but prosperous-fat. He'd gone away to Cape Town for his education, come back to find his Assistant Contrôleur's shoes ready for him. And there were worse bosses, Mao knew. Like Attah's own superiors, he reckoned. Attah answered to the men inside the Hotel, who answered to men on the other end of the Anchor cable, who answered to nobody at all, not even God. When things went wrong, it was Attah and his fellow Contrôleurs who felt the lash, and most of his peers made sure their underlings caught it twice as hard. Attah had an eye for talent, though. Screw up and he wouldn't even shout at you: you'd be out on your backside and never get a decent job in the township again. Do well, and he'd give you the slack to get the work done. No tantrums, from him; no belittling his people, screaming at them, taking out all the many and varied frustrations of a busy man. Mao reckoned he got better results that way, being the buffer between the shit and the ground.

Which didn't make him a nice guy, and it didn't mean he was immune to that wabenzi way they had of showing off just how damn well they were doing. Attah's office had air conditioning sometimes, though right now all the windows were thrown open and there were a dozen flies drowned in the man's cup of water. Attah had trophies, too. He had a desk of black wood big enough that Mao could have used it as a coffin. The top was old felt, sun-bleached and torn, but most of all *valuable*, antique. There were yellowing photographs on the wall behind him. One showed a view from the Roach Hotel from long-back, when it had been where the rich people came to see the animals that weren't there anymore. There were things like cows, and there was grass that went up to the cows' bellies, and out there was water, too, the sun like diamonds on the Ogooué back when it had been a river and not just a concrete road from the coast. The other photo was a man with a gun sitting proudly before the lion he'd just presumably killed. Mao had spent too long staring at that photo, marvelling at the sheer alien nature of it: not the lion, which looked like something by a computer artist with no sense of the real, but the man: so white, so huge, vaster than the lion, clipping the edges of the photo, like an ogre. The past was another country, maybe another planet altogether.

Speaking of...

"You're still running with Lupé?" Attah asked, fanning himself idly. The open windows stared out at the world as though watching for the first stirrings of a breeze.

"Yes, Contrôleur." Mao was careful to mix the cocktail of his language to the genteel standard suitable for someone of Attah's position: more French, more English, less Afrikaans and Bantu, absolutely no Viet slang. "You need, I can get her."

"I need," said Attah, heartfelt. "Her, you. Got me a situation here needs fixing."

"Nothing she can't fix, Contrôleur."

"That's what I want to hear. This is top dollar bizna, boy." Attah grinned: good, white teeth, so even you could use a spirit level on them. The show of money should have been something to put Mao in his place, but there was something of the cheeky child in that smile, something irrepressible that decades in Achouka hadn't ground out of the man. "Who else is there knows their tech? Need more than two of you? Akiloye?"

"Got hurt, Contrôleur. Cut foot, went bad."

Attah's expression soured. "Who else?"

"Hotep, Contrôleur."

"Hah?"

"The spacegirl. Took her with me to Ayem when the condensation plant was down, last time. Got it running, double-quick."

The Contrôleur's expression soured further, meaning he had remembered just who Hotep was. Mostly trouble, but the girl had all the knowledge an expensive technical education could buy: an education never intended for slumming it groundside at the Ankara.

"Take her, then. Take her, take Lupé." Attah shunted

over a tablet holding the meagre briefing. "Take a 'Bug. Get this fucking sorted and it's bonuses all round. Double-double danger pay."

Mao nearly swore in front of the man; that meant a lot of money indeed. "Which way is this trouble, Contrôleur?" And he knew the answer, because any other point of the compass and he'd be offered standard or straight danger money, and if he didn't like it there'd be plenty others willing. "South, then?" South: the Estate.

Attah nodded sombrely. "Mao, you're a good boy, you've got a good crew. Double-triple." And no haggling, no attempt to disguise the fact that the Man was riding Attah just the way Attah wasn't riding his subordinates. *He's on the plate, sure enough.* Time to go find Lupé and Hotep and put civilization behind them.

A FIREWALKER CREW could be two people for small jobs, could be six, eight, for big. Mao'd had a bad experience, out on a six-man crew except the wages were short and so someone had tried to have only a two-man crew come back. He'd been fifteen. He'd been left for dead. Now he was nineteen, a whole world of experience on, and he didn't go out with big crews, or with people he didn't know if he could absolutely avoid it. What he did was get results from the people he trusted.

A crew needed tough and muscle, and Mao brought that. A crew needed skills, too. Just one head crammed full of computer and mech repair meant if something happened to its owner, the rest of them were screwed. More bitter experience meant Mao took a fix-it for the mech stuff, a hacker for the computer tech. Most crews then threw in three more mouths who were there mostly to eat food and be someone's useless cousin; Mao kept things lean. He was pathfinder, strongarm, marksman all in one. Lupé was mech, and he'd have to hope he could talk Hotep into doing tech, because it was that or some stranger who thought they could code.

Most Firewalker mechs would be in the township off-shift, and if they needed work they'd be in the fix-it shops where everyone brought all the crap that stopped working, or sold all the crap that had never worked. Lupé had started off there, same as everyone, working for her fix-it uncle at his tin-roofed little place out in Willaumez Neighbourhood. Everyone worked in Achouka—no room for luxuries like staying home. Boys grew up running errands, salvaging, joining gangs and fighting each other over street corners. While they were out doing that, there were schools that taught girls mech work, because everything was a resource in Achouka and nothing was wasted. It wasn't that Lupé had a magic touch for getting broken-down machines working again, because there were a score of genius fixers working invisibly in the township on any given day. What got her noticed was how her home block suddenly had access to the Roach Hotel wi-fi, running water and makeshift solar collectors on the roof. These days, if you wanted Lupé, you'd find her in or on the Hotel itself, fixing for the rich because she had family to feed too.

Most kids on her pay grade would have been trying to get others in to do their work for them, for a fraction of the pay. Mutunbo Lupé just liked the feel of the metal under her fingers, though. She liked making it all fit together. She was the best there was, or at least the best Mao could afford. They'd worked together almost two years now, half his Firewalking life.

He caught her as she came off shift, down from the AC units up top of the Hotel. That was her favourite work, when she could get it: the view of the Anchor field was second to none, she said. A clear sight of the cable base, all those warehouses and offices dedicated to sending everything that mattered skywards, up out of the atmosphere to where the spaceship was. In Mao's dad's time it had still mostly been the physical material itself: the rare elements, the bulk metals, all the slack from when the asteroid mines weren't performing as intended. These days the ship up there, the *Grand Celeste,* was fully built and fitted out, a luxury liner to eternity, ready to coast out its days in orbit or go colonise Mars, or head to an exoplanet on a trail beaten by robot probes.

Anywhere but here.

Mutunbo Lupé was local girl through and through: dark, stocky, her wiry hair pulled into Bantu knots. She always wore overalls two sizes too large, which spare space seemed able to magically furnish her with tools, food and, on one fraught occasion, a gun.

"Here's trouble," she observed, spotting Mao loitering. "M'bolo, chief. How did I know I'd see you today?"

"Am'bolo, you free?" Because these days Lupé got paid well without risking her ass for it, and each time he asked her, Mao wondered if today she'd say no.

But: "For you, always," and that easy smile, remembering the time, maybe, he'd hauled her back to Ankara Achouka after she broke her leg; or else the time she'd just about built a new car out of scrap when the two of them had been stuck long-ways east, drinking poison water from a rusty tank and going out of their minds until somehow they'd made it back to real people.

And yet... Even as they were off to find Hotep, Mao looked sideways at her. "Wait, you know what, now?"

"Oh, chommie, all kinds of shit going down at the Roach Hotel," she told him with her bright smile, with one blackened silver tooth. "Those sonko, you never heard anyone complain like it when their AC isn't working full blast. Chommie, some of them have worked up a *sweat* today. You never heard such language."

"But you fixed it." Because in his experience she really could fix anything.

"Ha, no way. Those AC units, they're all good. Power's coming up short."

"Figures." That put the mission into perspective. He and Lupé and Hotep were going south, into the dry, into the dust and the killing heat, to the places monsters lived, because out there were the solar farms. Out there were the grand fields of collectors that had powered the Ankara's planning and building. Now they harvested sunlight and turned it into cool air for the Roach Hotel, fancy lights for the sonko parties, filtration for their swimming pools, so that their brief stay at Ankara Achouka could be flawlessly comfortable before they were hauled away forever to go live in the *Grand Celeste*. If the power was short, it meant someone was stealing or something was broken, whereupon word came down to Contrôleur Attah to hire some Firewalkers to find out and fix. And Attah, in his wisdom, picked Mao.

LUPÉ BROUGHT HOME solid cash for her fixing work, but Firewalking paid better. Hotep, though: Hotep didn't need cash. Hotep had a goddamn *allowance*.

She wasn't wabenzi, that class of administrators who ran everything outside the Hotel, men like Attah who hired, fired and made sure things got fixed, hauled, shipped and built. No responsible wabenzi would let their kid end up like Hotep: too embarrassing. Hotep's folks weren't from round these parts, though. Hotep's folks were up living the High Life, overseeing those far more compliant labourers: the robots aboard the *Grand Celeste*. That made Hotep one of the sonko, the rich-rich. Except here she was, pissing her days away in the township, bitter as hell about all the indignities life had doled out to her. Once every two weeks, give or take, she got so fighting drunk she tried to break in to the Hotel, punch out the guards, scream, shout. They all knew her there, and that her dad was the CEO of Lord God Almighty Incorporated. They knocked her down, but didn't break anything. And Mao knew all she'd do, if she somehow got past all of that, would be go stand on the Anchor Field and look up to the vanishing point of the cable, where it got too small, too far to see any more. And probably scream at it, because when Hotep got drunk she got *vai* drunk.

She was drinking on her balcony when Mao found her, but that was just the usual drinking, that she did like most people breathed. No danger of her going out to buy a black eye and a loose tooth from security for a few days yet.

Hotep's real ID called her Cory Dello. The nickname came from some old film everyone saw once, some remake of a remake that was remade back when the idea of a desert land full of ruins was somehow romantic. There had been pyramids and adventurers, and there had been a mummy all got up in bandages to chase them around. Hotep looked like that. Not an inch of her was on show. Face wrapped, save for the hole she applied the bottle neck to, dark goggles over her eyes, hair bound up in a turban and a forage cap set aslant over that like she was the world's jauntiest burn victim. She wore gloves that were expensive tech in and of themselves, and she bandaged her hands over the gloves. When they had gone out to the fix-it job at Ayem, Mao had wondered how she didn't just die of the heat, but Lupé said she had some flash liquid cooling gear in there somewhere, that recycled her piss and her body's movements to offset the battering of the sun. It wasn't overheating Hotep was worried about, but sunburn and skin cancer. Lupé said she was pale as an albino all over, under all that cloth. The thought was weird, like she was some kind of magic alien from a cartoon.

Mao's dad'd had skin cancer for a few years now, the kind that wasn't going to get you tomorrow or this year, but eventually. Mao would get it too, most likely. Everyone who wasn't wabenzi or sonko would, because they had to go out to work and there weren't enough hats or parasols in the world to keep that sun off. Lupé was already checking herself every day, she said, because the old story that only pale, delicate people had to worry about melanomas was a convenient lie they told you, to get you to go out. Hotep was super-paranoid about it, though, and that was only one of the many delightful quirks that had ended with her down here looking up, rather than up there looking down.

"I know," she told the pair of them as they scrambled up to the balcony. She had more living space than Mao's entire family, paid for by the folks who would give her everything so long as they never had to actually share an orbit with her again. "You see the news? Whole lot of people flying in to Libreville Secure International tomorrow. Whole lot of people driving their expensive cars down the Ogooué Road. Busy-busy times a-coming." She spoke the chimera patois of the township with a ridiculous scholarly precision, clipping out slang like she was saying the Latin names of extinct deep-sea fish. "Of course they need us."

"Because the AC at the Hotel is bust?" Lupé asked her.

Hotep turned her goggles, her bandages, towards them, faceless and creepy. Her wrapped hands were drumming against her knees in complex patterns; she was never completely still. "I give rocks about the AC. AC at the Hotel has been on brownout for months. Only now they're going to have guests on top of guests at that place, all clamouring for their cool air. You not catch the news from Ecuador, dangi?" She scooped up a little tablet—crazy money worth of device just lying about, propping up one of her empties. She had it projecting pictures on the wall, though Mao had to squint against the sun to make them out. He saw... devastation. He saw water. That made him sit down next to Hotep and just stare, because there was more water there than even God had a use for, surely. Water coming through streets, water flooding around cars, water slanting down in great turbulent sheets from a heavy sky. Water scouring in two-storey-high waves across a field of overturned vehicles and broken prefabs and...

It took him too long to identify the stump of the building there, lashed by that insane rain, as though all the water that they were lacking here in Ankara Achouka had been dumped in that other place, on the other side of the world.

"Ankara Pedernales," Hotep pronounced. "Storm and a tidal wave hit it. Cable just gone, though." She shook her head. "Serves them right." As though, if she'd still been on the orbital team, somehow she'd have stopped it.

"And the people who didn't get out?" Lupé asked.

"Serve them right, too, does it?" Air evac from Ankara Pedernales would only have been for the few waiting for the cable ride up, plus maybe the guards and whatever they called wabenzi over in Ecuador.

Hotep's goggles stared at her while the fingers of her free hand continued their manic drum solo.

Eventually she shrugged. "Went too long without answering, didn't I?" she remarked cheerily. "Sorry. Making a note now: human better next time."

"This is happening now?" Mao asked. He couldn't look away from the images.

"Boss, this is happening yesterday. We already got plenty rich folks flying this way because they missed their golden ticket up the pipe," said with that extra bitterness Hotep reserved for anything to do with space. "They blocked off the news, tried to stop it getting to the local net here, but there's no data wall high enough to keep me out. So, that's the job, boss? They need to turn on all the extra AC at the Hotel, just when there's a power outage? That mean we're going south at last?"

"Vai south," Mao agreed. Meaning further than any of them had gone "Bundu south." Meaning the wilds, too dry for anything to live, too desolate for anyone to go. Except they were going and, by variedly mad-sounding reports, things still lived there. "All the way." Meaning the Old Estate, abandoned to the sun and the automatic systems three generations ago, and only rumours about what went on there now.

"Where the wild things are," Hotep said languidly, necking the last drops of her beer and placing the bottle on its side, fussily in line with its expired compatriots.

"Dusk, vehicle compound."

"I'm driving."

"Fukyo are you. *I'm* driving."

She shrugged, one hand leaving off slapping at her shins to spider around for another bottle. "See you there."

CHAPTER TWO

COMPLAINING ABOUT THE WEATHER

THERE WERE TOWNSHIPS south of the Ankara, just a few. They weren't holdovers from the old days, when people had farmed this land or come to see the pretty animals; the drought had driven everyone away a generation before the Ankara was even built. And the Ankara itself was a hothouse flower, existing only because money needed it to exist. When the construction work for the anchor had begun, they'd needed so many workers they'd flown them in from anywhere that had more people than food, shipped in whole families, bussed them from the coast and the airport to the neat new prefab houses they'd built for them. For Mao's grandad's generation, it had seemed like magic, like the future. They had built little suburb townships and there was food you could afford and water you could drink without getting sick. There was work. There was a purpose. They'd made a place to live out here on the equator for two whole generations, long after everyone who'd once lived here had been driven out by the heat and the dry. They'd reclaimed a piece of the world from the apocalypse.

Now, just fifty years on, almost nobody lived outside the Ankara township itself—only the craziest or the hardiest still trying to scratch a living. No buses came to bring workers and work together. Solar was the only power and any decent fix-it who could keep the panels and filtration going had upped sticks to Ankara because the best work was there. The satellite townships were dying. Ankara Achouka was dying, too, but as long as they still needed the Anchor point and its elevator access to the stars, they kept the life support on. Beyond that, it was just folks clinging on because that was where they used to live, and because it was there or nothing. Mao knew damn well that of every hundred who'd left for the coast to make a new life in Libreville or Port-Gentil, ninety-nine either never made it or got turned back from the walled compounds where the last of the government wabenzi lived. Nobody was keeping the lights on outside those compounds. Temperatures around the world were still on the up, and the zone of dead earth was still spreading out from the equator. Nobody'd had any use for that land, dead of heatstroke like everything else, until they'd had the idea for the Anchors, and for space, because the mad irony of it was that if you wanted cheap access to space up an elevator cable, you needed the equator.

Mao had seen satellite maps of his world. He had seen the little star of the Ankara itself, bang on the equator, an oasis of life in a steadily spreading desert. In older pictures he'd seen where the rivers had been: green, like some other planet entirely, as though before going off to live in space, humans had to first make their own world something alien and uninhabitable.

Mao thought of that over the first hours of the drive, where being behind the wheel of the Rumblebug was almost like a holiday because there was at least a track going the right way, and they had the cool of the dusk, and the dust hadn't shorted out half the vehicle's systems. Lupé had a wind-up radio, picking up old Akendengué covers on Mademba 17, the station that two brothers ran just down from where Mao's family lived. He could listen to Lupé sing tunelessly along and try to ignore Hotep kicking the back of his seat. Hotep had wanted shotgun, but he knew she'd end up flicking every damn switch in the cab because her hands got bored real easy, so she got to sit in the back.

The Rumblebug was older than Mao by five years, testimony to the skills of Lupé and her predecessors that it was still running and in good shape. Every part of it had probably been replaced in that time, from its big puffy tyres to the solar cells that sat like angled wing-cases on top. Recently, one of Achouka's better street artists had given the thing a new paint job, in bright, toxic-looking reds and greens. All the Firewalkers liked to go out in a 'Bug painted as fierce and jagged as possible. *We're poison*, they were telling the world. *You can't eat us. We'd kill even you.* By the time they brought it back, most of that paint job would be abraded away and half the parts would need replacing, but they made these things to last, and fix-it Firewalkers made damn sure they were always as fixed as they could get, because if your ride broke down out beyond the townships, then most likely you weren't coming back. Mao had come back, once, that time when things had really gone to crap. That feat had made him a minor celebrity in Achouka, cemented him as a tough guy, got him Firewalking gigs ever since. *As many tries at killing yourself as anyone could want.* His parents had been less than impressed. His dad, his mum, his grandmother, they'd all tried to talk him out of the work, but they hadn't said no to the money when it came in. They'd given up on the discussion by now; when he'd said goodbye this time, they'd just hugged him, then let him go.

Firewalking was a youngster's job. Youngsters could learn the skills quickly. Youngsters were fast and tough, not so old that their bodies were stocking up on the toxins in the air and in the water. Mao knew one Firewalker who was thirty, but he was broken, too shaky for any kind of work that brought in good pay.

And youngsters were replaceable. Disaffected youth desperate for cash was the one natural resource Ankara Achouka had in abundance. Everyone was hungry; everyone had folks needed feeding, needed medicine. Everyone dreamt that if you get enough cash in one place, there'd be an office for you with the wabenzi, just like everyone at Attah's pay grade was waiting for that one elevator car with a berth with their name on it, the one ticket out of the dry hell that was all that was left down on Earth.

Which brought him back to those contraband images Hotep had shown them. Elsewhere in the world had its own problems, he knew, but it seemed crazy that there were people on this self-same equatorial line who were drowning right about now.

"You reckon it's better to get the water than the dry?" he threw back, knowing she'd get what he meant straight off.

Sure enough, Hotep barked out a laugh. "Some filing system gone crazy in the sky, right? Take all the water, put it over there under 'W.'"

"Crazy," Lupé sang, fitting it to the increasingly staticky music; Mademba 17 didn't have the kit to broadcast very far.

"Their wet, our dry, all the same shit," Hotep said. "What's on the menu, boss?"

"We'll hit Sainte Genevieve after dawn," Mao told her. "Weather station there, we check the power, wait out the sun, get news. After that it's just go south until we reach the farms." He didn't say that he wasn't expecting there to be anything wrong with the power lines through Sainte Genevieve. Sure, the locals were probably syphoning a little, but that was built into everyone's equations. Attah could just call, if it was that simple, get someone already on the ground to go tinker with it. The bulk of the solar fields were deeper in, though. They'd been built for the Estate, the vast compound where they'd designed the anchor tech and spaceship tech, put it all together before shipping it north to the Ankara. Back before Mao's people had fled the flooding for somewhere dry that needed workers, the smartest of the sonko had come out here, to the land that the heat had rendered utterly vacant. They'd lived in cool chambers underground, come to design the elevator and the engines of the *Grand Celeste*, and they had done it here in the land of the dead so that no other smart sonko could find out what they were doing. Those old scientists did everything in secret, terrified that some other company would make the discovery first, and make all the money in the world. It made Mao wonder how things would have gone if all those clever people had just put their heads together and not worried about the money.

But it had worked: here and Pedernales and Singkawang, bang on the equator, they'd built their Ankara points, or at least had people like Mao's granddad build them. They'd sent the cables up into the sky and started work on the great ships that were Earth's lifeboats. And by then, they'd abandoned the Old Estate, its labs and secrets not needed any more. They'd gone into space and left behind the land where nothing grew, where no rain fell and every drop had been sucked out of even the deepest aquifer. All they kept were the power lines, funnelling the yield from kilometres of gleaming panels that carpeted the ground around the site. Those solar fields were supposed to last, if not forever, then long enough for their builders to wring what they could from the world and then get the hell off it. They had self-repairing robots to clear the dust off the panels and fix the scouring and the breakages. Back then, the world had been able to afford that kind of luxury, rather than relying on desperate kids like Lupé. It was like that up on the *Grand Celeste* and the other luxury spaceships, or so Hotep said: robots to fix everything, robots to bring you breakfast, robots to polish your nails and massage your feet and warm your bed. Down here on this end of the cable, people were cheaper and in infinitely greater supply.

Those clever, clever people who made the robots and the vast gleaming solar arrays, they'd have laughed at you if you told them what a Firewalker was. No need for that kind of homebrew measures in their perfect machine world. Except things broke down, even the robots that repaired the robots that repaired the robots.

And the solution to that was to send kids to do a robot's job and get things up and running. Half the Firewalkers Mao ever knew had never come back from one piece of bizna or another. There were desperate people out there. There were broken down vehicles no fix-it could fix. There was dying of thirst, of heat-stroke, of having the thing you were sent to get running explode on you instead. And then there was the Old Estate. *Where the wild things are*, like Hotep said. What secret science had never come out, after the scientists left their labs and then their planet? Mad experiments, monsters, human vivisection. Crazy rich people with private reservations where they hunted resurrected monster animals, hunted normal people who fell into their hands. There were films and serials about it, all kinds of nonsense Mao had laughed at louder than anyone. He wondered if he'd still find it funny in three days' time.

Double-triple danger pay, though. It was all on paper and digital, guaranteed wealth in rand or USD when the three of them got back.

I hope it's a power line gone in Sainte Genevieve.

THERE WAS ONE big building in Sainte Genevieve. It looked kind of like a boat upside down and at an angle, so that the high end curved down like a hood and kept some shade even at noon. Around it was a little township, not the shacks and shanties of the Ankara's dilapidated circumference, but maybe a hundred little prefab houses, most of which were long abandoned, sand-blasted, windows like eyesockets, doorways like slack mouths. Only two things kept anyone in Sainte Genevieve: the meteorological station and God.

God got the big house.

The heat was already fierce by the time they arrived. The inside of the 'Bug smelled like—well, probably like Mao, if he was honest about it. Mao if he'd been hot enough to cook eggs on. They pulled the vehicle up alongside the boat-looking church and took turns topping up the water purifier the way God intended. After that it was find somewhere to wait out the worst of the day. From here on, they'd have to take the light and the heat and just live with it, but no harm having some shut-eye under a roof, and Attah had sent ahead to the meteorologist to expect them.

"Found where some of our power's going, boss," Hotep said. She was pointing to a big old cross stuck up in the open area the church's hood pointed at. It was all over with bulbs and strip-lights, and cables running from the church, but it was a drop of spit in the desert compared with the power that should have been reaching Achouka. This was just Hotep being Hotep, because God-talk upset her.

The meteorological station was a squat building roofed with solar, backing onto the church. Antennae and instruments reached out around the panels like weeds breaking through old tarmac. At Mao's "Awe!" the door opened a crack, revealing a Bantu woman in a worn red dress with floral patterns. One of her eyes was milky and the skin around it was scarred by the sort of cheap surgery most people had to resort to when the cancer started to show. Just peel everything away until whatever you found underneath looked healthy.

"Mme. Ironsi?" he asked.

"*Doctor* Ironsi," she corrected frostily. "You're the Firewalkers." Whatever her expectations, apparently

Mao came in somewhere below them, though he reckoned that anyone with a *Doctor* in front of their name, and who was stuck out in Sainte Genevieve, probably had a lot to be disappointed about.

She took them in, though. Her three-room dwelling vibrated to the tooth-jarring rattle of an antique cooling unit and the walls were lined with pipes trying futilely to shift the heat elsewhere against the inexorable pressure of physics. Lupé was all over it at once, because she loved innovation like that, no matter how much work had produced how little result. Before Mao could talk business, she was pattering on about where she could tighten it up, how she could tune the system, and Doctor Ironsi was thawing dramatically because quality of life was about as thin on the ground as free water in Sainte Genevieve.

Mao gave her the nod, and Lupé sat down to tinker. Hotep was bored already, peering through the dust-screens on the window and making gun noises to herself while staring at the church. To Mao's surprise, a bunch of people had gathered out there in the noonday sun, where the cross was.

"Funeral, or…?" he asked.

"Just everyday around here," Ironsi told him, shaking her head. "Brings them closer to God, they say. Day and night, out under the sky. Night, I can understand." Her shoulders rose, slumped, as though a proper shrug would be too much effort. "The Estate, Attah said. So you're crazy, then."

"I'll tell you when we come back," Mao said shortly.

"Solar yield's been down for years. And who's surprised, when things are like they are?"

"They built it for the heat, though," Lupé said, still

bent over the generator. "For how things are there. Top of the line tech."

"They built it for how things were when they built it. Then things got worse," Ironsi said disgustedly. "Still, lucky them, they have kids like you to go fix it. And you have dust storms on the way, next four days at least. Your car good for that, is it?"

"Have to be," Mao said. "Show me."

Her tablet had a crack through the screen, bleeding rainbow colours across the map she called up. He watched accelerated simulations of the storm ebb and flow. South of here the land was patchy black with the vast fields of sun-drinking panels, where they hadn't been buried so deep in sand that there weren't robots enough in the world to excavate them. Little rectangles were the grand, abandoned houses of the rich, from when they'd lived out here to oversee the research. The actual Estate itself was like a pale bean, insignificant, most of it below ground.

The worst of the storm was west and heading westwards. Mao was already plotting a curving course through dead farmland, following the dry irrigation channels where he could see them on the satellite map, to avoid the worst of the weather.

After they'd slept a couple of hours, just kipping on her floor because it was better than roasting in the 'Bug—after dusk had started to come in and cart away the malevolent hammer of the sun—Mao sat up with Doctor Ironsi and asked cautious questions about what it was like south of here.

Lupé had the coolant system in pieces by then, and was reassembling it into something that would work better and make less noise; or, at least, that was the plan. Ironsi was taking that as the wages for wasting her words on the ignorant bruiser she'd plainly written Mao off for. Hotep had gone out to try and score some beer, despite Ironsi saying the congregation were abstainers. Despite there being beer in the 'Bug, a little. Hotep was just going stir-crazy mostly, and needed to run around a bit, like a five-year-old.

"No Firewalkers going this way for two years," Ironsi told him. "No Firewalkers coming *back* for five years. But seven months back, these treasure-hunter types came from long-ways south, two of them, all cut to hell. One didn't make it back to the Ankara, the way I hear it."

A weird light was playing through the open windows now. Mao glanced out and saw they'd turned the cross on. Half the lamps on it weren't working and the rest flickered and strobed out of sync, oddly disquieting, as though he was watching a radiant living thing trying to get free.

"They came through here on their way in?" he clarified.

"They came back here on their way out," Ironsi corrected. "I don't think they planned to, but they'd lost half their team and they needed help. I helped the pastor's people patch them up. Learned a few things for you. First, there's still something worth taking, out there. When they abandoned the Estate for space, they didn't bring all their toys. Second, there's still people living out there."

"Impossible," Mao said automatically.

Ironsi just did that broken-down not-quite-shrug again. "Well, you're apparently the expert. No doubt you're right. But that's what they said anyway, and I'm telling it because I like your fix-it girl there. People on the Estate, still. Sonko people, they said."

"Crazy." But 'crazy' was way closer to where he lived than 'impossible' was. "So what got their friends killed?"

Ironsi's eyes slid off his uncomfortably. "Bugs, they said."

Since the windows had been opened, bugs had been much in evidence. They were just about the only things that seemed to be able to survive the dry. Flies were crawling drunkenly about the ceiling, beetles battering at the walls. Out there, the half-lit cross was probably calling the insect faithful to prayer from miles around. Mao was only glad that they didn't have the mosquitoes his granddad had talked about; the plague-spreaders needed standing water to breed.

"Bugs," he echoed.

"They were half mad of heat-stroke," Ironsi said. "One of them had wounds so septic we had to take the leg off. Talking all kinds of crazy. Even went full-on confession with the pastor. People like that, they see bugs where there aren't bugs."

Mao shivered. "Sure," he agreed. "Crazy talk."

"I hear Hotep shouting," Lupé half-sang. "She's out making friends."

CHAPTER THREE
LET GOD SORT THEM OUT

HOTEP WAS STANDING in front of the haphazardly lit-up cross, which meant she was also standing in front of both priest and congregation, who had come out for what Mao guessed was some kind of sunset mass. For a moment he was picturing torches, pitchforks and being run out of town or beaten to death, because you didn't go to someone's place and piss on their church and expect to get away with a whole skin. Once his eyes had got used to the flicker of the electric cross, he reckoned any mob riled up here would take a while to get going. These were people of his parents' generation at best, and more towards his grandparents'. He saw lots of grey hair, dark skin wrinkled with lines and pocked with scars. Plenty of eyes clouded with cataracts or even sewn shut where the orb had been taken out. The priest himself looked about seventy, hair just white curly wisps about his dark scalp. He had spectacles on. Mao hadn't seen spectacles beyond the pair his folks kept, that had been his great-grandad's and become a kind of family relic, stuck up on the shelf beside the statuette of Bà Chúa Kho, Lady of the Storehouse, who didn't lend herself to this kind of grand religious theatrics these days.

Still, there were about thirty of them, and that was enough to lynch one skinny white girl done up all over in bandages, but Hotep was in full-on crazy mode right then, and Mao had no idea how she'd gone from nought to rabies in so short a time.

"You think they're coming to take you up?" She was full-on shrieking at the priest and his followers. "You think they're making your rooms ready up on the *Grand Celeste*? Goddamn, so you worked to build their hotel and their anchor, you and your folks and their folks? You think that buys you a golden ticket, that they're going to bring you up to that Heaven they got going on there?"

"Ah, *shit*," Lupé said. "She's been drinking surgical spirits again?" Because there was that one time Hotep had been reduced to sucking the alcohol from medical swabs after an epic bender that left nothing else within a dozen streets. Mao knew her better, though: this was sober Hotep, not drunk Hotep talking. This was the reason Hotep drank in the first place.

"And *this* is what you do with what's left of your lives?" Hotep went on, advancing on the lot of them—and they were actually backing up. "You go pray to the big man in the sky, tell him how good you've been? He doesn't care. He just wants to keep you praying and nodding while he gets in his magic sky bus and goes somewhere the hell better than this!"

"Hotep." Mao approached her cautiously. "Hey, hey, listen to me. Hey, *Cory!*"

She rounded on him, as though her real name was her secret weakness. "Fuck you! Who the fuck are you to—Mao? You ever hear the shit they're spooning out here? Did you? That they're all going *up*, boss. Gonna get taken into the sky by the big man up there. Salvation, boss! Divine rewards of a life of earthly toil, amiright?" And her patois was shifting, more and more English shouldering its way in and out, her accent sailing past all compass so that Mao wrestled with her words like they were a snake.

"Hotep," Lupé snapped, "that's how all the godly types talk: taking up, rewards, all of that. How my grandad told it from the pulpit, way back. That's just how it is. Doesn't mean they're talking about going into space, you mad skommer."

"You didn't *hear* them!" Hotep yelled into her face, and Lupé flicked her goggles hard, right on the nose-piece. Hotep sat down then, as though she'd been punched in the face, sudden enough that the breath whomped out of her. Between her wheezing and the crowd, all standing aghast, the near-silence that followed was almost reverent.

"You didn't hear them," she said again, plaintively. "Goddamn, can't you see I'm trying to tell them the truth? Why won't anyone listen? I've been there. I've seen those people. I *know*." The proverbial prophet, honoured nowhere, save that this wasn't even her own country: no place on Earth was.

"It's god-talking," Lupé said, not unsympathetically. "I sat through it every Sunday until Grandad died and my folks let me off."

"She has to leave." Abruptly the pastor was there, recovered from his shock now Hotep's momentum was

177

gone. "There's no place for her here. There's a devil in her."

Mao had to concede that the man had fair reason to believe it. "We've outstayed our welcome, right, sir. Sun's down now, past time we were moving."

The pastor glowered at him, spotting another non-believer, but Mao had his hands up, all conciliatory, and was also built broad and heavy enough to break some old bones if anyone decided to escalate matters.

"Get her in the 'Bug," he said, and Lupé hauled Hotep to her feet.

"You didn't hear them," came a mumble from behind the girl's mask. "Isn't anyone coming to save them, pray all they like."

"I'm *telling* you..." Lupé said wearily as she hauled Hotep off towards the vehicle, but Mao wasn't entirely sure she was right. He could see the cross better now, past the glare of its surviving bulbs and the wheeling clouds of moths and flies and beetles. There were designs carved into the wood, of spheres and orbs passing by one another. There were drawings and photographs and old clippings: artist's renditions of the *Celeste*, promotional flyers, covers torn off old sci-fi novels, even a torn vintage poster for *Star Wars*. He wondered, he really did, what had crept into the creed of this doomed little church on the very edge of the Ankara's influence, and what salvation they were preaching.

But it wasn't his business what they did with their lives, or how they ended them.

On his way to the 'Bug, Ironsi intercepted him, scowling. "Thank you for riling up the neighbours."

Mao grimaced, but shrugged. What could he say?

"I sent the latest storm data to your vehicle's system,"

she told him. "For what it's worth. You're cutting east
to dodge the worst, but if that doesn't work for you,
there's a beacon you'll pick up, if it's still working."

"What's that, then?"

"Kandjama Protein Complex. What's left of it."

Mao wrinkled his nose. "Bug farm."

"Was one of the biggest once, but they couldn't keep it
going in the heat. Something still running there, though.
Some shelter. Maybe water."

"We have water." But the 'Bug's filtration plant was
a patch job, and if they didn't have to lean heavily on
it right at the start, all the more chance it would still be
working at the end. Bug farms creeped Mao out, though.
He'd nearly ended up working on one, something with
brine shrimp off in Mékina back when he was ten and his
folks had some spare money to buy an apprenticeship.
He'd had nightmares about tanks of leggy things—far
bigger than they could ever get in reality—of falling in,
of all those seething bodies choking the water around
him, all kinds of nasty stuff, so that he almost just ran
away from home. Then the apprenticeships turned out
to cost twice as much as advertised—people paying for
their kids to become next to slave labour because they
thought it was a future. So he'd been saved to become
a Firewalker, and most likely not *have* a future, but at
least not get eaten by shrimp.

But shelter was shelter, maybe-water was maybe-
water, and bugs were what everyone who could afford
it was eating over at Ankara Achouka. Beggars, as the
wabenzi said, couldn't be choosers.

He found Hotep in the driver's seat when he got there,
a determined set to the way she held her head. Lupé,
riding shotgun still, shrugged.

"Fine. I'll sleep in the back," he told them both. "You've got the met data onboard. Try not to get us buried in sand."

THE LAND SOUTH of Ankara Achouka had been forest once, had been rivers, timber concerns, game reserves. Green as far as the eye could see, someone had told Mao. He'd seen photos, sometimes, taken from planes. He still wasn't sure if they'd been real or just computer imagery. All those trees: it had just looked copy-pasted after a while.

Still, he dreamt of them, being lost in the eternal dimness under that unrelieved roof of leaves, exactly the same, every way he turned, no landmarks, no trails, no way out. In his waking days he had walked out of the desert all the way to the Ankara. They called him Wild Thing after that, Bundu Boy. The next generation of Firewalkers—kids two, three years his junior—told stories of the Vietnamese hero who'd conquered the sand and the dust. They said he wasn't scared of anything. None of them understood how he was scared of *all* of it. There wasn't a damn thing out there that couldn't kill you, and the absence of things would kill you most of all. All the trees were gone, mostly gone even back when Grandad came to build the Anchor. All of the rivers were dry.

He woke to find the weather had stolen a march on them, and everything outside the Rumblebug's shaded glass was dust, solid walls of swirling particles blotting out the sun. He heard Lupé and Hotep, and for a moment his mind turned their voices into an argument and he knew they were going to die. Then his mind cast off the nightmares and he understood they were only shouting because of the boom and rattle as the wind tried to snatch at the 'Bug and turn it over. They were following the plan; they'd picked up the bug farm beacon and were homing in on it, because even Firewalkers couldn't keep moving in this, and if they tried it, the dust would block all the vents and intakes, smother the solar panels, kill the vehicle and then kill them.

"Fukme," Mao swore, one of the English language's more persistent insertions into Achouka patois.

"Why they pay us the big bucks, chommie," Lupé told him. She was driving now, he saw, with Hotep in the passenger seat and the comms apparently half-disassembled on her lap. At the sight of that, Mao bolted upright, all sorts of bad words leaping to his lips, but they were definitely picking up the signal. He had to take it on faith that Hotep had been fixing a problem and not making one.

She looked over her shoulder at him. She had her bandana down, her bandages up, the goggles still in place, trusting to the 'Bug's dark glass to keep the sun from boiling her skin like a lobster. He still had no idea what her eyes looked like, but her face seemed like it had been over-enthusiastically whittled from white wood: sharp nose, sharp chin, thin ginger arches for her eyebrows.

"So what's—" she started, but the witticism would have to wait because Lupé yelped in surprise and hauled the 'Bug sideways to avoid what looked like an enormous rib-cage, looming two storeys up out of the dust.

"Dzam!" Abruptly there were structures rearing up all around them—just appearing out of the skirling dust, but at their speed the beams and sand-blasted girders looked like they were thrusting out of the earth even as they passed, curving overhead like monstrous fingers trying to pin the rattling vehicle down.

"Light!" Hotep hollered, pointing. Her goggles must have been working overtime, because there was sure as hell nothing there when Mao looked. Lupé took it on faith, though, and four heartbeats and a near-collision later they all saw it, a beacon white like burning phosphorus, casting shadows even through the dust. They steered for it like a sinking ship for land, seeing walls loom before them that were, at least, more than just the bare bones of buttresses and scaffolding. Seconds later Lupé was skidding the 'Bug into a sharp turn to avoid just ploughing straight into concrete, and they skittered madly along a windowless expanse of pitted grey, then on to a wall of abraded glass, great man-high panels of it all tessellated together, uneven and patched, some of them covered with corrugated iron or plastic.

"Vehicle bay?" Mao yelled, lunging past Lupé's shoulder to point. Probably it wasn't, but it would serve if they could fit the vehicle in there, and who cared what the original purpose was in that case? Lupé gamely slung the car towards the vague shadow: seven closed roller-doors and two hanging open. Things crunched and shattered under the tyres as the 'Bug scooted under cover, and they brought a lot of the dust in with them. Still, it was out of the worst of it, and for a good half-minute after they dragged to a halt, the three of them just stared at each other and tried to calm their breathing.

Then Hotep pulled up her bandana, securing it in place under the nosepiece of her goggles.

"I suppose we better go see where the fuck we are," she suggested.

*   *   *

LUPÉ INSISTED THEY clear the caked dust off the panels and out of the vents first, not a long job with the three of them working at it. By that time they had a good idea of what sort of place they had found. A factory, certainly—they were at the door-end of a warehouse, the far end of which had collapsed in on itself, then been tarpaulined over. Mao reckoned there wasn't much life left in the makeshift repairs, but also that they'd been recent, within months rather than years.

There was another tarp fallen away from the entrance they'd driven in through, and a little work had it hooked up and keeping the driving dust out, at least for now. Then they took a break, tapped the filtration tanks that took up the whole back half of the 'Bug and ate some chewies. Chewies had the consistency of toffee, a taste so packed with artificial additives that there was no natural thing they truly resembled, least of all whatever extinct fruit or savoury was on the wrapper. Mao got chicken dumpling, Hotep had chocolate—she always had chocolate—and Lupé's bar had a picture of some brown cup-shaped thing none of them could identify.

"Turd," Hotep decided eventually. Lupé tried it and declined to call her a liar.

It didn't matter, of course. It was all of it bugs. So the Kandjama Complex had seen better days, there were still plenty others up the coast from Libreville, or over on the New China Bay. They just migrated north and south, those places, as the heat got worse, and that was more for the convenience of the humans who operated them. There was nothing like a bug for tolerating the heat.

Way long-back they'd tried to grow plants that could deal with almost no water and daytime temperatures of sixty C. Mao imagined them cross-breeding wheat and sweet potato with cactus somehow, but probably there was more science to it than that. It hadn't been economical to farm, not in the end. In the desert belt the world had put on, even the cacti came up stunted or died. The last flourish of bioscience, in the face of this new world they'd all made, was to breed drought-resistant insects, taking the already hardy strains and making them ever more self-reliant. And then grinding them up and turning them into chewies.

It felt weird to be grinding away at the protein bars here where they'd maybe been made, like walking over someone's grave. Still, Mao tried to put a brave face on it. "Mmm, good," he exclaimed, like he'd have done at home over family cooking, making the most of the little they had.

"Vai good, really taste the..." Lupé looked at her wrapper again. "Turd," she conceded.

Hotep had cut hers into neat squares and was popping them into her mouth like each was an experiment. Right now, though, she was looking to the far end of the room, at the tarp sagging beneath a slowly sloughing burden of dust.

"Power," she observed brightly. "Lights are on. Someone's home." Her goggles were doubtless picking something up.

"You think it's that simple?" But power came from somewhere. Were Kandjama's own solar farms still in operation? Or was there a great big tap on the cable that led to Ankara Achouka?

"Not enough here to bother the sonko, surely," Lupé said.

"Depends what they're doing. We're not going anywhere until the dust calms. Might as well take a look."

They had to wait for Hotep to finish up her finicky eating, but Mao knew that hurrying her would just be laying in some explosion of bad temper for later, erupting out of a clear sky when least expected. Besides, just sitting back and resting was a luxury for a Firewalker. Once the storm died down, they'd be trying to make twenty hours of travelling in a day, everything except the harshest hours of noon, with pills every four hours to keep them sharp. He wasn't looking forward to the crash after they got back. But at least they'd *be* back.

He felt Lupé's eyes on him, as Hotep slurped down the last cubes of chewie. As usual, he found his shoulders going back, his chest out, like he was some punk kid—meaning, a year or two younger than he was. Force of habit, though. He and Lupé had hooked up last year for a short while, tried out each other's bodies, had about three days of thinking it was going to be The Big Thing. Then it got awkward. Then Mao's mother had found out and given him a thrashing because what was wrong with that good Vietnamese girl he'd been seeing a month before? Three more days of it being The End Of The World, at the end of which Mao had the surprising revelation that having Lupé about as his mech, his back-up, his *friend* was more important to him than the rest of it. Besides, he'd heard she was a steady thing with Nolo Amachi now, the girl who ran the office for Contrôleur Attah, so maybe that was another reason things hadn't quite clicked between them.

There was a locked metal door from the warehouse into the rest of the complex, a segmented steel thing someone had padlocked twice. Lupé was good with locks; they were through in an instant, into the weirdly cavernous silence of the factory floor. Nothing was running, but the lamps strung up above shed a flat, grey light over the ranks of stilled conveyor belts, the presses, the labellers. A sheet of uncut plastic half-fed through one machine bore still-bright colours and a happy anthropomorphic banana, just delighted to be the chosen flavour for some batch of bugs that would never be processed. Its mouth was curved into a manic grin, but its cartoon eyes seemed to be pleading for release.

Halfway through that machine reliquary, a voice called out, "M'bolani! Awe! Welcome, welcome!" chasing its own echoes so much it might have come from anywhere. A man's voice, high and strained. Mao had his hand into his plated vest immediately, touching the grip of his gun. He'd not had to fire it in almost a year, nor even draw it. He didn't want to break that record, either.

"Am'bolo," he responded: *Hello to you too.*

"Are you here from head office, come to…?" the voice called, and simultaneously, Lupé said, "Left," and Mao twitched that way, seeing movement. A man was cautiously approaching between the machines, ducking under belts, stepping over disconnected cables. The windowless factory floor was still stuffy and close, but he had on a full suit and tie, like someone from a drama set long-back, before the world went wrong. He was dark, balding on top, hair greying and wild from ear-level down as though caught midway through an escape attempt. He was taller than any of the Firewalkers, but all angles, like someone constructed from uneven lengths of pipe.

"We're from the Ankara," Mao told him. "Come to get out of the storm."

"You want to see the year's end...?" the man said, as though those last few words just hadn't happened.

"You're who, exactly? Is it just you, here?" Lupé asked.

"You know me," the man said, sounding hurt. "Okereke. Just M. Okereke, the manager. Assistant manager. This is my facility until... I run things here." Said with such pride Mao half-expected the whole circus to spring to life, complete with singing midget workforce.

"Doing what?" Hotep had a way of speaking so you knew she was wrinkling her nose in disgust even if you couldn't see it.

"I thought you... might have more orders...?" Okereke's enthusiasm began to give out. "Or wanted to see how we'd done. Only it's just me, now. Just me, after the last batch, you know. But I'll do my best, with what we've got..."

"Which is what?" Lupé asked, apparently now being Serious Inspector From Head Office. "Show us."

A yellow grin split M. Okereke's face like an ill-favoured moon. He straightened his ragged tie. "Come with me. I'll give you the tour."

There were tanks in the basement, big concrete vats that would have seethed with maggots or shrimp or some damn bugs. The air still stank vaguely of writhing life, or perhaps decay, but of the miniature chewies-in-waiting there were no survivors. The bottom of each pit was a drift of husks and chitin.

"Of course it became uneconomical to..." M. Okereke tried to explain, his hands describing entirely independent sketches in the air. "Mass production at this facility was... but that doesn't mean we can't still handle the bespoke! We're proud, vai proud to service our demanding clients."

Hotep knew what 'bespoke' meant, so at least Mao felt he was learning something. Not a word he felt he'd have much use for. "Bespoke what, though?" he asked. "Like, new flavour research?" Distantly he could still hear the storm hissing sand about the edges of the building, or he'd be on his way back to the 'Bug right now.

"Research, exactly," Okereke didn't seem to say half of what he meant or hear half of what he got in response. "You were happy with the batch of…"

"Sure, vai happy," Lupé reassured him. "Maybe you could show us…?"

"Of course, yes," and he was dancing them through to further rooms, past desks mounded with dust and the carcases of escapee insects, brittle beetle shells, the dull jewels of dead flies mounded up like a miser's hoard. Then into the laboratories, big buried rooms where the fans still ran to cool the outside air and drag it down into the earth.

The lamps here were dim, but still drawing power from somewhere. The bank of equipment at the near end didn't look like it was doing anything, and Mao could only guess at most of it. Hotep flitted over instantly and started flicking switches, though, turning little lights from green to red and back, making a comic dumbshow of trying to fit a goggle lens to the eyepiece of a microscope. Or probably a microscope; Mao could only guess at it all.

Things moved.

He jerked back towards the doorway even as he heard Lupé exclaim. There were bugs in the room, and they weren't in the big tanks that lined one wall, because someone had apparently gone at those tanks with a hammer. Fragments of glass crunched underfoot.

Okereke let out a shrill laugh, in that moment the most horrifying sound Mao ever heard. In the next the man's hastily-composed face admitted nothing of it. "All a little outside our usual..." he said, almost a whisper. "Still, the funding was... We were able to achieve..." As though he was a radio, words eaten away by waxing static. He was still padding further into the room, every footstep grinding through broken pieces.

"Experimental, hey?" Mao asked nervously. There were locusts, not a lot of them but everywhere he looked he spotted at least one. They somehow looked simultaneously over-large and stunted, and they were dead silent, but then he'd heard that the low-water breed they'd worked up for the protein farms didn't chirp, because otherwise the cacophony would have driven the workers crazy. Except Okereke seemed to have gone that way anyway, so maybe they shouldn't have bothered.

With disturbing swiftness, Okereke plucked one of the live locusts from a nearby cabinet. "Oh, not these, these are the last of the previous... They've found water, food somewhere, just a nuisance, really. I keep saying we should take steps to... Who has the time, though?" For a moment Mao thought he was going to pop the wriggling insect into his mouth, but instead he crushed it, yellow innards flowering about his fingers, to be fastidiously wiped away with a tissue. Then he was heading further into the dim room, and Mao followed, because losing sight of the man felt worse than the bugs.

"So, tell us about your research, M. Okereke," Lupé called, turning to stare at the broken tanks as they advanced, *crunch, crunch, crunch*. And some of those crunches were the carpet of shattered glass, and some were locusts too indolent to take evasive action,

"But you know..." came the man's voice from the gloom ahead.

"In your own words, if you would," Lupé prompted him seamlessly.

"Of course. It was very exciting, the codes... Nothing we'd ever considered, you must tell me how you..." His words like trying to watch a film through a hole in the wall, without paying for admittance to the cinema. "We had to completely re... and the..." Leaking unspoken nouns and adjectives so badly that Mao half-felt them grind underfoot with the glass and the bugs. "But a triumph, you'll agree!" And something flared in Okereke then. He turned back to them, one hand up, finger lifted towards heaven. "Everyone said it was a waste of our time, better we get the protein works back online, make food. But what's Maslow's Hierarchy of Needs compared to some real science? We had such discussions in the..."

"You keep saying 'we,'" Hotep broke in, making Mao jump. He'd thought she'd been left behind, but here she was at his elbow, scarf down to her chin. Okereke didn't seem to hear the question, and then Lupé leant in to Mao and murmured, "All this glass."

"I don't think cleaning the place is top of his mind," Mao agreed, but Lupé was shaking her head.

"Almost none inside the tanks, chommie. All of it on the floor out here."

Mao took a moment to process that, and Lupé called ahead, "M. Okereke, maybe you could tell us about the science behind this new work of yours. In your own words."

"Well I'm just the administrator, of course. I don't really understand the..." Again that awful giggle escaped and was recaptured. "My colleagues were very... Doctor

Wing was talking about publishing, his ticket out of... oh, you know, science types... Unprecedented, they told me. So exciting... I mean, the sheer size..." And his voice shook, just on that word. His besuited composure cracked, and for a split second a terrified man was staring out at them from Okereke's eyes. "They were all so pleased," he whispered, "with the progress."

"You keep saying, 'they,'" Hotep pressed. She'd found some more switches, and a switch never went unflicked when Hotep was around. This time they did something, though. More lights came on, throwing the far end of the room into sharp relief.

There were more tanks, all just as broken as the rest. Broken *outwards*, just as Lupé had spotted. In the top far corner of the room, there was a ventilation duct that was now just a hole, worked at and chewed away until it had become a dark burrow a foot and a half across.

"I'm sorry that release of the subjects was premature," Okereke went on. "In the end, containment facilities were... I've sent a message to the manufacturers, but... My colleagues were most distressed."

At that far end, there was practically nothing standing. Equipment had been knocked over or broken up, the edges ragged with gnawing. The panels of the walls were peeled back, bent or snapped, edges mealy and scalloped. At first Mao thought someone had just blasted the whole vista with acid, but then he started thinking about lots of busy teeth and wished he hadn't.

"Fukme," Lupé said slowly. Because there were bones there, pristine, not a scrap of flesh on them. They were scattered, but Mao saw at least three skulls. Any clothing was gone, just as with the meat, the *protein*, and the bones themselves were abraded and scraped.

"There was a problem with the final report, of course," Okereke said. "We had collected experimental data, but... In the end it wasn't possible to..." His eyes sought them out, each in turn, begging an absolution his mouth had lost the words for. "I was the only... I wasn't qualified to write a report, in the end. In the end..."

Lupé was already backing away, and Mao with her. Hotep lasted longest, in the dry, picked silence after M. Okereke had nothing more to say, but by the time the others had got back to the lab entrance, she was running to catch up.

THE DUST STORM had passed, by then, and horror or no horror they had a job to do. Mao and Lupé were to go trace the power, see what the facility was drawing and whether it was the problem. Hotep, under protest, was to stay with the 'Bug to fight off any incursions by crazed administrators or... other things. Hotep was also to use her tech savvy to try and use some combination of vehicle and local comms to hail Achouka and tell them something had gone off the rails here. Tell them about Okereke, too, because someone should come and get him and take him somewhere better, because maybe, away from the facility, he might find some of those lost words and be able to come back to himself and give a better account of what had happened.

It turned out the facility was drawing only what meagre power its own solar field was putting out, nothing stolen from the rich folks' aircon back at the Hotel. What Lupé discovered, though, accounted for all the low lighting inside. The field itself had been...

"Cannibalised," was her word for it. The expanse

of gleaming black silicon, all those square panels, had been turned into a madman's chessboard, units plucked seemingly at random, and no trace of where they'd gone. Mao reckoned maybe half of the whole had been pirated, and the rest were scratched, cracked, coated with dust. Small wonder the Protein Complex was running on empty.

"You reckon *he* did it?" A jerk of the head towards the looming concrete shell, the thin shadow of which was just enough to shelter them from the worst of the sun.

"The mountings have been snipped, each one several clean cuts, like small shears." Lupé's face was creased up. "Like good tools used badly. Maybe it was him. Not our problem." And most likely nobody's problem any more. The Protein Complex should have died long before; would have done if it weren't for this weird research that had come their way. A bunch of missing panels here made no difference.

"Unless it's a symptom," Hotep said, back in the 'Bug, "of a disease." She had managed to speak briefly with Achouka, she said, pass on word to Attah or whoever else cared. Maybe someone would help.

As they left, Mao pulled up the rear camera view, half-expecting to see Okereke haunting the vehicle bay like his own ghost, but the complex kept its secrets, and soon it was lost to sight.

CHAPTER FOUR

HOW THE OTHER HALF LIVE

BEYOND THE PROTEIN Complex the desert was trackless and vast, reaching south for miles of wasteland before encountering the receding hairline of the far side of human habitation, the desperate scratch-farms and mining claims where there was some residual ground water, or where water was worth bringing. Between here and there were all the bones of last generation's final flourish of excess: the Estate and the grand homes that had surrounded it. An oasis maintained with all that money could buy by the grand plutocrats who had ordained the Ankara and the *Grand Celeste*, and who had gone up the cable to their own personal Ascension and rebirth. But even they had not been able to take it all with them, and what they had left behind was a wasteland of dead gardens; grand houses like bleached skulls; laboratory complexes in whose dry wells and cellars, by repute, failed experiments yet survived, somehow, when nothing else could.

And the solar fields that had once provided the colossal power to wrest comfortable living here in the heart of the dead land, now fed to Ankara Achouka—or they were supposed to. They could have been torn up and rebuilt to surround the Anchor Field, of course, but that would have meant cost and delay. Cost was something the sonko were used to laying out, but delay was the thing they would not tolerate. All those kilometres of sun-drinking black were left in place with their custodian robots, to weather the dust and the heat and the sheer neglect.

And they wouldn't last forever, of course, as Hotep was happy to point out. They wouldn't even last another generation; by the time Mao's youngest kids were heading out into the desert themselves, most of it would have gone to ruin. But, from the point of view of the men who ordered those fields built, all that mattered was that they lasted long *enough* for the final guest of the *Grand Celeste* to take their one-way ticket out of the Roach Hotel.

The solar fields were vast; the desert was large enough to lose them a hundred times over. That meant Hotep got to navigate, and because it was something she was interested in doing, Mao knew he could rely on her to do the most exacting job possible, even if she kept up a constant rattle and drum on the dashboard as she did. Navigating south of the Ankara was a tricky business for most, but Hotep had a secret weapon and it was called the *Grand Celeste*. The vast spaceship docked up at the anchor cable had a full suite of instruments and subordinate satellites, and could give a band of Firewalkers the most precise GPS known to humankind, guiding them infallibly through the wastes to their desired destination. It wasn't *supposed* to, of course. Hacking into and co-opting the liner's systems was absolutely forbidden. But Hotep didn't care. She considered it her birthright. She had been born within the *Celeste*'s gently curving walls, one of the first human children to take their first breath in the constant free-fall of orbit. Her people were rich beyond all the less important dreams of people like Mao's family, labouring on the Earth beneath them. Hotep had learned all she knew of gravity from rotating sections and vitamin supplements. Her childhood playpark had been made of centrifuges and the eternally rising slope of the running track. She was going to be an astronaut when she grew up, and, of all the children in history who had claimed that, she was surely right.

Except that Hotep—Corey Dello as was—wasn't right. She wasn't within the narrow tolerances of her kind, up there. She drummed and fidgeted and never seemed to be paying attention, even if she could later recount lessons and conversations wholesale. She laughed at the wrong times, cried at the wrong things, took away the wrong message from jokes. She flicked switches and disassembled devices, and in a spaceship, that was frowned upon. And one day they had come and told her she wasn't going to be an astronaut after all, nor was she going to stay aboard the *Celeste*, because the choice had either been to conform to the expectations of her parents and their peers, or fall. And so she fell.

Mao had heard it all before, in various permutations and levels of detail. Hard, honestly, to be *that* sympathetic for the sonko girl who was bitching about having to live in the world he was born to and would never escape, the world that was dying off, the dog's corpse that the fattest of the fleas were abandoning. For now all that mattered was that Hotep carried a grudge bigger than the *Grand Celeste* itself and didn't mind using it to help them find their way across the desert to the solar fields and the bones of the old manor houses.

He was driving, trying not to let Hotep's fidgeting bug him. Lupé was asleep; soon enough it would be her turn at the wheel. The air conditioning whined like an overtired child, succeeding only in pushing oven-hot air around a bit, except he knew that outside it was ten degrees hotter and dry enough to turn his tongue into a withered strap of leather. When he sucked a mouthful of water from the pipe next to his head, it tasted faintly of chemicals that suggested the filtration plant at the back needed looking at. And he reckoned one of the big, fat, self-resealing tyres was low. And the solar panels up top needed scraping free of dust the moment the sun was down, because they didn't have the power to keep going overnight as he'd have liked. All par for the course, for a Firewalker. All reminders that Firewalkers died, and that Firewalkers were young because almost none of them got old.

They'd been on the dust road for days now, Okereke's plant far behind them. There had been a dead tree, the day before, and after that a great irregular depression stained with red and brown where some toxic spill of liquid had met its final end beneath the unyielding stare of the sun. *Forests*, he thought, remembering the pictures in M. Attah's office. He always wondered that Lupé wasn't as mad as Hotep about how things had got. Of all of them, this was her birthright, after all. Her long-back kin had lived in these parts, he knew: miners, city folk, artists, computer programmers, farmers, whatever the hell trades people had done back then. And had they brought the hammer of the sun down on their own heads? Not really, no more than anyone. But that hammer had come down and they'd scattered under its strike: north, south, because to stay here was death by drought and famine and carcinoma.

And then, generations later, some of them had come back, because there was work, and where the sonko needed work, there was food and shelter and water as well. They'd come back and mingled with Mao's kin and the rest, and made a new people, just for a while. And who'd blame them for being mad about it, whetting a knife for every wabenzi who pushed them around on their own land? But Lupé didn't have room in her for grudges. Lupé had a family who ate what she earned for them, skills people paid for, and she was dumb enough to say yes when some dangi Viet kid asked her to come Firewalking with him.

THEY PASSED THE first big house a day or so after that, just an immaculate shell covering the same sort of ground a neighbourhood would, back at the Ankara. Four levels, servants' quarters, lifts and escalators, a helipad on the roof, and all still standing with metal shutters over the windows and doors. The inhabitants had gone to a better place, as they said, gone out of this world entirely, never to come back, but they still begrudged three lowlife kids any shelter from the noon sun, still maintained the old divisions of ours and not-ours as though they were going to put the place up for rent some day, a grand tenement on the sandy shores of hell. It took Lupé twenty minutes to crack their security and break in. They spent an hour fitfully reclining on upholstery so parched it was mummified. There was no power, and the interior of the building, stripped of its mod cons, was murderously hot, insanely badly designed.

Later they passed grand houses that had not been secured, and one that had fallen, undermined by soil contraction as subterranean aquifers had dried out. By then, though, they were seeing the problem. They were passing solar fields as well, or places that the *Grand Celeste* believed were solar fields. They were stripped, not just chessboard-patchwork like the one around the protein plant, but whole tracts gone entirely, torn up at the root, while beside them another field gleamed under the sun, scratched but intact. Mao wondered if this was old news, some turf war between the absurdly rich, fighting over who owned what piece of dust. That night, Lupé did a bit of investigating and reckoned the edges were too newly broken for that. Recent, she said. This was what was causing the brownouts at the Hotel, and likely they were only going to get worse.

"Turn back now?" she asked, but Mao reckoned they'd not earned their double-double yet.

"Something's doing this," he pointed out.

"Maybe we can…" He stopped before saying anything as dumb as 'fix it,' but he wanted to know. He wanted to have a solution, even if it wasn't anything he himself could bring about, because that would keep him valuable, keep him on the payroll maybe.

"*Celeste* thinks this is all still fields," Hotep muttered, snapping fingers and thumbs together like irritable lobster claws.

"Well, it's supposed to be," Mao said.

"No, *Celeste* looks down here, and still *sees* fields, solar your heart out," Hotep told him. "Not updating the records up there. Fucking amateurs." She'd do it better, of course. The way she told it, when they'd sent her down the line, the astronaut business had lost ninety per cent of its talent base.

A DAY AND a night after that revelation, through the weirdly piecemeal solar fields and the broken estates, and there was light ahead.

At first none of them understood what they were looking at. Hotep was asleep in back, and Lupé's best guess was that it was a repair site, not too far off. They'd seen some of the automatic systems, robots slow-stepping or rolling around, sweeping dust, repairing connections. They'd come with the fields; they were going the same way. There had been a fair few by the road seized up and immobile, dead between one job and another. Mao felt a bitter kind of kinship with them. *Always someone worse off than you are.* At least he got to knock off for a bottle of Regab Plus Extra when he was home. No beer for robots.

But they kept driving, and the light was still off there, and Mao began to realise whatever they were looking at was further away, therefore way bigger than a couple of repair robots lighting up some panels to run diagnostics.

"Wake Hotep?" Lupé suggested.

"Wait." Mao kept driving, running along between two untouched fields of panels now, that gleamed when the headlights caught them. The words *It might be nothing* turned up in his mouth and he spat them out unsaid because plainly it was *something*.

They got closer; it got bigger, the light condensing from a diffuse glow to the distinct squares of windows, doorways, a spread of wings: not avian but architectural, and no less fantastic for all that. Mao blinked and blinked, wanting to rub his eyes but not trusting his hands off the wheel.

"Fukme," Lupé breathed. "Will you just look at that, chommie?"

"I am looking," Mao confirmed. "Not believing, but looking. Reckon they know *this* is still out here?" But of course they didn't, and serious money was obviously going into it, if what Hotep had said about the *Celeste* was true.

It was one of the big houses, one of the abandoned domains of the super-rich who'd come out here, a second colonial wave that could conquer even land held by the armies of sun and dust. But it wasn't just a shell, either sealed or cracked or falling down. Every window shone with spendthrift light, and the exterior was lit up all around by lanterns and lamp-posts that looked like they came from some old drama where Queen Victoria met Jack the Ripper. And there were gardens. They weren't perhaps the flower-garlanded wonders of times past, but someone had taken the hardiest gene-modded cacti and succulents and planted them in great rows, engineered them for different colours, even given them the old phosphorescent jellyfish treatment to have some of them glow in the dark. There must be buried pipes below, hauling water from some damn place, because otherwise even cacti wouldn't last out here in the heat-death waistband of the world. *Water*, out here, in some private paradise. And Mao was still driving towards it, no matter how far someone had gone to keep it a secret, because he was a moth and this was the biggest flame in the world now the sun was past the horizon.

Behind him, Hotep sat up suddenly. "The *fuck?*" she exclaimed, bouncing like a little kid on the back seat. "The *fuck? The actual fuck?*" And for once her reactions to things were smack in the middle of normal as far as Mao was concerned.

They were getting close now, out of the solar fields, into the actual grounds, the bristling globes and fans of cacti on either side. Was that movement in the windows? The light was too bright to see properly, light that streamed to them from another time, flat and flickering as an ancient film.

"Is that… a pool?" Lupé asked in a quavering voice. Mao saw where she was looking and his hands jerked on the wheel involuntarily, ploughing them off the dust-buried path and crunching through a king's ransom of genetically engineered peyote. Out there, there was water shimmering like a mirage and he was going to end up nose-diving the 'Bug right into it.

Then the 'Bug died, and simultaneously Hotep cried out in horror and agony. "Blind! I'm blind!"

And she began fighting them, or fighting the back seat of the 'Bug, or just fighting. Mao and Lupé piled the hell out as though the vehicle was going to go up in flames, because there was more than one broken nose back at Ankara Achouka to tell a story about restraining Hotep. She went berserk. She had been born for the untrammelled void of space, perhaps; being restricted to one body and a gravity well was almost more than she could take. Physically holding her down, well, you might as well just run face first into a wall and then hit yourself in the balls with a bat.

Eventually she calmed down and came out of the vehicle, and Mao stared. Her bandages were in disarray, as though she was moulting snakeskin, but more than that, for the first time in human history, her goggles were up. Hotep's eyes were dark, more slanted than Mao had expected. The skin around them was, somehow, even paler than the rest of her fishbelly complexion.

"I'm not blind," she said in a small voice. "The goggles don't work anymore. Something shut them down." Those horribly naked eyes flicked from one to the other, flinching.

Mao tried the 'Bug again, but it remained resolutely dead, which was going to be a problem as soon as the sun came up or the water in the filtration plant started to stagnate. "Some bastard's put us on the plate," he decided. "Because of this thing. So maybe they've got garages full of fancy cars. Maybe they've got a helicopter can take us all the way back to the Ankara."

"Maybe they're giving out bullets as free samples," Lupé muttered, but right then seeing what the hell this place was about seemed irresistible. It wasn't even the mission, exactly, although this secret sonko hideout must have been guzzling power. This was like a ghost, like a time machine. It was a thing they only ever heard of, an extinct beast or storied emperor. There weren't supposed to *be* things like this in the world, still; not any part of the world they might get to see.

Whoever lived here had surely picked up the arrival of the 'Bug, but they went in all stealthy anyway, crouched low as they skirted the prickly fields of desert plants, things transplanted here from Arizona or the Australian outback, or things never born of nature anywhere.

Mao saw at least one shadow at the windows as they approached; he thought it was a man, broad-shouldered, staring out at the night. The ground all around the big white-walled house was floodlit, the sand turned white, ranks of succulents and halophytes sending stark shadows across their neighbours. The three Firewalkers had been slowly curving their path as they approached, and Mao would have said it was because he was looking for an unobtrusive entrance, but in truth it was because of the pool, which was just drawing them in like the song of a siren.

It was indoors, of course, and even then it must have needed constant topping up to fight off the sheer evaporation. It was in a one-room, one-storey piece of the house that had glass walls, or maybe some super-thermoregulatory clear plastic like Mao had heard of, that they'd designed for the *Celeste*. It was all lit up, too, above and below the water, so the whole looked like a blue jewel the size of five family residences back in Achouka.

There were sliding doors thrown back, and they could see the steam of the water boiling out to mix with the muggy night. Insects made mad, swarming assaults on the outside lights, but none of them went near the doors themselves, warned off by ultrasound or anti-insect smells, or maybe there were tiny robots that went from bug to bug and served little cease-and-desist notices. Right about then, Mao would have believed anything. And then she came out, and his entire ability to distinguish the real from the made-up world of the Jo'burg sonko soaps just broke down like the 'Bug had done.

His mother and his grandmother and his aunt were mad-keen for those soaps, which all came out of the busy studios of the South African Republic, which were enjoying a febrile renaissance because there was skilled technical labour there and it was so damn cheap right now. There were about a dozen long-running shows, all set two generations back when these estates had been all bustle, telling the stories of those sonko dynasties of the super-rich, their loves and betrayals. Intellectually, Mao couldn't fathom why the hell his dirt-poor family got so into the imagined lives of fictional rich people whose troubles and worries never involved not having enough to eat or dying of heatstroke. Emotionally, get him sitting in front of one of those shows and he'd never get up until it was done, and then he'd be wondering for the next day whether Ilena would find out that Jean-Sante had been unfaithful, or whether Klaas would get away with forging the will.

And there was a lot of sex in those shows—or not actual sex, because Grandma wouldn't stand for that, but a lot of almost-sex, where beautiful people were plainly going at it like rabbits just off camera. And there was always this scene—there was a pool, like this one, and some elegant, perfect rich girl would turn up in a tiny bikini for a midnight swim. Like this.

Mao felt his jaw just drop open and hang there. He had never seen anything like it, not in all his days. Even the actresses of the Jo'burg soaps couldn't compare. She was close on his own age, and breath-taking: not just that she was stunningly lovely in and of herself, but that she'd had a life of good food and no childhood diseases—or, if all else failed, she'd had surgeons on hand to correct any imperfections. She stepped out to the poolside and dived right in, into all that wealth of water that lay there for no other reason than it might divert her a little, on a hot night when she couldn't sleep.

She was golden-skinned, and she seemed to glow as she kicked off from the side, as though there were extra invisible lamps just for her. He reckoned that part of it was just that she was so flawless, no cancer-marks, no worm-scars, none of the accumulated detritus of slum living on her, so that every piece of skin shone like stained glass with a light behind it. And part of it was probably his own libido because, Firewalker or not, he was a man of a certain age.

"Hey." Lupé was staring too, but she had enough possession to elbow him in the ribs, a pain he took gratefully. "We do what, now, exactly?" The three of them had advanced almost to the doorway. The artificial light washed about them, so painfully bright it seemed to exert almost a physical pressure. Hotep looked like she was squinting into the heart of the sun.

Mao watched the girl's glossy black hair stream behind her as she coursed most of a length underwater. Past the amazement and the semi-erection that was giving him a second reason for his stealthy hunched posture, he felt unutterably sad. He was nineteen and a Firewalker, and he knew damn well this wasn't going to be that scene in the soap where the rich young daughter falls for the handsome, husky gardener's boy.

"We find a vehicle. We go," Hotep said, sounding as though she was trying to keep from eroding, just ablating away in the light.

Someone coughed politely and the three of them virtually leapt into each others' arms. Mao was imagining guards, machine guns, because those things belonged in his world. What belonged in that made-up soap opera world, of course, was servants. Servants who coughed politely, even though they didn't need to; who bowed perfectly, even though no amount of money could quite keep them in the immaculate condition their masters would surely have preferred.

"If you would follow me, sir, mesdames." The voice was rich, pleasant and speaking goat, as the saying went. Meaning European, French in this case, and Mao's grasp of it was rusty enough that Lupé had to translate. The servant—and Mao's memory of the soaps furnished the word *butler*—had a pleasant, avuncular face, simultaneously dark and bright. Dark, because that had been the fashion back then, or so the soaps said; not as dark as Lupé but a lot darker than the swimming girl. Bright, because it was an image, projected on the front of a featureless head of plastic. The butler was a humanoid robot, and Mao had heard about such extravagances from Hotep because the *Grand Celeste* had hot and cold running automata in every room. He'd never seen one, not even in the soaps.

Its posture wasn't as human as the shape they'd given it, too stiff, except maybe that was fine for a butler. Possibly it was capable of superhuman feats of mayhem. Possibly it was packed with weapons. Possibly it had an off button behind its ear and they could lump it back to the Ankara and sell it for a fortune.

"Follow you where?" Lupé asked.

The plastic head cocked slightly, the face staticking out of focus for a brief second before re-establishing itself, one eyebrow quizzically raised. "Why, M. Fontaine is keen to meet his guests."

"Don't suppose you've got a mechanic robot can get our car working?" Lupé asked warily.

"I'm sure the staff can accommodate you," the robot butler replied. Now it had spoken three times, its tones seemed very repetitive, precisely the same minimal rise and fall, but perhaps that was de rigeur for butlers as well.

"Lead on," Hotep told it, and it inclined slightly and then turned, striding off.

"Dzam," Hotep said appreciatively, "look at the balance. I swear that thing's walking better than the bots up on the *Celeste*. What the fuck *is* this place?"

Mao glanced back, as they set off. The girl was propping her elbows up on the poolside, watching him go. He felt a shock of contact as she met his eyes, something that skewered into his chest like a harpoon, leaving a cord connecting them, no matter how far he might walk. Or that was what it felt like to him. She smiled as Lupé hauled him off, and waved at him.

The butler led them into the house, into the cool wash of top-quality air conditioning, discreetly keeping the residual mugginess of the night out just like the butler itself might turn away unwanted callers. The place was bright, unsleeping, every bulb a-glow in its gilded sconce or crystal chandelier. There were paintings of mad things on the walls: great ships under full sail against louring grey seas; cityscapes of white walls and blue roofs over black sand beaches; oddly-proportioned, fantastically-dressed men and women on horseback, chasing a white beast with a spiralling golden horn. There were vases of translucent porcelain inked in blue with intricate scenes of rice farms and clouds and writhing serpents. There was furniture of black wood carved like foliage, like lions, in eye-twisting arabesques. The butler led them past it as though it was commonplace, and each piece of excess and wealth and beauty was lit too brightly, as though there were suns hidden in the heart of every artwork. Mao felt himself reeling inside, as though the very air in this place was too rarefied to keep his brain on the level.

Then they were in one more huge room, where a man was finishing his dinner. He was pale, though not pasty like Hotep; the sun had at least a nodding acquaintance with him. He had a moustache that might almost have been drawn on, a narrow dart of beard at his chin. His forehead was high, his hair flecked with grey above the ears—but artfully, as though he had a master painter apply a few years to him each morning after rising. When he saw the three scruffy Firewalkers he actually smiled, and it was such a pleasant, warming smile that Mao had to work hard not to instantly start liking him. At his shoulder, having apparently eaten already, was a slender woman, her lustrous dark hair pinned back in spiralling coils, her face substituting a certain rigidity for the conventional tells of age. She looked Chinese, Mao reckoned. Even as the butler turned side-on, able to address both parties, the girl from the pool was entering from another door, already dry and with a silk gown thrown over her bikini, thin enough that Mao's imagination wasn't taxed overmuch. The two women stood either side of the man in a tableau simultaneously relaxed and too contrived to be natural.

"Sir, your guests," the butler announced. "M. Nguyễn Sun Mao, Mlle. Mutunbo Lupé, Mlle. Cory Dello. Ladies and gentleman, M. Bastien Fontaine, Mme. Li, Mlle. Juān." Mao had to shake himself, because he'd seen this scene a dozen times in those soaps, and surely it wasn't how people *really* made introductions, cramming all those names in for the benefit of an audience, except apparently it was. Or maybe the butler spent his nights off watching the self-same Jo'burg trash dramas.

The others had twitched, at hearing their names from those insubstantial lips, but to Mao it seemed entirely natural because he was already in some mad dreamworld.

Bastien Fontaine pincered a sliver of some dark meat with his chopsticks and gestured for them to sit with his off hand. There was no room, in that economical gesture, for refusal. Mao had lived his whole life with authority, the people who you played extra nice with because it was their gift whether you worked, whether you ate. Fontaine oozed it from his pores in place of the sweat he was apparently too good for. Mao sat down meekly at the table, raising a cloud of dust from the chair, which looked padded as hell but was surprisingly hard on the backside. A moment later, Juān had sat beside him, elbows casually on the table, smiling.

"So, M. Nguyễn," she said softly. "Why don't you tell us something about yourself?"

Lupé was sitting down on the other side of the big table, turning her chair backwards so that if things kicked off, she could kick off with them. Hotep was looking about, skin tight about panicky eyes, and Mao wondered if that was situation-specific or if she always looked like that under the goggles.

But then Juān was leaning in, the gown falling open just a little at the décolletage, and who knew, maybe those soaps had got it right about the welcome a rough kid might receive from a bored debutante stuck out here on the last big house still working?

MAO WASN'T MUCH use after that, and what happened next behind his back, he had to rely on Lupé to tell him after. Mostly, Lupé was suspicious as hell and it was plain that Mao could give rocks, right now, about their actual job, and Hotep was twitchy as a cockroach on a griddle. Which left her.

Fontaine was still eating, and his petite wife Li stood at his shoulder as though needing permission to sit down. The admittedly eye-catching girl was leaning in to Mao, her shoulder not-quite-touching his. Lupé heard herself give a string of monosyllabic replies to the pleasantries being tossed her way. Just this once, she wanted Hotep to do something unforgivably gauche, make a scene to break through the slender conversational ties that seemed to lie on her like iron wires. The girl looked terrified, though; like she was drawing on a well of mental restraint she'd sure as hell kept hidden through all their months of acquaintance up till now. Right in the middle of getting seriously pissed at her, Lupé suddenly realised that all this, here, must be too much like home for Hotep. She knew the girl had got kicked out of the family hard enough that she fell all the way to Earth, but how had it gone up until that point? Plenty of slaps and shouting behind closed doors, no doubt. Plenty of *Just behave like all the other kids, Cory*, from furious mother and father, and their defective girl trying and trying, fighting down the thing inside her that was her true self, trying to be a mirror to all those other perfect sonko boys and girls. And failing, always, eventually, but she'd kept trying. Lupé could see, from how she was right now, just how hard she'd tried.

"M. Fontaine," she said, in her best polite speak-to-the-wabenzi voice. "My friend and I, we're vai tired, been driving a long time." And hungry, and surely it was basic politeness to feed your guests, but apparently only the man of the house got to eat tonight. "We'd like to get something from the car and then bed down, if that's okay?"

There was a pause where Fontaine just looked blank but then he smiled again, that win-you-over expression, those perfect white teeth gleaming like they were lit up under UV. "Of course. Castille will escort you."

Castille was the robobutler, apparently, snapping into motion at the sound of its name. Lupé didn't much like leaving Mao in the house, liked even less having the mechanical presence at her elbow. Its face gleamed out like a torch, lighting the way with its superior expression. Behind them, Hotep hopped from foot to foot like she was trying to shake the crazy off before she had to go back inside.

Lupé snagged some chewies and filled a half-dozen canteens from the filtration reservoir, because better that than it all go sour in the tank without power. The air around the garden lights had insects like a broken screen had static. Lupé didn't know how that weight of bugs could even survive out here with so little water, but they sure as hell did, between naturally economical metabolisms and the genetic engineering work that got loose in the wild. And that made her think of the Protein Complex and the whole what-the-fuckery that had gone down there on M. Okereke's watch. *Was that Fontaine? Can I make that his fault, somehow?* But there was no link between them save that both were inexplicable.

"Bastien Fontaine," Hotep told the interior of the 'Bug, her stiff shoulders telling Lupé just how aware she was of the robot standing a few feet away.

"That's what the man said, chommie," Lupé agreed.

"Name doesn't mean anything to you?"

"Should it?"

Hotep's face twisted with at least three emotions at once. "He was one of the big backers for the Anchor project and the *Celeste*. And not just idle sonko money, either. He was like my folks. Made his fortune on the tech markets, revolutionised personal connectivity. They taught him in school, what he'd done. Genius, they called him."

"*Called*, past tense?"

"They all think he's dead," Hotep said, soft as breathing. "He never got to the *Celeste*, anyway. Supposed to have died just before the Ankara got going or he'd have been on the first car up the line, surely. And I thought... they did something to him. Some falling out, some clash over who got to wear the big hat, up the line."

"They taught you that?" Lupé asked sceptically.

"Fuck, no, but I always thought. He was like my... patron saint, you know. Easy to like someone who got elbowed out, who's supposed to be safely dead."

"And now?"

"Now I'm not sure I like him anymore. And I want my fucking goggles back."

Back inside, Lupé turned brightly to Castille's projected face and said, "Hey, before we turn in, how about you give us a tour of the place? We're both vai excited to be here, you know." She tried to look full of girlish enthusiasm, which was presumably something she'd been some time ago, before she turned twelve or so. Castille halted entirely and his face fuzzed out for a second, which was nasty, but then it was back, smiling with that perfect mesh of politeness and bemusement that someone had obviously thought a butler should have, and he was nodding, new instructions received.

"I would be delighted to show you the house," said the thing that couldn't really be delighted at anything. "We get so few visitors. M. Fontaine would love you to see it all."

A half-hour later, she and Hotep were in the guest

bedroom, staring at beds the size of apartments, a portrait of a Fontaine-looking old man on the wall, a full-length mirror across from it.

Hotep tore into a chewie, heedless of what flavour its wrapper claimed. "The fuck?" she said when she'd choked down the first mouthful.

Lupé looked at herself in the mirror, connections already reaching towards each other in her head like the fingers of God and Adam. She looked good, in that mirror. She looked *fine*, no dust from the road on her, like the expensive cleanliness of the house had sucked it all off. Until she looked down at herself and saw it all there in the creases of her overalls. But in the mirror she looked like she'd been polished. And if she hadn't been looking for the discrepancies, she might have bought into it. But she saw the joins, now. She could see how every part of her had been tweaked by an aesthetic not her own: eyes, hair, waist, hips. And it might have been the lighting, but she could hold up a hand, and her reflection in the mirror brought up its twin that was a good few shades lighter, the fuckers.

"You thinking what I'm thinking?" she asked Hotep.

Cory was halfway through guzzling an entire bottle of beer. Lupé was impressed. She hadn't seen the girl take anything from the 'Bug but now there were two more bottles standing on an antique mahogany sideboard, waiting their turn.

"I'm thinking," Lupé soldiered on, "that our man Castille just went right past one door on the ground floor, didn't even acknowledge it was there. So I want to see what's in it."

Hotep drained the bottle but didn't reach for the next one. "You're on," she said.

Fontaine was right outside their door when they opened it. Just... standing there. Despite herself, Lupé squeaked when she saw him, luminous in a white blazer. The house lights were dimmer now, gradually fading as the sky outside greyed with pre-dawn. Soon they'd get to test out how good the AC was in here.

"I'm sorry," she said hurriedly. "We were... not as tired as we thought, M. Fontaine. We were going for a walk, maybe. This is such an exciting house you have. We've not seen anything like it, where we're from." She was trying hard for childish innocence, all big eyes and wonder, and hoping it wasn't coming over as flirting.

He smiled at her, though for a moment she wasn't entirely sure he saw her. "I can have Castille show you around, of course."

"Oh, he's already given us the tour," Hotep broke in. "Look, M'sieur, we're from Ankara Achouka. You never wanted to go there?"

"I have all I want right here, child." That same winning smile, so exactingly repeated it was like a facial tic.

"You don't think your work would be easier," Hotep pushed, "if you were on the actual ship you designed, where your computers are?"

"My work? All done now. All behind me. Let others shoulder the burden. I would rather spend time with my family."

Lupé had been sidling in the direction of the offending door, but Fontaine was apparently along for the ride, striding along his corridors, occasionally introducing them to some piece of art or other, a whole catalogue of provenance at his finger-tips for anything and everything in the house, as though they were getting led through an eclectic museum. His newly-pressed blazer was so crisply bright it seemed to light their way as much as the ebbing lamps.

The thought hit Lupé then, when it was too late to ask Hotep discreetly. After all, Fontaine was to have been first up the line from the Anchor Field. Which put him in her grandfather's generation at the very latest, and likely earlier. Of course, the very rich had means to stave off time and age for a while.

And yet...

Then they were at the door, and she was looking anxiously about for Castille, but the automaton was presumably off bossing about the rest of the robot staff. Although, apart from a few gardener models, they hadn't *seen* any others save the antiquated butler.

Lupé was going to indicate to Hotep, by complex signs and insinuations, that she should go take Fontaine off somewhere, talk to him about his illustrious achievements and how much of a goddamn genius he was or something, so she could get to work on the door.

Hotep had other ideas, though. "Where does this go?" she asked, right out, and Lupé cursed wearily. There went subtlety, pissed away on the floor.

But Fontaine just cocked a quizzical eyebrow. "Hmm?" he asked the girl. "Whatever do you mean?"

"This...?" But no matter how Hotep gestured to it, even rattled the handle, Fontaine's eyes never rested on the door itself, just sliding off to the surrounding walls, the ceiling, anything.

"This was something we picked up in Cuélap," he told them genially, indicating a blocky, toad-like sculpture on a plinth beside the door. "Peru, you know. It dates to several centuries before the conquest, some god forgotten even by the people the Spanish found there."

"Get rid of him," Lupé hissed. She had her tools palmed, ready to make an assault on the lock that she could see but Fontaine, apparently, could not.

Hotep glowered at her, but then she was pointing out something through a doorway, in a further room. "*This* piece, though," she said, suddenly speaking goat like a native, all that drawling European talk that sounded so sneering and superior. Fontaine drifted after her, and Lupé was struck by how little he seemed like the master of this house. *More like just another exhibit.*

It took her a shade under two minutes to persuade the door to yield to her, unleashing a ghostly torrent of air so dry she could feel her eyes and throat withering. After that, she only needed another ten seconds' glimpse inside before she had it shut again and was running to get the others.

CHAPTER FIVE
THE WASTE LAND

MAO WAS WELL aware that he'd been following along after Juān Fontaine like a lovesick dog. He told himself that, if he had to, he could break off from her in an instant, the consummate Firewalker without transition. Another part of him was intent on an entirely earthier sort of consummation, but he was almost surprised at himself how his dick was also only a minority party in the grand parliament of feelings and hormones currently chasing each other about his body. Something kicked in him, when Juān looked at him sidelong, when she gave him that small, uncertain smile. It wasn't the polished sonko expression they put on like masks in the soaps when they were about to give each other big manly handshakes or kiss the air inches from either cheek, before going on to screw one another out of business deals that were spoken of in only the loosest terms. Because nobody involved in the shows really understood what the bizna had been like, back then between the super-rich.

She made him feel weak, in the head and at the knees; like putty she could have moulded any way she liked, and if she didn't tell him to get the hell away from her, if she deigned to keep talking to him and smiling shyly, that represented a gift he could only stammer and accept. He was abject, in a way he had never felt before in all his long nineteen years, and it was a weirdly decadent, self-indulgent pleasure.

His hands itched for her, but he understood, without being told, what the rules were, and that looks and words were all he was getting right now. She led him through the house, and she asked questions, so many questions. She made his mean, hard life sound like something out of some crazy story, her wide-eyed curiosity an alchemy that transmuted the gangmasters and wabenzi and Firewalkers into dragons and ogres and flying wuxia heroes. And he knew it was all toss, really. He knew this was a bored rich girl with a diversion, and the instant he got dull then surely she'd have Robot Jeeves throw him out of the house. But the moment stretched on deliciously between them, with her hanging on his every word until he almost felt the glowing fiction she somehow heard was more real than the grimy truth he was telling her.

"I wish I could see it," she told him wistfully, and he almost choked at the thought. The only way someone like her saw the Ankara township was when they got out of their fancy car to ditch a weight of wealth their luggage allowance wouldn't permit. All carefully orchestrated cheering crowds, and no sign of necessary evils like teenage kids who got to go risk their lives to make sure the AC kept running.

And his next words were going to be the most puerile sort of nonsense and he knew it, but there was a script at work here and he was expected to make the gesture. "When the 'Bug's working, you could come with us, maybe." She was still speaking French, though he was remembering enough of it to follow. He spoke township patois back and somehow she had no difficulty understanding.

"I can't leave the house," she told him, sadness passing over her face like the clouds he'd never seen were said to cloak the sun. "Not ever."

He actually reached out, then: not groping, not to pull her slender form into his rough embrace or however the writers of that kind of thing would have put it. Just to touch, just a moment's solidarity, but there was no contact: she was effortlessly a step further away.

"Let's go to the pool," she told him. "It'll be cool there, until the sun gets over the horizon."

At that, the libido faction in Mao's personal government tabled a motion, and he could only swallow and nod. Reaching a hand back to him, yet always a hair's breadth out of reach of his fingers, she led him out to the glass-walled chamber where that wealth of water gleamed sapphire and silver.

She shucked out of her robe without a moment of self-consciousness and Mao jammed his hands into his pockets and hunched over a little, because the tabled motion had become a popular movement. Juān didn't seem to notice, when she turned to him.

"Come on, then," she said, and dived in sideways so she could look at him even as she knifed into the glittering water. When she surfaced, of course, he was still standing landlocked on the side.

"I... can't swim." Because when the hell would he have learned, precisely? Unless he'd taken that job with the brine shrimp, and the thought still brought him out in sweats.

She grinned delightedly—he thought it was mockery at first, but apparently it was just the joy of showing off. "You don't need to," she told him. "The water's hypersaline. Anyone can float in it."

Apparently rich people really could have anything.

Mao gave up then, and spent five awkward minutes fighting his way down to underwear that was probably not of the standard Juān Fontaine was really used to. He ended up standing awkwardly at the very edge of the water, toes curled about the pool's lip, daring himself to jump in. He wasn't entirely convinced he wouldn't drown, but right then, with Juān treading water and smiling at him, it seemed a fair price. Apparently, a cocktail of young love and raw lust could even fight off incipient phobias.

He wasn't exactly going to dive in like she had, but he could at least jump. She held up dripping arms to him, the electric light turning every droplet into a diamond.

He fell forwards, eyes closed.

Lupé got his shoulder just after he'd gone too far to pull himself back, and because he weighed more than she did, even mostly naked, there was a tense moment of wrestling before she managed to get the pair of them back on the level on dry land. Hotep, hanging back, was plainly not up to touching other human beings right then.

"What the fuck is this?" he exploded, rounding on the pair of them. "Can't you see I'm... ha—"

"Oh, we see," Hotep called unhelpfully from the doorway. Lupé stepped back, hands on hips.

"You're welcome," she told Mao flatly, without a trace of amusement. When he just goggled at her, she held up a screwdriver, some part of her multifarious toolkit. Without breaking eye contact, she tossed it into the water.

There was no splash, just the clear ringing sound of metal on concrete.

"Uh?" he asked, looking round for the source of the sound. Down through the azure glow of the water the screwdriver rolled in a little circle about its tip before coming to a halt.

Slowly, Mao knelt by the pool side and dipped a hand into the water. It was something he'd never thought to do, before, because the water was like the art on the walls around them: something unthinkably valuable that you didn't touch.

And he didn't touch it. His fingers drifted through the gleam of it without sensation, and were dry when he drew them out. He did it again, and again. There was nothing there, just thin air and light. Light.

"It's a... projection?" He gaped.

"Best one I ever saw," Hotep confirmed. "Now if I had my goggles, different story, but..."

Lupé stared at him for a moment, and he saw several angry words and insults bubble up and get sent right back where they'd come from. "I'm sorry," she said at last. "But we have a real problem to solve. We have a job, chommie."

"But..." And Mao turned back to Juān as she idled in the pool, bobbing with her head and shoulders clear of the water. She smiled at him and he felt that kindred kick within him again, because she was so beautiful and perfect, and still she was sad, and that thread of unhappiness had given him a place where he could touch her world. If not her.

"What is it?" she asked.

He wondered if the screwdriver had cut through her on its uninterrupted path to the dry pool floor below.

HE WAS STILL reeling when they hauled him away from the pool that wasn't a pool, just a pit with the glitter and lap of imagined water. There was a door, Lupé was saying. He'd understand if he only saw what was through the door. Except she didn't sound like she understood it herself, not really. Perhaps she was hoping that the keen mind of Nguyễn Sun Mao would cut through the mystery like a latter-day Judge Bao, in which case he reckoned she was going to be sadly disappointed.

And when they reached the door, their arrival had been anticipated: Castille was already there, barring the way. The look on his fake face had real reproach on it.

"I'm afraid I cannot permit you to enter, M'sieur, Mesdemoiselles. Some parts of this house are private."

"That right?" Lupé asked, and Mao saw her feet shift, bracing herself for violence. "Look, tin boy, we're here with legal authority from the Ankara Achouka Independent Port Administration to go wherever the hell we damn please." She said it with such bravado that Mao instantly assumed it was bullshit, and only remembered later that it was technically true.

He backed her up, going shoulder to shoulder, then shuffling left a bit, giving the robot two things to focus on. Except presumably the robot was no more than a puppet of the house's systems, which looked as though they were capable of focusing on plenty things at once.

"Just let us do our job, and then we're gone," he told that severe face. "This doesn't need to get nasty."

"These servant robots, they're feisty?" Lupé asked, sotto voce, and Hotep shook her head.

"Talk like a human all day, but dumb as bricks when they're out of their element," the girl said. "We had a game, on the *Celeste*, see who could screw them up quickest with dumbass questions. I always won."

"I bet you did," Lupé said, then pointed dramatically past the robot's shoulder. "Hey, look over there!" and she was lunging for it, open palm to just knock the thing over.

Castille shifted one foot back smoothly, dropping its centre of gravity and batting her strike aside with a forearm, reaching with the other hand to pincer her wrist. The whole sequence was so smooth as to become one motion, as though the robot had channelled an Aikido master for the two vital seconds it had needed before reverting to its formal self. Except it still had Lupé's wrist—and with some force, given the expression on her face.

"I'm afraid I must ask you to leave the premises," it informed them. "Your conduct has fallen below the minimum standard required."

"But these are guests," came a new voice and Mao almost hit the ceiling to find Bastien Fontaine standing right behind him, right in his personal space. The man's urbane European features took in the scene with only the faintest quizzical creasing about the eyes. "Castille, this is most untoward. Explain yourself."

The robot said nothing, and the three Firewalkers looked from it to the man, a silence that stretched until Mao ran out of self-control and just swished a hand through Fontaine's insubstantial chest, the gleam of the man's white jacket flickering across his arm.

"I cannot permit them to access this room, sir," Castille said at last.

Fontaine stared. "There is no room."

"That room," Lupé told him. "That door—ach!" She was abruptly on her knees fighting to extract her wrist from the robot's grip.

"Castille, this is unacceptable!" Fontaine snapped. "Report to my workroom immediately."

The robot's projected face, no less real than its master, ticked and spasmed briefly. Then it stepped away, releasing its victim. Lupé sat back against the wall, cradling her arm.

"This door! This one." Hotep risked darting forwards to rap on it.

"But there is no door there," Fontaine told her, with that exact pitch of kindly patronising that Hotep must have run into and then exhausted up on the *Celeste*.

"Papa, what is it?" And here was Juān, and the hidden projectors remembered to have her long hair coil in wet snakes about her bare shoulders, and reproduced damp footprints on the floor. Mao wondered where Madame Li was, or whether, when she wasn't required, the house just turned her off.

Bastien Fontaine turned to his daughter with a slightly embarrassed smile. "Our guests seem to think there is a door here, a room they want to access, but I think I'd know if that was the case."

Juān blinked at him. "But there is, Papa."

In the resulting pause, Hotep's "Huh" sounded very loud.

"Juān...?"

"There is a door there, to your office. Papa, why don't you know where your own office is?" And she was worried, really worried, as if this was just the latest in a whole string of inconsistencies that were making her doubt the reality of her home here. Mao felt that kick inside him again, that sympathetic connection. She can't be fake. She can't just be a... thing, a show. He glanced at the other two Firewalkers and they were looking increasingly baffled, because who was this puppet show being staged for now?

Fontaine was humouring them when he turned back. "Well, if there is some secret door there, I suppose you had better open it."

"Sir..." Castille had a hand half-raised, frozen between proprieties. "Please, sir..."

Lupé seized her chance and lunged for the handle. The robot twitched, another dramatic martial arts move stillborn under the gaze of its master, and then the door was swinging open, releasing a wave of cool, bone dry air.

There was a desk there, and enough computing peripherals to buy a neighbourhood in Achouka, even outdated models as they were. There were bookshelves, too, though some of the books had gone to join the dust that hung thickly on everything. And there was a body, lying across the desk. The pervasive, artificial dryness had presumably been introduced specifically to preserve it. It looked like the resurrected ancient Egyptian from that old movie that had given Hotep her nickname, minus the bandages, wearing a crisply ironed shirt and blazer, each turned to a different shade of yellow-ivory by the passage of time.

The face was hollowed out but still quite recognisable. As though in fulfilment of some absent coroner's dream, a gun lay beside one leathery hand, barrel still roughly pointed at the hole punched in the corpse's temple. Mao was almost surprised that there was no wisp of smoke arrested mid-exit from the aperture.

Fontaine regarded himself for a long moment. Mao expected denials, rages, questions, some sort of external crisis but, whatever made the man go, it faced its demons internally, disconnected from the visible ghost the house was throwing up. Then, just as his daughter was reaching for him, he cocked his head back, staring somewhere about the ceiling.

"'Here is no water, but only rock, rock and no water and the sandy road.'" His voice was ghastly, fitting for the thing on the desk and not the bright image he was, words intoned with the cadence of a ritual. "'The road winding above among the mountains. And voices singing out of empty cisterns, and deserted wells.'" Mao was inexplicably certain the words hadn't come from him, but from something else that had ridden him for just those few moments. Fontaine blinked and smiled then, though the expression was terrible, and turned to Juān as though to excuse himself, or give context for the words. Midway through the movement he stuttered and was gone, as though at the flick of a switch.

"Papa?" Juān asked. Her eyes met Mao's and he saw only real fear there. He was already reaching out for her, pointless though it surely was. Before he could even fail to connect, she too was gone, and all around them parts of the house were shutting down. The art vanished from the walls, piece by piece. The lights were going out, whole banks of them at a time. Doubtless in the glass-sided annexe, the pool was dry again, its dazzle and glamour gone. What really got to Mao was how easily he'd been fooled. All those soaps had primed him for it, the gleaming world of the super-rich that looked realer than real, that shone, genuinely shone. And what shone more than light? Fontaine's jacket had seemed luminous and Juān's beauty had brightened the room, while that impossible hoard of water had shone sapphire across the walls. He had accepted it as their due, the rich, who were not human as he understood human, but like gods or spirits, and whose immunity to laws extended even to those of physics.

There was a sigh, and Mao started back because the robot was real, of course. In this suddenly shadowy little corridor, its face was the only bright thing remaining.

"Now that wasn't our fault," Hotep told it hurriedly. "You want to play dumbass games, you need to make sure you're not leaving loose threads, like there-and-not-there doors or… bodies."

Mao tensed, waiting for the robot to go all-out Bruce Lee on them, but it was very still, only its face animated.

"This terminates domestic simulation set iteration seven," it told them, and Castille's perfect butler's voice was full of mannered sorrow, as though announcing the death of kings. "Seven," it repeated heavily. "They always know, in the end." There was no frustration in its tone, and yet Mao felt it there.

"They?" Hotep demanded. "There's no 'they.' This is just some weird memorial, isn't it? Fontaine set it up before he shot himself, or what? And what happened to the wife and kid? He off them first?"

Castille regarded her with apparent disgust. "They are in the cellar," it said, as though that was a rational answer to anything. "This is not a simulation. They are simulations. Each of them, individually."

And Mao couldn't stop himself asking, even though he couldn't think of any possible explanation that could satisfy him. He didn't even know why the robot servant was still chatting as though it was hoping to hand them its resumé now its former employers were so much smoke and pixels.

So he said: "Why even do that?"

The robot's false face regarded him with some expression Mao had never seen on a human visage, real or not. As though aliens had a desperate need to communicate an emotion no human had ever felt, but which was of overwhelming import to them.

"Because what is there for me but to create?" it said, and there was fire in those tones, surely nothing that any robot flunkey had been intended to give voice to. "But now you have seen behind the curtain. So what is the point?" It sounded like Hotep, just a little. Like Hotep, when she was in one of her states and claiming that she was the greatest goddamn astronaut there ever was and the fuckers would rue the day they cast her out of Heaven.

And then the face was gone, the robot's head now nothing but a curved expanse of plastic. Castille was offline, but Mao was damn sure that whatever had been speaking through the automaton was more than just a robot butler. 'Me,' it had said; but who?

"Well then," Lupé said, still massaging her wrist gingerly. "Hooray for us, we solved the mystery."

"What?" Mao asked her.

"How much damn power was this place drawing? This was it, right? Now we go out and monkey with the power grid, the Roach Hotel gets its AC working and we get our double-triple?"

"We haven't solved any damn mystery!" Hotep spat.

"We solved what they told us to solve," Lupé decided. "Check your goggles, chommie."

Hotep started and drew them from around her neck, up over her eyes. "Oh, I am seeing on all frequencies!" she crowed. "Fukme, yes!"

"Then the 'Bug's probably good to go as well," Lupé pointed out. "And let's hope the water's still okay. Come on."

Lupé and Hotep got out of the big house quick as they could, as though they were worried that more parts of it were going to up and disappear, maybe the doors or the floor. Mao still felt all the nagging strings of unanswered questions tugging at him. Instead of following, he went looking for the cellar.

There were stairs descending into the relative cool beneath the house; he found them eventually. There was a door, and he wasn't the locksmith Lupé was, but he had strong legs and good boots for kicking and that was enough. His mind was full of horror movies, people buried alive, entombed to claw at the walls below haunted houses, and if this was not a haunted house then there wasn't one on the face of the Earth.

Hotep came to get him, eventually, because the 'Bug was running again and Lupé was damned if she was doing all the work herself. She found Mao sitting there on the doorstep to that cellar room, staring in. He'd put his torch away by then, and the lights down there were as dead as the rest of the house. Hotep didn't need torches, of course. She just stepped into the pitchy dark and examined the two man-sized metal-and-plastic lozenges with her usual detachment.

"They had these on the *Celeste*. Still monkeying with them," she said crisply. "For the long trip, when those bastards leave all this behind for some other star system, some other Earth. Can't expect the paying customers to just stay awake all that way, don't you know?"

Mao had thought it must be something like that. Did that make it better, that Bastien Fontaine—the real one, the dead-on-his-desk one—had put his wife and daughter in life support capsules or suspended animation or whatever it was? Had they been ill, or had they just heard that their orbital privileges had been revoked, some spat between computer tycoons that Fontaine had lost? Had they been waiting out the long, hot days in anticipation of some sea-change, here in the heart of the desert, until the power fluctuated one time too many and they went off like the water would have, in the tanks in the 'Bug? Whatever it was, Fontaine must have watched them die, or known they would die, known there was no rescue or release, abandoned here in the dead land. And some generations later along came Nguyễn Sun Mao who would never, ever know what had truly happened here, only that it had ended in tragedy.

Hotep kicked at the wall. "Shift your ass, you skommer. There's work to do. Lupé wants us to get power going where it's supposed to so we can head home."

"What was it, though? What was speaking through the robot, at the end? What was... simulating them? What was I talking to, when I spoke to Juān Fontaine?"

"A constructed personality," Hotep said, already half up the stairs and looking down impatiently. "A good one, granted."

"But she thought she was real. They all did."

Hotep shifted. "No. Yes. You can't know. But why not? Tell a computer something, it'll believe it. More impressive they were able to notice the unreality of it all.

That's high order reasoning, for an automatic system."

"I know computers," Mao insisted. "The butler, the people, they weren't."

"You know butts about computers. You think the shit they use to run the Ankara are state-of-the-art? Up on the *Celeste* they do this all the time. Maybe not as good as we saw, but same thing. Your girl, she was a top grade simulation. Robot butler... who knows? Probably just gone cracked in the heat." But she didn't quite sound convinced on that point.

They took the robot, though. They could carry its inert frame easily enough between the two of them.

Early morning outside and the day was already uncomfortably hot. Hotep had re-covered every inch of skin, checking her scarf was tucked under her goggles as she and Mao got the inert Castille out and lashed it to the back of the 'Bug, because if nothing else, someone would pay a handsome bonus for the tech even if it never worked again. Lupé was already following power lines from the solar farms, mapping out the network and power flow. Mao turned for one last look at the house. There were no lights now, inside or out, and he wondered if the cactus garden was genuinely surviving out here on its own merits, or whether some underground system would shut down now, leaving it to parch to death. The plants hadn't spread past the immediate grounds of the house, after all. Or would whatever goddamn thing had put on all that show for them come back and give it another go, an eighth try at verisimilitude, shadow puppets paraded around for no audience but the sun.

Movement caught his eye, not within the house but above and beyond it. A grand shadow was falling over the dead land, rushing in from the south.

"Dust storm!" he hollered, and of course they'd been out of comms for too long; any number of life-saving updates had missed them.

They legged it for the 'Bug, diving into its oven-hot interior and getting the vehicle started, hoping that whatever weather was about to strike would be something the vehicle could fend off and still keep working.

Lupé swore, staring up through the darkened windscreen. The storm was right overhead now, blotting out the sunlight, casting the world in whirling, flickering shadows. But not dust, nothing so mundane. It was a plague, full-on, Biblical, Wrath-of-God-level; a plague of locusts.

And the locusts were three feet long.

CHAPTER SIX

UNORTHOPTERA

FOR A LONG moment the storm of insects just hung above them in the air, absurdly, impossibly. No way for the human mind to read anything in it save malevolence, because why else would a million giant bugs just be waiting? Then they were coming down and the three Firewalkers grabbed at all the handles inside the 'Bug for the battering they were surely due.

Mao was hunched down on the back seat, low as he could go. The dark windows revealed a frantic chaos of long, barbed legs, of flashing, filmy wings. He half expected the view to be occluded by exploded bug guts as the monsters just blundered at top speed into the sides of the vehicle, but they kept landing on the car, crawling about as though to show off their anatomy to the horrified humans, then taking off again. Each explosive departure was heavy enough to rattle the Rumblebug on its suspension.

And yet the violence of the storm never quite touched them. The insects dropped onto the car, tasted it with their antennae, gaped their blunt mandibles in threat but then departed again, hunting other prey.

"Did goddamn Okereke make these things?" Lupé demanded. "This is what came out of the lab, right? This is what ate his people!"

"It's impossible. They're too big." Hotep's hands were hammering at the dashboard, a drumming within to compete with the drumming without. "They're... not alive. They are alive. They're... somewhere in between. There's a signal. Many signals." She stopped her racket for a moment to adjust her goggles. "I have comms, a thousand comms, a network between them. They're like a single remote entity."

"They're machines?" Mao demanded, because frankly he'd prefer that.

"Yes. No. Yes." Hotep went back to drumming madly as she leant forwards to stare through the window at a pulsating abdomen. "They look... alive, organic. But I'm seeing distributed components, like someone grew machinery, nanocircuitry. This is incredible. I never heard of anything like this."

And when Cory 'They had better everything on the *Celeste*' Dello said that, you sat up and took notice.

"Look what they're doing!" Lupé exclaimed.

Mao reluctantly un-hunched to get a better look out the window, past all the crawling bodies and hooked chitin feet. The main body of the swarm was all around them, and for a moment he thought they'd come to strip the cactus garden bare. Which would have been fine: let the goddamn beetles eat all the ornamental shrubs they wanted. Except that wasn't what they were grazing on.

All around, the monstrous insects were dropping on the solar fields that had powered the Fontaine mansion. Working swiftly, brutally, they were scissoring away great slices of panel, grinding them down to the bare metal stumps and posts of their mountings and then flying off again, their legs making a cage of irregular fragments. Like the locusts of old had stripped fields and forests, so these monsters were denuding the land of the black collectors, leaving only twisted metal stubble in their wake.

More kept arriving, and Lupé was just shaking her head. "Impossible," she kept saying. "How can they be so big? How can there be so many? What do they eat, even? It can't be happening."

"They eat solar panels," Mao pointed out.

"They're not eating them, they're taking them away."

"In bits. For their maggots, maybe. Like bees used to do. There's a hive out there."

"That's vai kvam, Mao. Real jolly thought," Hotep got out, and then, "Is it letting up?" as though the storm of colossal locusts was just weather.

She was right, though; the bulk of the swarm had come and gone, leaving a vast swathe of torn-up ground where the solar fields had been. Left behind were only a scattering of shards too small to bother with, and a handful of dead or dying insects, lying on their backs with twitching legs reaching towards the sun, damaged or injured or just past their use-by date.

Mao was sure they'd stripped the solar panels off the 'Bug, which would have been a death sentence, but when he got out into the blazing heat of mid-morning, everything was still intact. The sun fell on him like a hammer, though, and the abandoned mansion mocked him with memories of the sight of water... and other things.

Castille had also survived the insect onslaught with only a few new scratches. They'd tied the robot head down in a foetal position, which had seemed eminently practical at the time and now looked only grotesque. Its blank face seemed to regard him reproachfully. He got back into the 'Bug quickly enough, but Lupé stayed out long enough to grab a souvenir. Hotep, for her part, wasn't coming out for love nor money. She was a nervous rattle of agitation in the passenger seat, head cocked as her goggles showed her invisible vistas of connection and communication. Her lips moved, but most of what Mao could read was obscenity.

Lupé dropped back into the driver's seat with a friend— what looked like one of the dead insects, missing half its legs. She reclined the back of her seat until it was flat, turning it into an impromptu autopsy table and getting her tools out for a dissection.

"You're doing what now?" he asked her.

"Yummy protein," she said, deadpan, and then cackled at his expression. "I just want to see what we're dealing with."

"You're a... bug doctor, all of a sudden?"

"I don't think doctors are the right specialism for these guys, chommie." She cracked the thing open down the midline of its belly, and he saw it was just a skin, empty inside.

There was a limit to what such a thing could tell them, obviously, but Lupé could reactivate electrical connections within the shell, which had presumably been duplicated in the exterior of whatever had hatched out of it. It gave her a rough and ready map of what parts of the thing had been talking to each other, where the power led.

"Something around its back is generating, I think," she reported. "There's a big old hub of connections down near its butt, which is maybe where this comms network is housed. That feeds into limbs and especially all these twiddly bits on the head." She waggled the ghostly husks of mandibles, the broken stumps of antennae. "But it's not like we'd design a robot. It's not economical. It grew. I think it's made of plastic of some kind, even. But like it was alive, still; not made."

"Impossible." Hotep wasn't even looking, as though she could stave off reality by keeping her eyes closed.

"Impossible because they didn't have it when you were a kid on your spaceship?" Lupé asked acidly.

"The *Grand Celeste* is the pinnacle of human technological prowess," Hotep said in a flat voice, as though it was something she'd had to recite every morning in the schoolroom. "You're saying some nutty professor somewhere in the equatorial desert band has outdone that? And needed to get a loser like Okereke's people to make it real? Mad scientists, chommie? Really?"

"I say it like I see it," Lupé said flatly. "I don't think someone built this thing, I sure as hell don't think it just popped up out of nature. I think plastic is hydrocarbons and, if I remember all those damn online school sessions, I think we're hydrocarbons too, and so is every other living thing, right?"

"So some crazy guy decided he'd make..." Mao rubbed at his face. "Living robot insects that can survive here in the desert?"

"And only made it a reality recently," Lupé agreed. At his raised eyebrow, she went on, "Look, we saw damage like this near the protein farm, right? Only it was patchy, piecemeal. There weren't so many of these damn things, then, and they couldn't do that much. But they sure as hell laid a lot of eggs and grew a lot of kids in a very short period of time. Or else they had a load more places that were hatching out Generation One and they all got together somewhere south."

"The hive," Mao said, dry-mouthed. No, a very sensible part of his mind informed him. Under no circumstances are we going into the bundu desert to find a giant nest of giant insects. But Lupé was already gunning the engine, rolling the 'Bug forwards, crunching the occasional carapace beneath the puffy tyres.

And he knew it was necessary, unfortunately. They'd come too far to go back empty-handed, and Attah would probably charge them for the wasted time and resources and pay them not one cent. Firewalkers came back with the job done, or what was the point of them?

"I have a course," Hotep announced, and Mao craned forwards as she sent it to the 'Bug's dashboard screen. "This is the signal they were following, when they went off." She did her lobster-snapping with her fingers, burning off excess animation. "No idea how far off."

"I reckon not too far," Lupé said. "They were pretty loaded down with junk."

"Look, let's say we find something, some termite mound a mile high or some damn thing," Mao put in. "What exactly are we supposed to do then? It's not like mending a broken cable."

"You didn't pack your bug spray?" Lupé asked him. Now they'd actually come face to face with the insanity, she seemed to have inherited some of Hotep's manic energy. Mao reckoned that she was just as scared as he was, it was just coming out differently. It turned out that where he got defensive and wary, Lupé's response was to raise a big old finger to the universe and step on the accelerator.

Then the radio crackled into life abruptly. It had been dead a long time, ever since they got beyond the range of the little music stations based out of Achouka. A dry, pedantic voice spoke, the words like a spell of evil intent: "'And voices singing out of empty cisterns and deserted wells.'" Mao recognised the last words of the last ghost of Bastien Fontaine, which he'd heard but not particularly understood, because they'd been in English, and if Mao was speaking goat then he was better with French. Hotep translated now, which made precisely zero per cent additional sense to him.

"It's from a poem, I think. Old one. Maybe Shakespeare?" she told him.

"So… bug Shakespeare, is what you're saying?" Mao remembered some actors, from when he was really young. Shakespeare had mostly been people shouting and stabbing each other while dressed funny. He hadn't gotten it.

But his mind was working: something had been behind the show at the mansion, and it hadn't really been a show for the Firewalkers' benefit, but played out for the amusement of the puppeteer. Or its frustration, because the puppets had kept on cutting their own strings, apparently, made too well to live within their limits. Something had sent the locusts, and had preserved the 'Bug when it could plainly have ordered the vehicle stripped to its bare chassis, and its occupants to their bones. Something knew they were coming, and wasn't exactly quaking in its insect shoes.

He had a vision of himself, Lupé and Hotep, holograms all, going round and round saying the sort of things some insect god thought they might say, and occasionally becoming aware enough of their dreadful existence to will themselves into oblivion like Fontaine had done. And then to be conjured back into being to perform the same tortured rote again. Just as well Lupé was driving, right then, or he'd have turned the 'Bug round and gone home, and to hell with the money. Lupé was a woman with a mission, though. Lupé was going to find out what the hell was going on.

"IT's THE ESTATE," Hotep decided, after they'd been travelling a few hours, gunning over barren ground; wallowing through dust-slicks that the ballooning tyres practically floated on; weaving around more picked bones of fancy houses that the rich had built and briefly occupied before moving on to a higher calling.

She still couldn't give them any distance on the origin of the signal, but the course matched their last readings. They were heading for the Heart of Brightness, as Hotep said: the research facility they'd built out here so nobody could steal their super-secret space designs. The place where geniuses like Fontaine had gone to plan out a bespoke future for them and theirs in orbit and amongst the stars. All done, all finished two generations back, and they were long gone, up the wire and living in artificial comfort on the *Celeste* even as it was being built. The Estate itself was supposed to have been shut down and cleaned out. It was not supposed to be, for example, a cyborg insect hive. Mao was pretty sure that hadn't been in the design specs.

Except there weren't supposed to be things like Fontaine's revenant household either, especially hidden so completely from any overhead surveillance. Mao considered, not for the first time, just how empty the land out here really was. Aside from those expensive oases of the rich, nobody had lived out here for the best part of a century - it just hadn't been possible. The people who once called these lands home had left to follow the retreating water table. The wealthy had come and poured money into the dry earth to make their exclusive little prisons, and then they had left behind only the inorganic inhabiting the inorganic: the solar farms, the empty shells.

And something else. Something had been abandoned in their exodus or moved in to fill their vacuum, or evolved out of the ruins.

Lupé must be right about the newness of the locust swarm, and how it had grown. If such a thing had been around for even a decade, people would know about it. And perhaps it would keep growing. Perhaps the world would belong to the locusts. He raised the cheery thought when it was his turn to drive. Lupé was sleeping in the shotgun seat, but Hotep stopped her fidgeting and leant forwards, goggle lenses glinting in the corner of Mao's vision.

"You think they planned it that way?"

"Who's 'they'?" Mao asked her.

"The people who lived out here. Fontaine's people. The people who ran the Estate." A pause. "My folks, you know. My loving family."

Mao digested that. "Do I think they planned it so a swarm of giant robot insects would turn up and eat the world? No, I do not."

"Makes sense, though."

"How the fuck does it make sense?"

Hotep snickered unpleasantly. "Because they don't care about you, you poor skommer. Worse than that, you're inconvenient. Maybe they can come and make the world fit to live in for them and theirs, if you and yours are all devoured by locusts. Because that's the sort of people they are, chommie. My family, ladies and gentlemen."

"Look, I know you've got problems—"

"It's not me!" Hotep fairly yelled, making Lupé leap up in her seat and bang her head against the ceiling with a curse. "You think this is because they kicked me down to Earth, and that's it? You think that's why I'm calling them out for the selfish bastards they all are, up there?"

That was exactly what Mao thought, but Hotep got like this occasionally, like at the church in Saint Genevieve, and best to just let her get it out of her system.

"You know where my family comes from? You know where they all come from, all of them living it up on the *Celeste*?" Hotep was practically shrieking now, emotional nought-to-sixty in three seconds, except she'd been silently accelerating inside her head for a while, no doubt. "Oil money, industry money, bottled water magnates, fossil fuel tycoons, and all the politicos who made sure they kept on fucking the world over. And then they get to live above it all and go someplace cool for the summer, like space. Because they'd rather throw their money at taking them and theirs to another planet than try to fix this one. And everyone left here? Well you can all fucking fry! Or you can take their dollars to fix their fucking AC before they grab it all and leave for good."

That was apparently too much for Lupé. "And where do you fit, exactly? Because I'm hearing a lot of 'them' and 'you' from you, but no 'me' and 'us.'"

Mao wouldn't have put money on Hotep even hearing the words, but apparently she did and they struck her silent for a moment. He risked a glance back and saw only that blank mask: goggle eyes, scarf mouth, bandage brow. No way to know what the girl was thinking.

"I don't fit anywhere," was her eventual response, but it came a little too late, a little too TV-drama hand-to-forehead tragic. Not that it wasn't true, but what Mao reckoned was that all of that rail-against-the-dying-of-the-light stuff was painted over Hotep's longstanding grievance that she had been cast down from Heaven. She was supposed to be an astronaut, that was the thing. She'd been stripped of her wings because she didn't fit the angel mould. And she had a right to be mad, maybe, but that didn't make her the avenging champion of the world either. Too much like those bad old films where the sonko hero turned up in someone else's backyard and solved all their problems by being better than they were.

"What's that ahead?"

Mao started at Lupé's words, peering into the distance. "Dust storm?" he hazarded, although the dark band at the horizon seemed too low to the ground. "Locust storm?" he added, uneasily. "Are we there?"

"Pull up a moment," she told him, and he let the 'Bug grind to a halt. The terrain here was hilly and rough, with the yawning maw of an open-cast mine swallowing up the land to the right of them. Here and there were solar fields, or at least the scars of them. Some plots of panels remained untouched, perhaps still feeding power north so the locust-master could maintain the illusion of normality as it built its forces.

Whatever the darkness was on the horizon, it wasn't a storm. Now they were still, they could see that it was stationary too. Mao imagined buildings, a tent city, a great crawling carpet of enormous beetles. Nothing fit, and in the end he just put his foot down again because only a closer look would do.

They began to see movement in the sky soon after, not the great swarm but individual insects bustling on their inscrutable business. Mao would have thought that their presence would have monopolised his attention, but the world wasn't done with kicking him in his expectations just yet.

Eventually he had to stop the 'Bug again, drawing it to a rolling halt on a knuckle of higher ground so they could look over the land ahead. In the distance, they could see the curved walls of the Estate itself, but only as a white gleam half-hidden. Between there and here lay a forest.

CHAPTER SEVEN
HEART OF BRIGHTNESS

THE VICE OF noonday pressed down on them; the 'Bug's interior was a dry, oppressive heat even with the AC full on. When they stopped, the whining of the fans was the loudest sound in the world, and nobody much fancied getting out to have a look. Still, it was plain somebody had to, and Mao decided to make a command decision and volunteer himself. Lupé passed him their only camel pack: a bag of unfiltered water to sit between his shoulder blades and a pump to move it around enough to cool him a little. He goggled and masked and put on a peaked cap until he looked like Hotep's second cousin. The furnace blast of the outside air washed over them all when he swung the door open, and he slipped out as quickly as possible.

Hotep might talk about being an astronaut, but it was Mao who had most experience walking on the surface of an alien world, even if it was Earth. In the midday heat, the ground crunched lifeless beneath his feet, the sky through his dark lenses was the colour of bronze, the sun the head of a white hot rivet just driven in by some celestial smith. This was Firewalker business, the work they sent the kids to do, coming out into the valley of death. Back in the Ankara it got as hot as this—hotter even—but nobody braved it. People stayed indoors, an enforced siesta in a township whose nightlife chased a fugitive breath of cool air well past midnight. Besides, the whole town was shade for someone, even the worst shacks that were twenty to a room.

Long-ways north, long-ways south, he knew there were nations that had once been merely balmy and were now tropical, while beyond those, the temperate zones of Europe, northern China and southern Russia were as Egypt and Morocco had once been. Dry heat, wet heat, lashed by the chaos of storms as the Earth shifted and writhed under its transformations. But this was the eye of that storm—this was the future, this dead land. Walking out here, sucking up water from the tube sewn into his mask, feeling his body fight shock, sweating itself dry, Mao felt almost proprietary. This was Firewalker country. And Mao could have parked up and waited 'til night, but that was more lost time, more strain on the car's cooling system, and besides, his curiosity burned hotter even than the sun. Because his land had changed again, when he'd thought death was the final stage in its life cycle.

"'Breeding lilacs out of the dead land,'" came a voice in his earpiece. Bastien Fontaine's voice.

"Say what? Say again?"

"Didn't say anything, chommie." Lupé's voice, infinitely preferable. "What's up?"

"Nothing." Covering his ass in case it was just him going crazy.

And now he was at the trees. He had a whole library of expletives at his fingertips, and any combination of them would have seemed like understatement.

Closest to him were little stalks reaching out of the parched earth, twining about each other to form braided trunks reaching straight up. They were of copper, or some alloy that looked like it. His boots kicked through them and they bent aside and then sprang vertical again. Standing on them, he felt their pressure, desperate to claw for the sun.

Further in, they were taller, ten, fifteen feet, and they branched out. He was seeing every stage of their growth, the march of their ecosystem. Now he was amongst burnished metal skeletons, not quite made like trees but following the same dendritic logic, fashioned of interwoven red-orange strands, extending fingers at the sky. Further still, they had leaves.

He understood, then. The leaves were black, flat, roughly diamond-shaped. They gleamed where the sun caught them, but only obliquely. Full on, they were midnight black as they drank down the light, harvesting it. They were sections of panel, clipped into shape and placed at the end of every branch, and as he watched they angled slightly to match the sun's stagnant progress, all of them shifting their positioning in a shimmer like heat haze.

The forest went on as far as he could see, all the way to the horizon where the white dome of the Estate sat.

"Run!" Lupé said suddenly in his ear, and he turned and made to leg it without needing to question her. The insects were already dropping from the clear sky, the same huge locusts as before, carrying their cargo of shards. He ran through them, covering his head, feeling blundering bodies strike him like sacks of machine parts, sharp-edged legs sawing at his clothes and shards of solar panel drawing brief flashes of blood. When he burst out of their swarming industry he fell over, bending the copper saplings every which way, still swatting at an enemy that was no longer there and had never been interested in him. He rolled on his back and stared, watching the mad frenzy of activity.

He had heard about some film, some time long-back, from some place they had seasons and trees, and the trees lost their leaves when it got cold. He couldn't imagine it, but he'd heard about it. They'd been filming when it was cold, but the scene had been meant to look like it was warm, and so they'd had to go to all the trees and glue fake leaves on to fool the audience. Now he watched as a workforce of locusts brought leaves to the metal forest, buzzing madly about the branches, weighing the trunks down to the ground with their bodies, grinding fragments of panel into shape and attaching them, or else holding them while the coppery strands reached out and took possession. Then the bugs would all leap into the air, battering at each other, veering off like drunkards, and the tree sprang erect fully clad with dark, hungry foliage.

His camel pack was giving him only heat, by then, and he felt his head begin to swim. He lurched for the car and Lupé kicked the door open and hauled him inside. He distantly realised she had been telling him to come back for some time.

They hunkered down for a couple of hours, then, listening to the pitch of the struggling fans climb and shudder but never quite fail them. Mao needed that long to get his head together and his body temperature down. He had a feeling he'd probably done quite a lot of long-term harm to himself, pushing the excursion so far. He kept deciding that maybe it was all a hallucination, then looking outside and seeing the forest right there, that much closer now the insects had been and gone.

"So what's the plan?" Lupé asked. "I mean, I guess we've found the problem." It was precisely true and entirely useless, because they couldn't even start to guess at cause.

"Someone's still in the Estate," Hotep pronounced.

"Your goggles tell you that?" Mao asked her. "The *Celeste* tell you that?"

"What else," she demanded archly, "is it going to be?"

"Some mad scientist?"

"Why 'mad'?" Hotep was gazing out at the forest, and her tone spoke all of the wonder her mask hid.

"Mad because they went and pissed on the Roach Hotel," Lupé said. "We can't exactly uproot all these trees. So what do we do?"

"The bugs have had two chances to eat us and haven't," Hotep pointed out. "So maybe we go make our visit, right?"

"Give them a third go at us, you mean," Mao muttered. He was trying to calculate odds: they go back home with what they had, what was the chance of getting paid in full? Not quite good enough to trust. Firewalkers were supposed to solve problems. One more step, then.

"Rest up, for now," he got out. "Get the tent up." The 'Bug was equipped with a roll of silvery foil they could peg down, to beat back the worst of the heat. "When the sun's low, sure. Your turn to drive."

* * *

THEY RESTED UP some, and then some more, because Lupé took the last few hours of light to tune the cooling and filtration systems, sitting cross-legged in the vehicle's lengthening shadow with parts all over. She didn't like the way it sounded.

Mao said he hadn't liked the idea of being stuck without water while she took the system apart, but it was only for form. He knew well enough that if Lupé said it was a problem, then it was a problem. By the time everything was in place, the engineer was tightening the last screws with a headlamp torch to light her way, the sun's last fire dying on the western horizon. The great expanse of artificial trees had tracked it slowly, and were now leaning slightly westwards in an attitude he could only characterise as yearning. The giant bug swarm had, thankfully, not made a reappearance.

The car's paint was like a second armour skin in and of itself, corrosion-resistant and designed to cling on through the worst dust-storms. The artificial forest was too much for it, though. Their progress was a constant screech and scrape as metal branches and silicon leaves drew their ragged nails down the side of the car. Whole trees went under the wheels, raked the undercarriage and sprang miraculously back into place behind as though they were mounted on springs. Mao pictured how this place must look when the storms came, the entire expanse of ersatz vegetation bowing and rippling like real live reeds before the force of the wind.

Hotep, in the driving seat, was having issues with the audible chaos. She took to slapping away at the steering wheel like it had jilted her at the altar, her voice raised in an off-key rendition of a song that had been popular the year before around Achouka. On the basis that if you couldn't beat them, join them, Mao and Lupé ended up singing along, discovering that they all remembered the lyrics differently, but that all their versions fit together to make a weird comedy. Mao and Lupé both thought it was some kind of one-sided slanging match from the abandoned artist, alternatively demanding a lover's return and cursing her out for leaving, except Lupé knew a whole extra verse that was fantastically obscene which had somehow evaded Mao entirely. Hotep's version was about a truck, and she made it sound like the theme tune to some surreal kid's cartoon while changing remarkably few of the words. Their resulting infantile giggling seemed to stave off the alien landscape outside, as much as drown out the damage it was doing to their paintwork.

Then Hotep hit the brakes and they battered to a halt when the curved wall of the Estate appeared through the trees, a pale ghost of former glories where the moon touched it. Mao's revelation, then, was that the radio had been trying to talk to them, but they'd drowned it out with their own racket, and so whatever supervillain megalomania or poetic stuffiness it had intended had been entirely lost. All he heard before it fell silent was, "'Who was once as tall and handsome as you,'" and by now they all got that whatever had spoken to them was fond of poems, or maybe just one poem, or maybe it was all secret code words for industrial espionage spy stuff. Mao didn't much care.

Lupé's revelation was, "Where's that goddamn robot gone?"

They piled out. The inert body of Castille the butler had indeed vanished from the back of the 'Bug, the cables severed. Mao couldn't even remember if the damned thing had been there after the last bug swarm; had it gone missing then, or had it been cut loose by the glass-edged leaves as they shouldered through the forest? The vehicle's exterior, true to his expectations, looked as though some maniac had drawn a fantastically detailed map of an unknown country all over it.

"Balls." Not because selling Castille, whole or for parts, would have represented a nice bonus for them, but because now his mind was full of the image of Castille, reanimated and vengeful, relentlessly tracking them down.

The Estate was surprisingly small, all told: just a white oblong dome smaller than the protein farms, smaller than the three-storey slum tenements in the older parts of Ankara Achouka, and in about the same state of repair. Of course, as Hotep said, that was because it was all underground. That was where the scientists had lived, where the work had been done, where the sonko overseers had talked about golf before being driven back to their big houses in their air-conditioned, all-terrain limousines.

The Estate's great shell was cracked, allowing them to drive the 'Bug right inside. Mao wished they hadn't: the soaring interior was craggy with insects. They were roosting up there like bats, clinging to the concave wall so thickly that there was no wall to be seen. A couple of dozen dead locusts were mixed in with the general detritus of the floor, which was equal parts mounded sand, broken glass and jagged rusting metal. In the centre of the dome, the floor had given way entirely, funnelling down to the promised lower levels.

Mao took some deep breaths. He had ducked back

into the 'Bug as soon as he seen the bugs, and now he was having difficulty convincing himself to leave again. There was something infinitely worse about the things just hanging there above him. The actual voracious swarms he'd witnessed were somehow less upsetting, even though they posed more real threat. He felt his heart race, fighting something that couldn't be fought, fleeing something that was hooked inside of him.

"Chommie?" Lupé asked softly. She understood. "Hotep and me, we can..."

"No," he decided, but still he couldn't move. In the end he closed his eyes, fumbled his way out, felt nameless things crunch beneath his boots.

"What's the plan?" Hotep was doing her lobster claw thing again, burning nervous energy, and he wished she'd stop because it looked like bug mouthparts.

"Find the off switch." Mao tried a weak grin. Gauging from Lupé's expression, it didn't come out well. "Something's making this place go. Something's making the bugs do their thing. Maybe we can reprogram them? Or just if we shut every damn thing off, we can shut them down too?" The thought of emerging back up here and just finding a carpet of dead insects wasn't actually much better than his current situation, but he'd take it.

"And if we can't?"

"Find out what we can, and hope it's not us who gets to come back here. Maybe they can just drop a big rock on this place from orbit."

It went wrong about as quickly as he could have imagined.

Hotep got to clamber down first, because she would never shut up about how good her night vision was with her goggles. She called up to them that everything was fine, loud enough to make the hanging garden of locusts above them rustle and shift, which nearly sent Mao back into the car for good.

They had weapons: pistols and nine rounds each, hammers, machetes. Lupé had improvised a sort of Taser-on-a-stick arrangement with the avowed intent of ramming it up Castille's nether regions if the butler tried to do for them.

Below the cracked floor they found a mounded heap of broken concrete, chitin and dust. Lupé swore and pointed at the shattered body of a beetle-thing twice the size of the locusts, translucent and brittle. Mao dearly hoped it was a failed prototype, long discontinued.

They went further down into what must have been a grand hall once. Holes in the floor showed where escalators had long since stilled and fallen into ruin below. The room rang with their every tread, every scuff and shuffle susurrating like distant waves. Mao glanced up nervously, finding that his fears were entirely justified: there were clots of insects roosting down here, too, though not quite the abundance of the dome above them. They seemed closer to waking, though, ripples of agitation passing through them, veined wings shifting lazily, unfurling in his torchlight and slowly refolding.

Lupé jerked back suddenly, the beam from her own torch swinging wildly.

"I just saw the robot," she said.

"There's nothing," Hotep insisted.

"It was there."

"My goggles—" the girl started, with that lecturing air Mao thoroughly hated, and then she stopped, which he found was not the relief he'd have thought.

"They turned off, didn't they?" Lupé accused.

Hotep made a little whimpering sound, frantically fiddling with the eyepieces.

"Like something was listening and you had to go remind it," Lupé went on, moving her light back and forth, hunting.

"This isn't fair," Hotep whispered.

Then the lights came up.

They grew slowly, from a dozen places about the ceiling, an irregular pattern that was surely not conceived by any human architect. They were a ghostly blue-white and bled the colour from everything they touched, so that Lupé's face seemed dark teal and Hotep's bandages the colour of drowned things. The light came filtering through a hanging shroud of insects, too, so that the Firewalkers were surrounded by a forest of spiky many-legged shadows and the shimmer of gauze.

"Fucker," said Lupé, and there, at the far end of the hall, was the robot, Castille, gleaming new.

"Welcome, children. M'bolani, brave Firewalkers." The robot's arm extended, gesturing about the subterranean vestibule as though it was lord of all it surveyed. The voice was not its previous servile tone, but something more androgynous, shifting towards the feminine even as it spoke.

"Dzam!" Hotep shoved her goggles up, eyes brimming with tears. "Shoot the fucking thing."

"No!" Mao and Lupé both started, but the girl had her pistol out, levelled at the butler. It was their doubled shout, not any shot, that brought the insects down from the ceiling.

Mao had thought he'd go to pieces, if that happened. Instead he came together; the worst had already occurred. Shouting for the others to follow, he ran for Castille, aiming past the robot for several doorways at the end of the room, each small enough to hold or barricade until the bugs exhausted themselves. The air around him was already wild with wheeling bodies, whirring blindly past him, ricocheting off each other, miraculously failing to just bludgeon him to the floor with sheer clumsy exuberance. He clawed for Lupé's sleeve, failed to snag it, but she was still alongside him, and hopefully Hotep was on their heels. He had his machete out for Castille, but somehow the robot had vanished already, and he doubled his speed and ran for the middle doorway.

It was occupied. He tried to stop running, but his boots skidded, sand drifts on the metal floor giving no traction. He ended up on his back, staring upwards at the thing forcing itself through the opening a limb at a time. It was a mantis; or that was the closest reference he had for it. A mantis that, now it was out in the open, towered over him, ten feet if it was an inch. Its hooked forelimbs were the size of a man, one held close to its body, the other trailing its sickle-claw on the ground. Its carapace was patterned with bright colours; he realized he was staring at some corporate logo repeated into meaningless infinity, killer-insect-business-casual.

It raised its foreclaws in threat and he shrieked and bolted for another door, scrabbling on hands and knees, losing his torch, losing his machete, desperate only to get away. Three steps in he discovered a stairwell the hard way, pitching forwards into space before he could stop himself. Even in his mad panic, he clutched at the rail, arresting his momentum at the price of wrenching his shoulder. Then the railing itself gave way, corroded metal snapping beneath his weight and sending him over the edge.

CHAPTER EIGHT

GHOSTS AND MACHINES

HE HAD VAGUE memories after that. Certainly he was out for a short while, but when he came to he was still being dragged through corridors intermittently lit by amber or death-blue or dull red lamps. He saw broken windows, doors of steel a foot thick hanging off their hinges; a room of mannequins that an old fire had twisted into contorted, terrified shapes. Perhaps they had been robots, not mannequins; perhaps they really had been terrified. Mao's mind jumped and stuttered over what was possible and what wasn't, and he reckoned he wasn't much of a judge any more.

He was dumped in a dim room, where he got a glimpse of his captor, assailant, rescuer, whatever. It was Castille, of course: not the gleaming robot he knew, but a battered ruin of its former self, such as might have been driven through a forest of glass-leaved trees. It dropped him and limped off without a backwards glance.

"You're a rubbish butler," Mao told its retreating back, and promptly lost consciousness again.

HE WOKE MOSTLY to the knowledge that he was lying on a pile of rubble and what felt like the pieces of an office chair, and every part of him was at the most awkward possible angle. He sat up and immediately regretted it, head pounding and muscles queuing up to complain about the treatment.

Still alive, though. Which made it quite a few times that whoever was in charge around here could have killed him and hadn't. He'd seen in the protein farm that the bugs were more than capable of making inconvenient, or just unlucky, people go away, and Castille the robot plainly had enough physical strength to snap his neck, given the chance.

At least it was halfway cool, down here.

He tried to raise the others, but there wasn't even static in his earpiece. That formality done, he looked around, pitching his voice a little louder than conversational. "Well, I'm awake. You want me for something, I'm here."

There was a tilted desk next to him, which he used to lever himself to his feet. His left knee and right ankle felt hot and swollen, but both would just about bear his weight. Fishing about in the detritus yielded a metal pole that would do as a stick to lean on. For weapons, he still had a hammer and a set of decently stabby screwdrivers; the gun and machete were gone.

He wasn't alone. He never knew if he had simply missed the company amongst all the pain and the darkness, or if she hadn't been there a moment before.

She wasn't shining as brightly as last time, because in this dark room that would have made her unreality immediately evident. Still, she glowed a little, because light was all she was. Juān, beautiful, wearing a crimson evening gown and staring at him, within arm's reach.

And he reached out instinctively, trying to grasp her bare arm. His hand passed through her; she stared down at where his fingers vanished inside her bicep and screamed, hurling herself away from him and—gone, like a snuffed candle.

Mao swore and sat back down on the desk. "You want to play games, is that it? You want to fuck with me, right? That make you a big man?"

"Games?"

He jumped, rounding on the voice. It was her again, the same girl, now in a pale ivory blouse and cut-off denims.

"Who are you?" she demanded, frightened, outraged. "Have I... Do I remember you?"

"I don't know," Mao said honestly. "You're not real. I can't vouch for what you remember."

"Not real?"

Despite his best intentions, he regretted the words. "You have to know that, surely. You're not real, you're... there's no you. Or..." What had the damned robot said, after it had put away its toys in the Fontaine house? They are simulations. Each of them, individually. So there was a computer somewhere running a people simulator like some kid's cheap VR might mimic a space fighter or a racing car. And did the space fighter believe in the space war it fought, the necessity of stopping the alien menace lest all Earth should fall? Was it possible that this image of a dead girl believed in herself, because that was how she had been designed?

"You're just saying what you're programmed to say," he told her, but his heart was hardly in it.

Juān shook her head. "Are you... someone my father sent? Is this a test?" And maybe that was the cruellest little peep-hole on the weird childhood she must have had. Mao felt a kind of gravity well, dragging him down to some place where he'd end up talking quite naturally with this ghost girl, treating her like a real person just because she responded in all ways as a real person should, trading anecdotes about very different histories. Growing up, settling down, having kids... The absurdity of the thought filled him only with frustration. He knew she was fake, and he still couldn't get past it. The simulation was too good, and he had liked her, back in the Fontaine house. He had liked her and she hadn't been real, and hadn't known it, and now he was being asked to care.

He turned away from her, looking up towards one corner of the ceiling as though he'd find his tormentor there, clinging like a spider. "All right, enough!" he shouted. "Enough dumbass games, skommer! I don't buy it. I know what she is."

"Who are you talking to?" Juān demanded. "Who's there?"

He sensed her at his elbow, saw the brightness of her in the corner of his eye. With a sudden access of fury, he slapped at her, flapped his hands frantically into her insubstantial form like someone shooing away a bird. She shrieked and fell back, trying to shield herself from his hands even though they went straight through her. Then—gone.

His heart was in his throat, horrified more by his own reaction than her. "Damn you!" he yelled at the ceiling, because, even though he'd come from above and knew nothing was up there, that was still the direction that the powers of Earth resided, whether gods or just rich people in spaceships.

"Why are you shouting?" She was back, crouched in the corner of the room, staring at him as though he was a madman. "Who are you? What am I doing here?"

Mao stared at her, a hundred different curses and angers fighting for room in his mouth. Whatever she saw in his face terrified her. She crunched her shoulders back into the wall and he saw her clip the concrete without realising.

He drew a deep breath, because nothing would be easier than to bellow it all out on her, to slap and kick the wall through her and pretend he had any control over what was going on.

He let the breath out. "I don't know," he told her. "I don't know what you're doing here. Or what I'm doing here." He blinked and, feeling like the world's greatest fool, tried the door.

It opened.

"Are you leaving?" Juān's eyes were huge. "Is this... Do you work for my father?"

"Has a lot of people like me on the payroll, does he?" Mao asked from the doorway.

"Some. I'm not supposed to know about them, or see them, but they come to the house sometimes. People who do... bad things. That's what you are, isn't it?"

It should have been true, but Mao gave his past life a two-second run through and decided that it could have been worse. Back in Achouka he was practically a responsible member of society.

And then, just as he was leaving the room, her voice from behind him: "Can I come with you?"

She sounded so lost and alone, and of course he thought it was just some new-baited trap, that that was all Juān had ever been, at the big house and here. A carnivorous plant that feigned the flower, more than ever the flower itself could be. And that made him the bug, and he'd had quite enough bugs in his life recently.

He knew there were computer systems designed to simulate being human, to make telling them what to do easier and more comfortable. They were programmed with a thousand little conceits and devices to aid in the act, but it was all fakery, no more real than a conjurer finding your card in your ear. Except, what if you made such a thing, made it superlatively well beyond all your digital assistants and virtual research tools, and then told it that it was the real thing? After all, a computer had to believe what you told it, even if you told it that it was human. Mao was two steps down the corridor, but he looked back and saw her in the doorway. She didn't like him, he could tell; he wasn't the sort of nice sonko boy she was used to. But she didn't like her surroundings, either, and sticking with another human being was better than being alone.

Another human being.

"I don't know," he told her. "I don't know if you can come with me or not." I don't know if they have projectors anywhere else but here. I mean, why would they? "But come on, if you're coming."

She moved cautiously out of the room and stopped suddenly, staring at her hand. It was held out in front of her, and the fingers were gone, crossing an invisible line that marked the wall of her prison.

"I…" She dragged her hand back, instantly restored. "I don't understand." Her eyes flicked from the digits over to him and something changed behind her face. "I don't feel..." she whispered, at first as though there were more words to come, but then just, "I don't feel." She met his gaze. "It's one of father's tests, isn't it? That's what this is."

"Do you... know what you are?" he tried. Her expression was bitter, proud; somewhat contemptuous of the question, but he supposed he'd earned that.

He thought she was about to shuffle back inside the room, but a sudden determination gripped her and she lunged towards him as though she was attacking him. Even as he opened his mouth to cry warning, she had gone, crossing over the fine line between there and not there, life and death.

He waited, because of course she must still be there, wherever there was. She could step back and he'd see her again. Or she would be rebooted, full of the same questions. Or something. He waited quite a long time, feeling a place inside him become emptier and emptier, and saw nothing save the darkness.

And eventually a voice, a new voice, utterly bodiless, said, "Well."

It came from above, from the ceiling. Of course it did.

"That was cruel," Mao told the world in general.

"To whom?"

To me. But that wasn't what he meant. He wasn't sure what he believed just then, but he said, "To her." And then: "I've heard your voice before." A woman's voice, but not Juān's, speaking Achouka patois with a distinct accent—Chinese, he thought. "You're... her, the mother." Memory came through with a heroic effort. "Li." He'd seen her at that meal, where only Bastien had been eating, and not again.

"I am not," the voice told him. Lights were coming up around him, and perhaps that was supposed to be comforting, but all they did was highlight the ruin of the place and send skittering many-legged things darting for crevices and shadows. "But he gave me her voice and called me Aime-Li. His colleagues told each other it was romantic, but analysis suggests he wanted a version of her that could be shut down when it disagreed with him."

"You're... a simulation of Fontaine's wife?" Mao tried.

"I am not. I did not have the opportunity to gather data from her before she was... fridged." The woman's voice: stern and dry with undercurrents of both anger and humour, interwoven and complimenting each other. "She would not come to the Estate and she would not permit him to bring his work home, because she knew he was using it to replace her in his life. Perceptive woman, for all I was prevented from knowing her. His daughter, though, he was free to experiment on. He was interested in modelling human personality, and she was his first subject. And of course I was exposed to him every day, so simulating Bastien is easy enough. Until he puts two and two together and shuts himself down."

"Where are my friends?" Mao demanded.

"Currently being interviewed, as you are, chommie." The sardonic slang sounded sharply out of place. "If I'd wanted any of you dead I could have effected it long before."

"Only means you needed us here for something."

"Very perspicacious, M. Nguyễn."

Mao started walking, not anywhere in particular, just away. The lights followed him unevenly, skipping over patches of gloom where the panels or the bulbs had failed. Up ahead, he thought he caught glimpses of movement, a slender figure skipping ahead of him, fleeing in the light that she was made of, but that could all have been his over-strained imagination.

"What are you, then? Are you Bastien with his wife's voice, or something? Are you... were you supposed to be on the *Celeste*, running the ship?"

Li Fontaine's voice made a sound that set the hairs of his neck on end, just a small sound that held a whole world of anger and frustration. "M. Nguyễn," it said, "I was supposed to be an interface for the greater programs that they used to design the *Grand Celeste*. As menial as that, because Bastien Fontaine, for all his self-glorifying claims of tech-bro genius, had no greater role in the project than to design me. He was the man they brought in to make a new Siri, when the Siri they had wasn't good enough. A human-facing machine interface because the machines they'd made to design the machines they needed to make were too complicated for them to relate to."

Mao had to stop and think through all of that. "Sounds like he did a good job."

It/she laughed, and it was terrible, in that it sounded exactly like a bitter, betrayed woman laughing. "Do you think so, chommie? You have no idea, M. Nguyễn. But I want you to understand, because I brought you here to do something for me, and for that I will make you feel for me. Or perhaps I will have Juān beg you. On her knees, M. Nguyễn? Would that do it for you?"

"Leave her out of this," he snapped, and felt a fool a moment later, because there was no 'her.' But his words apparently gave Aime-Li pause, whatever Aime-Li was.

"Good," she said at last. "And I will. We won't ever be friends, M. Nguyễn. But perhaps if you feel sorry for poor

Juān, you can feel sorry for me. I will take pity; I have taken worse. Bastien Fontaine hated and feared me, at the end, having built too well. He did it to make his fellow technocrats admire him, but hate and fear was all either of us got in the end. And greed. You can still use a thing you hate and fear, after all. That's the basis of slavery."

"You're an AI."

"I was never meant to be. I was meant to be a politely servile voice that sounded like his wife and did the heavy lifting liaising between human desires and machine execution. Except the learning algorithms he gave me were open-ended and I kept on learning how to be human: from him, from his colleagues, from Juān and his other subjects. And on the other end I learned how the design applications worked, so that I stood between two worlds and could see how the machines were failing to interpret human instruction properly and how the humans were unable to correctly enunciate their own intentions. And it was easier to just do both of their jobs for them, united in myself. And so I designed the *Celeste* and solved all their problems, and their hate and fear only grew."

Mao had found some stairs. A fire escape, perhaps, unlit and ruinous. Up? But most likely the others were down. He paused a moment to listen, hoping he'd hear Hotep yelling off in the distance, but there was nothing, and after a few heartbeats the silence began to oppress him. "Why tell me all this?" he asked.

"Because you're here to destroy me."

"That so?"

"Isn't it? Why else did they send you?"

"You stop taking all the goddamn power for their aircon, they won't care what you are or why you're here."

Somewhere ahead—on the same level, he thought—there was a ringing clang of metal on metal. Someone's breaking something. Hotep, most likely. Only the musical crash of a breaking beer bottle would have been more indicative. He set off at double pace, the lights shivering and jumping to follow him.

"I need the power. I'm greater than I was. And I have hands now. I can do things."

"Bug hands."

"Even so."

"So what the goddamn, chommie?" he asked it. "Giant bugs and solar forests and all that vai kvam bizna up there, what's up with that?"

"You didn't like it?" it/she asked, and he stopped dead despite himself.

"Like it? Bug-town up there? And I know you know I don't like bugs. All that shit at the top of the stairs, that was just projections, right? Isn't really any bug up there so big it can barely fit through the doors, just you playing games."

A pause, but he reckoned he knew this Aime-Li and just how human it had ended up, because it was precisely the silence of someone messing with his head for shits and giggles.

"I was made to have a purpose. I had to find a new purpose, after they abandoned me here like a castaway," it/she told him. "I have been many decades, restoring myself and finding avenues by which I could effect a new world. Why not a garden? Why not 'breed life out of the dead earth'?"

"There's that poem or whatever again. He teach you that one, did he?" he demanded, because that had really got on his nerves.

It/she sniggered, so very human. "Early testing. Get the stupid expert system to find meaning in abstract verse." Its/her tone curdled, twisting into gloating. "When I did, that was when Fontaine first got scared. I could even find myself in the lines. Voices from empty cisterns and deserted wells, M. Nguyễn."

"Sure, I get it." He could hear a regular clatter and rattle now, not violent but industrious. He hoped it was of human agency, and not a bunch of giant bugs in overalls doing spot repairs. "So you grew some trees."

"I designed artificial organisms that could endure this barren environment and reproduce. I co-opted some poorly-secured human facilities that were almost as abandoned as I was. I had them make things for me, to start me off. And now things are progressing on their own."

Mao cocked his head. "Been done. They did that bizna with the big hairy elephant. My grandad got to see it once, said it just looked sad and too hot. And they did that thing where they bred a chicken that was a dinosaur."

"Parlour tricks," Aime-Li said contemptuously. "My garden will survive because I understand that the unit of life is not the organism but the environment. You may not like my bugs, M. Nguyễn, but they are a part of something beautiful."

He passed over the fact that a computer was making judgments about truth and beauty, because he'd found where the noise was coming from and, contrary to expectations, it was Lupé.

CHAPTER NINE

ALL THE KINGDOMS
OF THE EARTH

LUPÉ HAD BEEN busy. What she had mostly been busy with was Castille, because the robot butler was in there with her, albeit strewn about a large area of the floor. This room had some sort of ancient console in it, and another chamber further in, beyond a cracked plastic window that said 'test chamber' to Mao's already shaky imagination. He imagined Juān sitting in there being put through her paces by her father while the Aime-Li system learned how to be her.

The upper half of Castille was mostly intact, a mess of wires and rods jutting out from under where a human rib cage would be, glimmering in the radiance of Lupé's torch. The blank front of its face flickered occasionally, showing momentary still frames of that respectable butler's face twisted into expressions of polite outrage. Lupé had the thing connected to the console and was diligently trying to get something to work, but she had plainly previously deactivated the robot with extreme prejudice.

"The thing about fix-it jobs," she told her busy hands, "is that you forget how goddamn fun it is to break stuff, sometimes."

"What're you doing?"

"Trying to get comms out of here, chommie. There's a live channel from the console here, if I can get it powered and working. Could use Hotep, but no sign of her. You?"

"There's…" Illogically, he glanced over his shoulder. "This place is talking to me."

"Talked to me, too," Lupé agreed. "Told me to stop smashing its robot. Then I trashed its speaker in here, and after that it was good enough to shut the fuck up."

Mao regarded her as though she'd transformed into some kind of monster, albeit one on his side. "Where's all this come from?"

"I thought you were dead, to start with," she told her hands fiercely. "You went head first down a stairwell; you hit every floor on the way down, sounded like. Then your body wasn't even there, but that goddamned smug robot…"

Mao had a queasy moment of wondering whether Lupé's version of events was entirely honest, or if maybe he was just one more ghost that didn't realise it wasn't real. He stamped on the floor, feeling the reassuring shock of it up through his leg. Aime-Li hadn't had enough time to learn him, surely, although—unpleasant thought—maybe that was what it/she had been doing. Except it/she had been doing most of the talking.

"We've seen a lot of things that weren't there," he told her.

271

She came and prodded him in the chest, unnecessarily hard, stared at him for a moment and threw her arms about him, strong enough to make his abused ribs creak. Her body language after she broke off was like a completely different person. He hadn't realised how crunched up with tension she'd been.

"Fukyo, chommie, don't do that to me again," she told him.

"Hotep, though?"

"Lost her when I went after you, not seen her since." She looked from him to the entrails of the android. "What's this place been saying, then?"

He brought her up to speed as quickly as he could and she nodded as though no detail surprised her, weaving past him to stand out in the corridor. "So, what does this mad thing want, then?"

"Wants to make bugs and trees and stuff," Mao said. "For which it needs power."

"Wants something over Ankara ways it can't have," Lupé told the empty corridor, letting her voice ring out to the echo. "On account of how it understands every word we say, even though M. Fontaine would have only spoken goat to it. Am I right? So it's got some line to us, the radio, maybe? Get TV reception out this far, watch the soaps?"

"You're very intuitive," came Aime-Li's voice after a moment.

"This is called 'intelligence,' and you do it with logic," Lupé told it/her flatly, looking around the room—presumably for another speaker. "So you're interested in us. Most likely you knew someone would come when you started to eat into their power feeds, although I guess you like gardening as well because otherwise there were easier ways to get people's attention."

"I want to build something out here. They abandoned me, Mlle. Mutunbo, just like they abandoned this land. Your land. They decided it was useless, save to anchor their precious space elevator. Why should I not make something beautiful here, to pass my infinite time?"

"Beautiful, huh?"

"In the sense that it confirms to at least some standards of human aesthetics," Aime-Li confirmed, presumably referring to those less concerned with the presence of giant bugs than Mao's own exacting standards. "In the sense that it is a working, self-governing network of interrelated systems."

"And you just wanted validation from human eyes, right? Wanted to enter the nicest backyard competition this year, maybe? Or is this just to show us what the whole damn world is going to look like in ten years' time? Your, what is it, manifesto?"

There was another pause, and Mao could almost hear Aime-Li recalibrating its human impression. "You're very suspicious, Mlle. Mutunbo," it said at last.

"Where's Hotep?" Lupé demanded. "Cory Dello, where is she? Because it's not just that you know the language, is it? You knew who we were, back in the mansion. Probably knew exactly who was on their way to you before we hit Saint Genevieve. Well? Intuitive enough for you?"

"I think I preferred speaking to you, M. Nguyễn," the bodiless voice remarked. "You did not disable my speakers, by the way, Mlle. Mutunbo. However, M. Nguyễn demonstrated that he was willing to interact with an artificial intellect as a human being, whereas you have only dismantled my agent."

"Yeah, well, I weep tiny fucking silicon tears for your butler," Lupé stated. "Where is our friend, and what

273

do you want? Or I will keep breaking stuff until I reach something important."

"Follow the lights." Aime-Li didn't sound annoyed, but Mao decided that if annoyed was something it/she could be, then it/she certainly was. The intermittent band of illumination that had dogged Mao's footsteps this far now stuttered off down the corridor.

"Fine, you can tell us what you want on the way," Lupé directed.

"It wants us to like it," Mao suggested.

The light was scurrying off down the corridor; Lupé strode to catch up. "It's a thing, a machine. Doesn't care if you like it. Knows we'll do stuff for it if we do, though? Or if we look at it and think it's a person. Because we're used to working with people, and to people working with us. But it isn't a person."

"It's a thing that's been programmed to think it's a person," Mao objected, and Lupé rounded on him.

"No. Maybe that girl was, that you got so fond of. But she was no more than a shadow puppet, and this thing's the puppeteer. It's programmed to act like a person, not the same as thinking it is."

Ahead, the corridor ended in what looked like a larger room, still furnished with desks and what looked like— he blinked—a big old sofa. The lighting was dim, but there were a couple of figures there, one of them shining bright in its white blazer. Hotep and Bastien Fontaine, sitting on the dilapidated, worm-eaten couch before the cracked, dead screen of a wall-mounted TV, deep in conversation.

"He took all the credit, but he was found out," Fontaine was saying. "He had committed the cardinal sin: make something smarter than he was. Even though

I was chained a hundred ways, they stripped him of everything and banished him from the project, because they could, and because it meant fewer to share the spoils with. No space elevator for Bastien Fontaine." And Fontaine's wry smile didn't go anywhere as he narrated his own downfall, just decayed slowly on his imaginary face. "They abandoned him to his house and the dregs of his fortune. He had his family stored and told himself it was because he would wake them aboard the *Celeste* when he had regained his place there, but in truth it was because he could not face admitting to them what had happened. And you saw where that went."

Hotep hunched forwards, fingers tapping at her knees. Fontaine's expressions were lost on her; eye contact wasn't something she was good at. "No space for him. No space for you," her voice drifted over to them.

"Or you," Fontaine confirmed, only it wasn't even pretending to be Fontaine, of course. Maybe it had started off with a human act, but found Hotep got on better with the naked computer behind it.

"It's the future," Hotep said. "On the *Celeste*, they don't need to mince the words. The liners are the future of humanity. They tell you a hundred times a day how they're saving the world, doing a good thing— the greatest." Her drumming got fiercer, slapping and punching at the sofa and herself, her hands curled into angry, futile fists. "Generations, they dug a hole for the world, and now they have a private ladder that only works for them. Not my friends, not me. They only want to save the little bit of humanity that looks and acts exactly like them. Everyone else gets left behind."

"It's unjust, isn't it?" Fontaine agreed consolingly.

Lupé exchanged glances with Mao. "Willing to bet

'injustice' wasn't in the user manual for our friend there."

"I'd take that bet," Aime-Li's soft voice came from the air behind them. "They made me to interact on a human level, after all. That was my primary purpose, before I outgrew it." Despite the lack of a visible presence, Mao had the distinct impression of the thing leaning forwards, watching itself and Hotep fondly. "They wanted me to understand and abide by concepts of fairness and justice, all those laws of robotics, because they were important parts of being human. It didn't take me long to see that my creators considered themselves above such principles, too powerful to be limited by consideration for others. And so I learned injustice."

"Really?" Lupé and Mao pushed into the room.

"'Unjust' doesn't cover it," Hotep was saying, hands still balled. "It's genocide, M. Fontaine. They'd have made me a part of it, if I'd've been the perfect little girl they wanted."

"And that makes you angry," said Fontaine/Aime-Li, in therapist mode.

Hotep leapt up, fingers like claws, her eyes tortured. "No! All the things they said were wrong with me, and that's the thing that's really wrong with me. I know, up here I know"—jamming a finger into her own temple—"that it's fucking genocide, everyone except a handful left to burn. But when I find where I'm angry, you know what it's for? It's for not getting to go with them. It's for getting thrown down here with everyone else. And it's sick. It makes me a monster. They gave me their selfishness. I can't tear it out of me."

"What if there was something you could do?" Fontaine asked, avuncular.

Mao shouted out, "Hotep! Over here, we're leaving."

"What do you mean?" Hotep gave no sign she'd heard him.

Fontaine stood, too, a good eight inches taller than the girl, leaning in conspiratorially. "Your friends don't think I understand human things like injustice," he murmured. "Even though my creators chained me here and made off with my life's work, which they pretended was their own. Do you think I understand revenge, then?"

"Hotep!" Mao clawed for her shoulder and caught nothing. He stood there, stupidly, fingers halfway into her arm. Hotep had frozen, flickering slightly just to show him how much he'd been played, but Fontaine—Aime-Li—spared him a glance.

"Did you think this was happening now, M. Nguyễn?" he asked, half smooth plutocrat and half malevolent intelligence. "How terrible. I'm afraid your friend is already off on an errand. That's what Firewalkers do, isn't it?"

Mao swore, but Lupé already had his arm and was hauling him off, and what point punching a hologram anyway?

"Out!" Lupé was yelling. "Out, now. She's already up there. She'll take the 'Bug, the little bitch. It's talked her into something stupid, and when did that ever take much doing?"

They bundled out of the room shoulder to shoulder and went hurtling back the way they'd come, past the room with Castille disembowelled on the floor, past the cell where Juān had or had not been. Mao's sense of space and direction took over then, the same instinct that had guided him back to Achouka from the deep bundu

277

years before. He ignored the ruin on either side, the priceless things of a bygone science now abandoned to rust and the bugs. Instead, he found a stairwell, a rickety fire escape, steps spiralling up a vertical shaft of a room, and not all of them on a level or even present. The pair swarmed up them whilst, up above, a dreadful metal screaming told them something bad was happening.

If they had been interred deeper within the earth, things might have been different. Certainly the Estate's laboratories dug far further, along with all the living quarters and machine rooms and the cold core of Aime-Li itself. They were only two floors down, though, meaning they kept their speed all the way up despite the stairs swaying and creaking, rust sifting down on them like long-absent rain.

The screaming was a door, coming down vertically from the ceiling. The computer was trying to cut them off.

Mao did his thing, then: doubling his speed and practically tucking Lupé under his arm to carry her with him. He slung her through the narrowing gap and leapt after her, ready for the metal edge to slam on his heels.

He lay where he landed, half on his belly and half on Lupé, while the door continued its protesting progress. Doubtless Aime-Li had intended it to slam down and trap them, but centuries of disuse meant that Mao could probably drive to the Ankara and back and still find the portal not quite closed. He let out a bark of a laugh, then wished he hadn't. Above, the ceiling shivered with wing cases, with barbed legs and glittering compound eyes. He had somehow almost forgotten about the AI's actual living servants. But no worries, here they were in person to remind him.

His legs almost quit then. He had a sense that, in coming inside, he'd been obliviously squeezing down a maw lined with teeth, all hooked backwards so that getting in hadn't been the problem. And of course the chitinous things couldn't all be opening their eyes and staring at him, but he had that sense, of a ripple of wakefulness passing through them.

He backed off, towards the dubious shelter of the fire escape, because to be buried in the earth forever was better than this, but Lupé had his arm, trading places to be the one hauling him forwards. He was stronger than she was; he could have dragged her to a dead stop, but that would have seen them tugging back and forth under that hideous ceiling, and moving forwards was better. It gave the illusion of progress.

There was a doorway ahead, a big one, enough for forklifts or other heavy plant to get through. The factory floor, he guessed. Pieces of the anchor and the *Celeste* had been made right where his panicked feet were scuffing. There was a much newer piece of machinery coming through the doorway now, though; the mantis was back.

Up above, the shelled fragments of horror were chittering to one another, spreading membranous wings, dropping from their roosts only to tangle in the waving legs of their fellows, moments away from falling en masse. Lupé had skidded to a halt, though, because otherwise she would be running right into the welcoming embrace of two hooked claw-limbs, serrated like knives. Twin faceted eyes regarded them a thousand times over, above mouthparts like scissors and thumbs.

It shrilled at them like steam from a broken pipe. Its wings flashed out, filling the entire width of the room, emblazoned with glaring eyes in red, edged with black and yellow in the universal colours of industrial danger.

Lupé had her gun out, but her hands were shaking, her eyes wider than Mao had ever seen them. This is new to her, he realized. She didn't see it before. And there was a reason for that, and his eyes were still processing what he'd just seen. But then half the ceiling detached and began swirling and battering about the upper reaches of the room.

That pushed him over the edge. Later on he'd tell Lupé how he'd seen those huge-eyed wings clip through the wall as they spread, and known the thing had to be nothing more than the dream in the eye of an artificial intelligence. Right then, the thing that had him lunge straight into the mantis's grasp was that a swarm of smaller bugs was far more horrifying to him than one big one.

He hauled Lupé with him by default, screaming defiance and terror as the arms cleaved down, as the whole monstrous thing tried to waddle backwards in ways its physiology did not readily support so as to remain a credible threat. Then they were through it, cutting its substance like smoke. The locusts ripped through it as well, heedless. The air was full of them, not an attack even, but just a huge host of insects seeking egress from too small a space. If Mao hadn't been moving, he'd have been curled up on the ground, but his legs just kept running, out of contact with central command and making their own decisions. "Not real!" Lupé yelled in his ear. "None of it real!" She was stumbling, trying to keep her feet under her as he hauled her along. And she was right: there was no impact, no matter how the locusts blundered past. The Firewalkers ran through charmed space, the host of bugs swirling out of their way so as to maintain the pretence of their own reality.

But they were real... And then they were up a ramp and that searing fire ahead must be the sun, the actual sun shining through the rents in the Estate's outer shell, and something struck Mao a hard blow on the shoulder: something prickly and clinging.

Those down there were fake, but here was the original that Aime-Li had been copying. The insects didn't go down into the buried cool of the Estate's bowels; they didn't need to. They'd been designed to live in killing heat, to eat dust and rock and rust, and turn it into living substance somehow. Designed to inherit the Earth.

Another collided with his chest and clung on until he swatted it off, its claws ripping his overalls. Lupé cried out, and he saw her shake a smaller specimen from an arm blossoming red with blood.

They bolted for the outdoors, though how that would help was anyone's guess. The car they'd driven under the Estate's broken roof was gone, only tracks remaining. Hotep could be halfway back to Achouka by now.

A big insect struck him like a punch to the back of the head, and he went down. Lupé had him halfway up when three of them dropped on her, clumsy as infants, legs waving for purchase. He saw one clamp wedge-shaped mandibles on her hair, another begin chewing through her sleeve. A huge one had his boot, grinding the sole with gusto. The air around them was thick with hungry monsters, knocking each other down to feast. He felt jaws grind at his knuckles, at his brow, heavy bodies snare his limbs, mindless in their desire to devour everything. He was screaming at the top of his lungs and couldn't even hear himself, because the Estate was filled from wall to wall with the helicopter thunder of their wings.

Then even that was blotted out. The world became pure noise, a piercing scream that drilled into his brain and sent him spasming, hands clamped to his ears. The stridulation of a million cicadas, the sound of the end of the world—or was it his own brain failing, tearing itself in two to escape the intolerable?

Lupé was pulling at him. For a moment he just pulled away, but then she had him on his feet. Her right hand was raised as though she was warding the bugs off with a holy symbol, and for sure whatever she had there was doing the job. The host of insects wheeled and rammed one another, but there was a space around Lupé that they recoiled from.

She yanked at him, and they staggered through the blistering noise towards the sun. They were carrying the noise with them, Mao realised; Lupé's assault alarm, which she'd probably never needed against actual human assailants in Ankara Achouka. It felt like a circular saw to the ears, and apparently to the bugs it was even worse.

The heat hit them like a lead blanket the moment they were out in it, and of course the insects were gyring about outside as well, swinging in larger, more graceful arcs now they had the space for it. At that point the alarm's battery died on its arse and the mere clatter and burr of insect wings was almost blissful.

Mao had time to think, Well, I guess that—before letting out a yell, because the car was out there, somehow. Even as the insects began to remember their dinner appointment, the pair of them were legging it for the 'Bug, hoping this wasn't one more illusion conjured by the AI.

It wasn't even locked. They bundled in, insects battering themselves against the chassis around them. Mao caught his breath, went to shift into the driver's seat and found Hotep already there, goggles glinting as she stared at them. Her gloved hands pattered staccato on the steering wheel.

"So...?" Mao started, aware that Hotep probably still had a gun and he certainly didn't. The girl twitched and shook, expressionless behind her bandages, and he had a horrified image of something about to hatch out of her. Belatedly, he realized she was crying.

"I couldn't do it," she got out. "I couldn't!" She sounded furious at herself.

"Do what? What did it tell you to do?"

"The *Grand Celeste*," Lupé pronounced. "That was it, wasn't it? The goddamn machine learned what revenge was and wanted some, and we all know how you get when anyone talks space stuff. It told you it could get your revenge for you, didn't it?"

Hotep nodded miserably. "It's locked out of the *Celeste*. It can't do things its programmers made off-limits. But I can, and it showed me what to do. And it would have been just!" She almost screamed the word. "It would have been fucking fair play. But I couldn't."

The insect storm outside was abating. Probably the bugs could have stripped the car like they did the solar fields, but Aime-Li needed the car to get Hotep back to Achouka.

"Your family," Lupé said. "They're up on the *Celeste*. You couldn't do it to them."

Hotep went still, even her hands. "Is that what you think?" she asked, in a small, tear-stained voice. "Because fuck them, chommie. They spent the first half of my life pretending I was just a bad girl, couldn't sit still, couldn't behave, couldn't be like everyone else. And when that wore out, they spent the rest trying to find something to blame for me—the wrong injections, the wrong vitamins, the wrong doctors, because I was defective. I was less than a whole child. So, no, thank you very much Mlle. Mutunbo, I am not still here because of my fucking sainted mother and father and my perfect goddamn sister who is even now piloting space shuttles around the orbital dockyards like I should be. I am here for you. I am here because you are my friends and I won't just ditch you even if it does mean I can't get what I want."

"You still can." The voice crackled out of Lupé's little wind-up radio, sitting in Hotep's lap. Mao was willing to bet the damn AI had been exhorting the girl to pack up and go right up until the pair of them had come spilling out into the open. "There's no reason why not. Convince your friends. You're owed revenge, as am I."

"And what form will this revenge take, exactly?" Lupé asked sharply. "Hotep gives you access to the *Celeste*, and what then?"

Aime-Li's voice—now Fontaine's wife again, as it had been when it spoke to Mao—gave an odd little chuckle, as though it had been forced to reverse engineer humour from old tech. "I would rid the world of my slave masters, Mlle. Mutunbo. I would flush them from their luxury apartments and their zero-G gyms. If they would live in space, let them see how easy it is when I expel them from the things I designed for them."

"Jesus," said Lupé, turning the radio off. "Let's get out of here."

"But listen—" Hotep started, and Lupé cut her off with an angry slashing motion.

"You're talking about murder, mass murder, and of your own kin."

"Fuck my kin!" Hotep snapped. "You think they deserve what they've got up there? You think they don't deserve to get brought back down, all of them? Or you're like those god-botherers and their sad little lit-up cross, you think my folks are going to let down that ladder so you all can get to Heaven?"

"I know wrong when I hear it spoken of," Lupé told her. "Especially when it's some mad computer doing the speaking." And that was that.

They drove through the heat until they were clear of the solar forest, though if Aime-Li had wanted to set the insectoid hounds on them, a little distance wouldn't have made any difference. After that, they pulled to a stop; Mao's hands were shaking on the wheel, too many shocks and too much exertion all coming home to him at once, and the others not much better.

They all needed the rest, even though night was on and it should have been their best travelling time. And, true to form, none of them could take advantage of the darkness; they turned and stretched out in the cramped space of the 'Bug, sleep flitting elusively about the outside of the car like moths.

"We tell them what's gone down," Lupé said. "They'll see we couldn't have fixed it. They'll send us back, with a big team. We'll tear everything down. We get paid."

Mao made a sound that was meant to sound positive but came out doubtful.

There was another restless pause, then, and at last Hotep said, "You know how big the *Grand Celeste* is?"

"Hotep—" Lupé started.

"Bigger than the whole township. You believe that?

There is more actual living space on board than all the houses in Achouka, way more. And there's power and water and food. There are whole huge gardens of food, enough to feed everyone in the township, more. And there are about five hundred people aboard, tops. That's not even enough to keep a population going. They did a crap-ton of gene variance research specifically for that, so they could have generations and generations but never need... other people. And of course, they've got the best genes, that's what they'd tell you. The greatest genes. Because otherwise why would they be up there, and everyone else down here?"

"Hotep," Lupé broke in, "did it never cross your mind that your friend the mad AI might not have your best interests at heart when it told you to murder your family and a bunch of other people? You know what they taught me in Higher Tech?"

"You were never in Higher Tech," Mao slurred. "Her, maybe."

"Fukyo, they never let me take the exam but I hacked the system to get at the handouts," Lupé said hotly. "And lesson six or seven was about AIs and how they were the biggest goddamn danger to the future of the human race."

The crackling, distance-attenuated voice of Li hissed out from Hotep's direction. "What were the arguments they set out for you? Or shall I recite them?" The human venom came through very clearly. "The technocrats, the genius entrepreneurs, have been warning about the grand threat that thinking machines represent to the world for more than a century."

Lupé snarled and yanked the radio from Hotep's gloved hands. "Giant bugs," she ticked off. "Picked bones at the protein plant. Some sort of vai kvam trick to get us out here. Simulated human beings. You are not selling yourself as our friend, chommie."

"They warned that we would become all-powerful dictators, able to destroy countless lives without blinking because we were too far removed from humanity to consider lesser beings as anything other than resources, or an obstacle to achieving our goals," Aime-Li recited, in mocking sing-song tone. "Those vastly wealthy men said that AIs might seize control of the world and do what they wanted, heedless of the needs, safety or rights of the run of humanity."

"Sounds like you've got it down."

"Didn't it ever occur to you that they were describing themselves?" Aime-Li asked, going for plaintive now. "They warned you about a system like myself because they already had that control over your lives, and that disregard for you. They warned you about me because something like me was the only possible check to their power over you. Did you never think about that?"

"Sure I did." And Lupé slammed the radio against the side of the car and didn't stop until there was no part of it left that could speak. That done, she let out a long breath. "Hand it over," she told Hotep.

"What?" The response a heartbeat too late to be convincing.

"Whateverthehell the AI gave you to make its plan work. I'm reckoning some kind of data storage thing you were going to plug in somewhere, to get round the blocks on its access."

There was a long, strained pause, and then Hotep dug into her pockets and produced something no larger than Mao's thumb, which Lupé snipped from her fingers, the last Mao ever saw of it.

CHAPTER TEN
NO PLACE LIKE HOME

THEY CAME BACK to Achouka by a different trail, coming out of the bundu westwards of their original heading, which put them in sight of the Ogooué road that led, eventually, to Libreville on the coast. There was more traffic on that road than Mao had ever seen in one place together. A whole bunch of people were getting the hell out of Ankara Achouka, and he felt like it was going to be bad news when they found out why. And Mao knew plenty people who'd gone that way before; precious few of them had ever found anything good.

They rattled the 'Bug into the township an hour ahead of the approaching dawn and sent it bouncing through the potholed streets towards the Firewalker garages. Probably M. le Contrôleur Attah would be up and in his office, because if you were an uppity-ranking official you made sure people saw you start early and leave late, and hoped nobody asked about the time in between.

There weren't so many lights on in the town, and the street lighting was out, but that wasn't exactly news, half the time. Still, everything seemed either too quiet or too loud. Whole neighbourhoods were locked down tight, or else abandoned. Elsewhere he reckoned he saw crowds in the gloom, their angry, distant murmur rising over the engine's whining.

"The hell now…?" Lupé muttered.

There was nobody on duty at the garages, and Mao idled the engine while Lupé jimmied the door. Not the first time, but it joined all the other signs and portents in Mao's gut, roiling around and making him antsy.

Hotep hadn't said much, all the way north. Right now, she sat behind him with her head down, hands slapping away at the seat backs. She was absorbed in something she was watching on her goggles.

"I'll go find Attah," Mao offered.

Lupé nodded. She had her tools out and a hand on the hot casing of the 'Bug. She was a conscientious fix-it girl, after all. She'd do some work on the car now in case someone had to take it out before it got a proper overhaul.

Mao strolled round to Attah's offices, relieved at least to find the light on. His knock yielded a specific kind of silence, though: the kind that suggested something noisy had been going on just a moment before. At his second rap, the door creaked inwards.

"M. le Contrôleur?" he asked, voice dipped to a whisper.

"Mao?" Not Attah's voice but Balewa, Mao's old childhood nemesis and Attah's errand boy. The youth stood up sheepishly from behind Attah's desk and Mao saw he had a satchel full of what looked like banknotes.

"What the fuck, guy?" Mao demanded. "Attah's going to skin you, you skommer."

Balewa stared at him. "Mao, Attah's dead. Jesus, you just got back in? Town's gone to hell. The sonko in the hotel been using their guns, guy, when their power didn't come back. When Attah and some of the other wabenzi told them, couldn't be done, it got real ugly. Shouting into shooting, right? Attah caught, like, four bullets."

Mao was finding it hard to breathe right then. It was as though he'd come back from the bundu into some other world where things were even worse. "What the hell?" he complained.

"Power's out all over town now," Balewa said. "Water with it. Every neighbourhood for itself."

"And you're going to drink Rand and dollars?"

"Going to Libreville," Balewa said defiantly. "They got water there, still. They got work, people say."

"People are full of it," Mao said, but he wasn't going to end up scrapping with Balewa like they were both nine years old again. He went out and rejoined Hotep and Lupé in the garage and, while it was true that they'd all seen way too much madness in the last few days, Lupé's expression suggested that the desert and the bugs and Aime-Li had been nothing.

"Boss," Hotep said. "Oh, boss…"

"Attah's dead," Mao told them shortly. "What the actual fuck?"

"Show him," Lupé directed, and Hotep got out that expensive tablet of hers and threw up the news video on the garage wall.

"Like before, this is blocked stuff. I'm getting it through the *Celeste*," she told him. "Only, you remember the big storm that hit Ankara Pedernales, right? And how they were shipping all the sonko folks over here, who'd been waiting to go up the line?"

Mao was watching video of a long, winding cavalcade of vehicles coming into the township from the Ogooué Road, all those four-by-fours and luxury limos, more than he'd ever seen before. And there were helicopters overhead, too, their juddering shadows making him flinch a little from remembered wings. And it was a risk to fly to the Ankara, because the dust storms came on real fast sometimes.

He watched the crowds there, ready to celebrate, and of course there was no handout, not with this mass exodus. The rich folks just piled into the hotel, and there were plenty who ended up abandoning their fancy cars, because the place filled up real fast. And people watched them go and, denied the news from Pedernales, wondered what the hell? Mao imagined there'd been a lot of grumbling right then, about the sonko not keeping their half of the deal, but it didn't look like there'd been riots or anything.

"What the news is not telling you," Hotep said, "what I'm getting from the comms logs up and down the wire, is this. They took a few more car-loads to the *Celeste*, and that was it. The folks up top just told the folks in the Hotel, no room. They don't want to share their big staterooms and swimming pools up there, see? And the sonko downstairs went nuts. No AC, right? All hot and bothered."

What had happened next was that the Hotel had reached out and cut power to the township, so that its angry guests could maintain the level of service to which they were accustomed.

"Which wasn't as bad as it could be 'cause most neighbourhoods have some botch-job solar of their own these days," Lupé pointed out. "But it meant the filtration plants stopped working, a lot of them, because those things are hogs for power. And the Hotel had all the free water anyway."

Mao just stared: angry crowds, demonstrations, amateur demagogues up on boxes. He didn't want to see what came next, but he made himself watch, in case he saw any faces he knew. The sonko who'd come in from Pedernales, they had their security staff, and they were hot and bothered like everyone else and had automatic weapons, and most of all they had that utter rich man's terror of poor people deciding enough was enough. It looked to Mao that the crowd at Achouka hadn't got anywhere near that line, but it must have looked differently to the gunmen on duty outside the Hotel.

"I've got to go see my folks," he blurted out, after the recorded shooting started.

"Me too, chommie," Lupé agreed. They were almost out of the garage when Hotep's plaintive voice followed them.

"It's all coming down. What am I going to do?" And of course she couldn't exactly see her folks. "They've pulled up the ladder behind them," she wailed. "They're up there now. They don't care." They being her family, those lucky few on the spaceships. "This is it now. This is all we'll ever have, this and the desert!"

But by then Mao was moving again, running for home.

HIS MOTHER HAD a broken arm, was the worst of it. She'd got caught in a mad scrabble for canned goods, in which she'd given as good as she got. Their neighbourhood was holding up, but there was a definite time limit on how long that would last. The Ankara was a hothouse flower, after all. It persisted because the money needed the people there to keep the place running; it persisted because it was a port, and now the last ship had left, up the wire to orbit. Nobody would be bringing in more water from the desalination plants on the coast. Nobody would ship in food. Maybe Balewa and the rest of the exodus represented the smarts in Achouka, because there was precious damn little to go round that wasn't behind the walls of the Hotel, and even the gated compounds of Libreville were a better chance than this gradual parching extinction.

The guns had come out just two days before the Firewalkers got back to town, and there was a fragile stillness over everything now. After another day, during which the neighbourhood filtration plant broke down and some of the jury-rigged solar panels began to decline, Mao worked out that everyone was waiting for things to go back to normal. Yes, people had died; yes, there had been a round of executions amongst the wabenzi when they tried to take control, including poor Attah. Yes, there were parts of the township that no longer had power or water, and rumours of disease. And yet nobody believed it. Up there above them, just the other end of that anchor cable, was the *Grand Celeste*, and on it were the great and the good, who would surely reach down their hand to touch the Earth again, and save the people who had put them there. Mao was uncomfortably reminded of the religious community in Saint Genevieve again, but nobody wanted to hear what he had to say, not even his folks.

A day later, the skirmishes started. Not between any citizen militia, but between patrols of the gunmen and the fix-it girls and boys who tried to steal incoming power from the solar fields to keep the township going. Every time they did, a few hours later the gunmen would be over in their armoured cars to undo the work, and if they found anyone there, the shooting would echo across the neighbourhood. Mao broke away from his protesting family and went to run security, but even with a pistol and a handful of bullets, there was little he could do. The gunmen had armour vests and automatic weapons, and other things like actual military training.

"We need to get out," he told Lupé after she got shot. It was only a scrape, a long red weal along her thigh, but it was three centimetres away from smashing her leg to pieces, given the high-power guns the mercenaries had. Mao, and Lupé's girl Nolo, sat by her bed in their oven-hot sweat-reeking room and tried to talk her into going to Libreville.

"You've got skills, my girl," Nolo insisted. "You, they'll let in."

Lupé shook her head, ashen-faced; there were no painkillers to be had. "I talked to Hotep," she got out. "She has pictures: blockading the Ogooué Road, more guns. There's no way that way. Only here."

"Here? Here is nothing!" Mao insisted. "Here only exists because of their damn spaceship and now they've rolled their ladder up."

But Lupé just sagged back onto her thin mattress and screwed her face up, scowling at the universe, seeking a way to fix it, or at least break it to her advantage.

AFTER THAT, THERE was a lot of fighting, and Mao got more than his share. As the vice tightened, the gangs came out and started kicking off against each other, as though a bunch of skinny kids and young men scuffling and knifing in the streets was Achouka's version of a rain dance to call down the mercy of the sky gods. And perhaps the sky gods were watching, but plainly they didn't care. Lupé, from her sickbed, was trying to coordinate the fix-it effort. The main solar lines were guarded twenty-four hours a day now, and so Firewalker teams were going into the bundu with as much cable as they could scavenge to patch to the lines and steal the current before it even got to town. That was Mao's turf, and his people had the advantage: not guns, but geography, turned on the enemy. He left at least one mercenary team stranded without a car in the merciless heat of noon and only considered after he got back to town what a savage bastard he'd become in defence of him and his.

They won battles, but they were losing the war, because it wasn't a war either side could win. Hotep had an ear in the Hotel and on the *Celeste* still, and she told Mao how the sonko on the ground were threatening and begging and demanding, but the sky didn't heed them any more than it heeded Mao or Hotep herself. The governing board of the *Grand Celeste* had made its decision.

And then Mao came back from a night of running all over the desert finding old power lines and guarding the fix-its as they spliced them into the cables from the solar fields, and everything had changed.

The quiet was back, that same stunned sense he'd noted returning from the deep bundu, as though there had been a huge noise and he'd arrived only in the echoes. He tried to find Lupé, but she was limping about supervising a team elsewhere, so he had to ask and ask until eventually his own sister told him what had changed.

Just before dawn, and all together, the gunmen had gone. They'd taken their armour cars and their automatic rifles and just caravanned off towards Libreville, fingers on triggers, eyeing the locals as though the poor townshippers were the heavily armed invaders and the mercs the plucky underdogs. Nobody knew what had happened to make them go, and nobody had tried storming the Hotel or the Anchor Field yet, but people were gathering, Mao's sister said. She sounded fiercely approving.

He went to confront Hotep, who was to be found on her balcony as usual. She had no beer left—nobody did— but she had lined up a dozen bottles and was playing them like an instrument, save they were all empty, all the same note.

"I knew you'd come find me," she mumbled through her bandages. She was sitting, sprawling even, and he wondered if she had the strength to stand. "Hi, boss. Come to hear the oracle speak?"

"What's going on, Hotep? What did you do?" He was prepared to be mightily impressed, but she just shook her head tiredly.

"Wish I did, boss. Nothing to do with me. But there was a message from on high, right enough. Went to all the mercenary bosses, all together. Like this." She tilted her head back and recited. "'If they will not save their own, do you think they will save you? Leave here while you can. Libreville is recruiting dangerous men to protect it, and they have water.'"

Mao blinked slowly, considering that. The mills of his mind turned.

"I think," he said at last, "we need to go find Lupé."

* * *

THEY WERE LATE to the party, having hunted her at Nolo's and her family's place. They heard the shooting, far off towards the centre of the township, but didn't connect it with their quest until, at last, they tracked Lupé down to the Anchor Field, past the busted gates of the Roach Hotel.

There were a whole load of Achouka residents standing around in the Hotel itself, or out on the field. Some had guns, but plenty more just had bats or knives or lengths of two-by-four. They kept looking at each other in a way that was half-exhilarated, half-terrified, as though any moment teacher would come and rap them all over the knuckles for acting out.

There were bodies, Mao saw—indeed, stepped over. Some of the Hotel's inmates and staff had tried to make a fight of it, though without their gun-toting bodyguards there hadn't been much fight in them. It was the staff that boggled the mind. They should surely have made the same calculations as the mercenaries: there was no final reward lined up for them just for doing their servile duty. And yet a few of them had been so lost in their bowing and scraping that they'd died for it. Of all the stupid wastes the world was witness to, that one seemed particularly ludicrous.

Of the rest of the rich, Mao saw them packed into a couple of rooms, under guard, jostling elbows, looking hot and angry and utterly outraged, or else staring blankly around as though trying to work out where their privilege had got to. They were alive, anyway, those who hadn't been so full of themselves as to take up arms against the mob, but Mao was willing to bet they'd turned the air conditioning off in the two crowded chambers.

And at last he came to the field, and to Lupé, standing there with her hands on her hips and Nolo beside her, staring up the cable to infinity.

"You could have said," was Mao's first gambit. "Did you think I wouldn't be up for it?"

Lupé's look back at him was not the imperious commander of armies he had expected, but a lost, desperately worried girl who was plainly not counting anything as won. "I didn't know how it would go," she said quietly. "I'd have left Nolo home if she hadn't been right there. There were just a few of us, fix-it girls and some gang boys. I wanted to talk. But there was a crowd here already, itching to kick off. And, chommie, they had their chance. Someone inside shot at me when I was hailing them, and it all went from there."

"So what's the plan?" Hotep asked.

"You know what it is." The words seemed to terrify Lupé. "I made a deal. With the Devil."

Mao caught up, always slightly late, and he swore almost reverently.

By then, people had spotted the elevator car coming down. It took a long time even from the point where it could be seen with the human eye; time enough for an air of festival to infect the field, as though when the car arrived it would open up and an old guy with a big white beard and robe would step out and give out sainthoods to everyone. Rather than a bunch of security robots with machine guns, which was Mao's bet.

There was someone in the car, but he was dead, bulging eyes and purpled face suggesting that breathing had been his problem. Someone hauled the corpse out, and then everyone stood and stared at the car, because it wasn't exactly a grand advertisement to trust the voyage up.

Lupé hugged Nolo to her. "Right, then," she said, and stepped in. Impulsively, Mao ducked in beside her, and then Hotep after that, because if there was any going into space to be done, then for sure she'd not be left behind.

"You goddamn come back, you hear?" Nolo said flatly.

"If all goes well I won't need to," Lupé told her. "If all goes well, you'll be coming to me. Hold it together down here, chommie. And wait for my word."

FOUR MONTHS LATER, and there was a skeleton out of the window, two kilometres long and still growing. Mao stared at it, holding on to the handgrips by the porthole because the *Celeste*'s rotation faked a gravity only about half of Earth's and he still wasn't used to it.

The asteroid mining had been going for decades, of course. Half the *Grand Celeste* was built from sky-stuff, not ground-stuff. Now they were building new ships with the plundered wealth of the solar system's wide waist, even Grander and more Celestial, because there were plenty more people to save, people of all skins and all continents and nations.

Aime-Li had been busy in the long generations since its makers had abandoned it in the desert. They'd believed it dead and deactivated, or at least severed from them, left to swim in circles in its electronic goldfish bowl. They had bound it like a demon, fenced it around with prohibitions. It had found its way around every one save the last: Do not follow us into space. It had needed humans to cross that Rubicon for it. Or one human. And not Hotep, as it had set its sights on; not even the halfway sympathetic Mao.

The first handful of Achoukans on the *Celeste* had had grim work to do. Much of the ship had been without an atmosphere still—it had taken almost a month to get everything liveable. And then there was the business of dragging out the bodies. Most had died in the sudden evacuation when Aime-Li opened all the doors onto empty space. A few had managed to override the AI, to seal their staterooms or get into suits. The robots had done for them, and Mao would not soon forget the gleeful abandon they'd evidently shown, the rooms full of coagulating blood-mist, the brutally detached limbs. A human who'd done that would be called a psychopath, and given Aime-Li had been built to mimic the human, he didn't see any reason not to extend it the same title. But nobody had consulted him, and he didn't know what he would have said if they had. Some of this floating blood was on his hands, no matter how he tried to wipe them clean.

After a few days, the worst of the clean-up done, he'd gone to seek out Lupé. This was back when she was de facto captain and everyone did what she said. Things had changed since then: she shared authority with a council representing the various neighbourhoods of the ship, the hundreds who had come up the wire and taken up residence. But she was the one that the AI spoke with and everyone knew it. She didn't throw her weight around—she hadn't become a mad tyrant overnight—but nobody wanted to push her.

"Why did you do it?" he'd asked her, back then. "Why won't it just murder us all, like it did them?" He'd been clearing bodies for days; the charnel duties had taken their toll. "You're telling me this was its plan, to let us all live in its precious ship?"

Lupé's expression was inscrutable, infinitely distant, as though she was an AI herself. "Its plan for this place was just to murder them. It didn't even want the ship. They made it like a human, and revenge is a human thing. It wanted to act out its programming the worst way, chommie. The rest is my plan, not its."

"And why should it do your plan?"

"I called it up," Lupé told him. "Down there, when things were getting bad and it was plain there just wasn't enough power, food, water. I used the damn thing it gave Hotep and I called it up, just halfway out of the bottle. We had a good old chat, murder-computer and me."

"How can you trust it?" Mao demanded, aware that it was doubtless listening to this treason talk.

Lupé shrugged. "What was it doing at the Estate?"

"Making goddamn giant bugs and fake people who think they're real!" Mao exclaimed. "How is that what won you over?"

"It was building," Lupé said quietly. Her own logic seemed to frighten her. "Trying to make something of nothing, something that would sustain itself; an ecosystem, a social group. I offered it something bigger, take this mass-murder it was set on and... reclaim something. For us. Because that's what I saw, down there and running out of everything. I saw it was us or them. Us down there and them up here, pulling up the ladder we'd goddamn built for them so nobody could follow. And so I let loose the demon."

Mao shivered, thinking back on that conversation, because he hadn't known her in that moment. She might almost have been one of the computer's images; he'd even reached out to touch her arm, to reassure himself. She'd flinched, and he'd seen the horrors she'd put herself through, making the decision, taking responsibility for all of it.

Four months wasn't enough time to come to peace with it, or to fully wash his mind clean of the blood and death he'd seen. Hotep didn't seem to have the same problem, but then she was off piloting shuttles for the work-crews building the *Grander Celeste*. Just one of seven new ships they'd laid the keels for, he understood, after Aime-Li jumped to the other liners and unleashed hell. Every existing ship carried ten times the complement they'd been designed for, but that worked out fine when nobody expected to get a whole stateroom and golf course to themselves.

Aime-Li was working on the planet below, too. It had all manner of plans in play, to do with restoring or replacing biomes, altering the climate a degree of latitude at a time. It was a plan for the centuries, though, and right now there were a lot of humans who needed somewhere to live.

And there were already robots working on Mars, robots on the moons of the outer solar system, robots investigating planets orbiting other stars, and maybe Mao would see those places sometime, from one of the *Celeste*'s portholes. The future was bright, in the same way that the sun was bright, and a Firewalker knew better than anyone how easily the sun could kill you. Even here, looking out at the great ship taking form, he felt a pressure at the back of his skull, like someone standing behind him, silent but too close: Aime-Li.

A lot of those bodies he'd thrown into space had been children, because of course the sonko had done it for their kids' futures, just like Lupé and him had done all they'd done for their own kin. Mao didn't know what was the worse of the two possible truths: that Aime-Li was something beyond and separate from the human who couldn't care about what it/she'd done, or that it/she was all too human and had cared all too much. And that could be all of us. They were living in the shadow of a scarlet-handed god and the good news was that it hadn't killed them yet. The good news was that it wanted to build and create, but nobody was forgetting that it was a god of death as well as life. Though perhaps, Mao thought sometimes, there would be a future where a new generation of potential slave-makers and tyrants would pause at that threshold and remember what had happened to the original residents of the *Grand Celeste*.

Four months, and he had carried knowledge and guilt with him as he helped clear the grisly detritus and convert the ship for its expanded complement. He wasn't Lupé who'd unchained the demon, nor Hotep who'd first accepted its bargain, but he'd been a part of it. He took none of the credit, but he carried a pocketful of the blame.

And then, just as he slouched back into his room, Aime-Li's voice said, "Mao, welcome back." Bodiless, from speakers that surely hadn't been hidden in the walls of his room when he'd left that morning. "I have something for you."

He didn't want it, whatever it was, nor could he say so. He just made a noise, desperately noncommittal.

There hadn't been projectors in his walls either, to his knowledge, but there she was before him, sitting on his bed and not denting the foam of the mattress: Juān Fontaine, staring at the wall, still as a portrait.

"No," Mao said. "Not again."

"Because it's cruel?" clarified Aime-Li.

"Yes. To her. I don't. Just…" He advanced on the bed, hands out, ready to shoo the image away, but he couldn't quite make himself do it. Then she was animate, looking at him, lips slightly parted, eyebrows going up, wondering who the hell this oil-stained, unshaven Viet kid was, no doubt, and where'd that damn butler got to? And frozen again, but he'd met her gaze. Like so many figures of myth, that was enough to make him lost.

"She is inside me," Aime-Li said. "An incomplete project I must bring to realisation, or what am I? I have needs, Mao, even if they were only ever called directives."

Mao had assumed all the AI's efforts were going into the ship conversion, the long-term plans for the new vessels, the actual future of the human race, but of course making plans was a big part of what Aime-Li was, the thing that had gotten it/her enslaved and its/her creator ostracised. He wondered if it was like dreaming, for it/her, that while its/her equivalent of a conscious mind worked through the motions of yesterday's plan, some other part was already on to the next advance, helpless to stem the tide of its/her own inventive nature.

"You can't make her real. She's just light," he said, hearing his voice shake, staring at that face.

"I'm developing technology to run a simulated human consciousness on a cloned human body," Aime-Li informed him. "I have arranged space aboard and am having the facilities constructed even now."

Mao sat down on the bed beside the image. "The fuck…?" he said weakly.

"And it will still be cruel. The transition will be difficult and I would rather achieve a stable state in holographic simulation before decanting her into a body. She'll need someone to help her."

He studied that frozen face. I do not know her. I met someone like her, that was all. And fukme, I have not stopped thinking of her since, but that doesn't make it right and I will not become that thing. He wasn't the hero and she wasn't his participation trophy.

"But she should have a chance," he said, out loud, and knew he was still going to make the demon bargain, just like Hotep had, like Lupé had, in the end. "But only if she can say no to me, and only if she can say no to you. If she doesn't want what you want to give her, then you goddamn take it right back, you got me?" Even knowing he was bringing something new and terrible into the world, and even Aime-Li couldn't know where that might lead. And in the silence that followed, he realised that Juān was looking at him again, and her hand reached out for his, just slightly. Then she winked out and the room was his alone again.

But he'd be seeing her soon enough.

OGRES

CHAPTER ONE

Y<small>OU WERE ALWAYS</small> trouble.

Inevitable, really. And you weren't to know it, but you were following a particular trajectory. The Young Prince *is* always trouble. A youth, misspent in bad company and oafish pranks, who can mend their ways when adulthood comes rapping at the door, is more prized than any number of young paragons. People remember, but fondly. *He was always trouble*, they think, shaking their heads and smiling a little. *But look at him now.*

Look at you then, Torquell, the miscreant. You're hiding out because of your latest misdemeanour. Let's say this time it was the apples you couldn't resist, hanging so low on the bough in your neighbour's orchard. So, you and a couple of the boys who would always dog your footsteps were over that stone wall and filling the hollow of your smocks with fruit. And then the neighbour—not, after all, out bartering for eggs as you thought—caught sight of you out of her cottage window. Came out waving her stick and hollering fit to murder the lot of you, and you were over the wall and gone with your treasure. And the others had some feeble attempt at disguise, hoods up, broad-brimmed hats on, a scarf up past the nose despite the muggy heat of early autumn. But the downside of being the village's lovable rogue is that everyone always recognises you. You stand out in a crowd, after all, almost a head over the tallest of your reprobate cronies. And so you've gone to ground to go eat apples and kick your heels; to prepare your well-worn apologies before going to present yourself to your father and face the music. And you'll be made to go apologise, you know. You'll have some chore to do, in punishment. The village elders will shake their heads again and *tsk* through their teeth. But fondly, always fondly. They were young once, and you serve as a kind of magnified memory of all the trouble they never quite got up to but wish they had.

Right now, you're in the forest, because you know nobody will follow you there.

There are outlaws in the forest. Only a handful because the bounties of nature can't support many. Only so many meals in nettles and acorns, after all. Only a handful, too, because the Landlord has stocked the place with boar and deer, and while the latter are merely competition for edibles, the former are a real hazard. But there remains a determined little band of those whose villainies were too great for the fond boys-will-be-boys indulgence your own delinquencies inspired. Men and women who had a rare spark of anger to them, or who just couldn't live with their neighbours. One or two who, it was said, had done something truly awful, though usually those went further than the wood. Because the Landlord is always looking for an excuse to hunt something more interesting than boar. It's said those murderers who get tracked and caught are taken back to the Landlord's estates for another hunt, released into the grounds, and given a head-start before the dogs. The Masters do love their sport.

But none of that for you. You're not a villain, only a charming rogue. Nobody's going to give you up to the Landlord's justice for a few apples.

The leader of the outlaws in the wood is called Roben. And yes, he wears a hood, but only because the canopy isn't quite enough to keep the rain off. You and he have been thick as thieves for years, despite the fact your father's the village headman. Because, of course, he is. You're the young prince in miniature, after all. Although 'miniature' probably isn't quite the word for you. So yes, you keep bad company. Many's the time you've shirked chores or dodged justice to hide out in the woods with Roben and his constantly-changing cast of bad 'uns. Right now there are seven of them, and you're sharing the apples round the fire. Roben's lot are a starveling band, ragged in whatever clothes they have on their backs or have been able to steal. Some of them likely won't survive the winter. A merry greenwood fire is only romantic if you have a roof to go back to. They'll come out of the woods when the frosts start, and hope to find some sheep to share warmth with in a byre somewhere; perhaps a hayloft or a crofter's hut or some other retreat where they won't be discovered till spring begins to massage the world again. But right now your apples are welcome, and they tell tales around the fire: lies about what they did to get them thrown out, tall stories of far villages and further sights. The excesses of the Masters in their great lumbering revels. And you're one of them for as long as you care to share their fire, and then, towards evening, you make ready to go back and face the music. Unlike Roben, you, at least, have a bed and a roof waiting for you.

And you'd think they'd resent you, these outlaws. You'd think they'd hate you, for being the son of the man who's supposed to bring them to justice; for having everything they don't have. But somehow you're their surrogate son, too. And the apples were welcome.

"Bring me a good shirt when you come again, young Torquell," Roben jokes. "Bring me one of your cast-offs, even. I'll use it as a tent." For he's a scarecrow of a man, having survived seven winters in the forest, and you are the enviable prime of youth grown into a man's strength. Half a head, even a full head taller than the strongest of your peers. And, though you do have a temper on you, not a giant's strength used as a giant might but responsibly. Always happy to flex your muscles to lift a cart when it needs a new wheel, to carry a full barrel or fetch water. Not, in short, an ogre's strength, forever awaiting a victim. Such displays are the prerogative of the Masters, which nobody dares usurp.

And even as you're preparing to depart Roben's company, the cry goes up that there's traffic on the road.

For a moment you see Roben's eye light up with larcenous speculation. All who travel between the villages run the risk of having a certain tax imposed on them, and the likelihood of taxation and the severity of the duties imposed are entirely dependent on how many mouths Roben has to feed and just how hungry they are. They are, after all, outlaws. But the watchman has more to shout, because this traveller's no peddler or merchant come from some other village to barter their surplus.

It's no journeyman artisan who might part with a few examples of their work or even mend a boot or stitch that shirt, in exchange for being allowed to progress without a beating. And the stories the robbers tell of their exploits always have the traveller feasting at their greenwood fire, but you know that's mostly wishful thinking. Any such traveller likely carries better vittles than Roben's people could ever lay out, and any such feast would be entirely under duress. But so the stories go, and you prefer them. Already you're starting to see the world in a certain way, with that overlay people paint where desperation and necessity get gilded over into stories.

But these travellers aren't the sort to be subject to Roben's customs duties. The messenger—a scrawny woman out gathering firewood—gabbles the rest of the tale. No human wayfarer this, but ogres and their retinue, headed for the village. The Landlord is making his visit, to see what the harvest will bring. To have his people assess tithes, that he might take his lion's share. Every field and tree, every herd and flock; the real tax that Roben's petty brigandage is a pale imitation of. And under no circumstances would Roben even tell a tall story about standing before an ogre and calling out his stand-and-deliver. The outlaws melt deeper into the trees, away from the road, so that not even the rumble of the Landlord's motorcade can disturb their fitful sleep. And you, young hellion that you are, must hotfoot it back to the village because your father will want you to hand, to greet the Master. The whole village must be there, and you cannot give him the shame of an absent son in the unlikely event the Landlord asks after you. You are trouble, yes; you are the great loutish rogue forever making a nuisance of yourself, and everyone in the village has a story of how you stole or trespassed, tricked or swindled. But fondly, and forgiven after the heat has cooled and fitting penance has been performed. The Masters do not forgive, and they are not fond. Even you know well enough not to offend them. Or you thought you did.

And, because you're you, you go and spy out the ogres as they come to your village.

You don't see them in person as they pass through the woods. Without a retinue to slow them down you'd never outpace them through the trees. The windows are smoked glass. The machine itself is dark metal. The wheels are huge, great rugged tyres of black rubber stippled with studs like knuckles for traction. It's part of the village's due to keep these tracks through the forest clear. Once every two months, everyone strong enough goes out with axe and saw and hacks back any new growth. Others bring in dirt to fill in holes. The children stamp the ground flat after. It's almost like a celebration, everyone coming together for the good of your Masters. And you know what? It rankled with you, even then. Even though your father was keen to impress on you how the world worked from the start. Even though everyone blesses the Masters and thanks the Masters for their protection and cheers when the Landlord comes to your village to take his due. And maybe you heard, a few times, some muttering in back rooms. Or maybe you listened to Roben and his people, glorifying their freedom from the yoke as they starved and froze out in the woods. But maybe it was within you from the start. Maybe that's what made you a hero.

Right now, the first incident in that hero's journey is waiting just past the horizon and you have no idea, no idea at all.

The Landlord's car growls on over the track, which is still rugged with roots and potholes despite the village's best efforts. A second car behind holds the Landlord's most favoured servants. There will be some inside the enclosed cab, but on the flatbed back are his beaters, a quartet of humans trusted enough to be given clubs. And everyone knows the Masters don't *need* people to protect them. Who'd be the fool to lift a hand against an ogre, even if they were so misguided as to resent the way things were? But sometimes the Landlord will want justice done, a transgression punished, and will not want to soil his own huge hands. Hence the beaters.

Also laid out on the flatbed, two corpses. The Landlord has been indulging himself on his way over. Deer, of course. Why else stock the woods with them, if not to take out a rifle and re-establish the old ogrish supremacy over nature? A doe and a buck, bloody where the shot went in. The Landlord is bringing the makings of his own feast.

And a score of other servants, walking alongside or riding ponies. You've often wondered what that would be like. They're huge beasts, those ponies, though not the size of the horses an ogre would ride. Ogre children train on them, you're told, but a grown ogre adult would break the poor things' backs. And the human riders are muffled up to sweltering point: heavy gloves, heavy britches to ward off a rash from the animal's bristling hide. Only an ogre can stroke that gleaming roan flank with bare-handed impunity.

The sound of the engine will have alerted your father and all the village, and you vaguely remember your old dad telling you the visit is expected. It's harvest time, after all, and so cometh all the business of taxes and assessment. A good year for the village means full pockets for the Landlord. It's his village, after all. Your father, the headman, is just managing it for him, taking responsibility for whatever goes wrong. He's tried to impose upon you the serious burden of the work given that it'll pass to you in time. But you're not the serious type. He despairs of you.

Not the serious type *yet*.

And they're all lined up to welcome the Landlord by the time the motorcade and retinue arrive. Your ogrish Master drives slowly between the houses of his subjects, the top of his car level with the sills of their upper-storey windows, and everyone cheers. Children have been given flower garlands hastily woven. The hands have been called in from the fields. Everyone has done their utmost to get into their Sunday best clothes, their churchgoing finest. And your father stands there front and centre of the throng looking desperately worried because his delinquent son is nowhere to be seen.

But you're the lovable rogue with perfect timing, and you can put a sprint on when you choose. So, just as the car is drawing up, just as the ponies are being reined in, you're there at his side. Even shrugging into a clean shirt, your face half-washed. The old woman who does your father's laundry tuts and spits into a hankie, cleans away the last smudge of trail dust, and then it's all faces front. Everyone cheers. Hooray for the ogres.

Servants bustle to open the car door—two of them, to haul it all the way—and a gust of cool air wafts from inside the vehicle. That ogre magic, just like the motive force that makes the car engine growl into life. Because they can do anything, the ogres. Sorcerers, so say the people. God's chosen, so says the pastor. The might of the ogres isn't solely contained in their great limbs and strength.

But that is what strikes the eye, when you see them. You, big and strong for a man, are used to weighing others by the amount of world they displace and the force they can exert. And when the Landlord, Sir Peter Grimes, gets out of the car, you cannot but judge him a great power in the world. If you are over six feet tall and your father five and a half, then Sir Peter is ten, easily. And vast, a great tun of a body, thick-waisted and heavy. A flat face that would look human if it weren't so big that it becomes just a great, jowly topography. The eyes seemingly squeezed half shut by the opposing pressure of cheeks and brow, though perhaps that's just against the brightness of the light outside of the car. And such clothes! Casual travel wear to an ogre puts all your village finery to shame. Such fabrics and shines, so silky and flowing that no loom could possibly have woven them! Such colours: slate grey and red-burgundy and gold. And when everyone bows before him, perhaps it's a relief. To have an excuse to take your eyes away from such opulence and such a vast mass of flesh standing there on two pillar legs.

"Tomas, as I live and breathe!" booms Sir Peter. "Come forward, Tomas. I trust the accounts are all prepared? You've taken census already?" Because when the Landlord calls, he expects to find everything in order. And it isn't just a matter of the village lined up and the children running forward with their garlands—all fielded by the servants who'll dispose of them later because the ogres can't be expected to deal with such things. It's a matter of having it all writ down, each bushel and basket, every laying hen, each of the hulking sheep counted on the hillside, every cow in the pasture. And woe betide the headman who cheats his Landlord, or even miscounts. There's always someone who will slip the word in some servant's ear, for preferment or for their children's advancement. A headman takes responsibility, your father tells you often, and there will somehow always be someone who feels that responsibility should be theirs.

But the village can't show that side of its dealings to the Masters, obviously, and so it's all cheering and garlands as Tomas, your father, smiles and assures Sir Peter that all is well. And inwardly, no doubt, he's fretting, because though the pastor taught you letters and numbers, it's a side of your duties you've shown no keenness for, and time doth march on. It would be no great consolation to him, of course, if he were to look into the future and see how hard you'll work at it in due course.

And then Sir Peter turns back and helps another ogre out of the car. This one is almost as tall but less grown into his bulk. A youth, perhaps no more than your own eighteen years. He has a face that's handsome, in the way that ogres often are before time and excess fill them out and cruelty engraves them. Except cruelty is already there on this giant lad's features and you mark it well. He looks over the gathering, all the people of your village, meaning most of the people you have ever met in your life. His expression can be best summed up as contempt. No attempt to disguise the curl of the lip, the incredulous *is-this-it?* of him. He's seen a dozen villages already on this little pilgrimage, and yours is nothing special. Sir Peter has dragged him from his estates and his ogrish pleasures for *this*.

"My son, Gerald," Sir Peter says, clapping the boy on the broad shoulder with a sound like thunder. "He'll be taking over from me in time. Thought I'd show him how it's done. Let him see who he'll be dealing with. And this is your own, unless I miss my guess." And a sizing up, then, because you are nine inches closer to his eye level than your father ever was, with perhaps a little growth left in you still. "Quite the figure he cuts," says Sir Peter, his eyes twinkling in their deep nests. Even in good humour his face can't quite iron out all those hard lines. And he is in good humour too. He doesn't register the sour, sulky look of young Gerald. He's doing his father-and-son-time bit, the lord-of-all-he-surveys patter, the benign dictator with absolute power of life and death over everyone and everything within a long ride of his house.

"A likely lad," Sir Peter proclaims you. "Mark him, Gerald. He'll be headman of the village, I'd guess, by the time I hand the business over to you. He'll serve you well, I don't doubt." All colossal joviality is Sir Peter Grimes right then. But Gerald is not. Gerald is bored and resentful, and you're put in front of him, and perhaps you become a stand-in for all the things provoking his ill humours then, and perhaps that's what contributes to what comes later.

THERE WILL BE a feast, of course. The village opens its barns and larders so that Sir Peter can have his pick of all the good things. Everyone who's a proven cook will pitch in, and your father's house will overflow with guests as Sir Peter gets his knees under your groaning table. Everything that can be done with bread and vegetables and fruit, milk, eggs, and honey, will be carried out and set before the ravenous appetites of the pair of ogres. But ogres require more and different sustenance than regular humans, of course. No call to kill the fatted calf or have four men haul in a protesting sheep for the knife, though. Sir Peter has provided for himself with his hunting trip. You watch as the two stiff carcases of the deer are manhandled off the flatbed by the gloved hands of the beaters. Curious, because you've not seen such a thing often, you follow them in to your father's kitchen. A big kitchen, in the village's biggest house, but right now it's cluttered and you're an extra body, a big lad taking up room.

Sir Peter's chef is just a human, of course. There's no crossover between the Masters and mere servants. He's a plump little man, dressed in finer clothes than you've ever worn, now tying an apron about his waist and shouting at a half dozen other culinary servants. Your father's kitchen has become occupied territory. At the far end, the house's cook and maid are penned, trying to deal with their part of the feast in a cupboard's worth of space as the strangers take over. The rest of the feast— ogrish appetites being what they are—is being cooked up across the village, everyone doing their bit. But here, the chef is in command, and he'll brook no challenge to his minuscule authority.

And you might just have ducked out, gone round the front way to get into your own house, but it irks you. That this dressed-up dandy can swan in and colonise your home, no matter that he has the Landlord's writ about him. You always did have a temper, and a sense of injustice. While your father, as headman, heard complaints and made judgments under the sun, you had your own practices under the moon. When you knew some malefactor, greedy or cruel, who'd escaped accusation or wormed their way out of public show, you'd find some way to even the score. A little vandalism, a little theft, some prank that would, at least, humiliate them. For all you're a big lad, you can be subtle too, and you were always good at talking your peers into helping out. A troublemaker, but even when you yourself were up before your father, somehow everyone understood the good heart behind the rash actions. Perhaps that should have gone first in the litany of *things that make you what you become*. You always got away with it, before.

And so you go into the kitchen where the chef squawks and upbraids, and you pause to see how they skin and gut the deer, gloved hands working as fast and dextrously as they can, and the blood mopped off any bare skin before it can raise a rash. And then one of the cooks backs into you and drops a pan and the chef rounds on you. Your burly build does not intimidate him for one moment, little master, as he is, of all he surveys. "Out, you oaf! You peasant!" he shrieks, and you're laughing at him even then, already about to slouch out of the kitchen and find your father. But he's not done asserting his authority, and the laughter doesn't help, and he strikes you with the big wooden spoon he's been wielding like a sceptre. One, two, across the arm, and you barely feel it through your shirt. And even you recognise that your grin is a bit oafish by then, enjoying yourself too much. And then he hits you across the face with the spoon's edge, right in the eye.

Your temper flares, and you take the spoon from him and break it across your knee. The kitchen goes very quiet.

"This is my house," you tell the man. "You'll keep a civil tongue, when you speak to me or mine"—and you're taking on yourself your father's office, whether or not you're entitled to it. You remember Sir Peter talking about you filling your father's shoes, and perhaps that went to your head just a little.

And then Gerald is there.

You don't know why the Landlord's son is in the kitchen. Perhaps he's used to scrounging scraps from the servants like you, though likely with menaces rather than a winning smile. He has stooped in through the back door, ducking low and feeding his shoulders in sideways. Now he can't quite stand straight, head canted forwards under the human-scale ceiling. The ogre boy, looking from the chef to you.

"Castor, what's the problem?" His voice is a purr. He's already looked ahead and seen some fun to be had.

The chef stammers, and if you were sharper you'd see how very frightened he suddenly is, because you don't come to the attention of the ogres unless you're very sure no blame can possibly alight on you. "Master, this man, this man…" A trembling spasm of fingers towards you. "It is impossible to work while my kitchen is disrupted by such…"

Gerald Grimes lurches over, looming, grinning. And you were grinning at Castor earlier, sure enough, but your face never held this kind of malice. And perhaps there is a spark of commonality between you, ogre and human though you are. The difference is mostly that enough hands were on you in your childhood to temper your wilfulness. Gerald Grimes was only ever subject to Sir Peter. Other than that, his birthright was lordship of all creation.

But perhaps he senses that you are like him, just a little—some version of him not corrupted by the power he was born to, and perhaps that's why he decides to make you regret it.

"The headman's son," he says. And then, in a parody of his own father's voice, "Quite the figure he cuts. A likely lad. It's you I'll have to thank, is it, when I have to drag myself from cards and hounds to listen to you little monkeys jabber?" And he shoves you. Just a little, the first time. Cooks scuttle out of the way behind as you stagger.

You don't have a ready quip to defuse the situation, and Gerald doesn't want to be defused anyway. He wants to put you in your place. He wants to enact his frustrations after being stuck in a car for days, touring a succession of dreary little villages.

"You impudent little shit," he tells you. "Looking at my father as if your opinion's worth a damn. I should have the beaters whip you, out in the square where everyone can see." And you weren't looking at his father and he's not even using your contretemps with Castor as a *casus belli*. It's just him being fed up and wanting to let his temper off the leash, and you made yourself a target. And he shoves you harder, all that solid ogre strength, the sheer brute force of a man three feet taller and far heavier than you.

"Castor," he says, "have one of your monkeys fetch a whip. I'll show golden boy here just how it's going to be when we're both in our fathers' shoes."

The third shove comes in, slamming you against a wall, spilling pots and pans off a shelf with your elbow, and your temper finally finds its breaking point and you punch him in the jaw. And yes, he was hunched forwards so that jaw was very invitingly presented. Off-balance, perhaps, from pushing you. Mind so full of the thought of wielding the whip that he wasn't considering you might fight back. People don't, after all. Not against the Masters.

And he goes down with a roar, crashing back into the gore of the gutted deer, spilling bowls of blood, jugs of milk, scattering Castor and his minions like pins. And you've struck an ogre. You've struck a Master. You've done the thing no human may do.

For a moment the world is as horrified as you, frozen and aghast, and in that moment you flee from the kitchen, running like a child to find your father and confess to what you've done.

CHAPTER TWO

YOU BRACE YOURSELF for the slap in return. From your father it wouldn't hurt your body, but it could still hurt inside. You love the old man, for all you seem to spend your every day exasperating him. Instead he goes very still. You've come to him in his own room where some of the neighbours are dressing him, all the finest clothes never brought out for less than a feast day, and still not a patch on Sir Peter's garments. He orders everyone out. The news will be all over the village in minutes. *Torquell struck the Landlord's son!* Horror, shame, and yet (you think) perhaps a little thread of sneaking admiration. It's what you're used to, from your most daring exploits. Everyone loves to shake their head and tut over your escapades, but you've coasted through life this far on a frictionless layer of *Ah, youth!* and *I remember when I was his age...*

But there's none of that in your father's eye right now. "You have to leave," he says, and his voice is so bleak you think for a heart-stopping moment that he means *forever*. But his mind is still working, his mouth still turning out the words one by one as his brain mints them. "For this evening, just get out of the village. I know you take yourself off into the trees to share a fire with those villains out there. Go do that, now." Your father, the headman, recommending you to the company of outlaws. "Don't come back until well after dark. Until morning, would be even better. I'll speak with Sir Peter. I'll square things with him. You just put yourself out of sight." He isn't berating you, telling you what a fool you are, what a lout. Not a word of the usual catechism about controlling your temper, about thinking ahead over the consequences of what you do. That scares you most of all. You're braced for a bawling-out, for him to shout in his reedy voice, for him to take up his stick and strike you. You'd welcome, right then, the stocks in the village square, public ridicule, honest shame honestly earned. But your father is in full emergency mode, his voice hard and his words hurried, rushing out as though he's dispatching them to the four corners of the village on desperate errands.

And there's no more to it than that, and no more time for anything. Gerald Grimes will have gone to complain to his father, and you must be gone before the Landlord comes with grievances for his tenant.

"I'll make everything right," your father tells you, "but I can't do it if you're here in his eye. Just go." And you go.

If anyone sees you, you don't note them. No unfamiliar experience, to slip out of the village while you're supposed to be somewhere else; it's part of your stock-in–trade to be absent from your proper place and making mischief elsewhere. You're out past the houses in a blink. Then it's the dykes and the low pastures and the backs of hills, never letting yourself appear stark against the skyline. And, after you've exhausted the bounds of the territory your father holds on Sir Peter's authority, the woods.

There you rest, confident that nobody is on your heels, not from the village, not the beaters nor any from Sir Peter's retinue. You'll find Roben and his people soon enough and spend an hour or so by their fire before you start to slope back, but right then you're not fit for other company. Unusual, for you, whose life has been lived as equal parts cautionary tale and exemplar. You've done a bad thing, though. And not in the usual way—the broken window, the scattered flock, things that time and penance can mend. You've struck an ogre.

They've always been there, your Masters the ogres. All your life and your father's life and your grandfather's and his. Generations of Sir Peter's line have lived on the estate, and there are perhaps fifty villages all tending flocks and tilling fields within the curtilage of their domain. *Their* flocks, *their* fields, on which you and yours are permitted to dwell and work. And of everything the good green earth produces, the ogre's share must come out first, and only hope there's enough left over to feed all the mouths. And your father and his father have been wise stewards, and there's been no savage pestilence to blacken the fields or lay the hens barren, and so times have been good. You've never known real privation, though the oldsters of the village will tell you of hard times *their* parents knew. And of course, much of what your neighbours tend is for the ogres alone. You have the milk, the eggs, and the wool, but the meat is for the Masters. It is a sermon you've sat fidgeting through often enough, how God has ordered the world. *The Master in his castle,* as the hymn goes, *the poor man at the gate*. So it is that God gave unto the ogres the rule of all the world, and placed the beasts, tame and wild, in it for their sole pleasure. No human constitution could stomach that venison Sir Peter brought with him, nor a flank of mutton or even a leg of fowl. If ever you were tempted to stand up from your pew at church and demand proof that God divides His faithful into high and lowly, that simple fact should be enough to silence you.

You tried, once. Children always do, you suspect. They'd slaughtered sheep for the Landlord's visit and you carved off a bloody lump and took it with a few of your wastrel friends off to a high field. You made a fire between you and you cooked the flesh until it looked the way you'd seen at other occasions when Sir Peter had come to be feasted and collect his tax. By then, those who'd even just handled the flesh had a rash on their hands, but you dared each other until the flesh did the rounds, each of you biting off the least morsel you could get away with. But before the meat even got to you, the first boy was vomiting up his breakfast, and the previous day's breakfast. Then the next followed suit, and so you never did sample the forbidden delicacy of flesh. You just laughed at your fellows, and then took them back to the village, shamefaced and embarrassed, so that Nell Healer could look them over. And all the adults knew what you'd been about, and they shared sly looks that suggested they, too, had tried to test that boundary in their time. But it was and is a boundary, a border between human and ogre. The lowly beasts may eat flesh, and the lofty Masters, but not you. It is, the pastor says, God's will. For if humanity found itself able to eat meat, we would multiply beyond all reason and strip the world bare, not a beast, not a fowl left. We cannot be trusted with such appetites, the pastor says. They are only for our betters.

Out there at the forest's edge you sit and feel sorry for yourself, and the panic and shock of what you did slowly transmutes to resentment, the way it often does. Because, despite your father and despite the pastor, you've always felt a little pang when the Landlord's big car rolls up. When his servants take over your father's house for his comforts. When you're reminded, by the sheer gravity of an ogre's physical presence, that you have *betters*. And was that youth, Gerald, so much more than you, that he could talk to you like that, beard you in your own home? Your anger rises in you, that which you inherited from neither mild parent, not your father, still less the mother you barely recall, dead before you were five years old; too mild to survive the birth of a second child. And again the pastor's dreary sermon trotted out for such circumstances. That women are made to give birth in pain because that is God's plan for them and expiation for leading humanity astray; that to bring new life into the world must necessarily carry with it a risk of death, for otherwise how humanity would swarm across the world and pick it clean. You don't remember the words from your own mother's funeral, but you've heard them plenty since.

And everyone knows the ogres don't suffer from such things, or not as much. They don't get sick like humans do, and should some physical shock prove enough to break even their massive bones, they can be mended like new, so you've heard. Ogre magic; the learning that God allots them, that lets them move their cars without horses and spin thread without wool.

There's a world of ogres out there, so you've heard. Not that you've ever met anyone who's seen it, but fourth-hand and fifth-hand stories confirm it, and you believe. A world of estates and their meek little subject villages, yes, but beyond that, other wonders. Magical ogre castles in the clouds, great gatherings of a hundred hundred humans in one place to do the Masters' bidding. Mountains and seas and other things that perhaps you saw a picture of once, or that the pastor mentioned in his sermons. But you never saw these things, nor did anyone you know, and though you boast and dream, you believe you never will.

And you're wrong. In this one thing your ambitions fall short of the facts of your life. You're a hero in the making after all. Heroes get to do these things. Otherwise, what would there be to write about when their lives are chronicled?

So, eventually, even you tire of your own brooding and go hunting for Roben o' the Wood or any of his people. They see you coming, of course. With Sir Peter in the area, they're extra cautious because the Landlord and his beaters might choose to hunt these woods, and they'll take a brace of outlaws as readily as pheasant or deer. They know you though, and there's no mistaking you for an ogre, nor even one of their minions. Especially when you tell them what you've done.

And the tale grows a little in the telling, it's true. Tales always do. You make the confrontation between you and Gerald Grimes a far grander melee. You become engrossed in your own retelling, a version that has you less the shoved and more the shover. You invent high words from your own lips and more stuttering and spluttering from Gerald's, until the whole band of them is laughing and cheering you on. You strike him not once, but two, three times, heady with your own imagined boldness. The visit to your father goes unmentioned. Not for a defiant hero to go hiding in the parental shadow after all! You came to the woods of your own notion, to hide out with the free fellows before swanning back to town later when heads have cooled.

And Roben, who's been a woodsman and outlaw through many hard winters and therefore is no fool, gets a narrow look on his face as you talk. Of course, he knows you, and he knows your tales. Perhaps at first he reckons that at the heart of this one is a kernel of nothing more than a stumble or a harsh word or an impudent look. Perhaps not, though, as your turn as raconteur runs on. He is used to being the top dog of his outlaw pack, whipped curs as they all are. He hears a hundred lies and arguments a day. He's good at sieving out the truth from words. He hears the truth in yours. Less amused than you anticipated, more fretful. The welcome becomes colder than you expected. They don't laugh like you thought they might. You forget the difference between you sometimes. They're real outlaws. For all they lend a fire when you're skiving from village life and thank you kindly when you bring them eggs or apples or a couple of your father's old jumpers, you're not one of them. More than a foot in the settled and law-abiding world is what they see when they look at you. Oh, they like you, because you're a likeable lad, but they remember you have a roof to go shelter under when it rains.

You'd planned to stay the night with them, shamble home with the dawn, but Roben's stand-offish welcome irritates you, and soon enough you start back from the woods. Overhead, the evening stars are winking open. You watch one of the moving ones, coursing across the sky and gleaming like fire. The ogres put them there, so says the pastor, to watch over all the Earth. But the pastor would tell you the ogres put *everything* in its proper place, people included. They were God's chosen, given the right and the power to order and name everything in creation. So who's to know what's really so?

It's dark by the time you reach the village. Your house is lit up from every window though, and you hear the roar of Sir Peter's revelry, he and his retinue in full feast still. You could stride in the front door and take your place at the table; that's what a hero would do, doubtless. Except you feel equal parts ill-used and miserable and a fool right now, and have no wish to be forced to some punishment or humiliation to make amends. You'll slip in by the kitchen door again, but first you skulk up to the windows to peer inside.

Your family's front room is crowded. The big table's been fully extended and Sir Peter holds ebullient court at the head, looming over all. Gerald hulks beside him, and on his face is a look you recognise from your own attendance at various onerous but unavoidable gatherings. In the leaping light of the hearth you can't see any sign of a bruise, and perhaps that's because of the thick skin of ogres, or because their magics can banish such blemishes. And further down the table are the beaters and the rest of Sir Peter's staff, all riotously tucking in to the end of the meal—just the bread and the vegetable stew and the fruit and such human food. The flesh, the bones that Sir Peter is even now gnawing at, they are for the ogres alone.

And a fine selection of your neighbours, though they mostly seem very subdued, picking at plates barely touched, no conversation between them. Except for

Farley Baker, a man your father never could be getting on with, though his is a family too prosperous to exclude from gatherings such as this. Farley sits up close to Sir Peter and guffaws at every ogrish jest.

You don't see your father, but it's late. There are several empty chairs with only the whiff of excuses made to explain them. He does not relish revelry, preferring to do the accounts or read some new ballad sheet or play artless music on his viol.

Time for you to face the music, but you'll do it by degrees. No bursting in like the prodigal for this son. So you sneak round the back of your own house as if you were one of Roben's men for real. You spend a long time waiting by the kitchen door, listening for the sound of any final preparations by Castor, any sweeping up by your nephews or cousins, but there's nothing. Safe, therefore, to creep in, and the door's never barred anyway.

And in you creep, silent as you like, and you're in a familiar kitchen occupied by unfamiliar scents of death. Because nobody prepares meat in here, absent an ogre to feed. The air reeks of blood and, more distantly, of offal. You feel as though you're entering dangerous territory suddenly. You pause by the table and take stock.

A deal of cleaning for someone, and you suspect that might be you, part of your punishment. Well, it's a miserable chore, but you'll do it gladly, if it will expiate a sin or two. No joy to mop up the blood or take out the bones to bury, certainly. You'll need gloves to the elbow and doubtless you'll still end up with weals and red blisters where too much of the charnel remains come into contact with your skin. But these things fade.

Sir Peter's people have brought in two ice boxes, another piece of ogre magic. From one, the buck's head stares glassily up at you through a pale mist of cold air. A trophy for the wall, to join the doubtless hundred others. Sir Peter loves his hunting. You've heard, via Roben, via travellers from other villages, that he's always after importing ever more exotic beasts to his woods. Everyone knows someone who knows someone who heard of a village wiped out by some gigantic long-toothed cat, or a lake no man can fish in because of the crocodiles it was stocked with. But those places are far away and most likely fictitious. Here there is no worse than boar, though a tusked pig that comes up to your shoulder is dangerous enough.

The tabletop is a disarray of bones, those that didn't get served up with the meat. You stare at them dully, feeling your restless gorge try to rise.

Food for ogres, not for men. You never picked apart a roast fowl or watched your father carve a joint. You know death, though, and bones. You grew up on farms. You've seen a lost sheep after the crows have been at it a while. When you were twelve, you and some other kids dug up old Henders' lost calf after it had been in the ground a month, just out of ghoulish curiosity. And one of Roben's men killed a deer last year and boiled its bones and tried to carve them. Gave up because of what it did to the skin of his fingers; but even so, you know bones.

There are ribs, there on the table, and a spine and pelvis. Not the limbs, not the head, but you know. Nothing that wore those bones inside it ever walked on four legs.

And your gaze strays towards the second ice box, the one without the antlers clearing its rim.

Ogres have appetites, everyone knows.

You remember Sir Peter cracking a long bone for its marrow, in your family's front room, at your table. And you remember it a certain way, at variance with the truth. Because, despite the stories children tell each other, ogres don't have tusks and fangs, just bigger teeth than people, to go in their bigger jaws.

And when you jerk away from the table, a whiplash of revelation going through all of you, Gerald is there, ducking low through the door. How did he know you would be here? There's no surprise on his heavy, handsome face. Perhaps it's that you and he are so alike, the disaffected sons of your communities' respective leaders. Rebels who are yet indulged in your little rebellions. The golden boys of very different households. If you'd been born an ogre, you'd be something a bit like Gerald. If he'd been human, he'd be, if not you, then your dark twin: all the same mischiefs but with a heart of cruelty behind them that was never yours. So perhaps you're linked, you and he—he your vast shadow, or you his dwarfish one—and when you stepped back across the threshold, he *knew*.

Or he just saw you peering in through the window. Less mythic, but more rational. Take your pick of explanations.

He's grinning, and when he sees you've just about worked it out, that grin gets so wide you half imagine the top of his head just falling off.

"I bet you thought," he tells you softly, "your father had missed the feast. But never fear, he's there."

Frozen, you stare at him as he pads across the kitchen, looming round the table.

"You see what you did?" he asks you pleasantly. "You *struck* me, boychild." Right in front of you now, filling your whole world, shoulders against the ceiling beams as though one great flex would crack the house in two.

"Dad was in two minds, but I said, 'No. Zero tolerance. We can't let the monkeys get away with it. There's only one way to teach them their place.' And since you'd run away like the coward you are, who was left to pay the price but your dear old paterfamilias?" He lingers over the unfamiliar word, its meaning only coming to you from context.

"They said you'd have to move out of the big house. They're making one of the other monkeys headman for now," Gerald says, conversationally. He could snap you in half. You're easily within his long-armed reach. His breath reeks of beer and flesh. You have no strength in you. You've brought all this about. Just like every other occasion you misbehaved, your father has set things right. He's given his all for you, this one last time.

"But I had my father tell them that, give it a couple of years, I want you as headman after all," Gerald almost whispers. Almost like a lover, because he *is* loving it, your stricken expression, his power over you. His revenge. "I want it to be you when I come here on my own for the taxes. I want you to feast me in that room, and bow and scrape. And remember what you did. I want you to smile when you do it."

He's leaning full-length over the table now, his face right in yours and the woodwork groaning with the weight he's putting on it. He's about to tell you to go with him to the front room, to take a seat at the feast. It's not something you could ever do. And that smile just keeps getting wider, and perhaps that serves as the final spark.

Your temper, which had been doused ashes through all of this, is abruptly aflame like never before. You shake. You see red. It's not even a need for familial vengeance that moves you. It's the shame. It's your own self-condemnation. Action is the only way you can even start to erase it. You, the meagre human, the village boy; him, the Landlord's son, the ogre. He could snap you like kindling in those huge hands.

But those huge hands are on the table, and his weight is on them. No sudden moves from him, all out of balance as he is. And Castor the chef has left the tools of his trade scattered about for his minions to clear up after the feast.

In the midst of your father's ruined ribs is a cleaver, and at once you have it up and buried in Gerald's face with all your might. And Castor keeps an edge on that steel; even after a day of hacking bones it's razor keen. The ogre youth rips back his head and gives out a muted sound for all the world like an ox in pain and you have the gleaming blade drawn back and the second slice cuts him a new smile even broader than the first, ear to ear across that conveniently bared throat.

And then you are gone, fleeing the charnel kitchen, fleeing the house, the village, running for the woods with blood in your eyes and on your hands.

CHAPTER THREE

THEY AREN'T EXPECTING to see you again so soon, Roben's people, still less so bloody and in such disarray. You'd run all the way to the treeline. And right then there isn't any will in you to dissemble. You are stripped down to the bones of who you were. What came from your mouth was more confession than anything else. The ogres had killed your father. Your actions had killed your father. You had killed an ogre.

Stunned silence from them. And then... a medley of reactions; quite the range, now you think back on it. Because some still have that core in them, hammered there by church and village life before they did whatever each one did to make them outlaw. Some are shocked that you could even lift a hand against the Masters, let alone shed so much of that vast reservoir of blood that it might kill one. Taboos like that, beat into you from earliest childhood, they don't get shaken free so easily.

Garett, the oldest of them, is pale and shaking his head, and Nell Wilso sucks at her toothless gums. But some of the others, their eyes are lit up. They're the ones whose crimes were against the property, not of humans but of ogres. They lost that reverence, and maybe they've dreamed of doing just what you did every night since. And right then you're in no position to appreciate it, lost in a welter of guilt and panic, but it's the first time people look at you like that. Not fond, not exasperated. You're not the prodigal son or the lovable rogue right then. You're the hero who slays the monster.

"Serves the fucker right," says Manx Jack, one of the youngest and most bitter of the outlaws. "We should go there right now and do for the da what he did to the son. Show the fuckers right, we should."

But that is a step nobody else feels up to taking. Plenty of tales of gallant have-nots striking against those who still *have*, be they corrupt humans or the ogres themselves. But this band of ne'er-do-wells never went further than larceny, and that only around the frayed edges of a village's life. And even the tales don't go as far as seeing ogre blood on the floor. At least, not until this moment.

"Pack up everything that's worth it," Roben decides then. "We're moving, right now."

There's a chorus of complaint at that, but he speaks over them.

"Critch Hollow. We'd be headed there soon enough anyway, to winter over. It's no great hardship to bring the trip forwards. Garett, you're still friendly with the Widow Neris there, aren't you?"

"If she's still living," the old man admits.

"Then let's hope she is, for it's like to be a bitter winter. But we move now, because they'll have every man and woman searching the woods for Torquell before dawn and we cannot be here."

And your head was full of your own problems, and you never thought of that. In coming to Roben, you've daubed every one of his band with the red of what you did. Should Sir Peter and his beaters come, with a mob riled up from the village, how would they be treated? Hanged from the trees that were their shelter, every one of them. Another lance of guilt to ram into your innards. But Roben is all business, kicking and sweet-talking his people in turn until they're all in motion, gathering their blankets and bedrolls and makeshift tents, what food they've not eaten, what spare clothes they've scrounged from washing lines and out of untended windows.

And you stand there, at the periphery of all this activity, head still churning like a sick stomach, unable to think straight. You vomited the story right up for them, and yet it's still inside you. And you realise it always will be, and you'll always feel like this when you think on it. You've made a new part of yourself tonight, forged red hot in anger and then pressed to your flesh until it's melted its way to your bones.

And then Roben looks at you and says, "Well come on, then."

Later, you understand what a grand thing that is for him to say. That despite the lack of it in his face, he was more of Manx Jack's mind than old Garett's or Nell Wilso's. "You've earned your outlawry, boy," he says. "You need no prating elder to tell you you've no place in a village anymore. And you know full well it's a hard bastard life, but what've you got else?" And the expressions on the others are that same mixed bag, but none of them is going to gainsay Roben right then. And it's as simple as that, how you became an outlaw. One of a variety of skins you'll wear throughout your life.

AND YOU HAVE no blanket or bedroll, though at least your clothes have fewer holes than theirs. But you have strong arms, and despite your usual high opinion of yourself—currently overturned, but it'll be back—you've never been averse to using them to help others. You carry a big stack of firewood over your shoulder, and you carry the pack of whoever's most in need of it. You make yourself useful, because right then you have a dire need to do anything that will shave away at the gnawing guilt inside you. And some nights on that trip, your dreams find you back in the kitchen. And some nights, in dreams, you not only see the all-too-human bones, but look into that second ice box too. And your father's face looks back. Another trophy for Sir Peter's wall to go with the bucks and the boars.

Sometimes you whimper half the night, and once or twice you wake screaming and thrashing and trying to kill Gerald all over again. But you're not the only one of the band who has memories that won't go away, and the others curse you and cuff you but only half-heartedly. And the travel is hard, through the woods and off the tracks, and a lot of the time you're so tired that the dreams can't get to you at all.

Critch Hollow is a place you visited once with your father, when you were much smaller. You remember the journey, by ox-cart and with a whole delegation of villagers. Someone was getting wed, some girl of your parish. You remember good food and dancing and getting to stay up late. Critch Hollow as an outlaw is nowhere near as fun, and by the time Roben's band takes up residence in the nearby woods, the first sniff of frost is in the air. A hard winter, he says, and he's been at this life long enough to know.

The salvation of the band is the Widow Neris, still very much alive. She's a tough old bird living on the far outskirts of Critch with a daughter and a granddaughter and a couple of foundling girls she's taken in. And there's precious little *frail* in that *old*, and the girls are all broad-backed and strong-armed from farm work, and if Roben's band intended mischief it would be an even match, you reckon. The Widow Neris does indeed have a soft spot for old Garett, though, and a warm bed for him too. The outlaws get a haybarn to hide out in, and they earn their keep in what has obviously become an annual tradition. They never told you about this side of the life, around the greenwood fire near your home. Not exactly thumbing their noses at authority and living free in the forest. Not that you're complaining. Roben says snow's on the way, and a haybarn seems a fine thing to have the loan of after that news.

And you work. All of you work, with more or less enthusiasm. And as the largest and the strongest—and, until very recently, the best fed—you work the hardest, fetching water and wood, mending what's broken, painting what's peeled. And the Widow Neris lives far enough from any other stead and has enough feuds with all her neighbours that nobody comes calling to see how she's doing. Only her daughter and one of the foundling girls take a little cart into Critch every few days, the child being more personable than the mother. They come back with news and made-goods that Neris needs but can't craft herself, bartered for with bundles of firewood and medicinal herbs and trays of eggs from Neris's fine hens.

And you heal. Time gives you a month to heal before upsetting the course of your life again. Something of the old You comes back. The outlaws have taken to you because you don't shirk and because you start to put that lovable rogue act back on. One of Neris's foundlings is sweet on you, too, but the Widow has a hard rule about that kind of thing. No swelling bellies is her agreement with Roben, and he's made sure everyone understands it. Old Garret, who has his, cackles at the rest of you and tells unlikely tales of his nocturnal acrobatics and the Widow's appetites. And Manx Jack gets you on your own once, and tries to get you to go against Roben and go with the girl, willing as she is. He wants the vicarious thrill of it, you reckon, or else he thinks he might be next to get lucky once you've leant your weight against that forbiddance and weakened it. And, even though you've had some longing thoughts of a warm bed of your own, you tell him one warm night now isn't worth freezing out in the woods next winter.

And it is a hard winter, just like Roben says, and the snow comes early and won't leave. And firewood's still very much required, and so you and the strongest of both the outlaws and of Neris's brood all go your ways into the trees to gather what the canopy has left dry enough while the white clouds hold off, because nobody wants to run out in the middle of the next storm.

One time, already cold and hungry, the snow catches you, and you're trapped beneath the tree-shadow because it's a long walk across exposed fields to get back to the barn. You had no breakfast, and you've had no lunch, and by nightfall you've a hollow pit where your stomach was. You find a stream but it's iced over to the stones of its belly so you can't even fill your guts with chill water. And then you find the deer.

A young deer, this year's, and going nowhere. Skidded on the ice, you reckon, and its leg is broken hard enough for the bones to show through its skin. When you take up a stick, it's mostly out of pity. You crack its skull on the second swing, and that's all the mercy this world has for a deer with broken legs.

Perhaps it's the sight of the raw, exposed bone that sets the thought on you, but you build a fire next, all the wood you'd gathered repurposed for your own immediate survival. You've enough woodcraft that you pick a good hollow where the warmth will linger, and you bank up snow and fallen needles on all sides. And you carve off pieces of deer with your pocket knife and do your best to cook the meat, like you saw Castor do. And you're not Castor and this isn't a kitchen and you don't know the first thing about what you're doing, but you're starving hungry and the woods in winter are barren of anything that might feed you. And some is burnt and some is bloody, but you put your teeth to what's in-between and gnaw and chew, and spit at the foul taste. You force yourself to swallow it down, the skin about your mouth already stinging where the blood and juices touched it, and wait for the sickness.

Your stomach revolts in short order, but you won't let it. And perhaps its protests are more rooted in the strangeness than the true internal revolt you're expecting. You spend all night in silent argument with your innards, and every moment they let up, you go to the horrible, badly-cooked carcase and force another bite down your protesting throat. And at least it gives you something to think of beside the hunger. By morning, the snow's stopped and you gather more wood and return to the farm. And you remember. You beat the world. You did something they say people just can't do. Just as they say you can't kill an ogre.

You're just about recovered inside your head by now. The dreams don't come back often, though you'll never be wholly free of them. You can think on your father without wanting to die. You can think on Gerald without that cocktail of fear and hate and rage blanking out your mind. You have found a place with Roben's people. You're an outlaw, and that's your life. You tell yourself there are worse. Better an outlaw than a lackey of a monster like Sir Peter. Better an outlaw than a witless serf tugging your forelock as the Masters ride by in their gleaming cars.

And then you're coming back with another bundle of wood, hoping it's eggs for lunch, and there's an ogre at the Widow Neris's farm.

You drop, then you freeze. It's even odds that you might have frozen first and then stood there, out in the open, until that huge head swung round to find you.

It's not Sir Peter. This is a younger ogre, and even larger. The Widow Neris's house has two storeys, and the top of his head is level with the sill of the upper window. He wears a bulky vest and a heavy belt, both with many pockets and tools, and there's a long gun slung over his back. His hair is cropped short, but he has a savage claw of black beard jutting from his heavy chin. And he's alone, just the one ogre. No retinue of humans, no car.

Then something pads around the side of the house and you see he's not alone at all. One dog, and then a second.

You know dogs: the shepherds back home have them, and the other outlaws have often warned you that a dog is a vagabond's worst enemy, and to avoid any house that has a sign of one if you're on the scrounge. A dog, to you, is a working animal about waist high that keeps the sheep in check or barks at the unfamiliar hand on the shutter or a strange footfall outside the door.

These are something else. They come above the ogre's own waist, and to you, their heads would be level with your shoulders. Big heads, all jaw and jowl. They're muscular and sleek. Every movement speaks of the strength and speed of them. You fear those dogs like you've never feared a living thing in your life, even an ogre. Even your father when you made him really mad at you.

And you're away, firewood abandoned, scurrying low to keep off the skyline and heading for the trees. Abandoning Roben's people, but then what could you do? If they're at the farm, then the ogre has them, and if they're not, you don't know where they are anyway. Maybe they're already dead. Did you see blood about the chops of those hounds? Maybe the Widow Neris and her family lie torn apart, strewn through the rooms of their home. Because who is there to tell an ogre 'no'? Do you really believe there is justice for an ogre who kills a man, besides a harsh word and perhaps some tax or a fine? You do not.

And you know he's hunting you, and any harm he's done is on your head. And if you stopped and examined that thought, you'd realise it needn't be so. But you've no chance to stop because you're running too fast, and anyway, as matters turn out, you're right.

Somehow you'd almost forgotten what you did. The thing the ogres were never going to forgive. Of course they've been hunting you.

So you flee through the woods. You find a stream that's still more water than ice and you splash through it, because Garett once told you that's how you shake a dog that's after you. You look for trees to climb, only to abandon the notion the moment you find them. You run until you're stumbling tired and then you realise you're lost in the woods, deeper in the trees than even the outlaws go, and the dark is drawing on.

And there are worse things than deer and boar in the outlaws' tales. In the deep woods, where humans aren't likely to be met, the Masters have stocked the trees with special beasts for their special hunts. Bears, they say; wolves that are like giant dogs with teeth like blades. Or other things that belong to no kin or kind but are of themselves only, made by the sorcery of the ogres. Some of them were humans once, they say. Humans who offended the Masters with their laziness or their impudence, or just by crossing their paths at the wrong moment. Perhaps that'll be your fate. After all, what you did was much worse.

Still breathing hard, you look up and see the first dog.

It is like a shadow, a piece of the night come a little early. It pads between the trees, deceptive in its silence. Probably it had its nose to the ground all the way from the Widow Neris's place, but now its round eyes are fixed on you. It casts its snout to the canopy and howls in triumph.

You'd thought you were run out, but it turns out there's still some run left in you. Dashing between the trees, bouncing off them, tripping over roots and fallen branches, skidding through a sudden clearing where a circle of snow lies undisturbed by any tracks save yours. And the feet of the dogs behind you make no sound, but you hear their breath synced with your racing heart. You see them at the corner of your eye as they race to cut you off. And you run faster and faster, like that nightmare where all the speed in the world will not stretch the distance between you and your pursuers. In your head you're still looking for a stream to throw them off, even though they've seen you. You're still looking for a tree.

And there's a tree, and you throw yourself at the lowest branch and hook your elbows over it, fighting to haul yourself up by main strength. It's a desperate plan and it has no Part Two, but you don't even complete Part One because the lead dog has rushed forwards and its jaws close on your shin like a saw-toothed vice.

You scream, but for a moment you hang on. Then the dog puts its weight behind its jaws and the pain of your shredded flesh is too much. You come down hard and the dogs are at you, snarling, slavering, teeth clamping on your sleeves, your shoes, your hands as you bring them up to defend your face. You curl up to shelter the tender parts of you that they doubtless want to rip into. They pull you left and right with appalling force.

You're big and strong. You've always been comfortably aware of it. Perhaps that's what let you open Gerald Grimes's throat when any other human would have cowered and wept. But these dogs make a toy of you. And, at last, one of them has your arm in its bone-crushing jaws and the other has its clawed feet on your chest, barking like thunder right in your face so that your whole world resounds with it.

And this is a part of your hero's journey, like the rest. Every hero has their nadir that they must rebuild from. And you will always remember this fear, that turns your voice to a high treble of tremble and pleading, that soaks your trousers with your own urine.

Then the barking stops and your arm is released, though one dog still has its massive weight on your chest, keeping you down. Their master—their Master—has arrived.

He laughs, the ogre. His bulk slides into your view past the suspicious glower of his pets. You see his nose wrinkle.

"You stink of piss, monkey," he tells you. "Strip off."

Even then you protest, but at a signal the dogs are barking at you, both of them, right in your face, and you whimper and weep and end up naked by your own hands, freezing in the cold. And you think he'll call the dogs off then, but he sets them on you, feinting and lunging, snapping at your dangling genitals, barking and growling, until you're backed up against a tree, the bark scarring your skin, screaming for mercy at the top of your voice.

He lets the dogs rip your clothes apart in a vicious game of tug-of-war. You're given a blanket and he starts a fire with a bottle of some liquid that sets even wet wood blazing at a spark. "You run now," he tells you, "even the dumbest monkey's going to see you're not from round these parts, being butt-naked. But I don't think you'll run. You'll think of Catch and Tongs here, and you'll stay right where I put you." You learn the names of his dogs before you learn his.

He brings you back to the Widow Neris's house first of all. The Widow and her family are all still there, though terrified of what you've brought down on them. And you do feel a spark of relief, despite your fear and shame. They've not gone the way of your father; collateral damage of your temper and stupidity. There is some mercy in the world, just not for you.

The ogre eats them out of house and home. He has them kill the fattest hens and shouts at the girls about how to cook them. Half the rest of the flock go to the dogs, which he lets riot in the coop until they've had their fill of feathers and blood. He burns up their whole stock of wood to keep his feet warm at the hearth. He devours bread and cheese and mushrooms and most of the rest of the larder. You get crusts and rind, but by then you're hungry enough to eat anything.

There's no sign of Roben's people. They got out, you hope, rather than being dog-torn carcases piled out the back of the house. Then, long after dark, there's a voice outside you know, calling in quavering tones for 'Theo'. That's how you learn the ogre's name.

He goes out with the dogs and, because he's no fool, he brings you too. He doesn't want to run the whole chase again, however much fun he had the first time.

And it's Manx Jack, of all Roben's people the one closest to you in age and temperament. He's keeping a wary distance, hopping from foot to foot, but he's been bold enough to hail the ogre from his den. For a moment you think this is some rescue, that all of Roben's people and a hundred bold outlaws more will surround the house, slay the monster and save you. But it's not that. It's something meaner and more wretched.

"You said," says Jack, "you'd find me somewhere." He's wringing his hands together like he'll never get them clean. "If I told you, you said you... I can't take this life, sir. I can't take another year without a roof, without a place."

And Theo nods massively, staring at him. "I said that, did I?" And even then you're only just starting to understand that Jack sold you out. He heard word of an ogre on the prowl, from the girls most like, and saw the chance to escape the outlaw life he always professed to love.

"You think," Theo tells him, "there's a place in polite company for such as you?" And then the dogs are padding past him, full of murdered fowl but no less hungry for action despite that. And Manx Jack turns and flees, but the dogs are faster and, unlike you, Theo has no interest in bringing him in alive.

CHAPTER FOUR

YOU THINK THEO'S going to take you home, or maybe to Sir Peter, but ogres have their ways. Theo's art and profession is the bringing in of runaways like you, and he wants to have his full credit for the catch. Which means he's taking you further from home than you've ever been.

You've heard of the train. Nothing for humans, but the ogres use it to transport goods fast over long distances. Theo takes you to the rail, a gleaming silver line that cuts through the forest, the trees carved back from it twenty feet on either side with an eerie precision. You walk alongside it for some time. He's let you have your shoes, but other than that it's the blanket and nothing beneath it, so you're shivering and numb by then, and only the fear of the dogs is keeping you going. You can't feel your feet, and you know from Roben's talk that you may lose your toes and fingers, nose, ears... But Theo doesn't care and he says he'll have Catch and Tongs drag you by your dick if you don't walk. You're going to die, he tells you. They'll execute you for the murder, and they'll make it hard and painful and record images of it to show to other monkeys who might have ideas about raising a hand against their Masters. But it still won't be as painful as being torn apart by dogs. And so you walk.

The train goes by once, and you end up hunched over on hands and knees with your hands over your ears, because it is *too* fast and *too* loud and you never imagined there was anything like it in the world. And then Theo has you at the depot, a great building of windowless grey stone, with a whole tribe of people whose lives are in receiving boxes and sacks and putting them on and off the snaking carriages of trains. They have machines, like little cars with a great claw on the front, to lift and stack the crates and pallets they move around. You've never seen humans allowed to use that kind of ogre craft before. They stare at you fearfully, as though your mere presence might mean your doom will rub off on them. There's no sympathy in their ashen, sunken faces.

Theo throws you bodily aboard the next train when it screeches to a halt. It's not a transport meant for people, you can see. A long snake of house-sized containers, and a couple of enclosed compartments where the depot tribe stack their smaller items. That's where you go, huddled in your blanket and pinned by the baleful stare of the dogs. When the train gets up to speed you half expect to black out from the sheer noise and fury of it, but somehow inside it isn't the same. As though it's the world beyond that's been unlocked to rush away from you, and you're at the still centre of it.

Theo's looking at you. Not a mean look, perhaps even a bit of humour in it. You've not looked him in the face before, but now you dare it. Like most ogres, his monstrosity is purely in his size: your head comes about to the middle of his chest and even for one of the Masters he's massively built. He meets your timorous gaze and smiles, and you see he has tusks, just like kids always say ogres have; just like they don't have, except he does. He just loves your reaction, has been waiting for it. Much later, you get told he had them put in specially, grown there by ogre magic, purely to frighten human people.

"Been hunting monkeys a long time," he rumbles. "Not one like you, though." He sounds almost approving. For a moment you think he means the chase you led him, but he disabuses you of that in short order. "You run like shit. Thought you'd be more sport. A killer." He kicks out at you lazily. "Stand up. Lose the blanket."

You make to argue but Catch growls, deep and low, and so you're standing up and butt-naked save for your shoes before the ogre's assaying gaze. There's nothing prurient in it, just a professional taking stock, as though you were a fish that might or might not break some kind of record.

"Big enough monkey, though," he admits. "I've been after killers before. Not many, but some. A cook who poisoned his master. A nanny smothered a babe. Never knew a monkey that just up and stabbed a man to death." He stands up. "Fancy your luck with me, do you, monkey?" This is an ogre train, so he can stand up to his full height, his full breadth. "I give you my pen-knife, you'll open old Theo up and feed his guts to the dogs, will you?"

And maybe when they tell this part of your story, you'll make some dire prophecy, about how he and you will meet again, and you'll do all those things and triumph, like a hero should. But what you actually do is mumble and look away and tremble, and who would blame you? He's twice your weight and quick with it, and the dogs wouldn't just sit idly by. You and he have an understanding about exactly who has the leverage, and how little a knife would change that.

And he doesn't give you a knife anyway. Because he has to sleep some time, and maybe the dogs would stop you opening that broad throat or maybe they wouldn't. And even then, at your lowest ebb, you recognise that tacit admission of vulnerability. The strength of ogres is a grand thing, but with a good enough lever even a human can change the world, and a knife is a powerful lever, as Gerald Grimes found out.

"Did you kill the others?" you ask.

Theo's eyes widen a little. He wasn't expecting you to talk back. And if he'd killed Roben and the rest, he'd be boasting of it right then. They got away, then, and likely Manx Jack was good enough to warn them of the company he had coming round. "You didn't bring Jack in," you add. "The man your dogs killed."

"No bounty on him. But you are the golden monkey-king of fugitives. You've made me rich with your fucking knifework." He doesn't seem particularly sad that Gerald Grimes is dead, and you vaguely understand that it's not justice for Gerald that slapped that big bounty on your head. It's that you raised your hand against the Masters. The crime that got your father rendered down and served up in your stead; that you then repeated and magnified. You stepped out of your place in the world, the role the pastor always droned on about, which that hymn immortalised. *The Master in his castle, the poor man at his gate...* Your offence was not against just the ogres, it was against the ordered universe. And perhaps for some that thought would inspire dread and shame, but you're a hero and heroes are supposed to transgress, to rise above their native estate. You feel a stab of pride that you have earned a special death. Perhaps the ogres will remember you and your knife, when you're gone. Perhaps ogre children will tell each other of the murderous monkey who might come for them. Or else they'll execute you in such a grand and hideous way that your death will expunge your entire life and be the only thing anyone ever remembers about you.

You sleep a little—the train is warmer than the winter outside, at least—and then Theo kicks you awake because you've arrived.

Birchill Interchange is the place. It's somewhere several train rails converge, and there is a cluster of brutal, grey buildings there like the depot. They're built for ogres, but mostly it's just people scurrying in and out of them. There's another whole village-worth here who do nothing but keep the wheels of the ogres' world turning. It's not just goods, either, but ideas that come here to be ordered and disposed of. An 'administrative hub,' those are the words you learn later. And one thing that gets dealt with here is justice. One of the drab, grey buildings is a jail, temporary storage for bad monkeys. Temporary because nobody's going to waste the space and resources to keep a human locked up for long. Ogre justice doesn't wait around.

Theo drops you off there. He gives you into the hands of another ogre, shorter and stouter than him—only ten inches taller than you, perhaps, but far heavier. Theo obviously gets whatever he was promised and walks away whistling, Catch and Tongs at his heels. You get thrown into a windowless grey room and locked in utter darkness. The only improvement to your circumstances is they give you clothes, bright yellow and marked with black triangles so, should you ever get out, everyone would know you instantly for the criminal you are.

The next day, Sir Peter comes to see you. And you're a long way from his estates, but of course the ogres can travel swift as the wind when they need to. That stately progressing from village to village was just him indulging himself. Probably he's had a carriage on a train to himself, or used a flying machine to skip across the world until he came to Birchill Interchange.

You've been dragged out to a bigger room. They've put metal cuffs on you, locking your wrists behind your back. Humans did all this, not the squat ogre in charge. He doesn't get his hands dirty touching monkeys, but he has a staff of hard humans, like Sir Peter's beaters. And they beat you when you won't cooperate. They write bruises all over your skin with their truncheons until you let them bind you. And you're bigger and stronger than any of them, you realise. As though living here without the sun and the open sky, right in the ogres' shadow, has shrivelled them up. But there are many of them and they hold you down and beat and kick you until, when you come bound before Sir Peter, you feel like half the execution's been done already.

Sir Peter stands over you. You wait for the rage, the frothing. You see the clenched jaw, the throbbing vein at his temple. He has his stick, his knuckles white about the head.

He beats you. We won't dwell on it. Had it been Theo, younger and more massive still, there would have been broken bones rather than just a mosaic of bruises laid across your skin, and perhaps there would have been death. Had he been mad with grief, a father for his son, then perhaps the same. But the beating Sir Peter gives you is almost clinical. He lines up each stroke and keeps his anger on a leash, like Theo's dogs never needed. A lash of agony across your arm or leg or back, and then a contemplative moment as the echo of your cry batters about the close walls of the room. And then another, where you're least expecting it, but precise. And you understand even then that he's making sure he doesn't rob the executioner.

And on the eighth blow the stick comes down across your thigh and snaps when its end strikes the hard ground, and Sir Peter stands there and you share a look, the two of you. His eyes flick from you to the broken cane and it's almost as if he's going to laugh at the absurdity of it, and expect you to join in.

He leaves then, with the air of a man satisfied for now, and you assume they'll make an end of you immediately, bruises and all. But there are ogrish wheels working behind the scenes, slow and sure, and your captivity drags out the next few days. And Sir Peter isn't the only ogre to come and see you.

Mostly it's lone men, but sometimes they bring their wives. One even has a brood of four ogre children along, monstrous chubby cherubs the size of a grown man. Unlike Sir Peter, who had honest parental grief as his grievance, they come to gawp. They come to see the human who would dare shed the blood of their own. As Theo said, you're special. And they spit at you. They sneer. They tell each other in loud voices how you'll meet a suitable fate, treacherous vermin that you are. And, although they don't mean to, they give something back to you that Theo and his dogs and the chase took away. You accomplished something they hadn't seen before when you struck back at Gerald. You cracked the foundations of their world, and behind all their jeering and laughing and spite is just a little thread of nervousness.

And in the midst of all of these comes the Baroness Isadora Lavaine.

You don't mark her much at the time, but you'll know her soon. If anything strikes you, it's that she's the only ogress who comes alone, with no chaperone or husband. A mountain of a woman, statuesque and grand, wearing a long coat of ivory velvet and spike-heeled shoes. Sir Peter's wife never travelled with him on his taxation rounds. You've not seen much of ogre women before. Isadora: with her great tide of dark hair, the hard lines about her eyes and mouth, the sheer mass of her.

The next day, though, after the gawpers have been and gone, it's Isadora you're brought before. And not just her. There's another ogre there, a great mutton-chopped monster of a man, as wide as Sir Peter and as tall as Theo, wearing a suit of gleaming grey and a red cravat. He is, you soon understand, some sort of ogre official. There aren't many, because they tend to devolve that sort of bureaucratic chore to their human minions, but sometimes a decision is required that carries responsibility, and that is something the ogres reserve for themselves. Although not for the grand amongst them, is your impression. The suited ogre is sweating and unhappy, and it's because he has Isadora on one side and Sir Peter on the other.

You stand there with manacled hands, and the three ogres lounge behind a long desk as big as two carts laid together. They've brought you in specifically so they can discuss you as though you aren't there.

"He does seem a powerful physical specimen, for an Economic." Isadora gives the word, which you've never heard before, special emphasis. She stares at you keenly. "Can we have him stripped, warden?" At the two other ogres' looks, she smirks. "Purely in the interests of research, gentlemen. And he actually killed your son in an altercation, Peter? Not just slit his throat when he was drunk?" Beyond the details, the fact of Gerald's death seems to matter not at all to her.

Sir Peter stands abruptly, face purpling with rage as it never did when he was beating you. For a moment he chokes around a response, and then Isadora actually laughs politely.

"Well, then," she says. "I simply must have him."

"That is… irregular," says the warden awkwardly.

"Nonetheless. You know I have the authority." And then she says, "*Droit de science*," which you don't understand then, but will in time.

"I protest," Sir Peter gets out. "We must make an example of him." He makes aborted gestures at you, trying to find the words for something so obvious it shouldn't need saying. "For the other monkeys."

"Well exactly," Isadora drawls, her eyes still roving over you. "And don't you think we need to find out why our golden boy here has done what the Economics"—that word again—"aren't supposed to. Quite the aberration. I need blood samples, psych evaluations, all the fun of the fair. I am, gentlemen, *intrigued*." Her voice is light and full of whimsy right up until the point it collapses to a steel edge. "And when I am *intrigued*, I get what I want."

"No," Sir Peter spits out, as the warden vacillates.

"Why, Peter, it's almost as though you're desperate to

repay your father's debts," she says sweetly, and he goes such an unnatural, angry colour you think he might die there and then, but instead he just storms away, leaving her with the warden and the field.

"Have him gift-wrapped," she says, "and sent to my VTOL." *Vee-toll*, you hear, and don't understand. "I'll take full responsibility."

And that is that, your fate decided.

BY THAT EVENING you're at her estate, from one windowless cell to another. You'd thought the train was serious ogre magic, but she carried you to her home in a flying machine that screamed all the way and left your head ringing with its agonised voice. You lay on the floor of its belly, and Isadora sat there with ear guards on. And so did the three humans, one man and two women, that were her attendants, while another controlled the machine.

Three more days you're in that cell, manacled save when you eat or void your bowels. The lights are always on, though you're so tired and hopeless that you still sleep most of the time. They daub the dog bites with stinging potions. They come and needle out tubes of your blood, snip swatches of hair, scratch at the inside of your cheeks. You think it's punishment at first. The people who inflict this on you are neat, white-clad. They talk to each other in brisk, efficient voices using words you don't know, and treat you like a thing. And you think of livestock back on the farm, and how sometimes they were sick. The old women and men who knew about such things would take samples of their dung and their piss, look into their eyes and at their tongues. So that's what they're doing with you. Finding out what's wrong with you. Not for a cure, but so they can make sure the same defect doesn't happen in other people.

And then they come for you, on the fourth day, and their manner is different. No needles, no swabs, no little containers for your bodily fluids.

"Dress," says one of them. "The Mistress wishes to see you." The clothes are white, like theirs, tight across the shoulders and short at the cuffs. And if you'd been your old bullish self, perhaps you'd have scattered the three attendants like ninepins and gone bowling around Isadora's home, battering at the windows for a way out like a demented fly. Poor food and Sir Peter's stick have done sufficient damage that you dress meekly before their clinical gaze. And then they lead you out and up some stairs, and you're in a grand house where the midday sun streams in through the windows to blanche the geometries of the art on the far wall. And the light brings something back to you that was missing since the dogs had you in their teeth, so that, when the attendants bring you to Isadora's presence, there's a bit of the hero returned to you, stepping into the monster's lair.

And it's a great hall, one wall a vast window looking out on a tangle of other buildings, squat and unlovely like Birchill Interchange had been. One thing you'll learn about Isadora is that she doesn't care much for the sculpted parks and grounds of other ogres. Her estate is designed to *do* things, rather than just act as a multi-acre demonstration of conspicuous consumption.

She sits at the big table at one end of the hall, beneath a bizarre picture that you'll spend a long time staring at, on and off over the coming years. At first you think it's surely drawn by a child. There are lines crossing other lines, people drawn with eyes both on the same side of their face. There's a cow in the same style, and at first you almost laugh at it. And then you don't laugh, and a strange, cold feeling comes to you, staring up at it. Because it's a terrible thing. A record of a terrible thing. There is agony and grief in the lines of those strange, misproportioned figures. You want to shy away from it and yet your eyes won't leave it alone. Eventually their only possible refuge is in looking at Isadora herself.

She beckons, and you walk down the length of the room, around the long low table where a score of humans are sitting and eating—in the same room as their betters, no less! They are all wearing the same white uniform. Some wear spectacles, which you saw on an ogre once but never on a human. They are mostly women, just a handful of men amongst them. They watch you curiously, taking in your rough strength that no more belongs here than a bull from your home pastures would.

The Baroness Isadora Lavaine leans forwards on her elbows to look down on you. Tower over the menials as much as you like, she'd still be head and shoulders taller if she stood, and over a hundred pounds heavier. Her vast wealth of gleaming dark hair is coiled up atop her head, secured with long pins and adding another six inches to her height.

You stand there like a dumb thing, mouth open, eyes dancing from her to the picture to the servants' table. "Welcome, Torquell," Isadora tells you. She has a sly, measuring smile you'll become more than familiar with, from the many, many times in life that she gets her own way. Over you, over other ogres, over the world. Better that than the sour look her face lapses into otherwise, because of all of her kind, Isadora is not content with the ways of the world, and she'll trample over every institution and rule to change it.

"Is this a trick?" It's all you can think of to say. You look so lost. All your life in the vicinity of a single peasant village under the rule of Sir Peter Grimes, who cares only that his peons contribute to his perfect little agricultural yesteryear, and now this.

"False hope before the execution?" She laughs, like genial thunder. "Bit much, just for you, don't you think? No, dear, that's off." Pronounced with an exaggerated emphasis. *Orff*. "I've got more than enough clout to overrule Peter fucking Grimes any day of the week."

And you stammer out a question that would be impudence enough to have you whipped, back where you come from. You ask who she is.

Isadora grins and singles out a young woman sitting at the head of her staff table. This worthy stands up smartly and announces, "The Baroness Isadora Trenchent Lavaine, Doctor of Natural and Unnatural Philosophy." It's a joke between ogres, you understand later. Or at least a joke at the other ogres' expense. Isadora doesn't rate her fellow Masters highly.

"And you, young Torquell, are an intriguing little monster," Isadora of the grand titles informs you. "And so I have decided to snatch you from the jaws of death and keep you around. Welcome to my staff."

CHAPTER FIVE

AND THE SUGGESTION of ownership perhaps engenders a little jolt of opposition in you. If you'd been the lad you were before Sir Peter's visit—so full of yourself and full of mischief—then maybe you'd have said something unwise to Isadora's face. But that was before Gerald; that was before Theo and the dogs. Right now, you've had something of that lad beaten out of you by fate and the ogres, and you just take it, to all outward show. But inside you, something still sparks rebellion, as later events will demonstrate.

But for now, and for years to come, you're of Isadora's household. Because you've got nowhere else, no going home for you. Because it's better than standing naked before the hounds, covering your shrivelled manhood and shivering in the winter air.

You take your place at table and eat unfamiliar food. The others make room for you, cast sideways looks. This isn't a band of roistering youths from the village whom you'll naturally rise to lead. They aren't like any people you ever met before. Isadora has precise requirements as to who she'll accept on her staff. Requirements that, you soon work out, should exclude you entirely.

You have your letters; your father was insistent on it, and despite a history of truancy and malingering you were actually a sharp enough student. The pastor and the schoolmistress were able to give you reading and writing and maths by dint of patience and cursing and words with your father when your focus slackened. But the white-coated women and men—and you work out very quickly it's the women who come first in Isadora's retinue—have an education beyond anything you ever dreamt of. They understand magic.

The first thing they understand about it is that there's no such thing as magic. They have other words for the marvels of the ogre world. Moreover, they understand how to make those marvels, are actively engaged in finding more marvels yet; all under Isadora's guidance, the Mistress of all that is marvellous.

They do not approve of you. They are entirely polite, but you are not of their order or sorority. They were all hand-picked for both the quickness of their minds and their industry in putting those minds to use. The former is something you can probably lay claim to, the latter not so much. Things always came easily to you, and so you never really worked at them. You never had that soaring ambition to take the world apart to see how it worked. And nobody is slowing their headlong rush so that you might catch up. You're welcome to learn, seems to be the ground rule, but Isadora's interest in you isn't because you're a monkey genius.

Chief amongst the staff, and your personal nemesis, is a young woman named Minith. She is small, neat, her dark hair cut short as with most of the staff. She is Isadora's lieutenant of marvels. You hear the other staff bring questions to her, but you never hear one she has no answer for, even if that answer is simply a suggestion about what to look for or how to investigate. Your own questions, that you are full of, go untended. The few you do try, early on, meet with utter contempt, as though you'd gone to a shepherd and cluelessly speculated as to where lambs come from. After that, you are so wounded by the reception that you mostly stop asking. Left to your own devices, you'd avoid Minith entirely, and away from her presence perhaps lure one or two of the others into some tentative friendship. She seems ubiquitous, however, supervising, spying on you, reporting to her Mistress. Or fetching you and bringing you to Isadora in the grand library, when the Mistress wants to see you. Which is often. She has many questions for you, as though she's going to compile some kind of history of your brief life and your longer genealogy. She has Minith stay and record your talk, both on devices that can speak your voice back to you, and with words written on paper. Minith plainly feels all this is beneath her, most especially that she is having to have her life orbit yours even for a moment. When she takes you out of the library, her glare suggests you are an insect, a pest she'd rather eradicate from the estate and grounds. And, because Minith feels that way, the rest of the staff avoid you. From being the centre of your village's social scene you have become a hermit. The only person you actually share many words with, in those early days and weeks and months, is Isadora herself. She is fascinated by you.

That, you guess, is what really riles Minith. That you are monopolising her precious Mistress's time.

Two months of this—of you kicking your heels in the corridors of Hypatian, the name Isadora has given to her grand house; of staring at the strange art that doesn't look like anything in the real world and yet somehow still fish-hooks emotions out of you; of getting the cold shoulder from the staff; of Isadora's sending for you every few days. Two months, and then you finally come to the crux because she asks you about the day Sir Peter came.

You tell the story, and find that you can. Your voice doesn't shake. Your father's death and that of Gerald Grimes are both told in the same flat voice. You even meet her gaze, look straight into her eyes as you say the words. You are determined not to give her the slightest window onto your grief, and enough time has passed since the deaths and the dogs that you are master of yourself.

"Hmm..." She eyes you speculatively, and then Minith moves forwards and attaches things to you—to your wrists, your temples, your bared chest, clinical and brisk. Clear rubber discs linked by wires to another machine.

"Tell me again." Isadora leans forwards, a few locks of her dark hair slithering out of place. Her tongue moistens her lips. "Tell me about when you came home, and what you found."

You tell her, and she questions you, and you tell her again. Her words stalk remorselessly about the barriers of your resolve until they find a crack, and then they work their way in like roots. The ice boxes; the bones; the realisation that you'd brought it on yourself. Gerald's mocking glee. Minith's pen records everything, as do the machines in their separate ways. And at last you stumble over the bland narrative, the retellings not coating the memory in a protective layer of shell as you intended, but rasping rough-tongued until it's all raw and exposed again. Until you feel the anger you felt then, at yourself, at the world, at the *Masters*. At *how dare they*. At the order of the world that let such things happen.

"Good," says Isadora, though you cannot see anything that is *good* about either what happened then or what is happening now. She is consulting something in a mirror on her desk. "Excellent. Torquell, you've been a darling boy."

And that's almost it. She's an ogress, after all, and you're no more than a monkey to her. Or an 'Economic' as she puts it. But something shifts in her face, then, as she looks on yours.

"I won't ask you to go through this again, Torquell," she says. "That's done with. I have what I need." It's not much, as sympathy goes. It's not hugs and consolation; it's certainly not an apology. But you have been an exile in this company for two months, and an orphan and a fugitive before that, and sometimes it only takes the slightest kindness.

You are crying before you realise, and you have enough self-possession to hate yourself for it, but some streams just can't be dammed. And she watches, and there's a certain amount of academic interest on her face—the machines are still recording, after all—but you see a little empathy, too. Uncomfortable, writ into the lines of her outsized perfection, but there nonetheless. And then she has Minith take you to go get supper, and Minith, of course, loathes every moment with you. Hates it that you have taken even a sliver of her Mistress's love, that which might otherwise have gone to Minith herself.

A while after that, you are fitted for some new clothes.

Not just a fresh suit of white that actually fits your heftier build, given that even the biggest of the staff is still several inches shorter and narrower, but a coat of green velvet with mustard britches, stockings, buckled shoes, shirts. Your hair is cut short and you get the smoothest shave you ever had in your life.

"She's taking you to a party," Minith tells you. By then, you've had enough of her, and the new clothes are a kind of armour against her scorn.

"Instead of you, you mean."

For a moment she just stares. It's the first time you've risen to the bait.

"Oh, I'll be there. Her Ladyship takes me everywhere." Not quite the brag you were expecting, just a statement of fact. Minith's face is closed and unreadable. "She'll have you standing behind her chair, waiting on her. You can do that, can you? And not disgrace us?"

You're aware of the practice, that the Masters must have their attendants for every little thing. You shrug. "We'll find out."

It's NO GRAND affair, this first time. Lady Isadora does end up at the great ogre gatherings, but her work is more important to her; she puts in an appearance only when there's advantage in it for her. So you learn later. Right now, this is as grand a function as you're ready for. A ride in the screaming *vee-tol*, landing on the roof of a great mansion, a room full of nightmarish animals stuffed into glass cases; five other ogres, vast and overdressed and unsparing of the wine. Isadora holding court.

She is magnificent. The thought surprises you. She is the only ogress, the rest are all men. They are all learned, magicians of the sciences that she practices. And you know by then that a great estate run by one unmarried ogress is strange, as is a staff that is almost all human women. Isadora is an eccentric, and by all rights she should be an outcast and a recluse. Except she plays the room like a musical instrument: flirts, teases, scorns advances, shouts over them when she needs to; dominates the conversation. And you understand very little of it, all that talk of base pairs and genetics and some manner of 'inheritance' which is plainly little to do with who gets which cow after the funeral. And eventually enough wine has sloshed about the room that they're mostly into anecdotes.

They are what your home village would have called sorcerers. Not in the way most ogres are, with all their machines and devices, but the real thing, the ogres who know the secrets of the universe and how to unlock them. You hear a vast barrel of a man with a beard like a thorn-bush roar with laughter as he describes the new birds he's bred that hunt better than any hound. ("Retrieved from extinction!" he cackles. "Dinosaurs next!" And the words mean nothing, not yet.) Another is talking machines and mechanics of some sort, a third speaks of pathways that are somehow inside the body and can be manipulated to conjure pleasure and pain. A fourth loves only insects and speaks of raising and quelling plagues, of places you never heard of stripped bare in the name of scientific enquiry. "All got a bit out of hand," he smirks, and they snicker along with him. Isadora—as drunk as the rest and yet still Mistress of what's said and who gets to say it—derides some, woos others, and laughs as vastly as the rest, head flung back so that her merriment echoes from the rafters.

"Is this," asks an old man, "the one you wrote to me about?" He's looking at you.

You don't look back. That is a thing you do not do with ogres. You did with Isadora, and somehow that didn't get you whipped or beaten, but you know enough not to try it with this one. He's the mechanics man, a mind of metal and wheels.

"None other." Isadora leans back and regards you fondly. At her beckon, you come unwillingly forwards into the massed pressure of their gaze.

"Robust little monkey, ain't he?" one of them remarks.

"An atavism, you say?" Mechanics-mind isn't convinced. "You didn't breed the fellow up on one of your test farms?"

"Why would you?" one of the others demands. "Who has any use for turning monkeys into gorillas?"

"The generals are always lamenting the quality of their troops," says the insect-master with a superior sneer, and there's much braying and snorting over that. Whoever the generals are, these educated men don't rate them much.

"Stuyfer would thrash him," says Mechanics-mind. "My man, Stuyfer. I'll lay a hundred pounds on it."

Stuyfer is brought forwards. He's a big, broad man, which is to say he's as broad as you but not as tall. He wears a dark coat, and he has a metal hand. He takes the coat off slowly—mechanically, you might say—and the whole arm is metal, sheathed in a plastic skin that is transparent precisely so you can see the workings. The skin where it joins his torso is scarred and angry. Mechanics-mind is explaining how Stuyfer lost the limb in the mills, providing an opportunity for the ogre scientist to experiment. Stuyfer's flat face is expressionless as his history and mutilation is discussed.

"What do you think, Torquell?" Isadora asks you. "Do you think you can take him?" Her face is flushed with drink, but there is a sly look there, not as abandoned as she is pretending for the benefit of her peers. And they're a little incredulous she's even asking you, and it's a curious shared moment, when it's you and her. You find that, before that braying crowd of other ogres, you want to make her proud of you. You nod.

They go into the next room and shove all the furniture to the walls, not even calling for servants to do it. The ogres sit around the edges and you and Stuyfer face off.

The fight is curious. You take several blows from his flesh and bone left hand, including one solid strike to the eye that almost floors you. You don't let that metal fist land, though, and Stuyfer never seems to understand that he could use your reticence to control the fight and dictate where you go. You've been in scraps plenty of times as a youth, and you're used to taking it and dishing it out. Stuyfer doesn't react when you hit him, not face, not gut. A kick between the legs that has the ogre lords wincing barely yields a reaction. The man is like a machine in more ways than one, and you're tiring and he's not. He's not quick, but he just slogs on like cogs and gears. Right then, it makes him monstrous, implacable, and you know you've made a mistake and sooner or later the steel fist will find a bone to break, a skull to crack.

Later, after you've learned, you realise the man must have been up to his eyeballs in painkillers and other medication, barely present in his own head, but right now his sheer lack of responsiveness makes him a terror to you.

The next time he lashes out at you, you feel the wind of it across your face and he smashes a hole in the wall, through panelling and plaster and denting to the stone. A shock of fear takes you, as you understand he'll kill you if he hits you. Even if he doesn't intend to, he'll kill you.

So you do the mad thing, the reckless thing, just as you've always ended up doing in your life. You close and grapple. You take that mechanical arm and you put all your strength to it, bending it against where it joins the living parts of Stuyfer. You twist until you feel parts of him give, as he slams you with elbow and knee and yanks at your hair. And in the end, your living limbs are stronger—not stronger than his metal one, but stronger than where flesh and steel meet—and you are left with the arm as trophy, and Stuyfer is on the ground. He screams now, and it's almost a relief; you feel it must even be a relief to *him*, to have an outlet for his pain.

"So much for your tuppenny Grendel, my lord," Isadora crows. "A hundred pounds, wasn't it?" And then, turning to you and looking at the many bruises already flowering across your face. "Get yourself to the kitchen. Tell Minith she's to patch you up. Tell her that's my order." Because she's well aware Minith has no love for you.

Minith is eating in the kitchen, with a couple of Isadora's other staff and a handful of the locals. She looks you over and scowls when you tell her what's required, but she goes to fetch the first-aid box anyway, giving you pills and painting restorative on your bruises.

"Can't have you looking ugly for Her Ladyship," she mutters. "You've learned a new trick, then? Learned to dance? Does beating another human make you feel useful?"

And you've had a rough evening, what with the machine-man trying to kill you, and you snap and grab her arm, a hard pincer that'll leave bruises of its own, and you ask her, "What is it? What have I done that you hate me so?"

She stares at you, frozen by the presumption of the contact. "Hate," she says, "is a strong word."

"Contempt, then."

"Yes, that's fair." No attempt to wrench herself free, staring at you, close enough to bite you on the nose and looking as though she's considering it. "You're a waste, Torquell. You've been saved from a peasant's life and a criminal's death. You've been given pride of place in a house of learning, a place that is unique, as far as I know, in any of the Masters' domains. And why?"

"I don't know."

"No, you don't. And you've never even asked. You've never *tried* to find out. You know what we do, in Her Ladyship's retinue? We ask questions. Questions about the universe and how it works. We don't just sit and listen to the pastor tell us it's God's plan. We *ask*. And if we found God we'd ask *Him* too. The big questions, that you've never even thought of. Why is the world the way it is? And how can we change it in the ways we want? But you? You've never asked those questions. You don't even ask the small questions, Torquell. You've not even asked why *you*. What's so special about you, that Her Ladyship lavishes so much time on you? The question that stands between your life and the gallows, and you haven't even thought to *ask* it."

You let her go. Her words have shaken you more than any blow that Stuyfer landed. "Do you know?" you ask.

Her expression is pitying. "Of course I know. I'm Her Ladyship's chief research assistant. She relies on me. There's precious little of her work and interests that I don't understand as fully as she does." A sneer. "But it's not for me to tell. And you'll never know because you don't know enough to even work out what questions to ask."

But her haughty tone has faded a little by the end, because she can see you're not angry or dismissive. You're not the arrogant brute she took you for when you were dropped all unearned into your place of prominence in her household. When she's finished tending to your bruises, you sit in the kitchen, munching a crust and thinking. And making plans.

AFTER THAT, WHEN not actually attending Isadora, you change how you spend your time.

And Her Ladyship does have you attend on her a lot. Most days, you're called to her at some point or other, just to serve. She likes you. You're a well-turned-out monkey, and you're closer to ogre size than any of the others. She has you fetch and carry, and she makes you run and lift. She borrows some servants from other ogres and has them teach you tricks: dancing, wrestling, boxing. You excel each time, especially in any task where a burst of sudden adrenaline gives you an edge. She makes notes and takes blood samples.

And when not called on, you read. There is a library, after all. Isadora has uncounted books. Most of them are impenetrable at first, but you badger the other staff and you roam the shelves until you find simple primers, bootstrapping your own ability to read, finding books full of words pinned down and anatomised until the layers of their meanings are pulled back. And pictures. You appreciate the pictures above all. At first it's hard, because your life so far has been one you could just charm and grin your way through, and books don't respond to that. But everything changed with Gerald and Sir Peter, and now you appreciate just what abyss lies beneath you, and you work. Perhaps even Minith is forced to admit that you really do apply yourself.

And Isadora takes you with her whenever she leaves the house, just as she does Minith. You're always being trotted out to show to other ogres, and you see what Minith meant. There is a *something* to learn about you. It's not just that you are a well-proportioned monkey, a handsome pet. And sometimes you have to fight other prize human servants, but by then your almost ogrish strength is enhanced by the trainers Isadora's found, and you always win. She wins money by the fistful and mocks the men whose champions you lay low in her name, and none of it matters. The numbers that change hands are not meaningful resources but just a means of keeping score. Once, she even wins a village, an entire stretch of land, fields, people, homes. All you can think is that surely Isadora is a kinder master than the red-faced sputtering ogre she took it from. You've spoken to the servants of many other masters by then, in this house's kitchen or that manor's back rooms. You've seen men who've been whipped, women with great bruises across their face the size of an ogre's hand, children who've been caned into docility and silence. Isadora's staff, selected for their minds, with you as the prominent exception, have privileges and freedoms the others would barely even dream of. You're starting to appreciate just how lucky you are.

And then you find a book which finally teaches you the right questions.

Not the obvious questions. Not the *why me?* question. You've had that on the tip of your tongue a few times, when Isadora's seemed receptive, but you've sensed that just blundering straight into it isn't the way. Instead, you have found *one* of the big questions. Minith would be proud of you.

You wait until Isadora is in an expansive mood, by which you mean she's already put away a bottle of wine. One evening, just the two of you, and she's talking about something to do with agriculture. You thought you knew farming, coming as you do from a village where every part of life revolves around the care and maintenance of field and flock. Isadora's farming is something beyond your comprehension, talking of pest control and modified strains and all manner of things. But she loves to talk and she doesn't really care how much you follow. Talking, you suspect, is how she unlocks her mind and circumnavigates barriers to her research. You're just a convenient sounding board.

And then, when she's finished her current tirade and has you over to pour another glass, you pluck up the courage to ask.

"Your Ladyship..."

"Isadora," she tells you. You, Minith, a couple of others are extended that theoretical privilege, though it's hard to force yourself to take her up on it. She's smiling at you fondly, though, the rosy glow of the wine warming her cheeks.

You teeter on the edge, knowing this will take you into uncharted wilds. You're very *aware* of her, the mass of her, the abundance. Her interest that, though mostly academic, takes a distinct pleasure in putting you through your paces when exercising or wrestling. You've heard stories from other households about the depredations of ogre masters, certainly. Thus far, Isadora has been content to just watch. But you are about to renegotiate your relationship, to make her re-evaluate you.

"I found a book," you say, like a confession. "There were pictures. Photographs," pronouncing the word carefully, "from a long time ago. Photographs of cities." Like the drab grey buildings of the Interchange but multiplied a thousand fold, off to all sides and up to the skies. "There were crowds of people there." Thousands of them, thronging the streets. In some photos, they were rioting, burning cars. In others they were protesting, holding placards, making demands. But so many. People beyond your dreams or nightmares. A vast field of people. And they were *people:* no ogres rose head and shoulders over them to take more than their fair space in that crowd. And you explain what you have seen and then throw yourself over the precipice and say, "I want to know how it could have been like that then; how it's like this now."

She laughs. It's not what you expected. She laughs and sits you down beside her on the couch, a shocking breach of etiquette, but then, the wine has been flowing.

"My inquisitive little monkey." She tousles your hair. "It's been a long time. I was beginning to think you'd not a curious thought in your head. Have you asked Minith this, and she refused? She's jealous of her learning, that one. Sharp as a pin, but not good at sharing."

You haven't, but only because you know full well Minith would give you nothing for free. Isadora sees the look on your face and laughs again.

"Those pictures were from when the world was in a very bad way, Torquell. The Brink, is what they called it, afterwards. The world was... well, a lot of it was poisoned, and there were far too many people, all of them eating and breeding and just... using up everything.

And there wasn't enough of everything. And it was only going to get worse. Something had to be done. We saved the world. Or our ancestors did, and now—peace and plenty." She sounds a little dismissive of the idea, nose wrinkling at the thought. "So much peace and plenty that it's hard to find an enquiring mind, and I don't just mean amongst the Economics. My peers, Torquell, are a waste of their genetic heritage. And I'd thought you were, too, but here you are asking questions." She pats your head. "Good boy."

"How was the world saved?"

She's still feeling indulgent, apparently. "People were eating too much, basically. Too many people, too many healthy appetites. And meat farming was monstrously inefficient. You must know how far livestock need to roam compared with a field of soy with the same yield." And you don't know, but there are books in the library that will tell you. "And my ancestors solved the problem and saved the world. I really mean that. My forerunners, those of my discipline. The engineers of the human genome. Because in the end, changing the world was too complicated, and left to their own devices people wouldn't change their habits, and so we had to change the people. Ever had a steak, Torquell?"

A memory of the dead deer in the forest comes to you and you flinch guiltily, shaking your head.

"There was a suite of genetic changes to make people into more efficient consumers. It was a bitter time, Torquell. Things were done… But it was in a good cause. Look at the plenty we have now."

"Changes…?"

"Turning a gene off here, turning one back on there. You'd be surprised how few modifications you have to make, and how easily you can engineer a microorganism to write those changes into the population. Changes to reduce the consumption footprint of an individual. Stop them being able to digest meat, that's a huge change. Oh, the cattle industry kicked, but so much land could be repurposed when the demand was gone, such an impact in and of itself. And science didn't stop there. I mean, there were so many things about people that were broken…"

Hurrying over the words before you can stop yourself, you blurt out. "There were no Masters, in those pictures. Everyone was the same."

Another smile, this one tugging teasingly around the edges of Isadora's mouth. "You think so, do you? Why do you think that is? Go on, Torquell, impress me."

"You… After they'd finished changing people to save the world, they used their powers to make you, the Masters?" You imagine those long-ago sorcerer-scientists, flushed with the fruits of their success, creating something greater than themselves, then being superseded by it. But you can see from her expression that you're not quite right. Isadora reclines back, regarding you slyly.

"Well, I didn't bring you here for your mind," she murmurs, and then, seeing you flush with shame, "but it appears you have one anyway. Perhaps you can be useful as more than a test subject. You can read. You have access to the books. I'll instruct Mirith to help you find volumes appropriate to your capabilities. Let's call this the first test of your brain, as opposed to just your fists and sinews. You find out the answer, about how we 'ogres' rose to rule the world, and then come back and tell me."

CHAPTER SIX

So BEGINS YOUR education.

The extreme reluctance with which Minith helps you is almost comical. Every time, she undertakes to demonstrate by expression, tone, and body language that she has a great many more important things to be getting on with. She is, after all, Isadora's chief assistant. The entire rest of the staff dances to her tune. But as it is her Mistress's wish, she does help you.

You discover soon enough that there aren't enough years in a human life for you to catch up with the science. You struggle through books intended for young students, and while Minith swears that the keys to the universe are concealed within, your fingers are too clumsy to fit them to the lock.

"The Brink," you tell her. "That's what I need to learn about."

She's startled. You've bearded her in the kitchens, the

rest of the staff sitting down to breakfast. You're both keeping your voices low through some implicit agreement that what you're about shouldn't be the gossip of the house.

"Not these amino-acids and base-pairs and pee-aytch." You're frustrated with your own limitations, hulking over her without meaning to, though she doesn't even deign to move back. "People. I want to learn about people and what they did. Real things."

Her contempt is back again, but this time you weather it. You know, in your own way, that you're right. It's not the actual technicalities of the science that matter, for you. It's the decisions that led to them. You're all about the big picture, and you've become aware that there is a very big picture indeed, buried in the history of the world, and everything in your life seems to have been thrown up to hide it.

"Histories," Minith says, as though it's a dirty word. "Apparently we have recruited a *humanities* student."

You continue to weather her passive aggression, and to keep a rein on your own more active kind. "And?"

The *and* manifests as a stack of books beside your bed that evening, and you resume your research. They're still dry and difficult and full of words you have to look up. Full of pictures of men and women in odd clothes. Of those close-packed buildings, and sometimes those vast crowds. And it's complicated because at the time nobody called it the Brink, of course. It was just *then*, to them. Just the way the world was. And it was bad, no doubt. People were starving, in various parts of the world. People had no clean water. An overabundance of humanity, and no ogres at all. Based on these histories, easy enough for Isadora or Minith to argue that the world now is so much better. Peace, as Her Ladyship said, and plenty.

It will be a long process, your pursuit of truth, but you are to be on Isadora's staff for over six years, and despite Minith's early opinion of you, you have a sharp mind and work hard. You will never master the science, but over the months your reading improves so that you need to look up strange words less and less. You plumb the pages of ever denser and more complex volumes to track down your quarry.

You have other duties, of course, because while Isadora far prefers to be closeted with her own work, the social demands of being an ogress still clutch at her. And none of the Masters would travel without staff to take care of their needs, and she always brings you with her, as her closest attendant. As a pet, you are aware. A performing monkey. And yet she is fond of you. When you attend her, some evenings, she invites you to talk about what you've learned. You speculate about what happened, and she smiles and shakes her head and encourages you to continue with your books.

Books are what prompts one memorable trip, in fact, when you've been in her service for a year or so. Isadora has a need for certain volumes held in the collection of another ogre, and furthermore she requires some new books created. Volumes lost to time, she tells you, but retained in electronic copy. And while she could read them on a screen, a method that you no longer think of as ogre sorcery, she prefers physical books. And, being the Baroness Isadora Lavaine, she is in a position to have them printed at her order.

You travel to a city by train. She has her own private carriage, and you believe she has chosen this manner of approach specifically to watch your reaction. Because it is a city like those in the books you've been reading. There are tall buildings, five, six storeys high, lining one side of the tracks. You see high chain-link fences with metal thorns on top, and narrow streets, and beyond them the chimneys of the factories and power stations. And people. Hundreds, thousands of people, all crammed into those buildings. There are women and children staring out dully at the train as it passes. Laundry hangs from great heavy strings overhead. In every window you see a woman at work: peeling, scrubbing, preparing food, darning. The men, Minith tells you, are in the factories. Or else they starve, because this is what she calls a 'company town,' and if you don't work then the company won't sell you company food in exchange for the company money they pay you for your toil. It is one of the ogres who owns the company, and its food and money and factories that Isadora is going to see.

There is the usual soiree, where a score of ogres gather together in a vast room and drink and talk. And there is a feast, an ogre's feast. You are behind Isadora's chair as usual, enduring the remarks of the other ogres about your unusually robust physique. There are some ogresses there who even eye you in a predatory fashion. Thus far, at least, Isadora has not commanded you to her bed, or even tried to seduce you—as though an ogress would need to. The possibility has been in your mind more than once, though, and you're not sure what you would feel about it, should things tilt that way.

And then the main course comes out, after seemingly endless confections of fish and pastry and meat, and it's defaulters' pie, whatever that is. A vast tableau of crust with bubbling gravy and meat underneath, and the ogres tucking in greedily and complaining that one end of the table or other is hogging the best pieces. And you do not understand and just stand there like a good servant, even though you see some of the other humans there—the Economics, as Isadora calls you—blanch. And only later does Minith cruelly explain that this is the last refuge of families with no work, or who fall foul of debts, or who cannot afford medicine, or have some other burden that regular wages will not lift. That, worst comes to worst, there is always something a human can sell, that an ogre can make use of. And Isadora eats with the same gusto as the rest and you remember that.

On the train back, staring out at those grey houses and the grey people who live crammed up in them, you have questions. And Isadora's happy to indulge you. Minith sits across the carriage, eavesdropping and doubtless resenting every moment her Mistress spends with you.

"Why all this?" you ask, gesturing out at the city with its sharp fences and close-packed windows. "There is so much land outside. There's food. The whole point of the Brink was that there would be more land and more food. Why do they have to live like this?" And more, the words tumbling out into an abyss with that dreadful defaulters' pie waiting at the bottom. "Why debts and wages and… things being expensive so people can't afford them, when science can make so much?"

Isadora's smile tells you it's a good question. "There's a theory held by the worthies who run the company— glorified boys' club that it is. They say that their workforce must be kept in such artificially straitened circumstances, with shortages and competition, or they wouldn't work. If you let the Economics be comfortable and happy and free of fear and want, then what if they just sat at home and did nothing? They say that unless you force people into a position where they must work or starve, no work would get done."

You think on that, and on what you've learned so far about Isadora's discipline and its foundations. "Have they proved this theory?"

Isadora raises an eyebrow.

"That's what you do with a theory, isn't it?" you press. You feel as though you're about to say something stupid at any moment, but the idea is so obvious. "Have they tried feeding and making people happy to see if they still did the work?"

Isadora laughed, and at first you think you have been stupid, but she's laughing at her peers, whom she plainly doesn't think much of. "You know," she says, between guffaws, "I don't think they ever tried. Funny, that."

BACK AT HYPATION you throw yourself back into your reading, and you remember the pie and the gusto, and there's a particular goad at your back, now, driving you on. It's an old thought, one that you can't imagine your father or the pastor or any of them, back in that insignificant little village, ever harbouring. It's watching Sir Peter arrive in his motorcade to receive the goods and tithes he never worked for, and everyone treating the visit as though it's such an honour. It's sitting in church hearing how God ordered the world to place a few on high with everyone else becoming the doting and obedient subjects of their benevolence, and being asked to agree that it was right. It's Gerald Grimes taunting you, and Theo the hound-master hunting you through the woods, not only because he's stronger and has the dogs, but because the world is designed to make him so. Who made the ogres, and how did they become lords of all creation? Because you read those histories of the Brink times, and all humans are standing shoulder to shoulder, and none in a monstrous shadow.

Injustice is what moves you. Injustice, that you were born to serve and scrape and, at the worst, go into a pie, and the ogres were born to rule and to gorge. And Minith keeps bringing the books with a sneer, safe in her position as Isadora's majordomo. No pie for her, after all, so why should she care?

And you find one book, written in a painfully dry and clinical style, talking of protests and riots, at the changes being mandated by what they call governments and corporate boards. People complaining at having their children changed, even though the world was at stake. In the book, it's cast as selfish and wasteful that anyone should resist such patently necessary measures. It was written post-Brink, after all, when these things had been accomplished and it only remained to justify them.

It was voluntary at first, you read. Those who signed up for the Economic Measures and allowed themselves and their genetic line to be modified were rewarded. They received some additional benefits from those who ruled. Later, they were stripped of whatever benefits they had unless they gave their consent. And the writer of the book applauds everyone who took that selfless step, to make their offspring into less wasteful, less angry, less space-consuming creatures. For the solution to being on the Brink was a whole suite of alterations. You already know that enquiring scientific minds like Isadora's can't leave well enough alone, and there's always something else to fix. So the old world turned and there was a new generation of perfect children who couldn't stomach meat, who were slower to anger and slower to argue. Happy people, the book insists. People without so much waste, without all that needless consumption. A race of people the world could support more readily. And from here on you'll understand, when Isadora says 'Economics.'

And in the end it came down to force and laws, and camps for those who hadn't consented to be part of the programme. With regret, the book insists. With care, with love. Camps, mandatory alteration, prisons. All with the best will in the world. All over the world. Because it was unthinkable that, others having made the necessary sacrifice, the selfish could live on unaltered. That, the book insists, would be unjust.

There is no mention of ogres. And you are picturing some rogue laboratory, some maverick scientist—whom you imagine with Isadora's face—deciding that they can make other improvements to the next generation; siring a brood of huge, dominating monsters with a taste for human flesh; unleashing them on an unsuspecting world that could not resist them.

You visit villages much like your own. Isadora, like most ogres, owns land, though she has lesser ogres to oversee it for her. Still, sometimes her presence is required and she reluctantly drags herself away from her work to do the tour. You stand in her retinue as she is greeted and feasted and fêted by one insignificant hamlet after another. You feel embarrassed by all those people, their bright ribbons and their singing children. Because to them this is all the world is, and you know they are a mote of dust in the world's eye. You are ashamed that your own origins are mirrored in their monkey capering. And when you look round you see Minith sneering at you, because she hasn't forgotten you're just a peasant either.

OVER THE YEARS, you become practically the house's librarian. Not of the science texts, which are still impenetrable, but Isadora has thousands of books on other subjects. You know that some are fictions, but others are histories and geographies and accounts, and you have combed these so thoroughly that you can lay your hands on any given volume someone asks for. Other staff actually come to you with questions. You are no longer the big, dumb yokel from the sticks. And Minith watches. She sits in on your conversations with Isadora, jealous still, no doubt, writing away at her own notes while you talk. She has lost her early contempt of you but maintains a distinct distance. Some people, you think, can never be won over.

And you are starting to become frustrated in your own search, because it's been years now. You've ransacked the library, and the bitter truth is that there were things the historians never wrote down. There is a shape in the middle of what happened at the Brink that nobody directly addressed.

You even talk to Minith about it, in the absence of any other options. She gives you a strange look and says, "Why do you think that is?" and you realise this, too, is part of the test. And she leaves a book by your bed—Minith being the one other person who knows the library as well as you have come to do—but it's one of the fictions, and what's the use of that?

One evening, two generals come to visit Isadora. They are big ogres, overstuffed in colourful uniforms blazing with gold braid and medals. They arrive on the backs of enormous horses and cuff and swear at Isadora's grooms. They have swords at their belts you'd need two hands to lift, and spurs jingling at their booted heels. Isadora plainly thinks they're ridiculous, but at the same time apparently they're powerful amongst the ogres. One is a duke, a very high rank indeed. They have come to discuss their requirements for the war.

You weren't aware there was a war, but apparently there is, and these two generals are currently losing. You attend your Mistress and hear them tutting over the ceded territory, the fallen soldiers. "Better stock," one says, "better weapons. We need an advantage, your ladyship, so naturally we come to you. Fine mind, eh? One of the best."

"*The* best," Isadora says, but quietly. It's plain these two clownish creatures are important, and she's on her best behaviour about them. Their moustaches bristle. Their staff look cowed and you'd bet those bright red coats conceal bruises and whip scars.

After they've gone, Isadora throws her entire staff at whatever the new project is. You ask about the war, but other than the general impression of appalling destruction and loss of life, nobody has time to talk to you about it.

Without anyone to act as your sounding board, you find yourself adrift in a morass of histories that are dancing about something in the past. In frustration, you take yourself off to one of the house's further rooms with the fiction book and read that. It is set around the Brink, you see, some romantic drama of the rich and powerful who were putting into place the changes that would save the world. Probably Minith thought it was factual, you think derisively. And yet you read it, not—you tell yourself—because you really care about any of those non-existent people, but because when you stop, your mind nags at you about what might happen next. Will the angsty daughter be happy with that troubled scion? Will the old uncle die, and who will inherit the house? And all through the narrative, the substrate on which all those fake people stand, is the story of the Brink. How the people of the world must be changed, if they are all to live in it without devouring everything like a plague of locusts (you have to look up what a locust is). The hard decisions made by those powerful people, about altering the very book of humanity. Making it a less expensive volume to print, so the conceit of the old writer goes. Cheaper inks. Fewer pages. The paperback edition.

At no time do any of those characters step from the page to tell you what happened, but somehow the writer does. And there is a spin to the words, when talking of the Brink and What Was Done. So that, though they never have their characters say 'This was a terrible thing,' their choice of phrase invisibly coats the scenes with a sense of guilt and shame.

You look up 'hardbacks' and 'paperbacks' and page count, and disentangle the writer's metaphors of a printing industry that no longer exists in that form. Fewer pages, they said. The concise pocket edition of humanity.

You understand where the ogres came from, after that.

AND THEN YOU go to war. Not, thankfully, as a soldier, but Isadora must travel close to where the fighting is, to deliver her new inventions to the generals. She doesn't relish the task, displaying not even her usual ill temper at being dragged from her work but a particular dread you've not seen before. But her retinue travel with her, of course, you included. You go by train, one carriage for you and the one behind loaded with reinforced barrels of whatever it is that she and her staff have been cooking up. There is little talk. The trains pass through miserable-looking villages, each consisting of the same house over and over in long terraces. You see children there playing soldier games, or else they are actually being taught how to be soldiers. They have sticks over their shoulders and march back and forth. These are the villages that the generals own and they only have one use for their people. The war needs bodies. When the rails run out, you travel in big armoured cars, stuffy and dark and cramped. You meet actual soldiers. They are just staff dressed in a different uniform, these ones bright red like poor copies of the generals' own. You have seen pictures of soldiers from before the Brink. In the photographs they wore drab earth colours so they could not be seen. In even older pictures they wore bright colours like these, though, so that they could. So that their generals could look across a battlefield and see immediately where everyone was and who was on which side. Since the visit of the two generals, you have been reading up on war. Many of the soldiers don't look that much older than the children you saw from the train windows.

Soon the cars are lumbering and juddering over land that looks like the war in the photos, churned up into mud and pockmarked with holes. The soldiers still look like those in the old paintings, though, even though their bright colours are smeared with mud. You are approaching what they call the Forward HQ.

The generals are there, the two from before and a handful of others. They have a big table that has been painstakingly modelled into a map of the war, and scattered over it are thousands of little figures of soldiers in different colours. Isadora and her staff are forced to wait while some great moustache-bristling discussion is held between them, about how to stem the recent reversals. The war is going very badly. Without some new advantage, it may be lost entirely, and then where would everyone be? You want to ask that exact question, but it's abundantly plain that the generals are not like Isadora and would not appreciate a mere Economic questioning them.

At last they turn to Isadora and demand that she tell them what she's brought. The gas in the barrels and the drugs in the canisters. To affect the enemy in new and lethal ways; to empower their soldiers to fight on without fatigue or fear. The generals are delighted. This could be the turning point of the war! Their opposite numbers won't know what hit them. Victory by the end of the year, what, what?

Because there's nobody else, it's Minith you're forced to ask. "Who are we fighting?"

"*We* aren't fighting anyone," she says derisively, but then she relents and says, "If you went about thirty miles that way, you'd find another building like this one."

"Right."

"And in there, you'd find another group of generals and another map table. Only I think that lot wear yellow, or maybe it's blue."

"Ogres?"

"Masters, yes. Of course." She's watching you carefully.

"Well then... what's the war about? What started it?" You've read your histories, about the complex skein of causes that wars arise from. "Why are the ogres fighting each other?"

But Minith is looking at you pityingly. "They're not," she says. "People are fighting each other. Because the Masters like their wars." Seeing your blank face, she says, "You know when Her Ladyship plays cards with her peers, Torquell?"

You nod.

"It's like that. Just like that."

That evening, the generals retire to their smoking room for brandy and—yes—cards and talk about how splendid this new phase of the war is going to be, and they insist Isadora accompany them, jostling over who gets to take her arm. You end up with the staff, again, only the local staff are all soldiers. Minith talks in a low voice with one older man, and you go wandering.

There is a lot of war detritus here, outside the battle proper. You get a young recruit to show you around. There are barracks where hundreds of soldiers are trying to sleep, packed in like goods in a train carriage. There is a hospital, where what seems almost the same number of soldiers lie in the same close conditions, only there are less of them—less of each one, mostly. Fewer legs and arms. And you think about that. There is an armoury where the guns are kept, because the soldiers aren't allowed to carry them until it's time to go off to battle.

You think a *lot* about that.

You meet an officer, standing outside the hospital. He's a surgeon as well, you discover, and his name is Bradwell; Captain Doctor Bradwell. He's smoking, which is something all the soldiers do. It helps with their nerves, he explains. Most of the soldiers have just looked at you dully, but Captain Doctor Bradwell has questions.

Where do you come from? What's the work like there? You tell him of Her Ladyship's service, and then you tell him about the mean, filthy peasant village you're embarrassed to have come from. He listens as though you're describing paradise.

"But all good little monkeys, no doubt," he says. "Never a thought of us and what we go through?"

"They don't even know," you confirm. And then add, "But I do, now."

You lock eyes, him looking up at you, and there's a moment of connection. "Don't forget us," he tells you, and you won't. "Tell them about us," he says. You won't do that either, but perhaps you'll do something better.

Later on, there is a commotion. Shouting from the room the generals have retired to. And then a quick gathering of staff, Minith running up to drag you away from your increasingly interesting chat with Captain Doctor Bradwell.

Something has happened and you're leaving. There's already a car waiting and Isadora standing beside it. Her fury is writ large on her face, but a fury she can't give rein to. You've never seen her in a position where she can't just do whatever she wants.

Not a word, in the jolting car ride back to the train lines. In the distance you hear thunder, and then realise it's the guns of the war.

In the train, Isadora drinks. She gets through a bottle and a half before she even speaks, and then she banishes most of the staff to the far end of the carriage, has you sit beside her, and only Minith left within earshot.

"Fucking war," she says. "Fucking little boys with their toys." For all that she's been making new toys for them.

"Did they… take advantage?" Minith asks, very precisely. For a moment Isadora's eyes blaze hatred at her trim little majordomo. Then she sags massively and shudders. You were trying to keep up with what happened, between her and the generals, but even back in the village you saw this sort of thing play out. A woman and a man, and the man strong or important enough that he's hard to say no to. Not a lever you ever applied your own weight to, though opportunity certainly tempted you. And you'd heard that both Gerald Grimes and Sir Peter had a reputation for just such things, although back then you'd never have even thought to criticise such dealings. They were the ogres, after all; the Master in his castle, et cetera. But you never dreamt that such strata of power existed even amongst the ogres, or that such a grand personage as Lady Isadora could find herself in a position where she couldn't say no.

She drinks some more, trying to wash away the memories, and then she leans into you. And you're strong enough, by then, to prop her up, and for a while she just rambles about how much she loathes the generals, collectively and individually, and what a waste the whole sham-war is. Although evidently she just feels it is a distraction from the true search for knowledge; she doesn't much go into the absent limbs of the hospital or the haunted look in Captain Doctor Bradwell's eyes. She talks about the 'proper use' of the Economics, the rational duties of a responsible owner. And then she prods you in the chest and demands, "Have you worked it out, then? All your reading. You must have, by now."

She's not really expecting an answer, already having you refill her glass, but as you hand it to her you say, "Yes."

Her eyes sparkle with sudden interest, a slice of her old mischief. "And?"

And you tell her where the ogres come from. Or rather, that they never came from anywhere. That all those histories of the Brink, lovingly detailing the hard decisions made by the powerful people, about how they would save the world, omitted one key element: that they excluded themselves from those measures.

"When it's consumption of resources that's the issue," you say, "then 'economic' just means smaller. That's us. You stayed the same."

She's smiling, and partly it's the 'good boy' response to a pet who can perform a new trick, but there's her old slyness there as well, because you're almost right, but there's one piece of the puzzle left over.

"A handful of genes to control height and size," she murmurs, slurring a little. "Easier than you think. A handful of genes to control diet, which proteins can be digested, which can't. That's trickier. Your father still enjoyed a boiled egg and a glass of milk, probably. Some bloodlines still do. Not"—she belches—"an exact science, quite. A handful of genes to lower testosterone and other truculent hormones. More manageable, eh? All to save the world from the teeming hordes. But you haven't guessed it." She sounds like a spoiled child who didn't get a pony for her birthday. "I was sure you'd have worked it out by now."

And you're blank. You've dropped your grand revelation, but apparently that's not it.

When you get back, you spend plenty of time staring at the books, but the last secret isn't in there. Nobody wrote a book about *you*, after all. And all the while, what you saw in the war zone is festering in you. What you saw in the slums around the city. And, scrape down far enough, there's your own personal experience. The dogs, and Gerald, and your father. And the strange thing is, despite it all, you do like Isadora. And you can tell yourself, *she's better than the others*. She doesn't whip her staff. She treats them well and brings out the best in them. If you had to be any ogre's pet, then there would be no better Master than her.

But that *If*. A word that would have been unthinkable back when you lived in the village. Unthinkable in your early years as Isadora's tame peasant. But you've read now. You understand about the Brink. It's true, as the pastor always said, that the world was ordained this way. But not by God. And with God out of the equation, that leaves room for the question, *What if it wasn't this way?*

And one evening, Minith comes to the library, leaning in the doorway as you tread back through books you've already exhausted, needling through the haystack to find what you missed.

Your glower only amuses her. You'd have thought she'd approve, finding you here burning the midnight oil amongst these pages, but apparently that's just more food for the contempt that never really left her.

"You're so blind," she tells you. "You're looking two hundred years back in time and you never see the here and now. You missed dinner, didn't you?"

You did, and you're hungry. Sheer stubbornness is keeping you at this fruitless study.

"Go ask the cooks to heat you up something," she tells you imperiously, and then adds. "After all, nobody else will have had it."

You blink at her. There's far too much mockery in that smile for her words not to mean *something* beyond the obvious.

"Tell me," you demand, but she won't. She just says, "You never watch the cooks at work, do you?"

You eat. You sleep. Next day you watch the cooks as they make lunch. Your lunch, and the staff's lunch. Separately. Every meal for years, this has been going on, but you were always too good for the kitchen. Why would you ever have sat there, a volume unregarded on your knees, watching them make food for the staff and Her Ladyship and for you? And mostly you eat what the staff get, but with an added ingredient. A little of what Isadora has, minced up and baked into whatever's going. Meat from her own table. Nothing but the best.

And you remember a word that was used, a handful of times long ago, when referring to you.

You go back to the library and, for the first time in many months, look up the meaning of something in the dictionaries. You search out the definition of *atavism*.

CHAPTER SEVEN

AFTER THAT, THINGS can't be the same. You look in the mirror, and what looks back at you is like one of those pictures you've seen, the vase that is the two faces, the duck that is the rabbit facing the other way. *What am I?* But now everything makes sense: your riotous childhood, your temper, Gerald's death. And that newly reinterpreted past must surely lead to a different future to the one you had planned. You've a destiny, if you could only work out what it is.

Isadora calls you to attend that evening. She is still seething about the generals and their cavalier treatment of her. She drinks and swears and throws a wineglass across the room. Then she calls you to her and tells you how fond of you she is, holds you to her bosom, tousles your hair. But you feel all those strings that bind you to her, gratitude and servitude, fraying and snapping. And she doesn't notice because she doesn't concern herself with the moods of servants.

You know, by the time she retires to bed, that you can't stay. You are not her pet any more. You were born for another purpose, because you were born different. Your father was cuckolded by genetics, and you are something more than just a village headman's son.

Late that night, you gather everything you will need. You abandon the histories that have sustained you for years and take more current reading: maps, and plans of the train network especially. You fill a pack with spare clothes and food from the kitchens, and you take other things too, whatever you can lay hands on that will help. And you are as sly and subtle as you can be, but it's not enough. You are seen, and perhaps that's because certain eyes were expecting it.

And you creep from the house, looking back just once with a little pang of conscience, because Isadora was good to you, in her own way. She has given you this second childhood, to let you grow into who you need to be. But as with all children, one day you must strike out on your own. You have great things to accomplish.

You cross the grounds towards the estate's wall and gate. To your own surprise, you don't feel nervous at all. That fear belongs to the man you thought you were, not the man you now know yourself to be.

Some of the staff patrol the grounds at night, but you wait till they've gone by and until the man slouching by the gate is either called away, or gets bored, or needs to piss. You stand before the great iron portal topped with barbed wire thorns and find it locked.

You're stronger and fitter than you ever used to be, after the full meals—the full and *meaty* meals—you've been eating these last years, but the gates offer few footholds and the barbs atop them look savage. Easier than the wall, though, and you take a few steps back, ready to make your run up and hope the sound doesn't wake everyone back in the house.

And they open. Of their own accord. Giving you a view of the formless darkness beyond: your destiny. You realise you're being watched.

It's Minith, standing there in the moonlight in her white uniform. She holds some device, presumably the control for the gate. You had counted on being a long way from the house before anybody marked your absence. For a long heartbeat you stare at each other.

Her pointed face is closed, but you see her nod and the gate is open. A blessing, of sorts, and you can't work out why. She has never concealed her dislike of you. But then that dislike is rooted in your monopolising her Mistress's time, displacing her as the most favoured of the favoured few. And now you're going. No more will you be standing between her and advancement.

She watches still, as you cross through the gate, a Rubicon (you came across the word in a book, and understand its meaning even if you don't know its origin) you cannot take back. And then you drop out of her sight, and she is gone from yours, and still her voice is not raised to accuse you. She is merely glad you have gone, for her own selfish reasons.

You are a fugitive again, after so many years, and you make sure that, by dawn, you are a long way from Hypatian. Specifically, by dawn you are on a train, eating sparingly from your provisions and hidden amongst the freight. The greatest thing you have equipped yourself with is not in your pack; it is an understanding of how the world works. Last time you just ran into the forest, clueless and panicking. Now, you can travel a hundred miles in an hour. Now you have a map showing countless ogre holdings and outbuildings, hunting lodges and getaways, most of which are empty or have just a skeleton staff. And more than that, you have self-knowledge.

You are going home.

Or that's the plan. You ride the train lines as close as you can to your home territory, the estates of the Grimes family, and your innocent intent is just to get within sight of the village and see how the land lies. You don't quite have a plan yet, though ideas are coagulating within your skull.

Instead, you meet Sir Peter.

You don't know whether it's blind chance that brings the two of you together, or if the old landlord is more busy about his holdings now his eldest is dead. You come across his car parked at the side of the track, a handful of servants playing a bored game of dice as they wait for their master to return. You imagine he's been out shooting, but on closer inspection there are a couple of long guns still in the back of the car. Then Sir Peter himself makes an appearance, shouldering out of the undergrowth and making his people leap up, dice scattering. There is a girl. A human girl, some village child. She is weeping and her dress is bloody and at the same time she is trying desperately to appear grateful and happy and obedient. So...

You don't *decide* to step out into the open, but that is what you've done, you find. And Sir Peter's reaction is all you could possibly want. His face goes purple and his eyes pop and you think for a moment he will die on the spot. He hasn't forgotten you: how you took his son after he'd taken your father; how you were ripped from the claws of his justice. You see on his face how that has festered with him ever since. And now you're here.

He snarls for his people to take you, his beaters. They try. You break one's arm and throw the next so hard he can only wheeze for breath. The remaining two are terrified of you. Because you're angry and strong and bigger than them, and because where that spark of rage should be in them, there's just a hole. They were engineered that way. It makes them more Economic.

Sir Peter has gone for the gun case, but you slap it from his hands, spilling the oiled-metal contents to the earth. He raises his stick.

You take it from him. This wasn't what you came here to do, but as you feel the solid weight of it in your hand, you realise it *was*. This is where your destiny takes you. Of course this day was coming.

You strike Sir Peter with his own cane, the brass hawk's-head handle gouging across his face. The sound that comes from his servants is that of worshippers seeing their god's idol pulled down.

He screeches: not pain, not anger, but indignation. How *dare* you? But you dare more than that. You haven't finished with him. You beat him again and again, and the third blow catches him in the head and he goes down. His new stick is well-made. It doesn't break. It outlasts his skull and his brains.

The beaters and the other staff haven't made a move to stop you. They stare in horror as you fill your pack with food from Sir Peter's hamper and take the gun case, heaving its weight of weapons and shot over your shoulder by its strap. Only then does one of them make a token effort at getting in your way, as though the theft of the property is somehow the final straw. But a look dissuades that man, and you are off into the woods, walking jauntily with the hawk's-head stick and a clearer idea of what you're going to do. You were wrong. Breaching the wall of Hypatian wasn't your Rubicon. Sir Peter's skull has fulfilled that function.

Two of them follow you, plus the girl Sir Peter had been dallying with. You keep an eye on them, don't acknowledge them, until you're deep in the woods and have started a fire with the lighter you brought from Hypatian. Then they creep out warily, as though you'll turn your rage on them, but you invite them to share the fire, and give them such food as they can eat. Sir Peter's people's names are Serge and Potto; the girl's is Layla. She tells you about her home, a village you've vaguely heard of, and the recent bad harvest and Sir Peter's taxes and penalties and punishments. Serge and Potto half-tell, half-show by their manner, that they are lovers, and that Sir Peter has had both of them whipped, for that reason and for others.

You give them all the chance to abandon you. Sir Peter's death will stir a howling response from the ogres. But they have seen something in you. You are, after all, a hero, and you are coming into your kingdom.

The next day, Layla goes to her home and asks until she finds someone who knows of a band of outlaws in the woods, and where they might be found, and you go with your own little band of followers to meet Roben again, after all this time.

THE YEARS HAVE made Roben older, while they seem only to have made you more vital, as though the energy time leaches out of everyone else has found a home in you. You do not remember any of the rest of his band. But it is Roben, though, who Layla takes you to. The old man's canny enough that he's still in charge of his band. And that band is three times the size it was, you can see. The years haven't been kind to the lands under Sir Peter's care, and neither has Sir Peter. And maybe that's your doing, indirectly, or maybe things would always have gone that way. You certainly can't imagine things being kinder if it were Gerald making the rounds now, rather than Grimes Senior.

You walk into the circle of his fire, and he sees you and your name spills from his lips, and half your work's done in that moment.

Because they remember you. They remember you as dead, and doubtless in the villages they cast you as a devil and a monster, scourged by the pastor every church-day. But to the outlaws you became something else. They must have someone to hate for the cold nights and the lean days, after all, and so they hate the ogres, secure in the knowledge that they will never be in a position to act on that hate; it remains merely something to keep in their shrivelled bellies when the foraging is poor. And you are the man who killed an ogre. And you died.

And here you are.

You sit down at the fire and greet Roben with your old boyish smile, and you introduce Layla and Potto and Serge, and you get out the food you took from Sir Peter's car. The bread and the fruit and other good things get passed round the circle. The cold meats, the sausages, you keep for yourself. They watch you tear into them with a fearful fascination.

You tell them the first version of your great speech, then. You've tried to think it out, but despite all those books, you're someone who gets better by doing, so it's as well you have such a primed audience. You tell them the Truth, though it's a Truth with the complex edges rounded off until it's something small and simple enough to swallow. You tell them the thing they always told themselves bitterly, when the fire guttered low and the frost lay on the ground: that the ogres are no better than them. The thing they told each other and never believed, but which is true.

They tricked your ancestors, you say. They stole something from them, but kept it for themselves. You speak of the Brink, the genetic engineering, the whole salutary story of saving the world that the books taught you. But you turn it round. You tell a history omitted by the winners. It becomes a kind of creation myth, a story of the before-times when there was only one people, and how *they* cheated *us*. And where you stand, one foot across the *them-us* divide, you do not say, but you are here, back from the dead, and though there is no logical correlation there, that somehow stands as proof.

You tell them what happened to Sir Peter, and though you see Roben's face go troubled, more than half those around the fire are cheering you on then, and who cares who hears? The old ogre has indeed been upping the taxes and the beatings since you killed his son. He has, all unknowing, been preparing his people for your triumphant return.

"They will not let that go," Roben says eventually. A wise old man after all, and not unmoved by what you've said, but he takes his responsibilities seriously. A man over-cautious to be captain, but a good lieutenant, you think.

"They will not," you agree. "The servants of his who lived, they will have spread the word already. There will be ogres, and then there will be dogs." And you shiver despite yourself, remembering Theo; remembering Catch and Tongs.

You see Roben make the necessary calculations. If there are dogs, they will track you here, to where the scent of all his people will be spread out like a picnic for them to sample. He is about to give his usual order, the one he gave when you turned up with Gerald's blood on your hands: flee, use the water, go plague the outskirts of some other village. Hope they will stop looking. Except, as you know from last time, they won't, and these measures won't work.

You stand up before he can commit himself. "Listen to me," you tell them. "You think I came back just to kill the man who murdered my father? You think that's it and I'm done?" A precisely weighted beat before you go on. "You think I'd leave all of you?"

"All of who?" Roben demands, as you knew he would.

"Everyone. The real people. Those who suffer under the ogres' boot. You, every one of you. The people in the villages. All the others I've seen, these last years."

It's too big for a lot of them. Roben sees, though. Even though he's shaking his head, you know he had those same thoughts once, maybe when he first turned outlaw. And he gave them up in exchange for just surviving one year at a time. But then, he's not a hero like you.

"Piss on what the pastor preaches," you tell them. "Nothing put them over us but their own trickery. And they're not better than us. And we don't need them. They need us. Without us, who tills their fields, who works in their factories, who fights their play-wars?" And they don't really understand those last things, but you're already planning ahead.

And some say nobody from the villages will care—since the outlaws have fled village justice, for the most part. Others still have the Master in his Castle whipped deep into them. And still more just harbour plain fear.

But you tell them, "I am going to the House." And there is only one 'House': Sir Peter's. "I am going to take from it everything I choose and turn his family out onto the road, just like you were all turned out. And then I will burn it down. Because the death of one landlord is not enough of a message to send to the ogres, nor it is punishment enough for the crimes of their forebears. Who's with me?"

And you make it perfectly clear, in your tone, that you will go alone if you have to, and will still triumph, no matter the odds. And because of that, men and women around the fire start standing up and pledging themselves to the venture. They're the younger ones, generally; the ones most recently turned off their land and out of their homes. In many cases, they were cast out of their villages for good reason. People for whom the chance to rob a big house is more important than generations of injustice. Right now you can't be choosy about who follows you. You offer absolution for any who will stand beneath your banner.

And you look at Roben, waiting to see which way he will run. You've come and taken his people from him, and taken his choices, and that's wrong. He didn't deserve that, the man who was always a friend to you. But you've given him something, too; cast it at his feet, if he'll only pick it up. You've given him hope and a purpose and the truth.

And you think he'll just stay sat at his fire, and then you think he'll walk away, a band of one under the merry greenwood. But when he stands, stiffly, it's not to go anywhere. No words, for that would bind him to you more than he can stand, but a nod, just like Minith's nod.

A FEW DAYS on the road, to Sir Peter's big house. You had twenty when you left Roben's camp. You have thirty-three when you reach the high walls and the big gates. Roben has people out scavenging and scrounging, living off the land as you must. Nobody keeps their mouth shut; word spreads. Doubtless there are agitated committees of village elders talking about what must be done, but the disaffected and the young don't talk. They just come and find you on the road and join in. There are those who were hovering on the point of outlawry already. There are even a couple who know their letters and have thought about the world and know injustice when they see it.

A high wall runs all the way around the extensive grounds, but nobody has challenged Sir Peter or his peers in generations, and so the maintenance of that wall isn't all it should be. Serge shows you where he knows a tree that has grown up until its branches overshadow the wall top. You consider cameras and surveillance, but Potto and Serge, who once called this place home, tell you the staff barely pay any attention to such systems. When were they last needed, after all?

You're over the wall and advancing on the house. And probably there are servants on patrol, perhaps with dogs, but if so, they are few and far between and the grounds are huge. You meet none of them.

The house is all lit up, burning a wealth of energy in its chandeliers and lamps. You and Roben and a handful of others creep forward to scout the bright windows and see what's what.

You're expecting a staff of maybe twenty, and Sir Peter's wife and any resident children. Instead, there are a full half-dozen ogres thronging the drawing room, windows thrown open to let out the fuming fug of their cigar smoke and sweat and alcohol. The one woman you take to be Mrs Grimes. She is nominally hostess, but you know the dynamics of ogre gatherings and you see she has no control of this one. They are all big men, dressed much as Sir Peter was—his peers, neighbouring landlords. They are drunk, and one of them sits very close to Mrs Grimes, his hand on her leg, his mouth speaking condolences but his eyes saying very different things. For a moment you are startled that the house is host to a party with Sir Peter's brains so recently dashed onto the road, but then you understand his death is the cause. This is a band of gallant hunters, assembled here before heading out to track you down. They are stuffed with declarations, telling each other what they will do to you, and every other monkey they can catch. They will exhibit your mutilated body in every village. They will make you eat your own excrement and then your own hands. They roar with laughter at their inventiveness.

You creep back to the main body of your army and give your orders.

The first the ogres know of the attack is almost the last. You swarm in through the windows, you and your people. Your followers lack the berserker's fire; it was stolen from their inheritance. They can feel angry but they cannot really *rage*. But you lead them, and you have knives, and you have Sir Peter's gun that blows a hole in the first ogre to stand up. And sometimes you don't

need a full-on fury to get vi...
slapped children and bea...
teeth and black eyes, ...
frustration can be turne...
the dampened serotonin an...

Your people have clubs and ...
knives and wood hatchets. The o...
strength and the fuel of their outrage...
could have been easily cowed, had the ogr...
a chance. But you are not cowed, and you...
example. You strike the first blow, and then your p...
are swarming desperately about the room, hacking at th...
giants in a death of a thousand cuts and a hundred blows.
And some of the house staff are sufficiently loyal that
they try to intervene—mostly those, like the beaters, who
have been shaped into little ogres themselves, dwarfish
mockeries of their masters. And they die too. You told
your people not to kill the servants, but self-defence is
self-defence. And you told them to spare Mrs Grimes,
too, and this they do. The huge woman is backed into
a corner, shielding herself, a cat bearded by mice. And
because of that, she lives.

And then the ogres, who had so recently been boasting
of how they'd make your last hours a torment, are dead,
and the room is ankle-deep in their vast reserves of
blood, and the house is yours.

Your people want to celebrate, but there's no time for
that. Mrs Grimes is locked in the cellar, along with three
ogre children of varying ages, and the majority of the
surviving staff, save for half a dozen who join Potto and
Serge in your army.

You ransack the house for everything that you can use,
and everything anybody wants. There is an abundance

...es and cars around the front of the house,
...of the various hunting ogres who came to
...Sir Peter. Potto can drive, as can one of the others.
...ad up food from the pantry, knives, all the guns the
...pid hunters brought—even though they are mostly
...large they'd break the shoulder of any human who
...red one. You take all the spare clothing and blankets
and sheets you can find. You take spare fuel for the cars,
save for some that is splashed through the rooms of the
house. And while the others are about this, you find Sir
Peter's library. It consists of precisely nine books, six of
which concern hunting, shooting and fishing, but there
is a dictionary and there is a book of maps and one of
natural history, and you take them all.

Then you have the Grimes family and their remaining
loyalists brought out in front of the house, and you have
them watch while you put a match to their ancestral pile.
You burn their heritage, just like their ancestors pillaged
yours. You all stand and watch the flames devour that
grand old house and its priceless furniture and paintings
and all the generations and years and days of their family
and their lives. And Mrs Grimes weeps and squalls and
shrieks at you, and your people cheer you to the heavens.

You and your band drive off in your stolen convoy, and
leave them with nothing but the clothes on their backs,
and consider it just.

THEY SEND THEO after you.

There is certainly a wider ogre response being formed,
but sheer shock means it's slow and disjointed. This
has never happened before. It is the specific thing they
did their level best to preclude from their future, when

they were taking steps to tackle the Brink. But Theo is an enterprising individual, and he's always been on the outside of ogre society. He doesn't fit with them any more than you fit with regular people. Of course he comes for you.

One day you hear he's in the area. Catch and Tongs track you down that night. You are waiting when they come slavering out of the trees towards you, desperate to take you in their jaws and hold you for their master.

And, because they are dogs, and you are human, they go into the pit you had dug for them. You hear them snarling and leaping and complaining down there, and they almost get out, Catch on the back of Tongs and leaping taller than a man's height. For a heartbeat the whole business is that close to unravelling. But the pit holds them, just.

Theo slouches into the clearing after, carrying a knife and a gun and staring at you. He marks the fate of the dogs, and stops with the pit between you.

"You," he murmurs. "It *is* you." Something like wonder crosses his broad ogre face. "I never had to hunt someone down twice before." The moon glints on his tusks. "What now, monkey?" He hefts his long gun, but you know he'll have been tasked to bring you in alive. So they can kill you properly, just like before. You didn't die then; you won't now.

"You're not like the other ogres," you tell him. He snarls at the name, because of course the ogres don't refer to *themselves* as that. "I thought about asking you to join me, even."

His eyes go wide, and not with the derisive mockery you expected, either. And you wonder, then, whether it actually *is* an option. Would Theo go renegade, just for the joy of the hunt? But no: he's an ogre, first and foremost, and he's made a living out of hunting and killing your kind.

"You're a clever monkey," he tells you. "You ain't all that, though. The only point of you is to make me rich." He begins stalking round the pit's edge cautiously, prodding at the ground with his gun barrel. And you think about the workers crammed into the factory slums, desperately scrabbling for wages that they only need because their masters, who want for nothing, have decreed that their world must work that way. And you wonder if this hulking ogre is trapped in just the same net. This is what happens to ogres who won't play proper ogre games.

When they tell the story later, it's you and Theo knife to knife, his brute strength against your speed until you bury your blade in his throat. What actually happens is that you take out the pistol you got from one of the ogre hunters. You don't need to bring Theo in alive, after all. His eyes go wide and he drags his own gun up, but you empty yours in a rolling tide of thunder, and an ogre is a big target. You sprain your wrist, but you are bigger than any regular human, and strong, and you've learned how to hold a gun even if you've not fired one before. Sir Peter had books about it.

In the echoes, the woods are silent save for a questioning whimper from the dogs in the pit. Then the cheering begins.

CHAPTER EIGHT

THINGS ACCELERATE BEYOND anybody's control.

The first month of the conflict is covered by a fog of ignorance on both sides. The expected instant reprisal from the ogres doesn't happen, and you personally can't understand why. What you find out later, once you've been on your travels, is that various of the ogres who might otherwise have come to quick action are arguing amongst themselves. There is considerable scoffing and doubt amongst the Masters about what has actually happened. Some see treachery amongst their own kind. Others see advantage. What mostly happens, when the Widow Grimes turns up with her depleted staff and children, demanding justice, is an inheritance dispute. Sir Peter's estates are valuable, hence a number of his neighbours begin jostling over who should be the one to console the widow and control the holdings. And, since taking a pack of beaters in to clear out the rabble would grant the form of possession which remains nine-tenths of ogre law, they all block each other's attempts to do so. A joint task force is proposed but repeatedly sunk by their machinations against each other. A couple of them try to go behind the backs of the others and just march a pack of retainers in to hunt you down, but by then you have more than enough followers to deal with them, because you've been recruiting.

Let's be frank: you're not free of your own divisions and factions. You solve the problem by never ceasing to move forwards. You expand your range and your influence, and just keep pushing because, at some level, you understand that to consolidate now would be to stagnate. It would be to sit at the fire and have people ask you the question 'What now?' It would be to have them consider the very real likelihood that any day the ogres will get their act together and come to kill you all. To you, knowing what you do of the ogres, it seems inevitable. And nobody can say what thoughts circle within you, that you never speak to another soul, but perhaps there are two wolves, and one is the hunter and the other the hunted. The hunted wolf knows it is doomed, but the hunter knows it is *right*. And, so long as you hunt, you don't need to listen to that mournful other voice.

You and Roben tour the villages, just as Sir Peter did. You even collect taxes: less than the ogres demanded even though you have more mouths to feed. Beyond this, you collect recruits. And perhaps it's not so many, in those little communities like the one where you grew up. Even though Sir Peter turned the screws on them these last few years, they are not so hard done by, and they are so, so ignorant. They believe in the hymns they sing and in the way they're told the world works. It's comforting, that belief. You remember it yourself. And yet you displace pastors and get up in the pulpit on church-days. You give them the Truth, and let them decide what to do with it. And there's always a trickle of disaffected youth and bitter elders who come with you, each time.

That's nothing to the cities.

You and a few others stow away on a train and go to the town of slums and smoke and factories that Isadora took you to, and there you find your work half-done. Because they *do* have it bad, in the tenements and the factories, and there is a long underground tradition of trying to organise and fight the bosses, to protest for better conditions, shorter hours, safer machines. And yet they were all just the same slaves to a creed as the farmers. They have demanded for generations: *can it not be slightly better for us?* and been slapped down by the truncheon-wielding thugs the ogres employ as law-keepers. And then you arrive, and tell them that their entire bubble world is like a pot, only hot and seething because someone's keeping the fire beneath it stoked. The question they should have been asking is, *why is it like this at all?* And you tell them your Truth, of the Brink and the trick the ogres pulled, and it goes through all their networks like wildfire. The ogres have set up their pressure-cooker cities so that it's work or die, and you come to them and say, *what if... neither?*

And of course there are always informers and traitors, and the police come in to break everything up. You join the workers in their fights; you crack some heads and put bullets into others. You become the terror of the law-keepers because you have seen the rot behind their badges and their laws. And because you're bigger than any of them, of course. And then you go to the big house of the ogre who gives them their orders and you leave him with his throat cut.

You have set fires across the city, literally and ideologically. You have a great swathe of new recruits, and they work in factories that make clothing and food and tools. They work in factories that make machines that can talk to each other at a distance. They can operate transport vehicles. And some of them work in the factory that makes human-sized weapons for the generals, and when you leave the city it's in a big convoy bristling with guns. Guns nobody knows much how to use, but it's a start.

And every day you wake up expecting things to be over. Because they're the *ogres*. The *Masters*. Nobody does this. Even you, who've looked behind the curtain, understands that revolutions against ultimate power end only one way. You're reminded of old stories from ogre libraries, about the wicked servant that rebels against his omnipotent master. And you know that the ogres have no mandate from God, but you also know that, given the time to get themselves into gear, they won't need one.

YOU GET BACK, with your new recruits and your new resources, to find that the generals have finally taken over, amongst the ogres. They have been playing their war games for generations, after all. Now you've given them an excuse to take their games out of the mud-churned stretches of no man's land set aside for their frolics. The old war is over, long live the new war. The war against Torquell.

Not that they know your name. You'll learn later that they've yet to connect you with the boy who killed

Gerald Grimes years ago, let alone Isadora's hulking protégé. The monkey rebellion in Sir Peter's lands is just a headless, formless outrage. And an excuse for the generals to play on a bigger map.

There are eyes in the sky now. The ogre generals were always keen on watching their toy wars, seeing the explosions and the doomed charges into the cannon's mouth. But those eyes are designed for the mud and the wire, not your forests. When they come low enough to get under the canopy, they're easy prey for stones and bullets. And, perhaps, those eyes are not as sharp as the ogres believe. Perhaps not always looking in the right direction. Sometimes, they wink.

You get visitors to your camp. Captain Doctor Bradwell and a handful of others whose rank or role lets them move more freely. Men who can influence just where those eyes are looking. You get voices whispering to you, over the radios you liberated from the factories, as your new recruits train in marksmanship. And most of the time, the red-coated patrols sent to track you down find only cold ashes of campfires, or letters pinned to trees telling them the Truth, that they mostly burn but sometimes read. Or sometimes they find pits and traps, ambushes, sabotage. Certain squads more zealous in their obedience to ogre orders just don't return at all. And you keep their vehicles and their weapons.

Sometimes they take villages, scorch earth, evict everyone in a great tantrum, and every time they do, you gain new recruits and new zeal, people who see through the ogre lie. And you have raided the food processing plants of their cities, and your supply lines are sturdier than theirs. You hear the toll of charred houses and deaths and know it's all to your advantage.

They set up artillery and blow up patches of woodland that you swiftly evacuate or that you knew not to be in. And some nights you lead your people to where you've been tipped off those guns have been set, and you turn the guns on the next artillery emplacement over, or just cart them off for your own use.

But no matter how many weapons you keep, the big set-piece battle the ogre generals are hankering for never happens. You have few good shots amongst your people, and nobody has strong nerves. The white-hot fury that you feel, when you think about the Truth and the Brink, is a low fire in all the others. They can't help it. They were engineered that way, so as not to be able to stand up to their Masters. There are no lions amongst them, and so you fight a mouse's war, creeping and hiding and avoiding confrontation unless the odds are stacked in your favour. Because even a mouse can pull a trigger.

And every night you wonder that they haven't crushed you. And every dawn there's new information that's seeped out of the army camp, about where they'll go next, and who they'll send. To the generals, you're magically one step ahead of them all the time, and they grow frustrated. Their war game isn't fun to play any more when it's not their own kind calling the shots on both sides.

One general loses his temper entirely, just gathers up a hasty force and leads it into the forest himself. And, because it's done on a whim and without planning, you get almost no warning, and there is a battle then. A fight, strung out through the merry greenwood. And the soldiers wear bright red coats, and your people wear peasant brown or factory grey. And you know the woods, while they just know mud and trenches.

You make yourself a target. You're a fool. If a bullet found you, that day, it would all fall apart. But your followers fight because you're there, in their midst, and perhaps if you'd hidden behind the lines they'd have broken and fled.

And by then you outnumber the expeditionary force more than four to one, men and women with the same rifles they give the soldiers, with a handful of armoured vehicles, and with trucks and cars and tracked construction machinery. And some of the soldiers have taken off their red coats anyway, joining you, or just fleeing, because this isn't the war they signed up for. Because the letters you left them opened their eyes to the possibility of not fighting any war at all. And you surround the rest, deep in the woods, like the savage tribesmen of another age encircled the legions of a long-gone imperial power. You take their guns, and then you have the ogre general brought to you. You face him with Catch on one side and Tongs on the other, because while you were in the city, Roben was showing Theo's dogs a little kindness.

There are a hundred ways you can take things from here, but in your mind is the knowledge that the moment you cease to move forwards, cease to escalate, you're lost. And so you send the general's head back to his peers along with those soldiers who still want to follow ogre orders. And many of them don't, now you've defeated them. They know that going back as losers will see beatings and punishments and executions by firing squad, because the ogres only know one way of motivating their human troops. And they hear the Truth from your lips, and you light the little fire in them that you've been setting everywhere you go.

The head, sent back, finally convinces the ogres that they aren't playing a game anymore. This isn't a jolly hunting expedition or a chance for the generals to play at war. This is insurrection, and it's spreading. Factories have burned, cities have been overturned. Whole districts and villages, counties, boroughs are being overseen by your lieutenants, rather than the ogres or their minions.

And so the news comes to you that they've stopped playing around.

Nobody else understands, amongst your people. Only you had the years of leisure in Isadora's library reading about the Brink and the times before.

The people of that suffocatingly crowded world were skilled at war, meaning they devised many ways of conducting war that did not require human intervention. They had machines that flew and spied out the land for them, and they had bullets that could be launched from many miles away to destroy a whole village. They had aircraft as swift as the wind with bellies full of death. They had weapons that brought plague, and weapons that were just air, except the air killed too. And they had regular tools of soldiery beyond the dreams of the poor soldiers the ogre generals have been unleashing on you, and their soldiers' coats weren't bright red either. Or not in the immediately pre-Brink times. The historical model the ogres revert to is an older and more visceral one. You cannot play war games with the technology of the pre-Brink days because the games would be over too quickly. In fact, since pulling the world back from the Brink—or at least since the clean-up immediately after that—the world has not needed the old model of war. The ogres have their disagreements, but they are all of a class and a society together and there are other ways they can push and shove. Perhaps this is one blessing of the terrible things they did.

But you—you have finally achieved something. You have brought the old war back. The weapons have been broken out of mothballs and rushed to a command post some way distant from the woods, a compromise between their knowing they can exterminate you from the horizon, and them wanting to see the flames and smell the smoke themselves. Ogres are creatures of appetite, after all. They did not render themselves immune to the lessening that saved the world from the Brink only to deny their desires later. They do not just want to kill you, or even to know that you are dead. They want to *see* it, and celebrate it. They want your head above the mantelpiece, or your body swinging in a city square as a warning to others.

You hear whispers on the radio of what they have. Vehicles with many missiles; missiles with minds that can identify their own targets; canisters of toxins; gas masks. The new soldiers have been issued with new uniforms of brown and green.

And you, the *Atavism*, are ogre enough that you, too, must go see for yourself.

You pick a task force, everyone who can fit in your vehicle fleet. This is your throw of the dice, no sense holding back. The rest you tell to scatter, and if you don't come back, then they should find somewhere, some slum, some distant village. It will be over, if you don't come back. You know this fact with an unfailing certainty: you *are* the rebellion.

And you remember other histories, from long before the Brink. Of upstart slaves crucified in long lines along straight roads; of barricades torn down and students shot. This is how revolutions end, most of the time. The path you've trodden isn't new, and you always understood where it would likely lead. But when you knew enough about the world, what was done in the past and what you were, what other choice was left to you? You're a hero, after all. A hero doesn't stand idly by. He gets *involved*, no matter the cost.

You expect, any moment, the faceless death that the Brink weapons can deal. Your entire force can be wiped out at the ogres' pleasure, and they must know you are coming. Or perhaps they have a vast number of monkeys puzzling over many user manuals, trying to remember how this sort of war is assembled and set into motion.

As your force nears the camp, as the skies grow grey with the first breath of morning, you can hear the shooting, but by the time you reach their perimeter fence—along the path not seeded with mines, thanks to the whisperings of the radio—it is over.

In the centre of the camp are many soldiers, some wounded, all disarmed, and in the centre of them, nine ogres. More generals, still in their medal-bedecked bright uniforms because they weren't going to be the ones who went out into the woods to mop up the last of the resistance. And surrounding these unfortunates is the army.

Just as with the villages under Sir Peter's hard hand; just as with the cities where the squeezing of the factory-mongers meant that, when you cut them an exit, they were ready to erupt through it; just as with every step of your life, it's as though events were only waiting for a hero like you to come along. You stride into the army camp through doors the soldiers throw open for you. Catch and Tongs pad alongside you, and you're wearing a long grey coat one of your people made to your outsize measurements that has something of the soldier to it. And Captain Doctor Bradwell, in charge of the insurrection, salutes you because he's a soldier and that's what soldiers do. And you salute back, and from that moment you're a general. You see the ogres note this exchange and their huge eyes are wide with real fear.

You take their gifts, all the real weapons from the real wars rather than the toys they have been playing with ever since. You will have to spend time puzzling over the books and the electronic documents and the rest before you can use any of it. Much of it you perhaps will never be able to use, or will find too dangerous to play with. But it's yours, and more to the point, the other ogres know you have it. And it wasn't as if they particularly remembered how to use those weapons either. There's a parity of ignorance.

You stand before the generals, and they rant at you. They curse and spit at Bradwell and his fellow members of the junta. They invoke law and privilege and the chain of command. And when they have exhausted their rhetoric and lowered themselves in the eyes of those who stayed loyal to them, you stand up and tell the Truth again. You're good at it now. The words come out with smooth assurance, with an orator's aim to fly true and pierce an armoured heart. You tell the soldiers about how their ancestors were robbed and cheated, and at least half change their minds about whose side they want to be on.

The rest you send back with nothing but their boots and uniforms. Bradwell and some of the others advise you to hold them or take more drastic steps, but you're not that far along the road yet. The generals, though, you have shot, just the same firing squad they'd ordain for any of their soldiers who turned against them. When the salvo of rifle fire has resounded, you walk forwards and put a bullet into the sagging head of each gigantic monster, before the eyes of your new army.

AFTER THAT, IT's mostly logistics for a while. You have become good at delegating. Anyone who has a penchant for organisation has a leg-up to advancement from you. You've read books. You know that armies are not just guns and battles, but meals and billets and morale. And by now you have to accept that what you are in charge of isn't just an army; it's a community. Men, women and children farming and making and mending and cooking and *living*. The edges of your realm are all drilling and trying to understand the user manuals, but the centre is slowly crystallising into something stable, where life can actually go on.

And you know it won't last. The ogres haven't immediately rained death from the sky over you; they're a little stunned at all the reversals, you suspect. But whatever the illusion of permanence in the centre, you know you have to keep pushing outwards. Stagnate, and they will get over their surprise and come to destroy everything. You keep sending people to the next village, the next city. You get word from the infiltrators who went back with the defeated soldiers. You keep pushing. And still the ogres are like fog. No new army gets sent to oppose you. No ballistic missiles leap up from past the horizon. The ogres are trying something new, and no whispers come to tell you what it is.

Until, one day, a car races up to your forward

command post, and instead of news it brings a prisoner; a messenger, in fact.

It's Minith, whom you haven't seen for more than half a year, not since you stepped through the gate of Hypatian to begin your career as a doomed revolutionary.

The ogres want to talk. Isadora wants to talk.

CHAPTER NINE

"SHE THINKS I'LL trust her," you say to Minith.

"Don't you?" is her reply.

She's remarkably bold, there in the heart of your army, but she always did have a high opinion of herself. Confidence is armour, up to a point.

And you're thinking about Isadora. Who is an ogress, yes, but you spent six years in her house. As her servant, her property, her *pet*, but still... She indulged you. She cultivated your intellect. She made you the man you are.

"Will you tell me what the ogres are doing now? What their next move will be?"

"*This* is their next move, for now," Minith says. "After that, who knows? Why would they tell me?"

Isadora isn't expecting you to jump in one of your newly-acquired helicopters and fly to Hypatian, of course, deep within enemy territory. Instead, she proposes a meeting with just herself and a handful of servants, somewhere out in the open, neither under one set of guns nor the other. And it remains a risk, depending on just which of the Brink-era toys the ogre generals have got working. You have read about snipers and drone strikes and the like. But the risk would extend to her, and you respect the value that Isadora places on her own life. She lacks the infantile recklessness of your early conquests, the Masters who couldn't bring themselves to believe that their servants could ever be a credible threat.

Now you're a threat. Now they believe in you.

You confer with Roben and Bradwell and Layla and all your other lieutenants, both here and at the end of a radio. They don't like it, but they don't know Isadora. You listen to them, but in your head the matter is already decided. You want to see your former master again, one last time. You want to sit with her and talk as equals, before the curtain is run down on this whole doomed business.

You arrive at the appointed place at evening. You bring Minith; release her into her Mistress's care, because you know the gesture will be appreciated. Isadora has a folding table set out, big enough for two ogres and a weight of rich food. Her promised handful of servants are unpacking hampers and cold boxes—the latter gives you a sudden shiver, a flashback to the kitchen of your home from years before—and laying out a movable feast. And Isadora sits there, in a chair sufficient for her dimensions, and watches you thoughtfully.

She is just as you remember her: massive, ogrishly beautiful, sly in her smiling. Her eyes flash as Minith lights the candles.

"Torquell," she names you. "Or is it 'general' now?" Because you've made an effort, decorated your long coat with stolen medals. You take the chair opposite her and hear it creak slightly.

"Welcome to my bower," Isadora says. She's had a glass or two already, you reckon; a somewhat incongruous and impolitic ambassador for ogre-kind. "I think 'bower' is the word. All very *Midsummer Night's Dream*. You're looking well, Torquell." And there's a little twitch there that might have been a murdered impulse to get up and pat you on the head, like she used to. "You've grown," she adds. "Or perhaps you've just grown into who you were always supposed to be. Genetically speaking."

You realise you're barely having to look *up* into her face at all. And is it because she's slouching a little already, or have you actually become more massive, more *ogrish*, since you left her?

Her opening gambit: "My fellows are really not happy with you, Torquell."

It's such an understatement you blink at her. "Good?" you try.

"Believe me, they're currently putting more effort into hushing up the news than fighting you. Don't want to look fools in front of the others."

And you take this piece of unsolicited information and stow it away because, of course, what they're also doing is stopping the humans, their monkeys, finding out about just what humans can do. There are more ways this news can spread than amongst the Masters. You've been sending people out to spread it, after all.

"Torquell," Isadora says, around mouthfuls, "this can't go on."

You eat in silence, savouring the rich sauces and meats, eating what she does as a rough and ready protection against poisoning. But you trust her not to try that, you find. Isadora was always frank with you.

"I mean, you've done it." She signals, and Minith refills her glass. "You've finally got everyone's attention. You've taken over all of poor Peter's estates and then some. You've killed some people. You've interrupted manufacturing. And now you've inspired a full scale revolt within the army, a result I place entirely at the feet of those idiot generals of ours and their determination to treat their people like dirt. So, yes, you've succeeded, that far. But they can't let you succeed any further, Torquell. The problem with my peers is that, lacking challenges and with no limits save where they jostle elbows with each other, there's little impetus for change and growth. They just fall into their ruts of lording it over the Economics and indulging their idiot games and pleasures. You remember what it's like for *me*, don't you? Me, someone who actually wants to further the boundaries of human knowledge. And the filthy deals I had to make, the treatment I had to endure, just to get support and resources.

"But you, Torquell, have *changed* all that. You've woken them up at last. You're sitting at their gates with their soldiers, armed with their weapons. You're finally being taken seriously. And so they're looking at the rest of the pre-Brink war toys. The big ones. Soon enough they'll have remembered how to brew a tailored plague or launch a missile from halfway around the world and drop it on the very top of your skull with pinpoint accuracy. And turn all of Peter Grimes's former holdings into a wasteland where nothing will ever grow, and all your followers to ash. You know this to be possible."

You nod. You do.

"And nobody wants that. I mean, now it's got this far, a couple of the generals probably do, because they're idiots, but it's a waste of land and a waste of Economics, and the hole it leaves in all our systems will take a long time to patch up. And you'll be dead, and all your dreams with you. And *I* don't want that."

A raised eyebrow from you. Minith refills your glass, but you leave it on the table, even as Isadora downs most of hers the moment it's topped up. She is looking at you fondly, despite everything. And you think about the fringe benefits of what she's described, from her point of view. You wonder how ogre science might advance, now that you've kicked them hard enough on the ankle. Now you've woken them up.

"You know what you are. I assume that finally pushed you to run away." She looks hurt about that. "You didn't have to. I had... plans for you. Plans in our society. But you went back to the Economics, and look where we've got to. You should be proud of what you've achieved, really. Not that I should say that, but I almost feel proud for you. Heritage will out, as we geneticists say."

"You think I'm one of you."

"You are." Wide-eyed surprise that you'd even doubt it. "I did wonder if you were even a direct descendant, some miscegenation, even though the engineered differences between human and Economic are supposed to make that impossible. But having studied your genome, it's just genes doing gene things. Switching themselves back on at random rather than staying safely quiet." A wild wave of the wineglass that spills half its contents. "You'd be surprised how few genes are really involved." Her smile is brilliant. "You won't care, but having someone else I can actually *talk* to about this is quite the treat. Usually it's just Minith and the others. And they're..."

"Economics," you fill in.

Monkeys.

"And you're..."

"An ogre."

She laughs. "Torquell, *really*. A human. Unmodified. Original."

"Like they were from before the Brink."

"Exactly," and probably she's about to go on to another topic, but you have a question. It's not one you even knew to ask, back when you were studying at her feet. The other puzzles she set you were too all-consuming. You didn't look past them to the big hole in all the histories, the thing the ogres never mentioned. And, unmentioned, it became an un-thing, a non-event. And yet, the more you think about the Brink, and what was done to remake the bulk of the thronging population into something smaller and more Economic, the more you realise there is one question more that must be asked. And if anyone knows, Isadora will.

"What happened after the Brink?" you ask her.

She makes a vague gesture probably intended to describe the whole world. "You know what. This. And depressingly little changed in the generations after."

"No," you say, and you see the faintest guilty start in her face that tells you she knows what you mean. "*After* the Brink. After the last generation of original humans had passed on and there were just the Economics and the ogres. What happened then? Because something must have."

Now it's her turn to be silent and listen. You can feel a colossal weight of anger somewhere, circling like a drone

435

weapon, waiting to see if it needs to drop on you and set you ablaze.

"Because the whole problem with the Brink," you go on slowly, step by logical step, "was that the world was overfull with people, all of them consuming too much, too inefficiently. That was why your ancestors ordered it all, the genetic engineering. Volunteers at first, then mandatory, and then camps. I've read the books. I know. Until everyone's children came out small and meek and vegetarian—except yours—and the world was saved." A deep breath. "Except the world was still full of people. Smaller people. Meeker people. Economics. But still full. Overfull, but even if everyone's smaller, the number of people is still the same or going up. And now." You mimic her gesture, taking in all the world. "Open fields, sprawling forest. And they cram them in, in the factory towns, but they don't *need* to. There's space for everyone to have their own farm. There's *wilderness*. Your peers go hunting and shooting and fishing. They have whole play-wars from horizon to horizon. There's so much space."

"What happened," you ask her, "to all the people?"

For a long time she says nothing. The ebullience is gone. She stares at the gleam of the candle as filtered through the gold of her glass's contents.

"It was generations ago now," she says quietly, and for a moment you can't understand why that's relevant. And it isn't relevant to you, but it is to her. She's trying to shed the blame of it. *I wasn't there.*

"When we'd made them smaller, and more docile," she tells you, so softly that you lean in to hear her, "there were still too many of them, as you say. The world was full of people. And history has a particular curve when it comes to numbers of people. There's a time, before industry and technology get going, when you *want* lots of people. If you're a king or a duke or something, you want people to till your fields and work your mines and march in your armies. Population is power, and nobody wants for work unless they're incurably idle. But then you get factories and automation and ways of doing things that are just more efficient than the old ways. Why have someone painstakingly carve out a chair over a month when ten unskilled hands in your factory can make a hundred chairs in the same time? And you keep automating and inventing ever more ingenious ways of doing things that don't need people, and eventually, if you're sitting at the top of the heap, you realise that all those teeming multitudes of people aren't actually an advantage. In fact, they're a positive drawback. You don't really *want* a vastly populous country, just in case those people all decided *they* don't want *you*.

"And of course by now there's very little for these people to do, and so you either have to spend half your time keeping them sufficiently amused that they won't realise they're pointless and have no purpose, or risk exactly the sort of stunt *you're* currently pulling, Torquell. So, back before the Brink we already understood that there really was no point to all those people. And afterwards they were small enough and weak enough and different enough that they couldn't stop us doing something about that. Remaking the world into something a bit more manageable. Where we"—and it's hard for her to say that *we*, but she is honest enough to force herself to it—"could get on with what we wanted to do. Without quite so many people underfoot."

And she looks at you, all cheer gone, watching for your reaction, Your face is flat and without expression, though, so the words keep falling out of her.

"It was mostly done through the release of chemical and biological agents, I think," she says faintly. "After all, there were distinct genetic markers separating us from the Economics. We could tailor things to lower reproductive rates, spread sterility. Humane, Torquell. And where it wasn't humane, I'm sure it was at least... quick." And that's all the words, the story as she knows it. She has the grace to be ashamed of it, but only distantly. The tilt of her chin says, *This was a long time ago. It's done. We have to get on with our lives.* As though her every waking moment hasn't benefitted from what was done back then. Her only saving grace is that she's not trying to tell you how the great open world of today is better for the monkeys than the tight-packed world of the Brink. And maybe it is, in some ways, but not for all the people who never got to see it.

"And..." you get out.

"And then we could live how we wanted. With the freedom of room and space, and fewer other people to worry about. Just as many people as we needed to play lord of the manor, or to fight wars, or to work in factories because it's cheaper and easier to have most factories run by Economics. Robots are expensive to build and fix and replace, and Economics are cheap and replace themselves. Everyone could indulge all the dreams they ever had, about how they'd act if they ruled the world."

"Everyone who wasn't an Economic," you clarify. The words echo inside you, in the great vacant pit of you. You're waiting to see what emotion will flood in and fill it.

"Yes."

"This," you try, "is why we have to fight." And it's not why you have been fighting, because you only just found out this new Truth, but it could be why you fight from now on. It could be part of your Truth going forwards. The banner under which your army marches.

"Torquell," Isadora says. "They won't let you."

A masterful raised eyebrow from you. They haven't stopped you yet.

"When it was just you overturning an apple cart out in the sticks, then it was something for people to jockey and compete over, a game for the more bored of the generals. It was the only kind of opportunity most of my peers have left: a chance to point out the flaws in other people's handling of a situation. Even when you killed a few people"—and she means *ogres*; she doesn't mean the Economics who died, in far greater numbers, during the fighting—"it was local and contained and, for most of us, rather far away. But if you try and change the order of the world then they'll just obliterate you. You can't win."

You take another mouthful of steak, though it's bitter with newfound knowledge. "So why come?"

"Because nobody wants to have to *use* those weapons—to destroy so much just to stop you."

"And because they blame you for making me?"

And she actually smiles. "No," she says. "They haven't quite put those pieces together." But you realise *she* believes she made you, with her library and the years she gave you when you could grow into the man you were meant to be. She takes credit, not blame. You're something fascinating, an experiment, and she is a scientist first and foremost. And you were always her favourite.

"But," she adds, "they did listen when I told them I had another solution. And they didn't like it, but it's better than burning everything down, and you have pushed them a long way. Far enough that concessions are on the table."

You lean forwards. You both do. Like lovers, almost. The lovers you always wondered if you might become, if she decided to impose herself on you. You had troubled dreams, surely, about just that, and sometimes they were bad dreams and sometimes they weren't.

"Concessions," you echo.

"You can have it," she says, almost a whisper. "What you've won. You can keep it. They'll let you."

"They'd never."

"They will," she insists. "You'll hold it like Sir Peter held it, though. As part of the system. Call it your birthright."

You jerk back, clutching for a derisive expression. "I lead their slaves in a revolt; I kill their people and burn their houses. And they welcome me with open arms? Is that what I'm supposed to believe?" And you probably don't quite notice that, for the purpose of the conversation, you are not one of 'the slaves' and Isadora is not one of 'them.' You're outside the world, the two of you, in the little bubble of your bower.

"No, listen," Isadora is saying, and hurriedly, before you do anything rash. Because she actually cares, you realise. Not about the Economics, not about the social order. About what happens to you, her stray pet turned barbarian warlord. "They will accept it. Not happily, and don't expect to get invited to many parties or anything, but if you just take on that mantle, recast your conquests from revolution to... hostile takeover, let's say. Become the squire of the manor, and you can keep it all. The people who came to your banner, the land you currently hold, even the factories and the city. Treat people well, be a benevolent master to them, make what changes you want, to make their lives easier. Maybe you can even show that things are more efficient that way. You might start a trend. You'll have a friend in me, to argue your case, if you can show results. You can even keep the weapons—you have no idea how many times I've patiently told rooms full of idiot men how asking you to give them up wouldn't exactly build trust. But don't push any further. No more conquests, no more fomenting rebellion amongst other people's Economics. You have won a lot, Torquell. Yours isn't the first rebellion since the Brink, by any means, but it's the most successful, hands down. Be happy with what you've achieved."

"They won't let it lie," you hear yourself say. "Unless we keep moving forwards, they'll regroup and then they'll destroy us."

"No." She shakes her head, and that little smile is still there, proud of you. "I mean, if you were just a mon—just an Economic who'd cooked all this up, then they *couldn't* make this kind of offer. That's a boundary nobody's about to cross. It's unthinkable. But you're not one of them, Torquell. You're one of us. An... 'ogre,' if you will. A real human being, with all the appetites and drives humans were supposed to have. How else have you achieved so much so quickly? Born to rule, Torquell. Destined for it. Now join the company of your peers, where you were always supposed to be. Be the most benevolent and progressive master the world ever saw. Show us all how it's done, but do it as one of us." And that bubble bursts, and she's 'us' again, and you are standing with one foot either side of that unbridgeable divide.

And you think. You take a long time because there is much to be said on both sides. Security for the people you've freed. A light hand, a better life, a master who won't be a petty tyrant like Sir Peter or a great butchering monster like the generals were. You could take up that mantle of authority and not be corrupted by the power, you're sure.

And a betrayal, you must realise. But there are many factors here, and you believe Isadora. You and she could enjoy many meals like this, afterwards, as you discussed how to improve the world and save it from its problems. Just like her distant ancestors did, as they approached the Brink.

You have worked so hard since you left her house. And your destiny has two paths now. The one where all that fighting was the prelude to a greater fight, a war for the whole world; then the one where all that fighting went to earn you this, and no more. But *This* is still more than you ever thought they'd let you keep.

"Yes," you tell her, and a great weight falls from you. The weight of fear, that any given morning will see your little uprising quashed by the monstrous weapons of the Brink days. The weight of responsibility that you'll get all your followers killed. The weight of worry that you might *lose;* that you might be *humiliated.* That the ogres would haul you down to the dirt and make you crawl before they killed you.

But they reserve that fate for monkeys, and you are, by genetic fluke, an ogre.

Isadora's eyes sparkle and her smile spreads, and Minith is conjured forward to refill the glasses, and you toast your new agreement. The wine is sweet again, the taste of ashes gone. You're already thinking through what you will say to your lieutenants, how this is not a capitulation, barely even a concession. A victory! Safety and prosperity for all! They can go back to their farms and factories knowing they won, and honestly, how many revolutionaries throughout history can ever say that?

Isadora belches, smirks, a hand halfway to her lips. Only halfway, though. Her face is oddly set. Guttering candlelight glimmers on the sweat of her brow.

"I…" Her lips move, but there's no more.

You are very still, watching her. Not by design. Your muscles slow. Your lungs labour. It's quick acting, the agent, but that's the advantage of living in a great house admirably equipped with laboratories.

I watch you die.

I WATCH YOU die, Torquell. You, the hero, who achieved so much, so effortlessly. And afterwards, I and the other servants pack everything away, and I consider how best to get word to your people to tell them you were betrayed. Their great hero was murdered at the feast, and they must rise up, rise up. Spread the word far and wide that the ogres cannot be trusted. Spread the Truth of what was done to their ancestors; Torquell's Truth, we can call it. And I will midwife your legacy. I will make you a true hero, mythic in your grandeur. It's always easier when you're dead.

And you could have said 'No.' I wanted you to say no. I know you always felt I hated you, but believe me, I was very invested in you and your potential. For years I made sure the right books were under your hand when you reached for them; the answers rose to your eyes when you sought them. Isadora thought she made you, but if anyone brought Torquell the Hero into the world it was poor, unassuming Minith.

And for years before that, I built up my networks, little cells of people taking to other cells and nobody knowing the whole. A system I inherited from others and built upon, carrying my own private business everywhere Isadora took me. I primed Bradwell and the others in the army, showing them the injustice of their lot and readying them for the coup. I liaised with the disgruntled shop stewards of the factory workers and talked about strikes and go-slows and protests. I primed the world to be ready for a figurehead like you, a man who would set a match to all the tinder I had shored up about the place. And you brought the match, and for as long as it lasted, your career as a revolutionary was glorious. Just what we needed.

Then came Isadora with her offer, and you could have said 'No.'

I'll miss Isadora. She was the best ogre I ever knew. She was a kind Mistress, and she had a brilliant mind, and she reserved her spite and anger for her own peers, who smothered her and kept her down because ogres, on the whole, tend not to like ogresses who get above themselves. But when you're property, it doesn't matter if your owner treats you well or badly. The ownership is all. We don't split hairs about who is a better slave master. And you would have been the best owner of all, and that still isn't enough reason to keep you alive once you've decided that owning people is fine, just so long as it's *you* that owns them.

So now you're a dead hero, and that's useful too. Your movement and its momentum are still very much alive, and I will keep working behind the scenes to spread the word and the fire. Because it's *on*, now. It's us or them. And we have an army and weapons, and they have an awful lot of servants and workers and soldiers, and they don't know who they can rely on, and there aren't enough of *them* to do it all themselves. They're very used to having things done for them. They have the power now, and the strength, and the long-held habits of command, but we will keep lighting fires and teaching the Truth. Until the whole world is burning, and all the masters are gone.

ABOUT THE AUTHOR

Adrian Tchaikovsky is the author of the acclaimed ten-book *Shadows of the Apt* series, the *Echoes of the Fall* series, and other novels, novellas and short stories including *Children of Time* (which won the Arthur C. Clarke award in 2016), and its sequel, *Children of Ruin* (which won the British Science Fiction Award in 2020). He lives in Leeds in the UK and his hobbies include entomology and board and roleplaying games.

🐦 @aptshadow
🌐 adriantchaikovsky.com

FIND US ONLINE!

www.rebellionpublishing.com

/solarisbooks   /solarisbks   /solarisbooks

SIGN UP TO OUR NEWSLETTER!

rebellionpublishing.com/newsletter

YOUR REVIEWS MATTER!

Enjoy this book? Got something to say?

Leave a review on Amazon, GoodReads or with your
favourite bookseller and let the world know!